More Praise for
Live from Cairo

"Bassingthwaighte renders his characters and Cairo itself with a You-Are-Here intensity."

— The Seattle Times

"There are far too many great things about this book to list in this small space."

— Kirkus Reviews (starred review)

"Absorbing and important reading."

— Library Journal (starred review)

"Expansive . . . Searing . . . The author paints a deep and empathetic picture of the inner struggles of his courageous, flawed characters, who in the midst of mortal danger and insurmountable odds, grapple with the most fundamental questions of right and wrong. The answers follow neither rules nor laws, making the climax to this novel breathtaking and heartrending."

— Publishers Weekly

"Remarkable . . . There is so much to like about this book, from brilliant characterization to exceptional writing."

— Bookpage

"Relevant, funny, and moving."

— San Diego Magazine

"A positive and highly successful attempt at helping readers grasp the enormity of the refugee problem, not through statistics and investigative reports, but by pinpointing one individual's struggles."

— *New York Journal of Books*

"Packed with action, history, and heartbreak, this debut novel rings authentic."

— *Inside Jersey*

"This ambitious and darkly comic novel captures, in its multiple perspectives, the tangled pains of a refugee crisis. Like Joseph Heller and Adam Johnson, Bassingthwaighte brilliantly illuminates the absurdity of a tragic situation."

— Andrea Barrett, author of *Archangel* and *Servants of the Map*

"Ian Bassingthwaighte's *Live from Cairo* is, as the title suggests, a living, animate, remarkable novel written with an energy rarely found in debut novels. With its sweeping eye for sizzling detail, this portrait of wanderers from different lands in a troubled Middle East is urgent and fiercely engaging."

— Chigozie Obioma, author of *The Fishermen*

"My favorite thing about this book is the focus on love — love for country, for self, for mothers, for brothers, for each other. That at the heart of this novel is the deep, aching love between an Arab woman and an Arab man gives me goosebumps. We need this book. We need it on every shelf."

— Randa Jarrar, author of *A Map of Home*

LIVE FROM CAIRO

A NOVEL

IAN BASSINGTHWAIGHTE

SCRIBNER

New York   London   Toronto   Sydney   New Delhi

Scribner
An Imprint of Simon & Schuster, Inc.
1230 Avenue of the Americas
New York, NY 10020

Copyright © 2017 by Ian Bassingthwaighte

First Scribner trade paperback edition July 2018

SCRIBNER and design are registered trademarks of The Gale Group, Inc.,
used under license by Simon & Schuster, Inc., the publisher of this work.

For information about special discounts for bulk purchases,
please contact Simon & Schuster Special Sales at 1-866-506-1949
or business@simonandschuster.com.

The Simon & Schuster Speakers Bureau can bring authors to
your live event. For more information or to book an event, contact
the Simon & Schuster Speakers Bureau at 1-866-248-3049 or visit
our website at www.simonspeakers.com.

Interior design by Kyle Kabel
Map by David Atkinson/Hand Made Maps Ltd

Manufactured in the United States of America

1   3   5   7   9   10   8   6   4   2

Library of Congress Cataloging-in-Publication Data is available.

ISBN 978-1-5011-4687-9
ISBN 978-1-5011-4688-6 (pbk)
ISBN 978-1-5011-4689-3 (ebook)

To all those still waiting.

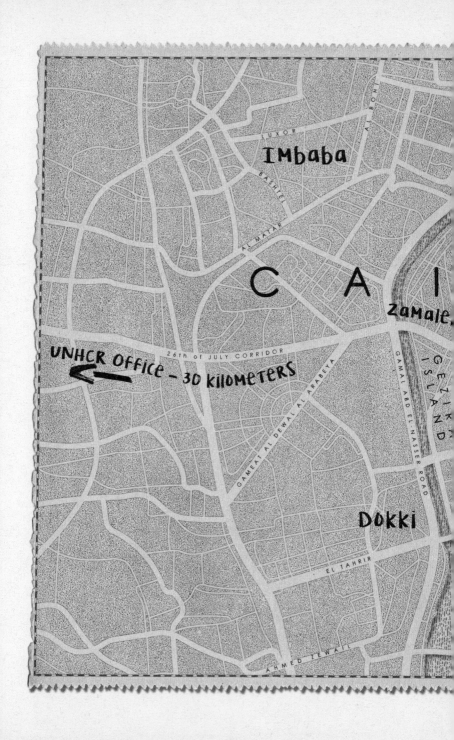

PART I

THE PITCH

1

Hana slipped on the wet linoleum leading from baggage claim to Arrival Hall 1. No warning sign; no warning mop. She landed in the sitting position and watched her wheeled luggage roll unattended through customs. The fall ousted Hana from the trance caused by long, seemingly motionless travel; a curious lack of turbulence made it feel as if she'd spent all night pinned in the black yonder. Hana remembered waking full of dread somewhere over the Mediterranean. Her nightmare had been that she wasn't moving. Move now, thought Hana. Stand up. She stood without making eye contact with onlookers. Then, unburdened of embarrassment, she chased her bags. "As-salamu alaikum," said Hana as she passed the customs agent. Her rogue luggage had come to rest against a frosted-glass wall the height and width of the room. Installed therein was a frosted-glass door, beyond which lay her job, her purpose, her happiness. Finally, her life. Hana sped to the door, which slid open automatically. An air conditioner, mounted above and aimed straight down, blasted her kempt hair into a style more befitting her mood. She tucked the restive wisps behind her ears.

The arrival hall was almost empty, so Hana had no trouble finding the paper sign with her name on it. A tight cap hugged the driver's fat head. "Welcome to Egypt!" he said. "Everything was invented here. Poetry, science, math. The calendar, the plow." Hana reached to shake his hand, but retracted at the last second. This wasn't America, after all. She ought not to touch men she didn't know. The driver led Hana at a brisk pace to the parking lot, where an ancient black Peugeot sat exactly parallel to the curb. "Please," said the driver, gesturing to the back door. He loaded Hana's bags into the trunk, then himself into the driver's seat. "Here we go," he said. In the mirror, the driver looked proud. As if God had delivered this task. You, drive! The car started begrudgingly but came to life when the driver throttled. The airport was suddenly a dim light in the rearview.

"Is there a seat belt back here?" asked Hana, fishing in the crevice of the seat. She quit fishing after concluding that, at this speed, the belt's value was purely psychological.

"Don't worry," said the driver. "I'm Mustafa. Thirty years of legendary driving experience."

The dark cinder-block city blurred past. Night even seeped into the main drags and busy intersections, as if streetlamps were designed to accentuate the dark instead of defend against it. The lamps whipped by so fast they appeared to stand at odd angles.

"Some people, they're afraid of the revolution," said Mustafa, as if he could sense Hana's anxiety but couldn't see it was his own fault. "I know it is a good thing coming. Mubarak is gone. God willing, the army will go soon. Oy, the army."

Hana relaxed. Or told herself to relax while looking out the window for signs of protest. All the news, the viral imagery – everything she'd seen and read in the weeks preceding her arrival – suggested evidence of the uprising lay rampant in the streets. One photo had depicted a whole avenue blocked off by huge cement cubes that had been stacked into a wall by the army. Protesters had used that unyielding canvas to paint the exact image of the street that lay beyond. The optical illusion was itself an act of rebellion, as if to say, *This wall doesn't really exist.* Hana thought there'd be more glass, more tires, more paper strewn on the sidewalks. The paper would be leaflets and poetry and meeting places listed with dates and times, and xeroxed photos of martyrs.

"Do you mind?" asked Mustafa, tuning his radio. "My show is on." White noise poured into the back of the cab. Eventually he found the station. A soap opera full of exaggerated crying sounds. "I hope you don't mind. I have been waiting all week to find out what happens."

Hana listened for stray words and phrases she remembered from her mother's militant Arabic lessons. She'd only endured those lessons until she'd been old enough to mount an articulate protest against them. Hana had been seven at the time. "I don't have any-one to talk to in this language but you," she'd said. Now the radio offered a garbled story. Hana heard *Please kiss me* and *Don't leave*. Then a struggle of some kind followed by a loud slap. The discrepancy between the number of words spoken and the number of words she understood was so severe that Hana leaned back into the seat cushion and regretted childhood. The rest of the drive passed at a speed enabled by that languor. The highway became a labyrinth of one-way streets. Downtown appeared around them.

"Ah," said Mustafa as if he'd returned home after a long journey. "We've arrived." Parallel parking required a surgical touch, though Mustafa made it look effortless. "Over there." He gestured. "Sharia Mohammad Mahmoud. Mansour. That building."

Hana recognized the cream bricks. Her new employer, the United Nations High Commissioner for Refugees — mercifully referred to by its acronym, UNHCR — had sent pictures, a floor plan, a key. She reached into her pocket to confirm the key was still there. The crummy prison retained its tinny captive, which was strangely cold to the touch. Hana was so relieved she threw open the wrong door. The graver of her two mistakes was not looking for traffic. A passing car made contact, but just barely. The edge of her door peeled the blue paint off the passing car like dead skin. Screech owls would've sounded less piercing. The door, pulled open beyond the hinges' limit, was stuck now at a gruesome angle. Brake lights bled red as the passing car came to a stop. Dust kicked up by the tires had a spectral quality and wouldn't settle. A sudden calm grew eerie amid the billow. Then, just as Hana was beginning to think she was having another nightmare – could dust really hang that way in the air without time having come to a stop? – the front door of the passing car cracked open. The driver rolled out. When he hit the pavement, he kept rolling. Back and forth as if he was in pain. Perhaps even near death. Oh shit, thought Hana. Oh shit, oh shit, oh shit. She tried to shut her door in an attempt to seclude herself from the mystery unfolding before her. Why did the man fall? How was he injured? Hana's door wouldn't shut, so she pulled harder. Her hands slipped off the plastic handle. The plastic felt like wax. Her palms were too sweaty.

Mustafa yelled out the window and honked his horn until the man writhing in the street reluctantly ended his act. Aha! thought Hana. You're not dying. You're not even injured. You fraud! You cheat! Relief preceded anger and the sound of her own heart beating her eardrums. What did he want? Money? How much money? The fraud sat, stood, then started toward them. He hesitated as he passed through the headlights, appearing both afraid and enraged. "Oh, no," said Hana when he proceeded to the stuck door. She tried desperately to close it again, to no avail. "Jesus Christ," said Hana to the waxy plastic handle. The fraud leaned over and peered in. He seemed shocked and saddened to see a woman in the backseat. His fingers were rolled in a fist. Mustafa shook his own fist out the window and threatened to get out. Hana didn't understand the Arabic, but Mustafa's tone suggested a threat. Her spine prickled when the fraud moved from the back door to the front. Loud words were exchanged before the fraud lunged through the open window into Mustafa's lap. His entire torso was now inside the car. He and Mustafa grappled in the space between the driver's seat and the steering wheel, both men vying for air. Hana wanted to run, but guilt kept her ass planted. What had she done to Mustafa's taxi? To his livelihood? What would the fraud do to his body? To his face?

Grunting and keys jangling in the ignition gave way to a popping sound and, at the same time, a yelp. Hana, ashamed to discover how low she'd sunk in her seat, peered through the space between Mustafa's seatback and the headrest. The tussle had come to an end. By the look of it, Mustafa had landed a punch square on the fraud's box nose, which was flatter than it had been and was now bleeding. The fraud was so dazed that he hung listlessly in the window. Not that Mustafa squandered any time waiting for the fraud to extract himself; he shoved open the door and thus ejected him. The fraud landed with a thump in the street. Mustafa got out, grabbed the fraud by the arm, and dragged him back to his well-used Volkswagen. All the while muttering something like, "I warned you. I did warn you." The Volkswagen must've been manufactured in the '70s. The aesthetic damage Hana had caused, now that she had time to look, blended seamlessly into the car's long and presumably storied history. Mustafa lifted the fraud into the driver's seat and said, "Yallah" so loud he sounded like a foghorn. The fraud, though grimacing, didn't overtly protest; he sat up straight, closed his door, and slowly rolled up his window. Mustafa slapped the roof to hurry the rolling along. The fraud, like a whipped horse, sped away.

"Now the hard part," said Mustafa, traipsing back to his cab. His contrived smile was still there, like a scar from thirty years spent earning tips. "Shutting a door that does not want to be shut." He leaned with all his weight, dug his heels into the hot tar, and shoved the back door until it submitted to the pressure of his will and what must've remained of his anger. The door wouldn't latch until Mustafa kicked it. "Best not to lean on the . . . ," he said, kicking the door a second time.

Quiet, suddenly. The joints in Hana's body began to unfix, so she could again move. Her fingers uncurled, nails leaving tiny red crescents on her palms. She pulled out her wallet even though the fare had been paid in advance. "For the door," she said desperately. But Mustafa said no money. How could he blame Hana for what God willed? "Oy," he said about God. "I don't know what He does to my car. Yesterday I drove all morning with no gas." Mustafa landed in the driver's seat. He rested his head on the steering wheel. He breathed and sweated heavily.

"I'm sorry," said Hana after a few seconds. "Really, I didn't mean . . ." Her words seemed to evaporate before reaching him. A sick, empty feeling lodged in her stomach as she exited the vehicle on the sidewalk side of the car.

"Please, take my card." Mustafa leaned across the front seat and extended his arm through the far window, presenting a copy. "Call every day for best fare, best service, best safety record."

Hana accepted the card by way of apology. Mustafa didn't want her money, but at least he'd accept her business. She dragged her bags across the sidewalk as if they contained both her clothes and her guilt. "I'll just pay for the door by tipping excessively over time," she said, turning back to him. "You know that, right?"

"Very good," said Mustafa. He exited the parking spot as if he drove less by sight than muscle memory. An unconscious finesse. "Please remember to call," he said out the window. "Otherwise I go out of business."

Hana watched Mustafa's taillights fly away before dragging her bags up the stairs and into her building. A tile floor led to a rickety-looking elevator: the manual glass door had to be latched before the buttons lit up; the wooden floor managed her slight weight by curving into a shallow bowl; and the whole apparatus whined during ascent. Not that Hana had energy left to consider what the whining implied. The elevator stopped abruptly at the seventh floor, revealing polished concrete walls leading to dark-colored doors. Hers was brown, inlaid with carved wooden polygons forming a complicated geometric pattern. The apartment beyond a door like that, thought Hana, must be really special. Unlocking the door proved difficult. Her hands shook just enough that her key kept missing the keyhole. She ordered her hands to stop shaking by glaring at them. "Calm down," she said to herself. When Hana finally got her door open, she met a dark room. She navigated by colliding with and bouncing off waist-high furniture. After locating the light switch on the far wall – an odd spot, yet it added character – she discovered the apartment looked the same in life as it did in pictures. Hana was almost disappointed that her expectations were met. A tortoiselike tour of the apartment revealed a single surprise: bath towels stacked neatly in the hall closet. Thick and, she thought, absorbent. She counted them. Three, the perfect number. One for using, one for using while the first was in the wash, and a third for backup or in case of company.

A cold shower washed away the shock, the sweat, the smell of peanuts, even the lethargy. No way could Hana sleep now. At least, not until her hair dried. In the meantime she began unpacking. Her bags were jammed so tightly they exploded when she unzipped them. While sifting through the mess, Hana found a note her mother had secretly packed. Her mother's name was Ishtar, same as the Assyrian goddess of love and war. A goddess who, according to myth, descended into the underworld, kicked down the front gates, and wreaked havoc in hell. The note said, *Have a good time!* in huge, messy cursive. *Love, The only mother you'll ever get. P.S. Thanks for waiting so long to leave me. I know you wanted to go earlier.*

True, thought Hana. But not very nice to point out. What was Ishtar's motive? To solicit pity? To implant regret? Hana refolded the note before returning it to its hiding place. Then she ducked her pensive mood by lying down. In bed, Hana resolved not to miss or even think about Ishtar. Now wasn't the time. She needed to sleep. It was past midnight. Way past, almost morning. Hana closed her eyes and tried to think of nothing. Her idea of nothing was the black area between stars. That scared her the same way thinking about death scared her. She tried to think about something else. Her sore arms were the obvious candidates. Why were her arms sore? Dragging her bags, probably. Or yanking the car door. Her arms felt as if they'd gone to the gym without the rest of her body. Hana wondered if there were gyms in Cairo. Surely, there must be. But gyms for women? Hana tried to think of nothing again. God damn her wet hair. Not that her hair was really the problem. The urge to sleep was precluded by a body drained of the ability to feel even tiredness. Her endorphins had poured out with the whiskey and were all used up. The whiskey had been free on the international legs of her flight. Hana had indulged in a desperate attempt to block out her fear of burning up or drowning in the cold black ocean. Then went her adrenaline, left back in the cab. The only thing she could feel now was the firmness of the pillow and the weight of the air. Not the weight, exactly, but the thickness of it, so that her body was again covered in a thin layer of sweat. Hana got out of bed and walked to her balcony. The dark and the loneliness — or aloneness, since she felt no longing for companionship — went well together. She didn't have to worry about waking Ishtar or stepping on Pen, the family spaniel. The old dog, at his own peril, loved feet.

When Hana reached her balcony, she sat in a plastic chair and witnessed the sun's meek declaration. A red blemish in the eastern sky. She watched the red spread out and change color as traffic noises amplified. The city, seen now in the light of the morning, looked different from in the light of the television. Where was the tear gas? Where were the tanks? Satellite dishes large and small capped every building. Cairo, thought Hana, was surprisingly well connected to space. A strange, happy fact. Like how all the buildings in Chefchaouen were painted blue; and how, in Beirut, dried sea horses could be found along the promenade. The feeling of having arrived in a new place finally settled upon her, like a bird landing.

Later that morning, Hana visited her office in 6th October City — an hour's drive west, though Mustafa's lead foot shortened the drive to forty minutes — where she matched names with faces, which Hana found easier to memorize. A penchant for sketching people had trained her how to see them. Mostly she sketched older women, whose treacherous lives were plainly declared in lines, scars, spots, and other dermatological anomalies. The faces at the

UNHCR, however, had less to tell; they were much younger. Employees included Yezin, whose giant eyebrows met in a tuft above his nose. His beard was neatly trimmed and his outfit was clearly ironed. There was Fadwa, who wore a scarf, and Noha, who didn't. Fadwa had chapped lips and long arms she hid by crossing. Noha had wire-rimmed glasses and bloodshot eyes that betrayed the rigor of her work. Not that she looked unhappy. There was also Joseph, another American. His bow tie overshadowed his face. Silk, by the look of it; navy, pindot. Either the bow tie was too loose or he just loved talking. He listed every famous Joseph he could name. Saint Joseph. Joseph Stalin. Joseph Conrad. Chief Joseph. Jerry Lewis, whose birth name was Joseph. And finally Napoléon Bonaparte, who married Joséphine. Upon finishing his list, Joseph disclosed his motive. The names inspired him to do more with his life. By *do more* he meant "work harder." His eyes were even more bloodshot than Noha's.

After the awkward introductions came an awkward lunch. Or a lecture disguised as a lunch. The lecture happened at Margret's desk. Margret was the office coordinator and the liaison between the UNHCR and the Egyptian government. She spent most of her time on the phone with the Refugee Affairs Department of the Ministry of Foreign Affairs and the secretive, sometimes intimidating Ministry of the Interior. Margret was a German who spoke English and Arabic with almost no accent. She was feisty, tall, and her skin was a painful shade of pink – a combination of heatstroke, sunburn, and stress.

"I brought kofta and ful," said Margret, gesturing to the spread on her desk. "That's meatballs and mashed fava beans. Well, not exactly mashed. More like stirred aggressively. Dig in. How was your flight?"

"It landed, at least." Hana took beans by the heap. The idea being to cure or at least bury her hangover.

Margret stabbed two meatballs with a fork, then took great pains to cut them evenly. "You almost look like you're from here. Pretend you are and you'll get hassled less. In the street, I mean. Not much less, but some."

"My parents are Iraqi."

"That's right." Margret raised her index finger to excuse her chewing. "Assyrian."

There'd been a background check. Hana had gladly signed the consent form when applying for the job, for it relieved her of the duty to explain who she was and where she came from. Her life story had been distilled into a series of facts. Her father was blown up in Baghdad, Iraq, in 1980, a few months before Hana was born, when an Iranian missile dropped like a shot bird. Her mother fled to America. What other choice but to run? The war had compounded a more historical danger: the persecution of Assyrian Christians at the hands of the Baathists. Not that Hana could remember what she hadn't witnessed. The pain her mother told was just a story.

"Mm," said Hana, finally setting in on her beans. "The ful is . . ."

"Tastier than it looks? I know, it looks disgusting."

Margret looked relaxed as she was eating. Hana found this impressive — Margret's ability to eat and talk and look relaxed at the same time, and to simultaneously be a boss with authority and probably a rule book. If you crossed Margret, she'd hit you with the rule book so hard you'd wake up years later having learned how to follow orders. Impressive. Also, frightening. Hana was impressed and frightened and happy. Frightened because she was finally in Cairo and had to prove she deserved to be. She had theoretical, but not practical, experience — what Hana thought of as "too much school." Could she do the job? Could she do the job well? Could she do the job well over time? The job would be reading and evaluating resettlement petitions, filed by refugees on the run. On paper, a plain duty. But in practice?

"Well," said Margret, eyeing her half-cleared plate with conflicted interest, "I'm probably fuller than I think. I better stop." She cast her plate aside, but not into the trash; maybe her decision wasn't final. The pause in conversation was thus filled by the sweet feeling of discovery. Margret wasn't just a boss, nor just a leader. She was an actual person with insecurities that leaked out at weird times. Hana counted her discovery as one more reason she was happy to be in Cairo now, in the thick of it. Summer was coming and the revolution was still a spark suspended over a pool of gasoline. The office was air-conditioned, the employees were curious, and the boss was more human than most.

"I might as well get on with the spiel I give new hires." Margret cleared her throat to make way. "Your goal, like mine, is to send every refugee to a safer place. Sound about right? Sadly, that won't happen. Not now. Probably not ever. There's not room, politically speaking. Not in any country. We're talking about an onslaught. Tens of millions worldwide. Worse still, not every person who petitions to resettle is even a refugee. Insofar as that word is officially defined. Egyptians or Jordanians will pose as Iraqis. They'll say their houses were bulldozed or bombed. They'll burn themselves with a lighter and say it's really a bullet wound that hasn't healed yet. No matter how sincere a story sounds, or what it makes you feel, remember that tears don't qualify as evidence. We need proof of origin, proof of trauma, proof of flight. That means source documents. Identity cards, medical records, pay stubs, death threats, even the envelopes in which the death threats were sent."

By not talking, Margret allowed the background noise to assert itself. People wrestling with the copy machine; phones ringing; cold air blown in by old fans. The noise made it easy for Hana to remember what she'd learned in law school. The truth paled in comparison to the paper trail. With paper, you could prove anything.

"Something else," said Margret finally. "Most resettlement cases are filed by nonprofits on behalf of refugees who don't normally apply for resettlement themselves. Not everyone knows English or has a computer. Or even the right forms. Information is surprisingly hard to disseminate. You'll be dealing with a few resettlement lawyers, most of whom are foreigners and all of whom are a pain in the ass. My ass, especially. One is gifted in that regard. Charlie Wells. He calls and e-mails relentlessly. As soon as he figures out we've got a new hire, he's going to zero in."

Hana believed herself to be a hard target. Evasive by nature.

Calls could be ignored. E-mails could be deleted. "He can try. But I'm very . . ."

Margret didn't appear to be listening. "The last thing that you need to know . . ." She paused as if her own speech had sped ahead of her. "Ah! I remember. Feel free to stop by my office whenever my door is physically, actually open." Her smile suggested her friendliness had a limit. "Just don't knock on my door if it's shut."

"I will. And I won't, ever. Not even in an emergency."

Margret laughed, a little. "Go find Joseph." She finally slid her plate into the trash. "He'll show you how to do your job. Or at least where to do it."

Hana shook Margret's hand with what she hoped was a firm grip. But not too firm, lest she seem eager. Then she cruised the halls in search of Joseph, whom she eventually found in the kitchen eating lunch by himself. At one time he must've had company. Several empty chairs were pushed back from the table, giving the kitchen an abandoned look. More like Chernobyl than a ghost town in the Old West. It wasn't as if people had moved out over time as the town died. Something had made people run.

"Folks here take their jobs very seriously." Joseph turned and gestured to the chairs with his foot. "Badr, Fadwa, Noha, Hend. The list goes on. We're all victims of a collective office ego, which has run amok. Who can do more work faster? Who can eat lunch in two minutes without choking?" Joseph lifted his applesauce; he'd been irrevocably changed by his environment. "Recently I discovered I'm less happy than I want to be. I want to be more like Yezin. He's the only one who eats lunch at a normal speed. He gets more work done than the rest of us combined. An infuriating paradox."

"Yezin." Hana recalled each of the faces she'd seen. "He's got . . . big eyebrows?"

"One giant eyebrow, actually. You'll see him around. Or hear him, more likely. Humming while he cleans lint off the hard drives. I think it's some kind of Zen-like activity – polishing, the way he does, with the cloth."

Hana felt as if she'd entered a world that had existed for a long time without her. She relished that and imagined, months from now, being invited into the fold. "Margret said you'd show me the ropes."

"The ropes. Of course. One second." Joseph made quick work of his applesauce before pushing his chair and every other chair back under the table. Then he led the way down the hall. "The office is an assembly line. You're at the beginning of it with me and Yezin." Joseph pointed through a doorway as they breezed past; Hana caught a glimpse of Yezin waving. "We read and evaluate testimonies, which are the narrative portion of each refugee's petition to resettle. There are thousands of these documents in this office at all times. They never stop coming. We keep them over there and over there."

Joseph pointed at two lines of filing cabinets, which in no way hinted at the catastrophes they contained. Then he gestured through another doorway to Hana's desk: "All yours."

Hana walked in and sat down in her chair. The memory foam had already forgotten whoever had last sat there.

"How does it feel?"

"Pretty comfortable." Hana thought she could sit there all day and feel no pain.

Refugees came like dust blown from other deserts. Iraq, Sudan, Somalia. The men survived abduction and torture. The women survived abduction and torture and rape. Aggravating circumstances included missing relatives or children, various psychological disorders, and a high rate of arrhythmia. The average heart, it seemed, was unable to normalize after the shock of learning what people could do. Testimonies arrived in stacks, but Hana moved through them one page at a time, so slowly that she never had to lick her finger. She knew the UNHCR processed hundreds of thousands of resettlement petitions each year, but only a fraction were approved and even fewer were actually resettled. Her burden, then, was to choose carefully.

There were two categories of reading. The good kind and the other kind. The good reading contained electricity, causing the hair on Hana's arms to stand up. Such as when she read about an Iraqi family whose story was awful and true as far as she could tell. Not only did the timeline add up, but the case had urgency. The mother's terrible heart condition satisfied that requirement. Not just arrhythmia, but a severe prolapse requiring surgical replacement of the mitral valve. The supporting documents proved everything, and Hana got to pass the case along for further review. Maybe the family would be vetted, approved by the American embassy, and flown to Philadelphia or Boston or Detroit. A hard life would await them, but so would physical security, which the family hadn't known since before the war. Plus, the mother would get her surgery. Her fear of death would be replaced by other, lesser fears. Would she miss hearing the call to prayer so much that she'd hear it spontaneously — a kind of muscle memory, but in her ear? Would she find a job? Would her son make friends? Would he be happy?

The other kind of reading had a less tactile, more insidious effect on Hana's mood and overall happiness. Such as when Hana revoked a Sudanese woman's refugee status after reviewing her case. Not by choice, thank God; by mandate, which slightly reduced the considerable feeling of guilt. That woman, named Rita, was from southern Sudan and not Darfur. The United Nations had declared the region safe for repatriation even though there was no peace or even ceasefire. Now Rita's petition to resettle would become a one-way plane ticket home. The worst part? Her village was still controlled by the militiamen who'd stormed into her life on horseback while she and her boys had slept all those years ago. Time had a way of sharpening bad memories. The rape, the theft of her livestock, the burning of her hut. Most of all, the murder of her children. The facts were in plain English on white paper. The children had tried to flee, but there'd been nothing to hide behind. The children had been thin, but not thinner than the grass and the trees. The sound of gunfire had drowned in the sound of horses galloping.

———————

It was, all of a sudden, two weeks since Hana had arrived in Egypt. She'd done nothing but work. Hana interpreted that as a good sign. She liked her job. Or saw how she might like her job one day after her skin thickened. The process had already begun. Now she could read testimonies without crinkling the paper by gripping it too hard. A marked improvement. Not that Hana could enjoy the feeling of having changed. Not today, at least. Today she was late for work. Ten minutes late, to be exact. She burst through the office doors out of breath and off-balance, causing a racket by steadying herself against the wind chime. Why would Margret hang a wind chime by the door if not to know when it opened?

"There you are," said a voice from down the hall. Margret's head appeared from a doorway, followed by the rest of her body. "Exactly who I needed to see."

"There was a jam on the bridge." Hana was still new and felt she had no right to be so late. Ten minutes was too many. "The army was shooting protesters with water cannons. The weird part? Protesters ran toward the water – "

"To indicate they're not scared," said Margret coolly. How could anything surprise her after such a long career in the conflict business? "By the way, do you want to conduct a resettlement interview? You've been here . . . uh, a while. I think it's time."

Hana didn't ignore the question. She placed it in the queue of things to process. Other questions came first. Such as, why show the army you're not scared? Wouldn't that compel the army to change tactics? Wouldn't water become rubber? Or even metal? Not to mention, Hana's lunch, her coffee, and her work – a stack of testimonies, thick as a phone book – were slipping from her grip. She couldn't hold everything much longer. How to decide what to drop? Not the coffee, for the carpet's sake. Nor the stack of testimonies. How long would that take to clean up? That left only her lunch, which she let slip from her fingers. "Ugh," said Hana when the bag fell. She set the testimonies and the coffee on the filing cabinet, then set about collecting her lunch. Hana hoped the yogurt's seal didn't break when the bag landed. The yogurt offered relief from the heat, the pressure, the stress. In the afternoon, when Hana felt like a dead dinosaur being compressed into a fossil fuel, she escaped to the kitchen, ate her yogurt, and played Tetris on her phone until she achieved the high score. If the high score was too high, she reset it to zero. That way she could forever best herself. But if the yogurt's seal had broken, she had no way to carry out her ritual. Hana peered forlornly into her bag, where a gruesome murder scene lay in wait. A quarter strawberry, aloft on her baguette, looked like a tiny heart with a yogurt coating.

"About the interview," said Margret. Her calmness alerted Hana to the absurdity of the situation. The yogurt didn't matter. The protesters were none of her business.

"By 'interview' you mean . . . ?"

"The other half of your job description," joked Margret. Or maybe she wasn't joking. With Margret, it was hard to tell. "You can't just read, not forever. You'll burn out if you keep reading."

"I love to read," said Hana. Should she describe exactly how much she loved reading? How her mother used to work in a library? How Hana had spent every day after school in the stacks? How she'd taken home Kafka, Woolf, and Mahfouz? How she'd lingered so long in the pages that her mother was reprimanded for excessive use of the blind eye? The *blind eye* was library lingo for refunding the late fee, an off-the-books employee benefit.

"Variety is related, I think, to job satisfaction," said Margret.

In a last-ditch effort to avoid the inevitable, Hana finally confessed. "I'm not ready. Just knowing the names . . ." Hana thought suddenly of Rita. How blessed she felt to have never met the woman.

Margret gave Hana a sorry look. Also the testimony. Just printed and still warm to the touch. "Joseph offered initial approval. My feeling? The case isn't dire enough. Either the interview will change my mind or it won't. It's scheduled for three o'clock. I trust you'll be ready by then?"

"Yes," said Hana without believing it true or even possible. The UNHCR handbook described what the interview entailed from a mechanical standpoint, but suggested no tips on how to maintain poise, distance, and objectivity in the face of traumas that were technically in the past but lived on, even grew, in the memory. Hana was, she realized, totally alone in the task of becoming reticent. And had only hours to change. She speed-read the testimony and took notes – Dalia, thirty-four, fled Baghdad – while pacing her office, but the wind of her own movement failed to blow away the feeling that she was about to jump off a cliff.

When Margret reappeared that afternoon, her presence automatically drew Hana into the hall. A kind of tractor beam. "Follow me," said Margret. They walked to a sparsely furnished conference room, which neatly presented an oblong table, matching chairs, a fake plant with waxed leaves, many of which had detached from the plant – the illusion of wilting gave life to the room – and two framed pictures of Gandhi. Technically one picture of Gandhi and one picture of his possessions at the time of his death. Two pairs of sandals, two bowls, a wooden fork and spoon, three porcelain monkeys, his diary, his glasses, his prayer book, a spittoon, a watch, and two letter openers. What couldn't fit in a single pocket could be carried in a single hand. Margret said she loved the photo because it depressed the hell out of her. "Not in a bad way," she'd said. The photo clarified what possessions had true value – time, family, home, and health – and served as a reminder that every refugee had lost at least one, often several.

Hana and Margret sat across from Dalia, who sat by herself. Hana knew the no-lawyer rule – people trained to obscure the truth were not welcome – but it seemed now like an extraordinary caution, and patently unfair. Especially unfair given the size of the table, which could've sat ten people comfortably. "Do you need a translator?" asked Hana, irked by her paltry offer. Yet she had to ask. "Also, nice to meet you. My name is – "

"No," said Dalia, somehow interrupting without seeming rude.

"My parents taught me English when I was young." Her skin looked the right age, but her eyes were much older. "I studied in college, too. And taught my husband. That's how he got the job with the Americans. Not only did he work hard, but he could speak their language."

Hana didn't want to disturb what she hoped was a happy memory—Dalia had shut her eyes and seemed to withdraw from her body—but Margret, tapping her watch, threw Hana a stern look. Hana said, "Ahem." Then, "Excuse me. Ahem." The silence grew until it draped the table. Hana had no choice but to jolt Dalia from her pensive state. "What happened in Baghdad?" blurted Hana. "Why did you flee?" Sensing her questions had accomplished their task, Hana added, "I'm sorry, I don't mean to be . . ."

"The war," said Dalia. "It wasn't safe."

Hana saw now that doing her job—extracting Dalia's horror story in its peculiar form—would be difficult and, by nature, unkind. Hana hoped she'd be able to forgive herself. "That's what happened to your country. I'm asking what happened to you."

Dalia's hesitation was so slight Hana wondered if she'd imagined it. "We were walking to our home. From the market. We carried bread and vegetables. On the walk, Omran asked if I thought we'd have electricity that night to cook food. The electricity came and went with the water. 'Don't worry,' I said. 'The potatoes will be washed, one way or another. If I can't wash them in the sink, you can rub them clean on your shirt. I will find some way to cook them.' What I really meant was that I loved Omran, but it came out that way about the potatoes. Then a truck pulled up to the curb. The brakes screamed. A man screamed out the window. Another man flew out the door. He hit Omran in the head with a rock. Omran fell over."

"When?" asked Hana.

"Right after the rock," said Dalia, as if that were so obvious it almost hurt to say. "They hit him so hard."

"I mean, the date."

Dalia cocked her head. "August," she said coldly. "I don't know what day."

Hana listened to the sound of Margret scribbling notes on her legal pad.

"That's all right," said Hana after a few seconds. "Please, continue."

Dalia inhaled as if relief might be found in the air. "Omran fell and there was blood on the sidewalk. I sat by him and grabbed his arm and held tighter than I've held anything. 'Omran, wake up!' I screamed. The men from the army approached and kicked me right here." Dalia put her hand on her stomach. "I couldn't breathe. I couldn't scream again."

Hana said, "By 'army' you mean . . . ?"

Dalia's eyes widened and Margret's pen scribbled madly. "Militia. Young men with guns, but no fear or even restraint."

"What militia?"

"How can I know?" cried Dalia. "Maybe the Lightning Brigade of Ansar al-Sunna. Maybe al-Qaeda. Even the mujahideen. I didn't care at the time and had no fear except in losing Omran. Finally, I stood up. I fought back. I hit the nose of the one who was closest, a young man. So young he had no beard. I think not even the ability to grow one. I balled my fist and hit so hard he fell onto the ground and made a whimpering noise. His friend, the much larger man, hit me with the stock of his gun and said, 'Damn you.' I can't be sure what he said, but I think he said 'Damn you' and 'whore' and 'bitch' before he hit me a second time in the face with his gun."

"Were you injured?" asked Hana.

"I woke up later and my husband was gone. That is an injury."

"Did you break any bones? Was your eyesight affected? Your memory? Do you get headaches? Nightmares? Flashbacks?"

Dalia's disgust, indicated by her blank face and her refusal to say more, prevented Hana from making meaningful eye contact.

"Okay," said Hana. "So you don't know who took Omran."

"I told you. I don't know."

"Do you know why, at least?"

"Yes. Why, I can tell you. Omran worked for the American army. He rebuilt water mains after they were blown up. The militias say, whoever helps the enemy is also the enemy. Even the worse enemy for betraying their home."

"Did you receive any threats before the kidnapping? Some warning? A letter of some kind?"

"Yes, a letter. I found the letter in the trash. I think Omran didn't want me to know."

"What did the letter say?" asked Hana. "Do you have a copy?"

"The words won't leave me alone. Even after I burned the letter. I suffered once the threat and suffer a thousand times the crime in my imagination."

"Please, if you don't mind . . . will you . . ."

" 'Leave now you atheist, with no God in your heart. Take your whore wife out of our country. Leave now or die. Your wife, too, will die after we ravage her. God's will be done by our hands if you don't go.' "

Margret had warned Hana about rape. That warning was really instruction on how to broach the subject. "Caution should be matched by persistence," Margret had said — aware, if not comfortable, with the irony. "Few refugees volunteer the information. So few I've never met one myself. The shame is too great."

"Was the threat of rape just a threat, or . . . ?" The whole story was already in the testimony, but that didn't save Dalia from Hana's prodding. The truth of her story would be determined, at least in part, by any disparity between the written testimony and the verbal interview. Facts would align; lies would reveal themselves as small divergences in the story. When Dalia presented a blank stare, Hana tried rephrasing her question. "It says here that you — well, is that something you experienced? I'm not referring just to the men who took Omran. I'm referring to any men, anytime in Baghdad."

Dalia's face changed. There was a sickness in it. "Omran is the one I love."

Hana couldn't stop thinking about her choice of words. What a horrible, empty way to ask that question. "I know you love him," said Hana in a vain attempt to repent. The instinct to offer a few more kind words, or even her hand, was curbed by Margret's insane scribbling. "Please, I need to know. Ahem. Dalia." Hana felt sick to her stomach for saying *ahem* so many times. "I need to know if you were ever . . ."

"I got Omran back," said Dalia, more coldly than before. "After paying all the money we ever saved and selling whatever possessions we owned that were worth anything to anyone with money. That's the important part, that Omran came back alive in good health considering. Blinded in one eye, but not both. And not dead. What else do you possibly need to know that's not written in front of you? You keep reading the sheet. I see you reading."

Hana didn't know how to explain the methodology. What could she say? That institutional distrust compelled her to ask questions to which she already had answers? No, Hana would never say that. At least, not in present company. Not with Mute Margret wielding her black pen.

"At least, tell me about Omran," said Hana. "Why did he go to America without you? Boston, right? That's where he resettled?"

"He didn't abandon me, if that's what you mean. I told him to go."

"I don't mean to suggest . . ."

"Omran worked for the Americans. He qualified for a special program. If we had legal documents to prove our marriage, I would have gone with him. We had no papers, so I didn't go."

"What papers?"

"That's what I want to know." Dalia wore the sort of despair that looked from afar like apathy. "Our marriage was a religious one, in the village. We didn't sign anything or even take a picture. The memory of the people who were present, and the memory of God, was enough. Why didn't the US embassy permit that history? 'It's a fraud issue,' they said. I could've been anybody. Omran's neighbor. Omran's cousin. Omran's friend. I am his friend! The one he loves! That's why we married!"

Hana, who'd been holding her breath, sought to release the pressure without making any noise. Controlling her breathing that way proved Hana wrong about herself. Maybe she could calm down. Maybe she could finish the interview. To that end, Hana rushed the rest of her questions. Dalia did her part by answering tersely. She'd fled Baghdad when the violence got worse. Life was slightly better in Cairo, but not good. Not good at all. As a noncitizen, she had no rights. She couldn't work or buy property. Not that she had or would ever have that kind of money. The revolution made things much worse. A rising sense of nationalism – reflected in the street by flag-waving, but taking more insidious forms at night, in the metro, on buses – meant trouble for immigrants such as her. "It's not safe to reveal my origin." Her accent, Dalia said, was enough. What was she supposed to do? Stop talking? That's where the interview ended, with the feeling – belonging to no one specifically, but floating in the air above the table – that the only way to change Dalia's fate was to change her location.

After the interview, Margret used her tractor beam to pull Hana into her office for an informal debrief. Hana stood under the ceiling fan, which made an obnoxious clicking noise. Click, click. Her hair kept blowing into her mouth. "The testimony says she was raped," clamored Hana, words dislodged by the pressure of waiting to speak privately. "That has to count for something."

"I wish it did," said Margret, master of the relaxed look. "Unfortunately, if her verbal testimony contradicts the written one, or even presents omissions, we have to strike the relevant details from the file and flag her for reliability issues. Now, tell me what to do with her case."

"How can we strike that? Wasn't the proof on her face? Didn't you see how she reacted?" Hana knew, suddenly, what Joseph had been thinking. Or feeling, at least. A compulsion to approve the case. As if there were no other way to spend his empathy. "Every bone in my body tells me she needs our help. She can't work. She can't own property."

Margret had dexterous fingers. She rolled a pen cap from one side of her hand to the other like a gambler with a coin or a poker chip. The behavior seemed utterly unconscious. "What about her husband? Can't he work? Can't he send money?"

"Hypothetically," said Hana. "But that doesn't mean – "

"My point is that Dalia's case doesn't exist in a vacuum. Is her poverty more compelling than another's destitution? Is her broken heart more compelling than another's broken spine? Is her rape more compelling than another's fall into sex trafficking? I hate to juxtapose tragedies with greater tragedies, but there's no other just way to fill the quota. Now, tell me what to do with her case."

A single-file queue almost a million people long appeared in Hana's mind. Dalia was an invisible dot in the distance, with no chance whatsoever of leaving Egypt.

2

D alia needed to cross the street if she wanted to catch a minibus. The walk home was too far and the cab ride was too costly. But the street was four lanes wide with a de facto fifth lane called the sidewalk. There were no stoplights. No crosswalks. Not even a median. Dalia's head swiveled in search of a gap in traffic. Black taxis from gone decades blasted past, and minibus drivers, who ate amphetamines to stay awake, didn't bother honking. When there finally was a gap, she darted beyond the first row of cars. Vehicles were now on both sides, whizzing past. Instead of praying before darting across the next lane, Dalia thought of Baghdad for good luck. Why would that city bring good luck? Nothing good had happened there recently. Though everything good had happened there at some point. The memory of her alley – clotheslines hung low with wet dresses, dropping rain that smelled like soap – was a painful camera flash. She saw things that didn't exist anymore. Omran sitting outside with the neighbor eating pastries, and the neighbor's children playing war games in the street. It had been hard to watch them point plastic guns at each other. Not emulating the militias, but executing the terrorist. The boys had achieved victory when the boy terrorist played dead. They'd made popping sounds with their lips as they shot the body.

Dalia heard a similar popping sound now and turned toward the source. A man's car had run out of gas and was now blocking the road. He kicked the front tire with enough anger to fill ten men. Pop, pop. Obstructed drivers took pleasure in scolding him with their car horns. Dalia took the opportunity to cross the rest of the street in a single fluid movement. She reached the other sidewalk just as a few pedestrians helped push the stuck car out of the way, releasing a surge of vehicles. The wind of their passing brought a temporary reprieve from the heat. So temporary that Dalia didn't register the coolness until the air was hot again. She looked at the stranded driver, who looked depressed. He sat next to his car, rested his elbows on his knees, and grumbled to himself. Dalia imagined he was praying angrily for a tow truck or, if he was more sensible, a time machine. She imagined borrowing his time machine and using it for her own purposes. She'd go back and kiss Omran. She'd go back and kiss him again. She'd go back, much further this time, and tell a younger version of herself to leave Iraq before the war started. When the younger version protested – the disbelief, the pride, the desire to finish school – Dalia would slap her so hard the pain would knock her and Omran north into Turkey or west into Syria.

A minibus sped by every minute or so with a man hanging out the window shouting the destination into the cacophony of car horns. Gezira! Maadi! Shubra! El-Manial! Dalia threw her hand in the air when she heard a man shout, "Imbaba!" The minibus swung toward the curb and the sliding door swung open from the inside. People were packed in like books on shelves, pressed against each other. Dalia pushed in, taking the only available seat: the one nearest the door and, lamentably, by the man who shouted the route. His breath smelled like cigarettes and what must've been gum disease. Every time the bus turned right, his body, pulled by the gravity of the turn, moved toward her. Each turn, slightly closer. When his arm finally grazed Dalia's chest, she pushed him as hard as she could. It was an automatic reaction. The repulsion was so immense and instantaneous. The man stopped shouting the route to express both surprise and dismay, as if Dalia were wrong for rebuffing him. His stare was even worse than his breath. Sadly, there was no obvious way to escape. No empty seats. Not even enough empty space for Dalia to lean away from him. A body blocked her. Another woman. Dalia leaned against her anyway. Maybe no room would become a few spare inches. Even one spare inch. When Dalia leaned into the woman, she leaned back with equal pressure. Why wouldn't she make room? Dalia was hopeless and mad only until she saw another man – using more space than he needed, with a briefcase inexplicably between his knees – on the woman's far side. So they were trapped. Dalia kept leaning into the woman, who kept leaning back. Any increase in pressure was matched exactly. Dalia told herself they weren't locked in battle; they were commiserating. The calmness brought on by the contact was very real. Dalia's anger blew out the window. Not all of it, but some. The residual anger became an acute spatial awareness. She cut an inch from her width by stacking one thigh on top of the other and twisting her hips so that facing forward didn't require seeing, even out of the corner of her eye, the man who shouted the route. Though it did require intruding further on the woman against whom she leaned. Dalia hoped the woman wouldn't mind; thankfully, she seemed not to. Dalia gazed past her, out the side window. She was yet denied her peace. A faint reflection in the glass proved the man shouting the route still had something to say. "Whore," he croaked at Dalia's back. She didn't acknowledge the slight much less fling one back at him. It was enough to know that one day he'd meet God. Probably while hanging out the window of the minibus. He'd get hit by the side mirror of a parked car or, better yet, a road sign. His head would fly straight off.

Dalia used the rest of the drive, nearly an hour – or longer, on account of its zigzaggedness – to commit more of Cairo to memory. Before the revolution, she'd done her learning on foot. The traffic circle at Sadat to the market at Saad Zaghloul, with a detour through Garden City if she wanted to see the trees. Or Dokki, by the theater, to Gezira, by the opera house, if she wanted to see the water. Really, the fishermen. Really, the fish in their buckets. Twenty-four hours a day, every day — before, after, even during prayer — fishermen dangled bait off the bridge. She used to walk past them and had loved looking down at the catches, watching fish splash in bids to return to the river. A few times she'd even bought a fish — small, a single serving of meat — cooking it almost beyond recognition. Omran used to say, "The skin is the best part. Fry until it's crispy." She'd cooked the fish and eaten the skin to feel closer to him.

The revolution put an end to that wandering. Dalia had no way to avoid the army, the protesters, the police. There was no real difference between them in her mind. One brought the other into chaos. Police carried sticks and guns. Protesters carried signs and rocks. Soldiers carried bigger guns and radios. Each radio could turn one soldier into a truckload. The worst of the violence had ended, but the memory kept Dalia inside. Her memory was of Mubarak's regime killing protesters out-of-uniform or using hired men. That way the regime couldn't be blamed for civilian casualties. Her memory was of embassies closing and the resettlement process grinding to a halt. Hundreds of thousands of refugees who'd escaped war only to find themselves stuck in a street fight had prayed for miracles. Dalia had prayed with more anger than hope. Her prayers had gotten lost in a city full of protests, full of smoke. Cigarettes, car engines, piles of wood, and glass bottles filled with flammable liquids had all contributed to the haze that hung over the city. Her memory was of many police stations burning along with at least one library.

Dalia left her apartment now for only three reasons: phone cards, food from the corner store, and, as of today, her resettlement interview. Thinking about the interview caused in Dalia the urge to feel something other than sorrow, but trying to avoid the inevitable only hastened its arrival. She tried not to cry; she tried to hide the crying; she tried to stop. If only to prevent the man who shouted the route from thinking he'd wounded her. Dalia thought of her age, which made her happy. In six years she'd be forty, halfway through a full life. Only halfway! If she could come into existence, grow up, and become herself in less than half a life, what could she do with the rest? Row a boat to America? Swim, if necessary? The crying mixed now with laughter, which produced a sound. Something between a cough and hiccup. The hair on the arm of the woman sitting next to Dalia stood up. Dalia saw the hair and knew her neighbor was listening. At the base of each hair, a goose bump. The goose bumps were a divine gift. Their multitude gave Dalia hope. If her hiccup could solicit compassion from a stranger, couldn't also her story? If so, then Hana might approve Dalia's case. And Dalia might see Omran again.

She thought of more divine gifts in order to stop the silliness. Crying on the minibus, thought Dalia, was silly. Stupid, even. Crying begged her neighbors to stare. Their attention was the last thing she wanted. Divine gifts included Omran's humor. He was always doing funny things with deeper meaning, such as naming their cat George after the first American president. Every time the cat had meowed, Omran had saluted the four-legged war hero. The cat had been a war hero because he hadn't feared bomb blasts or power outages or gunshots that sounded like fireworks through the walls. The animal ignorance, or deafness probably, had made Omran and Dalia feel braver. That feeling, as if they'd survive the war no matter how long it lasted, made it easier to love, fuck, cook dinner, eat dinner, and clean up. Dalia had abandoned the cat after fleeing Baghdad, but kept photos as penance for the crime of leaving him. She couldn't bear to forget. Other divine gifts included Alexander Graham Bell, inventor of the telephone, and Rumi, inventor of love. Now, in lieu of sex, Dalia and Omran read his poems to each other, back and forth until some ecstatic and altogether mysterious satisfaction brought the call to an end.

The minibus swung to the curb, exchanged passengers, and re-entered traffic; then swung to the curb, exchanged passengers, and reentered traffic. So on to what felt like infinity. When the minibus finally reached Dalia's stop on the southern edge of Imbaba, she was brain-dead from the dull pain of holding her legs in such an uncomfortable position. Passengers had already disembarked and

the man who shouted the route had reached to swing the door
closed by the time Dalia realized she needed to get out. She made
her getaway at lightning speed, ducking under his arm. The door
slammed shut with such force that the tail of her scarf flipped in
the wind. As the minibus sped off, the man who normally shouted
the route out the window shouted something else at Dalia. Where
his hands would fit on her body. The list of her anatomy was loud
and strangely comprehensive. Not just her breasts. Her neck, her
stomach. The immense and instantaneous repulsion from before
resurfaced as the urge to throw something. Dalia picked up a rock
and threw it after the minibus, now several blocks up the street.
The sound of rock hitting pavement offered little satisfaction.
She wanted to hear glass break. Dalia turned away from the smog
trail of the minibus, expecting the immensity of the city and the
anonymity of the sidewalk to produce the sick feeling one might
get if stranded alone on the Moon—with the ability to see Earth,
but not travel there. The exact feeling presented itself. Strangely,
it wasn't entirely unpleasant. More awe than grief. The distance
was unimaginable.

Dalia walked east along Al Matar Street, then hung left into the
labyrinth. Buildings without distinct characteristics enveloped her.
They were tall, but not very tall, rectangular, and made of brick.
Her building was no different. Not the home she wanted, but the
home she had: the heart of Imbaba, or Embaba in the Tigre language of the camel traders who once plied their trade in the great
Friday market, where an animal's value had been determined in
part by the distance it could spit. Imbaba had since been paved
and built upon. The district had become a knot of corridors, both
poor and poorly lit. Dalia found some comfort in the narrowness
of the corridors, which recalled alleys. She cherished the moments
in which she could trick herself into thinking she was back in
Baghdad before the war.

A neighbor, another Iraqi, sat on the front steps of her building.
Dalia didn't know his name even though she saw him often. He

never seemed to move from that spot. Though he'd only spoken to her once, months ago. The night she'd first arrived. "Today from Baghdad?" he'd asked. The question had contained the pain of a hundred thousand journeys, reminding Dalia that her loss was nothing special. She'd hated the neighbor, perched on the stairs with a cigarette in his lips and a warm Coke in his hand, for asking such a presumptive question. The hate hadn't lasted long. He'd run, too. Had lost someone. Dalia had seen that much in his face and realized her own face must've contained such information. "I love history," he'd said, his body a black shadow on the steps. Yellow light from the building behind him had poured down the stairs. "This street is very famous. Napoléon once declared war on the Mamluk chieftains living here. The street was desert back then. The dead were everywhere. These buildings" – he'd paused, motioned to all of Cairo – "were constructed on top of the bones. This is what I've learned. Every famous city is a graveyard." He'd flicked the butt of his cigarette onto the sidewalk, and the orange sparks went dancing.

That evening, Dalia passed her neighbor the same way she always passed him. No words exchanged on the stairs, but thoughts of regret sent back from inside the building. She was never able to ask his name or hear his story. Dalia feared that speaking to him wouldn't alleviate her loneliness. If she said nothing, there was at least the illusion her isolation was her own fault. A poor choice she could stop making if she needed to. Inside, more stairs waited for Dalia. Five flights, leading to a long hall, leading to a red door. The sound of the dead bolt unlocking welcomed Dalia back to her cramped apartment. By now, she was almost drawn to its smallness. Dalia lay on the only notable piece of furniture. The couch had been in the apartment when she'd rented it and smelled of past inhabitants. Their sweat, their troubles, their smoke. At first, the smell had bothered her. Now it offered companionship. She looked up at the ceiling and tried to decide whether it was gray or pale blue. The debate had raged for a while. In every light the ceiling looked different.

"Blue," Dalia said to the paint. "Right now you're blue." She turned on her side. That way she couldn't second-guess herself. At eye level was a low-standing table, upon which sat her stuff: a phone, a bank card, a book. The phone beguiled Dalia. She wanted to call Omran. She wanted to confess her fear that the interview hadn't gone well, but also the hope that it might have gone very well. She wanted to hear Omran sigh, weep, or reassure her. Knowing Omran, he would reassure her with a joke. "Yes, I know it went well," he'd say. "I feel it somehow in the air. Like how some people can feel lightning before it strikes. 'Run!' they scream. This causes a stampede." Omran would laugh to make time; he would use time to find meaning. "There is no way to stop you from coming." he'd say finally. Then: "I better wash the dishes. I want you to come home to a clean place. Ha, ha. It's very dirty. The kitchen, particularly. I'm sorry to inform you. There's an ant farm in the sugar bowl." The kitchen, in Dalia's mind, had come to symbolize something important about Omran. Not that he loved food so much as he loved the occasion of eating every night with his wife, telling jokes, reading the newspaper out loud, and very occasionally, after the food on the plates had devolved into morsels, surprising Dalia with some kind of dessert. Kleicha, baklava, halvah, or – her favorite – kleichat joz, a pastry filled with nuts, covered in rose water, and cut in the shape of a waning moon. Every bite had been an escape from the war and led directly to the frenetic sex normally reserved for Eid al-Fitr – when, after the month of Ramadan, God lifted His restrictions. They would spend that night and the entirety of the next day completely naked.

Dalia picked up the phone but couldn't bring herself to actually call Omran. What if their conversation didn't unfold the way she'd imagined it? What if they argued? Dalia had felt for some time that an argument was percolating. Something about the nature of patience. How long would Omran wait before moving on? Dalia would never ask such a hostile question. Either Omran would be offended or he'd be hurt. Knowing him, he'd say something like "I know what I want." More than likely, in a tone. A little surly. His point would be that he'd wait until he was decrepit or even dead to be with her. Still, Dalia couldn't shake the feeling that he was growing anxious. He talked often about the children they didn't have and therefore still needed. The sooner, the better. He'd just turned forty. "Halfway through a full life," he'd said like it was an unwelcome milestone. "Quite old to start a family. Soon it will be too late." The opinion, declared as fact, had frightened Dalia. There was no way to know when or even if they'd be together.

Eventually Dalia returned the phone to its cradle. Immediately the phone rang. She startled from the sharpness of the sound and the strangeness of the timing. It was as if Omran, having sensed her distress, had called to say *Hello* and *I miss you* and *I'm here*. Dalia waited a few seconds to be sure the phone was actually ringing and not just ringing inside her head. Ring, ring. She startled again. Not from the sound so much as the idea that she'd imagined something into reality.

"Hello?"

"Yes, Dalia! It's Charlie." A few seconds passed. He cleared his throat. "Hello? Are you there?"

Dalia couldn't tell if she was furious at Charlie for not being Omran or if she was furious at Omran for not having called. "Yes, it's Dalia. I'm here."

There was no response. Maybe Charlie had pulled what he figured was a broken phone away from his face to glare at it angrily. He'd never been a patient man. But Dalia had met few patient men in her life, so she couldn't really blame him. It wasn't a personal failure so much as a biological inadequacy.

"Hello?" said Charlie again. At least he didn't give up easily.

"I said I'm here."

"Sorry, my phone is . . ." He sounded disappointed in the quality.

"Never mind. I'm here."

Dalia knew there was only one thing they had to discuss. Waiting for Charlie to bring it up felt like wanting to breathe and for some reason not being able to.

"The interview!" said Charlie, expertly feigning optimism. "Did it go well? Or did it go very well?"

Dalia had learned to forgive the careless way Charlie spoke to her. He was better at law than conversation. His single-mindedness rendered him unaware of everything outside his purview. That purview didn't include handling touchy subjects with much finesse. Charlie atoned for that shortcoming through devotedness. He labored without rest or even remittance. Dalia didn't pay him, anyway. She wasn't quite sure who did. His clients were asylum seekers and refugees who'd lost jobs, assets, limbs, even members of their families. This insolvent community was bound by the kindred suffering of its constituents. From them, Dalia had learned Charlie's name. She'd learned the Refugee Relief Project was where you went if you wanted to leave Egypt.

"I don't know." The more Dalia thought about the interview, the worse she felt.

"Come on. Not that bad."

Charlie had always been mysteriously devoted to and inexplicably optimistic about her case, which made Dalia worry that nothing would come of it. She'd never had good luck before. Why now, all of a sudden?

"How can I know? I answered their questions. I tried my best to answer them."

"Good. That's good news. Now we wait. I'll let you know when I hear something. Meanwhile, call Omran. Calm him down, please. He's very anxious."

"I will." Dalia hung up. Though she didn't plan to keep her promise. Not today, at least. The argument buried in Boston wasn't the only thing she hoped to avoid. More difficult, possibly related conversations awaited her. Such as what would happen if her petition to resettle was denied. Fall out of love from distance and time and stress and lack of money? Hear later that Omran had remarried? And had kids? Dalia was fixed on avoiding those questions entirely. If she didn't voice her fears, maybe they'd die inside her. That theory, like a mayfly, lived a short life. An oppressive stillness filled the room. Suddenly Dalia needed to call Omran. Not tomorrow. Not later that night. Not ten minutes from now. Her fingers, cured by necessity of their paralysis, punched the phone so fast she dialed the wrong number. She tried again. Ring, ring. Dalia loved that sound almost as much as she hated it.

"Hello?"

"Omran?"

"Hello?"

"Hello, Omran."

The long delay revealed the call's tired journey.

"Hello?" they said at the same time.

Dalia wanted to cry. The business with the phones had grown so old.

"There you are," said Omran after the delay worked itself out. The drone of his voice had a calming effect. "Can you hear me? Or do I sound like . . ." He mumbled unintelligibly.

"I can hear you."

"Thank God. I had a dream last night that you called. I was trying to tell you something important, but you kept saying, 'What?' That's all you were able to say. What, what, what."

A thousand conversations beginning with the same inescapable misunderstanding had trained them to force their communion along. This to prevent awkward silences from becoming lonely moments. Omran made the first move by saying that nothing was to be learned from his dream. He just worried the way all people worried in the absence of whom they loved. Dalia made the next move by changing the subject. She asked Omran what he'd done that day. The boring question betrayed her want for normalcy. Omran said his day was still young. He deplored the time difference. "I just ate lunch. Before that I ate breakfast. I also watched the morning news." The news was painful to watch. He always said that about the news. It caused him pain to see the conflict, to know – and be reminded – where his wife lived. He was ashamed of leaving her. Omran never said so explicitly, but the truth hid poorly in the long drawl of his sadness. Dalia sought to cheer him up by telling what she feared was a lie. That the interview had gone well. "Really?" asked Omran. He sounded much younger and suddenly free of constraint. "Are you sure?" Withholding the whole of the truth – Dalia wasn't sure or even confident – wasn't entirely selfless. She enjoyed her power to affect Omran almost as much as she enjoyed winning arguments or having sex. A sorry inkling alleged that sex would be changed. The inkling bit with such force that Dalia couldn't think about anything else. She envisioned Omran sitting naked on her couch. It was more strange than sexy. Time made everything unfamiliar, even a body. So did trauma, distance, secrets. Dalia knew things that Omran didn't and could never. How might the violence she'd endured come back later as a shadow or even a bright, painful light? Would that haunting affect where she put her hands? Or what she felt when she touched him?

To celebrate the good news about the interview, Omran read a poem by Rumi. He read two lines with particular yearning. "If one asks you how the Messiah revived the dead, before / him kiss me on the lips – 'Like this.'" Dalia blamed the effect of the poem on her mood; it made her skin itch, which made her heart sunder.

3

The Refugee Relief Project, located six blocks north of Tahrir, lived in a one-story cinder-block building guarded on all sides by a wall. Natural light was provided by four windows Charlie called fire exits, all of which were painted shut. The project's nickname was the Oven, and the joke was you could hard-boil an egg in the air. The reality was less dramatic. People inside tended to sweat, but not from heat alone. Clients sweat because they were asked to recount a tortured past they desperately wanted to forget. Interns sweat after discovering they weren't made for nonprofit or third world. Aos, the translator, sweat because he was underpaid. He overdressed to compensate. Two junior lawyers — Sabah, an Egyptian, and Michael, a Brit — sweat because law school hadn't taught them to work so hard or fail so often. Charlie, nothing if not a comrade, sweat to share their pain.

Clients were Africans and Arabs from all walks of life. War, in every form it came, was the great equalizer. Bricklayers, professors, novelists, engineers, thieves, accountants, and men and women who'd dedicated entire lives to prayer with nothing to show for their prostration. All running from something. The fear of deportation. The nightmares. The physical traumas endured. The psychological traumas developed. The fucking boredom of waiting around all the time. They wanted to leave Egypt. Charlie's imagined job was to make that happen; his real job was to very occasionally make that happen. He took solace in the daily grind to forget the likely outcome. The grind included interviews, testimonies, phone calls, and what he referred to as Calamity Management. Last week a man without an appointment, filled with some anger but more fear, had burst through the door holding a knife against his neck. He'd said his name was Ali. Then he'd named his wife and his children: Ramlah, Sabri, Shazi, and Hassan. He'd asked for a stamp in his passport and the four passports in his back pocket. He'd turned to show the bulge. He wanted to go to America and threatened to cut his own throat if he couldn't go. The blade had rested firmly on Ali's skin. Charlie had urged him to drop the knife, to sit down, to begin the long application process. That had only made Ali more agitated. He said he knew the truth. Nobody ever got to leave. Or so few he'd never seen it happen. Charlie had begged Ali to be reasonable. It had been a poor choice of words. To such a perturbed man, the implications must've been sinister. Go home! Give up! Get it over with! Ali had backed away from the office wearing a frightened look on his face. Charlie begged him to wait, but it was no use. Ali turned and ultimately fled the building, knife caressing his neck as he ran. Since then Charlie had suffered from wondering. Where did Ali go? Was he still alive? Is it my fault if he isn't?

The latest calamity had arrived that morning in the form of a rejection letter from the UNHCR. Charlie held the letter—addressed to him, but regarding Dalia—in his hands. He'd read it several times already but read it again while slouching in his chair so that passersby would think he was dead or drunk and wouldn't bother him. He hoped that by the time he finished reading the letter, the world would've ceased to exist. Sucked into a black hole. Burned up in the sun.

"Are you all right?" asked Aos, appearing suddenly. In addition to being Charlie's only translator, he was Charlie's only friend. At least the only friend he saw outside working hours. Still, Charlie found himself hiding the rejection letter in his desk drawer instead of declaring that another case had gone belly-up like a bloated fish in a toilet bowl.

"Fine." Charlie grinned. A poor disguise, but he couldn't think of a better one.

"I saw you reading a letter. In complete despair."

A few weeks had passed since Charlie had called Dalia to ask about her interview. He'd made the mistake of confessing his good feeling. Charlie wondered how many times he'd done that before. Offered false hope as petty consolation.

"Do you think I'm cruel?" asked Charlie.

"Cruel how?"

Behind Aos, Charlie spied a moving body. An intern! Charlie loved the interns. They were unpaid and not bothered by that. Hopeless romantics, all of them. Italians with a taste for adventure; Swedes who wanted to practice their Arabic; Americans with something to prove to their parents. Charlie squinted. It was Rupert, from London, with red hair.

"You told us to convene in the courtyard for lunch." Rupert looked excited and tired and fucking hungry. Maybe a little sorry for interrupting. "For the party boat? Right? That's today? I thought it might not be today, but then it was marked on the calendar."

Charlie forgot it was Monday. He forgot he'd rented a party boat for the interns and that Aos had picked up sweet treats from El Abd, the famous bakery. Also kofta sandwiches from some hole-in-the-wall operated by a man with only six fingers, who claimed a propane explosion had blown the other four clean off. Charlie had forgotten the party boat would play loud Arab pop from Beirut and loud Persian pop from Tehran and would circle the island of Zamalek for three hours while the interns ate their fill and danced their hearts out beneath multicolored twinkle lights strung up in lieu of a canopy. The boat was really a floating dance floor with a motor attached; the captain was really a young man with no prospects. Charlie had even forgotten that he'd prepared a speech. He wanted to thank the interns. After all, they conducted introductory interviews and wrote draft testimonies so Charlie, Sabah, and Michael could spend their time on more important things. As three nonprofit crusaders, they would've preferred to slave in their own salt mines, but their desire to do everything was precluded by the volume of work. Charlie also wanted to thank the interns for not going home. At least, what remained of the interns. Many had abandoned post when the revolution started. Some were frightened and left. Others had frightened parents and left begrudgingly. Charlie had no idea what differentiated the interns who went from the interns who stayed. All he knew was the interns who stayed deserved recognition in the form of a party boat.

"Is everyone outside?" It occurred to Charlie that the answer to his question was clear. The office was quiet. The desks were empty.

"Yes," said Rupert. "Rose-Marie is so excited she's stammering."

Rose-Marie, from Stockholm, who spoke four languages, who had thick-rimmed black glasses, who'd traveled through or studied in more countries than she cared to count — the display of counting seemed to embarrass her — had several nervous tics. Among them, an affection in English for gerunds. In her mouth, *I'm leaving for the night* became *I'm leaving-ing-ing . . . for the night.* Followed by an exhausted look, as if Rose-Marie were tired of waiting for her speech to correct itself and had recently decided to stop making an effort.

"Give us five minutes," said Charlie.

"Okay," said Rupert.

Charlie listened to the sound of the young man retreating on the balls of his feet. A soft walker. The office door opened, then swung closed on spring hinges. "Do you think he was trained to walk so quietly?" asked Charlie. "Or was he born that way?"

"Impossible to say," said Aos. "Now, to that letter . . ."

Charlie loved the sound of the spring hinges, which indicated the front door was in use, that the office served a purpose, that Charlie's life, by proxy, meant something. He checked the clock on the wall. "I can't believe I forgot about the party boat."

Aos' ambiguous gaze – where, exactly, was he looking? – made Charlie feel as if he were secreting information through his pores and Aos was absorbing that information straight out of the air like a sponge.

"Was it a rejection?" asked Aos after a few seconds.

"How do you do that?"

"Do what?"

"Know things before I tell you."

Charlie frowned when Aos noted certain patterns in the mail. Such as how rejections arrived on Mondays, normally. Today was . . .

"Fine. It's a rejection." Saying so aloud caused an intangible ache. Charlie couldn't feel it, exactly. Or rub the spot. The ache existed everywhere and hid itself in its own abundance.

"Whose case?"

"Dalia's," said Charlie, seeing her. Either his memory was getting more visceral or Dalia had left her shadow in the room. Charlie wanted to believe she'd left her shadow, as a gift. He shrugged to obscure any injury caused by failing her.

"Don't pretend this doesn't hurt you."

"Please stop reading my mind. You're only making things worse."

An entire friendship – years old, with scars – declared itself. A hand on a shoulder, left there for too long; awkward laughing; finally, an embrace.

Aos said, "We don't have to give up," and Charlie said, "I know. I won't. I love her."

The music blared nonstop as the party boat cruised up the smooth, brown river. The food was already gone. Thank God, thought Charlie. He was bursting. The sandwiches and sweet treats existed now only as aromas for those dancing near the take-out bags. Charlie's memory was two-faced. Bliss, regret. He'd eaten too much, too quickly. He could still taste the pistachios and the honey. Or maybe the rose water. Charlie probed with his tongue, desperately trying to dislodge whatever piece of nut or pastry haunted him. Failing to erase the flavor, Charlie resigned himself to the sad fate of remembering.

The city looked strange from on the water. Taller, cleaner, less populated. The Sheraton and the Grand Nile Tower feigned grandeur; houseboats and floating restaurants feigned the same. Charlie's favorite floating restaurant – importantly, not for its food – was installed in a permanently moored river cruiser now coming into view. A gallant old vessel that once plied south from Cairo all the way to Aswan. Three stories of pure white wood and a grand deck with lawn chairs spread everywhere. What famous explorers, academics, and travelers, who were all dead now, had leaned against the railings of that cruiser while the hot wind blew their tan hats into the Nile? Charlie loved to wonder and loved more to chuckle at the distance of that history. The cruiser had since been converted into a Chili's, complete with neon sign and bad salad. Charlie had been dismayed upon discovering that fact, but had since then learned to accept that ancient Egypt wasn't a modern country. Ancient Egypt was an illustrated children's book. Now every time he saw the sign – when he crossed the bridge or walked the length of the corniche – he solemnly said to himself, "I wasn't even alive when that boat sailed to Aswan." The basic math, subtracting his age from the length of history, offered comfort. Not much comfort, but some.

"Ah!" cried the captain over the sound of the engine sputtering. The engine died and the music stopped. Had they run out of gas? Had the fan belt torn? Do party boats even have fan belts? The boat drifted north with the current toward the Mediterranean. With no music left to propel the interns, they became ecstatic statues. One intern had been giving swing lessons to the rest. Even Sabah and Michael, buckling under the pressure of seeing others have fun, had participated. Now everyone was stuck at weird angles. The interns finally sat down on wood benches tracing the perimeter of the boat. The men first, awkwardly; then the women, less so, with some laughing. Michael and Sabah moved to the prow, where they leaned against the railing and flicked crumbs into the river for the fish. Their contentedness struck Charlie as unfair. Their jobs were hard. They had no money. Why was Charlie so miserable when he was literally and figuratively in the same boat? Maybe they were fucking. Obviously they were fucking. They'd probably been fucking for months.

Only two sounds survived the death of the engine: the captain cursing in Arabic and Aos trying to light his cigarette with a spent lighter, to no avail. Click, click. Charlie wiped the sweat off his face with his sleeve and said, "Is it just me or does the light have actual mass today? Like if you put your bathroom scale in the sun, it would cry out in pain. A pound! Five pounds!" Nobody answered, but Charlie didn't take offense. He hadn't indicated to whom his question was directed or whether it was rhetorical.

"Would you look at that," said Michael, pointing up at the Qasr al-Nil Bridge just as they floated beneath it. Heads tilted back, but the only visible thing was the underside of the bridge – blackened by smoke, time, weather, and brightened slightly by the twinkle lights. When the boat popped out the other side, it became clear the bridge was occupied by protesters. The music had drowned out their shouting, but no more. The protesters flew flags from many nations. Egypt alongside Libya alongside Syria alongside Yemen. There was no visible military presence. No revolutionary guards in red berets. No heads popping from the tops of armored vehicles. Charlie did, however, notice a single helicopter circling overhead – the faint *whoosh whoosh* drew his eye – but didn't mention it lest it affect the mood. The interns yelled greetings to the protesters. The protesters yelled greetings in return, sharing their surprise, wonder, and excitement in the form of delirious flag-waving.

"Ah!" cried the captain again. Something important had been discovered in the belly of the boat. Charlie hoped the engine would start up and pour fumes, and the music would pour from the speakers at high volume. The sooner the party continued, the sooner it ended. Then Charlie could get back to work. But the captain had only found a box of matches. Aos, at least, was glad; now he could light his cigarette. He smoked it halfway through, then gave the rest to the captain. They joked in Arabic before slipping into more serious conversation. Evidently the revolution had come up. Charlie knew Aos' position from hearing it so many times. The army couldn't be trusted, the Muslim Brotherhood was the wrong party to take power, Mubarak should be imprisoned for life. Presumably the captain disagreed. Both men looked incredibly distressed. Aos lit but didn't share another cigarette.

The protesters on the bridge no longer appeared to be people. The party boat had drifted too far away. The protesters were a single mass stretching from Zamalek to the east bank of the Nile. Yet the interns aimed their eyes at the bridge and spoke in excited terms about the people they'd seen and would perhaps remember as symbols of their time in Cairo. The man who'd dropped a flower in the boat and blessed his country by chanting, "Misr, Misr!"; a boy, aloft on his father's shoulders, who'd chanted the same word at a higher pitch; the woman who'd shouted loudly that the revolution would end when Mubarak was dead, and not before. She'd gripped her sign as if it had meant everything to her. NO EXILE, it read. NO EXONERATION. Charlie hoped this was the extent of the interns' exposure to the revolution. They had been instructed to avoid Tahrir, to avoid crowds more generally, to stay indoors after dark. There was a citywide curfew, after all. They were also encouraged to skip work if they woke up with a sense of dread. Even the lesser sense of foreboding. There was no way to know with certainty if the interns obeyed these commands, but looking at their faces now, full of awe and surprise, there was little doubt. Charlie was relieved. He didn't want to worry about their safety in addition to everything else he worried about. He told himself to stop worrying about so many things. Pick one thing, he told himself, that you're worrying about right now. And stop worrying.

Bang! A column of black smoke shot out of a metal tube. The captain's tense shoulders relaxed as the black smoke dissipated. He rubbed his hands together. "I have a good boat. The engine is . . . eh, not as good." The boat tugged back to the bridge. The interns, brightened by the prospect of floating under the protesters again, talked in the same excited terms about the revolution. How great it was to be in Cairo at this historically significant time. How it wasn't history yet, but one day people would look back. But the interns fell mute on approach, despite the same delirious flag-waving. Charlie saw disappointment on their faces. Maybe repeating what had been a powerful moment had revealed the artifice. The interns on the boat were small fries and had no role to play in the movement occurring on the bridge, except to wave at it.

Several hours disappeared in the same frightening manner as the weeks preceding them, with no trace. The party boat returned safely to dock and the staff hurried back to the office, which was technically open for another twenty minutes. Not that Charlie had patience left to wait for a silent, abandoned place in which to work and think. He cleared his throat before anyone got too comfortable. "I hope you all enjoyed the party boat." Charlie meant what he said, but didn't sound as if he meant it. He sounded depressed. "Let's call it a night. Come back tomorrow feeling relaxed and optimistic." The forlorn display confused the interns, so Charlie said, "Chop-chop." When that didn't work, he unleashed his famous death stare. The interns dispersed under the weight of his gaze, but Michael and Sabah wouldn't leave so easily. His death stare hadn't worked on them since – well, not in a long time. Sabah said she needed to finish Hassan's case, which was too urgent and awful; Michael, nodding in agreement, said he was neck deep on account of the party boat. "Now I'm a half day behind," he said with more regret than his words deserved. The maneuver was so predictable that it had no effect on Charlie. He crossed his arms to show he was impervious to Michael's entreaties.

Coercing Michael and Sabah to go home had been a nightly ritual for almost two years, a term of service much longer than that of the handful of lawyers who'd come before them. Those predecessors, who'd enjoyed playing Charlie's second-in-command far more than they'd enjoyed doing the work, hadn't stayed long. Sabah and Michael were different. Both had arrived during the seasonal burning of rice straw in 2009, when smoke the color of ink hung in the sky above Cairo. Sabah had just finished law school at American University and had refused to leave Egypt despite having the clear opportunity. "I was born here," she'd told Charlie with a conviction he'd never experienced. Sabah had started working the same day she was interviewed. The same hour, truth be told. Michael had come a month later after the smoke was beginning to thin. Winds had blown the ink clouds west into the desert. He told a short version of what he'd called a love saga. He'd met a girl at Cambridge, where they'd both studied law. She was British Egyptian, born in London, with a heart that brought her back to her roots. Michael's heart, beating wildly, had said follow her. So he'd followed her. The love saga had ended a few months later after the love interest decided she didn't like Egypt. Or Michael, for that matter.

"Get out," said Charlie in a stern voice. "Come back tomorrow feeling relaxed and . . ."

Sabah grimaced and Michael waved absentmindedly. Still, they acquiesced. Michael shoved papers into his briefcase willy-nilly while Sabah took a more ordered approach to her packing. The unspoken slight being they wouldn't relax. They wouldn't even try to relax. They'd work from home late into the night and return tomorrow having neither slept nor showered. And likely cantankerous. Charlie's punishment would be enduring them.

Aos was the only permitted exception to the nightly exodus. Charlie's office, Charlie's rules. Not because he owned the office, but because he'd been there since 2007. Considering the pay and conditions, four years was a long tenure. Charlie had arrived immediately after the US troop surge in Iraq. After his brother deployed for the second time to a country that was already contending for the top spot on the Failed States Index, the Fund for Peace's list of countries that best met a set of horrible criteria, including the inability to maintain control of sovereign territory, corruption, lawlessness, the nonprovision of public services, and the involuntary movement of people, meaning refugees. Timothy Wells, brother and army specialist, off to make things worse. In Charlie's opinion, at least. And things did get worse in Iraq. The US Department of Defense claimed to observe security and economic improvements after the surge, but the discrepancy between officially counted civilian deaths and actual civilian deaths increased. Charlie didn't blame the entire war on his brother, but only because that would've been irrational. He did, however, consider his brother an accomplice to war crimes. Turning a sovereign country into a war zone over weapons of mass destruction that didn't exist. Inciting a forced migration, the scale of which was beyond comprehension, only to make that migration physically and legally precarious. Most nights Charlie worked so late one day inadvertently became the next as he tried to undo what his brother had done.

"I've always loved my work," said Charlie after Michael's and Sabah's chairs had lost the body heat contained deep within their padding. "This is the first time I've loved a client. It's not like I have a choice. The heart wants what it wants."

"I've heard that before," said Aos. "Who said that?"

"Emily Dickinson, Woody Allen. Other people."

"It's bad advice."

"Still, you see why I can't give up."

What else could Charlie say to untangle the knot of his affections? That he'd always been attracted to slightly older women, as if they knew something he didn't? That Dalia had more than age, fortitude, and beauty on her side? Though he'd be lying if he said there wasn't some physical element that drew him to her. It was, even to Charlie, a little strange. All but her hands and face were covered. Unless the office was especially sweltering, in which case Dalia would bare her forearms and untuck her scarf from her shirt. It wasn't sexy in the American sense of the word, but watching Dalia roll up her sleeves nonetheless made Charlie feel as if he were bearing witness to a private act. He'd reflexively look away and pretend to write on his legal pad. Somehow Dalia had crawled under his skin despite Charlie's thinking his skin was too thick to crawl under. It was both fantastic and utterly terrifying. He knew he shouldn't love her. It was, among other things, unprofessional. Then again, he did love her. The whole thing surprised Charlie just as it must've surprised Aos. Normally Charlie reacted less intensely to his work. If not by choice, then by necessity; the onslaught demanded he jump from case to case to case. Now, in lieu of jumping, he was flailing. His mind was elsewhere. He couldn't write fast enough. Sometimes he couldn't write at all. He was busy aching and plotting and begging God to help Dalia. Why beg God when Charlie was on the skeptical side of agnostic? It was irrational. No, it was completely insane.

Aos raised his eyebrows. "We never give up. We can appeal the case, same as always. Or find another way to help. A job, a resident visa."

"Appeals never work," said Charlie. "And bah humbug to the other stuff. What good are temporary measures? We need to get her out of Egypt as soon as possible. Not five years from now. Not even one year from now." The sense of urgency was informed by circumstances beyond Charlie's control: the longer Dalia stayed, the more he wanted her; also, the more other clients suffered the spoils of his distraction.

"Well, occasionally the appeal process – "

"Never."

"Very rarely, I'll admit."

"We need to do something else." Charlie stood from his chair with such force that the chair rolled into the wall. He paced and wrung his hands. "Something that might actually work."

"What, exactly?"

"I don't know."

The pacing continued, picked up speed.

"Will you sit down? I'm getting sick from watching you."

"Stop watching!"

"Habibi," said Aos, grabbing Charlie by the arm. My friend. "We can't do anything tonight. The workday ended two hours ago, officially. Let's talk more tomorrow, after you've had a chance to — "

"Are you going to tell me to calm down? Don't say that. It's not meaningful."

Aos was particular when it came to choosing battles. Charlie knew that, so didn't blame him for walking away. A few minutes later, Charlie heard water boiling. Then a cup of tea appeared at his desk.

"Are you calm yet?" asked Aos.

"It's hard to know for sure." Charlie blew the steam off the hot water. More steam appeared, so he blew again. Then more steam appeared. "God damn it," he said, blowing the steam off his cup.

The next morning Charlie showed up unannounced at the UNHCR in 6th October City. The trick to sneaking inside any building, according to every heist movie he'd ever seen, was confidence. Charlie didn't ask where to find Hana's office; he just walked assuredly until he found it. All he had to do now was resist the urge to pontificate, to disparage Hana's work, to impugn her conscience. Control yourself, thought Charlie. Swiftly arrive at your point. Don't argue. Make space in the conversation for Hana to speak. Don't interrupt. Don't rebut in a tone. Remember why you're here. Remember Dalia. Don't dress up her tale; the truth itself is monstrous. Say plainly what you think Hana should know. Ask plainly for help. Don't beg. Don't ever beg. No matter what happens, leave on good terms. You never know when a person may prove useful.

Hana's office was void of life, but that didn't stop Charlie from entering. The door had been left open. There might as well have been a welcome mat. Sunlight busted through the windows in massive beams that seemed to bleach the carpet. The office was much hotter than the hall. Charlie felt like a grape becoming a raisin. He hated raisins. He hated desserts with raisins in them. He even hated his tie, which was the color of a raisin. A deep, textured purple. And a little tight. Charlie tried to loosen his tie, but the knot wouldn't cooperate. Every frustration and failure channeled into his hands. He tried to yank the tie off his neck. In doing so, Charlie dragged himself toward Hana's desk. He leaned against it for leverage. Then tried yanking again. He yanked so hard he couldn't breathe for a second. It was a peaceful feeling.

"You're going to strangle yourself," said Hana, guardedly entering her own office. "If you keep doing that."

Charlie, aghast to be caught off guard, looked up. Dear God, he thought. He'd been ambushed. Wasn't he supposed to be the one ambushing her? It was a shame to give away the upper hand so easily, but Charlie had nobody to blame except himself. He threw his tie over his shoulder to be rid of it. "Hana?" he said, trying hard to sound dispassionate. As if he were here on official business. As if he'd called ahead. As if they'd planned this meeting. "Are you Hana?"

"That's right. Why are you . . . ?" She gestured to his choice of seats.

"Oh." Charlie stood up. Leaning against the desk had prompted him to sit on top of it. The desk had been the perfect height. He'd barely had to lift his body. "God, I'm sorry. Really. I didn't mean . . ."

Part of Charlie regretted coming now that he'd embarrassed himself. He'd never known what to do with that feeling. Were you supposed to learn from it? Were you supposed to pretend it didn't bother you? The same part blamed Aos for having failed to dissuade him. Aos had tried, of course. Last night when Charlie had shared his simple, lambent idea: he'd solicit help from a mole inside the UNHCR; the only way to get a mole was to go there and get one. "Oh, Jesus," Aos had said. "That won't work. Not even with luck, karma, and God on your side will that work." Charlie hadn't listened. Charlie hadn't been able to listen. The only thing he'd been able to think about was why Aos had taken Christ's name in vain when he could've, and perhaps to greater effect, taken Muhammad's.

"Do I know you?" asked Hana after the silence dragged on for a duration bordering on the uncomfortable. "I mean, should I know who you are? Do you work here? Are you delivering something?"

"I run the aid office near the Nasser metro stop," said Charlie, trying and failing to achieve nonchalance. "The Refugee Relief Project."

"Ah, Charlie," said Hana as if there were no one else on Earth he could be.

Charlie felt he was being insulted somehow, but tried not to let it bother him. If his mood got any worse, it would enter that unpredictable territory where he said things as soon as he thought of them. Nothing good had ever come of that. "I received a letter from your office about Dalia. It was a rejection notice with your name on top. To be honest, it ruined my day. Not that I blame you. You're just doing your job." Though he did blame her, didn't he? For sacrificing her scruples out of loyalty to some enigmatic machine? The UNHCR. Headquartered in Geneva. Jam-packed with human-shaped administrative robots.

"It's no fun sending bad news."

"That's true," bemoaned Charlie. Every time he got bad news from the UNHCR, he passed it on to his clients. Often crushing them beyond recognition. They wouldn't move; they wouldn't speak.

"Is there something you want?" Hana asked eventually. Her cluttered desk implied she was a busy woman.

Charlie didn't *want* anything, per se; he *needed* to get Dalia the fuck out of Egypt. There were so many reasons she needed to leave. Her safety, her marriage, the efficacy of Charlie's office. His weird feelings for her, he thought, were not relevant. Were his feelings really that weird? Was it wrong to love someone you'd come to know deeply, who'd told you the story of her life? The long and arduous telling had taught Charlie about the intimidating and remarkable teller: a woman with resplendent forearms, impeccable language skills, and strength beyond even the toughest wood. Hickory, pecan, hard maple. She loved her husband more than Charlie had loved anything. At first, he'd admired what she had. Then part of him wanted it. The other part wanted to get it away from him. "I'm just here about the rejection letter." Charlie's dispassionate tone was beyond reclaiming. "It was – I'm sure you know, since you wrote it – a little vague. There was a check mark in a box labeled *not urgent* and another check mark in a box labeled *not medically necessary*. The former is untrue; the latter is more or less gibberish. What does that mean? 'Not medically necessary'?"

"There's a set of criteria. I can send you the list."

"You know," said Charlie, no longer trying to hide his disdain, "most of my clients don't have the capacity to move on with their lives without physically moving on. Like, to another country."

"We can't resettle everybody," said Hana. She pulled two bottles of cold water out of her minifridge, offering one to Charlie.

How disarming. The room was hot, after all; he was thirsty. "Thanks," said Charlie. The bottle cap resisted slightly. Breaking the seal was crisp, satisfying. "But I'm not asking you to resettle everybody."

"I think you are."

Charlie winced from the sting of the truth. Or what the truth used to be. "Right now I'm hoping we can focus on Dalia." That was the problem, wasn't it? His eyesight? It was as if Charlie had developed some kind of lovesick tunnel vision.

"There's nothing more I can do. I'm sorry. Not that it's actually my fault."

Exactly what Charlie hated about systems. No human was ever to blame.

"You can change your mind." Charlie struggled to articulate why; the reason, like a primary color, was too elemental. "Edward de Bono once said, 'If you never change your mind, why have one?' He makes a good point."

"Am I supposed to know who Edward de Bono is? Or are you trying to make me feel stupid for not knowing?"

"No, you shouldn't know. I'm not even sure how I know. He's an obscure Maltese philosopher. Unless, I guess, you're from Malta. Perhaps then he's slightly less obscure. Anyway, he invented lateral thinking. Like outside the box. Way outside. Once he posited the source of the Arab-Israeli conflict wasn't land or even religion, but low zinc blood levels in the local populations. This from eating too much unleavened bread. Low zinc causes aggression, and aggression causes war. He advised the British government to stop selling weapons to the region and ship jars of zinc-heavy food spread instead. Have you ever eaten Marmite?"

"I think this conversation might be illegal," said Hana. "A conflict of interests, at least."

Charlie relished the moment when Hana glanced out the door and down the hall as if she expected her boss to swing by any second. Her worry indicated the upper hand was shifting in Charlie's favor. "Dalia deserves to leave this country," he said, relaxing slightly. "If you knew her, you'd agree. It's obvious. Really, she's wonderful. Nice and very smart. Doesn't America need more smart people? Who know more than one language? Who can feel empathy? Isn't our country getting dumber and colder as we speak?" Charlie recalled why he'd left Montana; not because he had somewhere to go, but because he couldn't bear living amid selfish white similitude. My land, my God, my gun.

"Urgent cases go first. It's the only just way to fill the quota."

"What do you mean, *urgent*? You keep saying that."

"I mean a credible threat on her life. Is she dying from some injury or disease? Is she suicidal? I mean, has she actually tried to kill herself? Are there scars on her wrists?"

The sound of Hana's words contained compassion, but the words themselves were merciless. Charlie thought saying them must feel like stabbing yourself with a pen – to admit aloud that your job was to measure trauma, then rank it, like a popularity contest in which the winner was crowned Most Hurt Person.

"That's a high bar you're setting," said Charlie.

"It's not my bar. It's policy. How else to evaluate resettlement claims? Knowing the quotas fail to meet demand by a factor of . . . ?" Hana made an imprecise gesture with her hands. "I'm not sure exactly. It's a lot. Most refugees have to integrate locally or repatriate to their home countries. Only extraordinary cases qualify for resettlement."

"Extraordinary? What do you mean *extraordinary*? Like better written?"

Hana looked annoyed by the semantics, but also somehow penitent for resisting them. "Why put Dalia's case above others?" The question, sharp and fast, was clearly designed to kill the conversation instantly. Hana might've accomplished her task had she not tried to slam-dunk with a second zinger. "What do you know that I don't?" The second zinger morphed into less-effective versions of itself as Hana lost steam. Charlie saw a breach developing in what was otherwise her impermeable exoskeleton. It was as if some part of her wanted to help. "That I didn't read in Dalia's testimony? That I didn't learn in her interview? That would change my mind? That would change Margret's mind? Margret, by the way, is my boss."

"It's a long story." Charlie exhumed a letter from his pocket and read what his verboten love had written: a fateful tale scribbled on pages that had been folded and unfolded more times than bore counting. The pages should've torn months ago. Charlie's tender handling was all that had kept the seams intact.

4

Six months ago, Dalia walked into Charlie's office for the first time. Her anxiety had condensed in her legs. "I can't sit," she said. "My legs are . . ." Dalia waved at them. "I would just need to stand up again." Dalia examined the room as if she might find a lost article pinned to the wall or left on a shelf. A letter, a picture, a key. The search delayed but didn't preclude her introduction. At last, Dalia offered her name. She said she was from Baghdad and had lost her husband. Not because he'd died, but because he'd left her. "Not his choice. I told him to go." A world map was on the wall. Dalia put her finger where her husband fled to. Her finger covered the entire state of Massachusetts. Her arm crossed the Atlantic. "It looks so close, doesn't it?"

"Well, it's a small map," said Charlie.

Years of her suffering and years of his loneliness met where they stared at the wall.

"Can you help?" Dalia turned. "Please, the truth."

"I can write your testimony and submit your case. The rest is up to other people, who don't work here. Sometimes I think they don't work at all. They're very slow."

"How slow?"

"For an initial decision? Just from the UN?" Charlie hesitated. "Six months. A year. Maybe longer."

Hearing time discussed that way — as if it moved slowly, but no matter what — actually comforted Dalia, a little. "What do you need from me? A signature? A payment?" Please, not a payment. If Charlie asked for a payment, what would she do? Promise to pay later? Never pay?

"Just where you came from and why you left."

The relief was immense, but temporary. Dalia had always thought of her life as simple, short, often tragic, but punctuated by moments of such joy that she couldn't imagine changing much. A line running from the past to the present. Describing that line, however, was precarious. She couldn't tell the whole story. Not to a stranger. Not to a man. "There are things I can't say." Dalia thought she might never be able to say them.

Charlie offered Dalia a ballpoint and a legal pad. He was practiced, it seemed, in handling such a predicament. Dalia thought his pen trick might work. A pen would allow her to move at her own pace without a live audience. Clarity and chronology were no longer pressing issues. The only downside, so far as she could tell, was that speaking the words let them dissipate in the air, whereas writing preserved them. "Are you going to read this?" asked Dalia. "Can a woman read it instead?"

"I'm sorry. Sabah's desk is . . ." Charlie gestured to his own desk by way of example; it was buried in paper. "She has no bandwidth. Not today. Maybe never again." Charlie laughed, or tried to laugh. His fake laugh was so obvious. He turned red. "Plus, whoever reads what you write — me or someone else — will pass the information along to the UNHCR in the form of a written testimony. From there, the information is public record. Not generally public, but a lot of eyes will read your story. It's the nature of the beast, I'm afraid. I'll wait outside. Don't rush. Write everything."

Dalia pressed the tip of her pen into the legal pad. The black dot grew over time as ink soaked into the paper. Her mind wandered to Omran's missing eye; the bruised socket had been almost as dark. Dalia thought she might as well start there. The origin of that physical injury could be identified and the cost could be described. It was an easy entrance to a darker place, where much worse things had happened. The ink dot grew into a line, a letter, a word, a sentence, and finally the story Dalia never wanted to tell:

My husband's abduction began with a dent in his head. At least, that's how Omran remembered it. He said he woke up with what felt like a dent. He couldn't touch the spot with his hands. They were tied behind him. But his head felt dented. Or broke open, with the brain coming out. A headache, he said, like no other. The ache ran all the way down his neck into his spine. Even his ears hurt like he was deep underwater. The skin surrounding the point of impact – he'd been clubbed with a rock – burned, and the pain radiated outward from there, like someone had scratched raw a large area of skin and rubbed salt in the wound. No light penetrated the bag over Omran's head. He tried to pray and scream and stand up in order to escape. His captors were smart, or at least systematic. In addition to tying his hands, they'd also tied his feet. They'd tied his hands to his feet. He couldn't even sit up comfortably. They drove Omran to a cellar somewhere in the city. Right away they dug out his eye. They provided a single mercy during what Omran called the "prolonged extraction." Each time he woke up, they beat him to sleep again. A few words he remembered only because they shouted them so many times in his face. Traitor! Atheist! American!

Omran talked about the experience only once, shortly after his release. I cried the whole night while he sat at the kitchen table and shook with tremors. The morphine, the shock, the pain of trying to explain how he survived. I couldn't endure his bewilderment. I asked him to stop so I could vomit. Cruel, I think, to ask him that. I didn't vomit. I just stood over the sink for a long time spitting. He didn't know and couldn't ever know what I'd done to free him. He only knew what he felt. The gag, the blindfold, the beating. The feeling of being thrown from a moving car. He felt his skin rub away on the pavement. He felt the sun beating him. He felt my hands lifting him into the sitting position. He felt more hands lifting him into a car. He felt the doctor cleaning his eye socket. He screamed that he needed to see me. The doctor turned his head. Omran saw me in the chair and he wept.

Maybe that's too close to the end of my story. Maybe it's better to start with the war. When the Americans came, Omran said to me, "The sooner they win, the sooner it's finished. God willing." He gestured out the window at the Green Zone. We couldn't see the Green Zone from our window, but we both knew it was there. "There must be something I can do to help." I said he didn't know how to shoot a gun, fly a helicopter, or read a map. War maps are more complicated. How could he possibly help? What if he found danger? What if he died? "If you die, I'll find another man," I said. Not to cause pain, but to dissuade him. "To kiss, to marry, to have children." Omran laughed and touched my wrist. He said his bones told him he wouldn't die. (His whole family had strange bones. His father had bones that found water; his mother had bones that found lies. Prognostic bones were Omran's inheritance.)

Construction. That's what Omran did. He rebuilt exploded pipes and sewers for contractors working for the US Army. An engineer brigade. When my city turned inward and started shooting itself, when it turned inward and blew up its own infrastructure, Omran dug ditches, poured cement, and brought back the water. "For washing," he'd say. "Hands, vegetables, dishes. Infants in the sink." Infants appealed to Omran more than they'd ever appealed to me, but I still promised we'd have one. "Several?" he asked every time the subject came up. "By *one* you mean 'several.'"

Neighbors knew Omran moved dirt with an American shovel and disapproved. What neighbors, I don't know. What militia they contacted, I don't know. Maybe no neighbors. Maybe militias gathered information another way. I don't mean to blame my neighbors with no evidence except a betrayed feeling. Feeling betrayed isn't evidence, is it? Omran was abducted in the name of God, which they screamed in his face when they stole him. Who, exactly? And why? All I knew was that my husband was gone, feared dead. My only hope was that he was held for ransom. Not executed. What good was Omran shot dead? His body had no value and his death would convey no message that hadn't been conveyed already, a thousand times.

I expected the Americans would say one of their own went missing. Omran had labored and made friends and had worked for their army for months. Did Omran not deserve rescue or the money to secure his release? The embassy cited limited resources and a policy of non-negotiation. The soldier watching the door said, "I'll pray for you." I don't remember the young man's name or even the sorry look on his face, except to say it was sorry. At the time, I couldn't bear to observe such a bad omen.

How could I secure Omran's release without money? I sold the jewelry, the computer, the furniture. The cash in my pocket was my only hope for my husband. I sought him by seeking the nearest cleric to our house, who people said had abandoned God for more profitable opportunities. Like connecting militias to recruits. I had not gone to that mosque in some time, since before the war. When I saw him again, he didn't hide who he'd become. He barely greeted me. I told him what happened. I handed him cash. He shook his head like he couldn't help, but I could see the truth in his eyes. He wanted more money. I had nothing left to sell except myself. "Is that worth something to you?" I asked. He didn't even hesitate. His hands fell like rocks upon me.

What to do next besides clean myself? Go home? Wait in despair? No, I couldn't. I couldn't bear the stillness. So I continued my search. I searched for Omran every day by walking and shouting his name, and shouting the cleric's name at the door of his holy hiding place to embarrass him; he would have to keep his promise to quiet me. His face beat red until I found my husband gagged and blindfolded in an alleyway after more than a week, when even my heart said he was dead. A note was stapled to his chest: *Leave now in the name of God.* The blood around Omran's eye had dried and the wound was closed by its own swelling. My heart swelled with love and gratitude and surprise and hate and regret. At the hospital, the doctor said Omran's eye socket was, considering the circumstances, in good shape. The captors, he said, must've given antibiotics. The doctor asked Omran if he'd taken pills during his captivity. Did he know what kind? For pain or infection? Omran said, "I don't remember. I can't remember. The information has gone." He cried my name when he saw me.

Soon after, I packed the car – Omran in the backseat so he could lie down – and drove around the city in a kind of delirium. We had nowhere to go except back to the Americans. They took some responsibility. Not all, but some. Contractors had been persecuted before for their association with the US Army. Had been shot, had been tortured. There was a special, expedited resettlement program for survivors like us. The caveat being violence must've resulted from an association with the US Army. Not religious beliefs or pre-existing ethnic tensions. Not even ethnic tensions exacerbated by the American war. The embassy wanted proof that Omran's blood was their responsibility. And that more blood would spill soon. Written threats, corroborating witnesses, police reports. The only threat we had was *leave now or die* written in pencil. No reason was listed and no sender was marked. We had no witness. No police report. How could we go to the police? Who loved to punish victims, not perpetrators? Who said rape was adultery? And the woman was whipped? What evidence could we present them? Omran's empty eye socket? Only to be laughed out or arrested for lying?

We didn't leave our country because we were barred from doing so. We didn't leave our city because we had nowhere to go. Home, then, for lack of other options, where an unknown enemy lay in wait. The intruders came to our house the same night. They shot the wall, the floor, the window, and finally Omran. Once in the shoulder and again in the meat of his thigh. He held his stomach to fool them into thinking they'd struck his gut. He moaned for a few seconds and stopped breathing. The intruders saw a man killed by his wounds; they saw a wife killed by her grief. "God is great," they said, fleeing.

We didn't go to the hospital. I looked at Omran's wounds and told him he wouldn't die. He didn't have permission to leave me. Omran said, "The pain." I said, "The morphine." Prescribed by the doctor for his eye. Omran took a large dose and said, very disoriented, that we needed to get into the car before he fell over. If he fell over, I would have to carry him. He apologized for being fatter than he was at a younger age and less handsome. "My bones," he lamented. "My bones don't work. They haven't worked in a long time. I'm sorry I lied to you." I plugged the wounds with cotton balls and tied scarves around to stop the bleeding. He could only walk on his right leg, so I bore the rest of his weight. I drove to the Americans at a speed enabled by my terror. "Look what they've done!" I yelled from the far side of the gate. "You didn't believe us before, but look!" I shouted so loud that I spit. The spit convinced the Americans of what the truth had not. That Omran's service had put his life in danger, and also my life. Thank God, for they expedited his paperwork. My husband was granted the right to go to America. But the good news came with a catch. Omran could go, but I couldn't. Not without a marriage certificate issued by the Social Status Court.

The what? I said we were born in a village where the memory of our pledge was enough. We didn't marry in the same village, but one like it. Not Baghdad. Not close to Baghdad. Not anywhere near the Social Status Court. "What else can I do to prove I love my husband?" I asked. "I don't have those papers. There's no way to get those papers. Those papers don't even exist." The Americans said proof of love was not required, but proof of marriage; a document, rather than a feeling or the memory of an event. Unless I could produce the guests who were there and those guests would submit to questioning. The Americans had forgotten they'd started a war! That people had died! That people had scattered!

Omran held my arm like a cane. "I won't leave you," he said. "Don't bother asking." I wanted to peel his hand away, but I let him rest. "If you don't go," I said, "the intruders will return. Ten bullets in your head, Omran. Not even you can survive that. You're stubborn, not immortal." He wept and finally had to sit down. I gave him no option. I told him to go. Thank God his departure was swift. I had no time to fear his absence. It was suddenly before me.

I remained in Baghdad for one month. I couldn't stand it anymore. I couldn't sleep. So I got in my car and drove to the border of Jordan, then along the King's Highway through the Sinai to Cairo. Visas didn't matter by then. People were flooding out. Every border had a queue. You could pay money to skip the queue, but what money did I have that I didn't need for food and water and gas? The only thing I wanted was to make it to Cairo alive. When I finally arrived days later, I found Cairo was only safe in comparison. I was an immigrant in a land that didn't want me. I meant to steal work they didn't have. To implant my sorrow in a place that had too much grown from its own troubles. One night on the train, a man pinched my breast and told me to go back to Iraq. "Go home," he said. And I wanted to, badly. Except home stopped being a place the day I met Omran. Not the same day, but one day, ambiguously, when I discovered I loved him. I was so young. That day I knew I would marry Omran and saw in his eyes that he'd known his whole life that God had pushed him, hard and fast, toward me. Now that he'd arrived, he was so glad. Gladder still that his affections were returned. And that I would be with him.

———————

"Is there more?" asked Charlie when he finished reading the letter. The pages displayed ink smears where tears had fallen and been wiped away. "Please tell me there's more."

"Halas," said Dalia. "It's finished." She watched Charlie's heart beating through his shirt until she realized it was just a fan blowing the fabric.

"Why'd you flee Baghdad after Omran left? What's life like in Cairo? Why can't you stay here?"

"I told you. You're holding it."

Charlie scrutinized the pages, front and back. The backs were blank except for the ink that had bled through the paper. "More specifically. The details matter. More than they should, I'm afraid."

Dalia waved away his request. Telling stories was lonely work. Charlie pretended not to see the gesture. Or needed glasses, badly. He asked the same three questions again. Why'd you flee Baghdad? What's life like in Cairo? Why can't you stay here?

"Telling stories is lonely work," said Dalia, and not politely.

"Hm. I'm sorry, but I need to know."

"Today? Right now?"

"Well . . ."

Dalia couldn't endure his calmness. She walked down the hall to the door, down the street, down the stairs to the metro. The train went down under the river. An hour later Dalia lay down on her bed. Really, her couch. A week passed before she could will herself to go back to the office. How to get to America without Charlie's help? How to get Charlie's help without trusting him? How to trust him without telling him everything? Dalia continued the exhausting process — hour-long meetings scheduled over several weeks — by explaining where pain lives. "In the clothes Omran didn't take with him. In pictures from before the war. Even in George's despondent meow. The poor cat. He never liked me very much, but he loved Omran."

Later Dalia told the story of her flight to Egypt. Not a flight so much as a long, troubled car ride. Her desire to survive weighed more than her fear of driving the dangerous route from Baghdad. The car broke down in the Sinai. Dalia had to walk twenty kilometers before she saw another vehicle. She carried food and water and pictures, minus the frames and the glass panels. The cat stayed behind in the car. "How wicked," she said, "to leave George." Dalia shielded her face with her hands and wept for several minutes before she could speak again. "I shut the windows so he'd die faster. I didn't want him to wander around in the sun and be afraid and suffer for hours. He would've died anyway. It would've been worse."

That wasn't even the most dismal part of her story. Before Dalia took the King's Highway to Cairo, the cleric she'd once bribed with her body returned and raped her again. He didn't knock on her door. He just opened it. "Don't look at me like that," said Dalia, rebuffing Charlie's pitiful gaze. "I didn't even want to tell you." Nor did she want him to tell Omran. What if Omran didn't understand? Her entire being said he would understand, except for the part of her brain where fear lived and reason couldn't penetrate. "Don't tell him. He can't know."

In time Charlie circled back to his hardest question, though he was shrewd enough to change its verbiage. *Why can't you stay here?* became *Why isn't Cairo a durable solution?* Dalia was still annoyed but nevertheless had an answer prepared. It had taken her a few sessions to distill the myriad reasons into one immutable truth: "I can't work. If I try to work, I'll be arrested. If I'm arrested, then . . ." Charlie nodded as if he already knew what would happen. Then why ask? He took copious notes and even recorded the conversations on tape. "For backup," said Charlie, gesturing to shelves full of cassettes. He appeared overwhelmed by the sheer number. "If only our system weren't so . . . antiquated."

Dalia didn't want to know who Charlie was, where he came from, or what kept him at his desk all day. Obsessive-compulsive disorder? Glue? She only wanted to know what the lines on his face meant. Was he affected by her story? Was that empathy? Not fatigue? No, thought Dalia. It wasn't possible that her story had affected him. Charlie must've heard the same story, and ones much worse, a thousand times. More than a thousand times, judging by the number of tapes. Charlie was just tired. Her story meant nothing to him.

5

I n a less professional setting, Hana would've punched Charlie in the stomach. No, the face. What right did he have planting his sorrow in her heart? A fertile, crowded ground.

"I'm not asking you to help me," said Charlie from the floor. Somewhere amid his story, he'd sat. The telling must've burdened him. "I'm asking you to help Dalia."

Hana envisioned Dalia's pain as a sphere rolling behind her. How else to bear so much, so far? If only Dalia's pain were more square. If only she were weaker and more depressed and sicker and poorer and less articulate. If only her entire being screamed her suffering. Then Hana would have a chance in hell of convincing Margret to change her mind. Presently there was no way. "You can appeal the decision." Hana's sadness took a stern form lest it reveal itself. "You have that right. But the same people will review the same case, evaluating its merit using the same policy. I'm sorry. I wish I could help."

"Why don't you?" Charlie tried handing Dalia's letter, which he'd read in its entirety, to Hana. "Please, I'm asking . . ."

"What, exactly?" Hana wouldn't take the paper.

"Well, if there's no chance an appeal . . ."

"There's no chance."

Hana could see Charlie's mind whirling in the way he wrung his hands. "Then a new yellow card. Please, it's the only way."

A yellow card was, at first glance, a Holy Grail. A refugee bearing one, who'd not only endured Refugee Status Determination, but had, by the end of the process, been deemed worthy of the title of Refugee, was allowed to petition the UNHCR for the right to resettle abroad. But the rate of approval was abysmal and each card was tied to a single application; therefore, one chance to resettle. That made a yellow card more like a lottery ticket. If Dalia wanted to play again, she needed to start over. That required a fresh story, a false name, a forged case file. More than anything, it required a new yellow card. There was no way to get one without stealing it.

"You can't be serious," said Hana. "That's illegal. That's *very* illegal."

"It's the right thing."

Hana reached for the phone as if she would call Margret or even security. The threat was enough to dislodge Charlie from his spot on the floor. He stood up, dusted the seat of his pants, and raised both hands in the air as if he were surrendering to an armed guard. He walked that way to the door, only putting his arms down so they didn't bang the frame. "So long," said Charlie as if his last hope had been shot dead; it was a sober, mortal parting.

Relief struck Hana like a spritz of cold water. At last, she thought. The bother was gone. A few minutes later, she saw Charlie again through the window. He was standing on the sidewalk outside. "Jesus Christ," Hana said to herself. "Why are you still here?" She wondered if Charlie could sense her staring at him through the glass. His posture – rigid, as if each arm were made of a single bone; long, and slightly curved, but otherwise unable to bend – indicated as much. A taxi hurtled toward him, but Charlie didn't flinch. Nor did he flinch when the car stopped so close to his body that he needed to step back to open the door. Presumably he knew what Hana was still learning. That taxi drivers were street surgeons. They never hit customers and rarely hit pedestrians. When they did, it was pragmatic: drivers used their bumpers to part crowds or push teenagers, who belonged on the sidewalk, out of the street. Charlie ducked into the taxi, which merged into the heat shimmer bouncing off the road; traffic in the distance appeared to undulate.

Hana sought to think no more of that man, diving back into her work like a suicidal person anxious to jump off something. She found what she always found in the testimonies stacked on her desk. Lists of physical injuries inflicted by gangs, militias, police, and soldiers. Fingernails torn away. Whippings. In one case, an electrical wire was inserted into a woman's genitals and connected to a battery. The captor, who operated the battery, repeatedly whispered, "You'll die soon," into the captive's ear. The shocks caused internal burning. The captor was pleased but not finished. He removed the wire, pinched the genitals, and asked, "How tender?" He took a picture with his cell phone, then sent the picture to the woman's family for ransom. These and other physical injuries manifested later as stutters, twitches, shakes, nightmares, headaches, and uncontrollable weeping. One man described his weeping as a failed cleansing of his memory, his body's desperate attempt to remove toxins that refused to pass in his urine, his sweat, or his shit. Formerly, Hana had read these testimonies as separate accounts. Now they seemed to stack upon one another. Yusuf upon Hakim; Hakim upon Sanaa. Finally, Hana turned away from her desk. To imagine something else, she needed to see something else. Date palms flanked her window from the outside, a kind of natural framing. The date palms, with long leaves, shook even in a light wind. When a vehicle barreled past, for example; or, more rarely, during a weather event. Cairo, thought Hana, had almost no weather. Just as she had almost no purpose in life. What was her purpose? To resettle a few refugees in the time it took to make a multitude? To categorically deny people the right to migrate? The right to migrate was really the right to move on from your suffering. The right to joy, to reunion. The right to forget. Hana felt like the worst person on Earth until a knock on the door proffered the needed distraction. It was Joseph. As ever, his sullen demeanor hid well in his bewitching choice of bow ties. Azalea mélange. And wool, by the look of it.

"I saw Charlie sneak in," said Joseph. "I wanted to see how it went."

If Joseph saw Charlie, why didn't he stop him? Or at least warn Hana before she was assailed in her own office? Hana was miffed, but only a little. It would be petty to mention it. "I'm just glad he's gone."

"He likes to ruffle feathers."

"To guilt-trip."

"To henpeck."

"To beleaguer and displease."

The game ended when Hana realized she was smiling. How callow of her to diminish Charlie. His methods were unorthodox and even offensive, but his intentions – well, it seemed to Hana that intentions mattered. Her own intentions were good. She wasn't to blame. Not for war. Not for quotas. Not even for rejecting Dalia's petition to resettle. Hana was just doing her job, disgusting as it might seem to people who couldn't see the big picture.

Next, Yezin appeared wearing a curious look. "Ah, you survived. I knew you would."

Did the whole office know Charlie had snuck in? Hana would've been angry if Yezin's thick eyebrows weren't so easy to like. Maybe Charlie was a rite of passage. Maybe this was their way of inviting Hana into the fold, by initiation. Maybe they'd be good friends after this.

"Also, for weeks I've been meaning to thank you," said Yezin. "I keep forgetting. Now is the time."

"Thank me? For what?" In Hana's mind, she hadn't done anything. Her greatest fear was that she never would. That she lacked gumption. That her life would pass without impact or meaning.

"For coming here. God knows we needed the help. You've seen the filing cabinets. Soon the cabinets will need another row, another room, another building."

"You're welcome." Hana didn't know what else to say.

"Next week we'll celebrate with cake. Your one-month anniversary. Some people don't make it so long."

"No!" cried Joseph. He put his hands on Yezin's shoulders and shook him lightly. "You've ruined the surprise."

Margret appeared in the same suspicious way as her predecessors. As if she'd happened past and, now that she was here, wanted to get a word in edgewise. "That man's a rite of passage." Margret seemed to think she was revealing something. "By the way, you set a record for most time spent in his presence."

Oh, no, thought Hana. I'm being reprimanded. "I'll send him away next time. Before he sits. Before he even speaks." Would there be a next time? Hana had mixed feelings about the idea of seeing Charlie again. She had mixed feelings about her mixed feelings, so that by the time she untied what she really felt – that she wouldn't mind seeing him – she'd changed her mind and decided to never see Charlie again. He was shortsighted, selfish, theatrical.

"I wanted to make sure he didn't crush your spirits," said Margret. "I'm sure he tried."

"He tried very – "

"Exactly. I knew you'd resist his pageantry. That's why I pulled your résumé from the pile." Margret's gesture indicated the pile was enormous. "I said, 'This woman's the one.' "

Margret smiled before she left and Joseph shrugged before he followed her. Meanwhile, Yezin did something strange with his eyes. As if he was trying to express regret or empathy. Maybe he felt guilty for letting Charlie sit on her desk but couldn't apologize without breaking rank. The best he could do was indicate his heart wasn't a dead place. That he felt something. A difficult, awkward task, thought Hana. His eyes were wide-open with eyebrows lifted so that he looked assaulted by surprise. A loud sound, a sharp pain, a sudden gust of wind pushing him toward a precipice.

———————

At 6:00 p.m., Hana jammed papers into her briefcase and called Mustafa for a ride home. For three reasons she had yet to call another driver. In ascending order of importance: she still needed to pay for his door; he never asked intrusive questions; he never gawked at her in the rearview mirror. Plus, if she matched his energy – yakking back and forth as if at some point they'd become friends – the forty-minute commute became a window into Mustafa's life and times. In traffic jams, or when the army blocked the road, Mustafa idled and told Hana about his family, the protesters, the army generals, even the Egyptian Museum. Some people said the Egyptian Museum had become a makeshift prison. At night, police hauled protesters to the basement and tortured them next to a hundred sunken reliefs depicting Ra, the sun god. Mustafa said these facts as if they were speculations; with the hope, perhaps, that they weren't true.

Did he fear the revolution as much as he claimed to welcome it? The question swirled in Hana's mind, but she never dared release it into the wild world of Mustafa's taxi – a wheeled collection of oddities that defined its driver. Every time Hana got a ride, she noticed something new. A box of tissues was glued to the dash and pictures of Mustafa's family were glued to the box. "For easy seeing," he'd said. There was the flag of Egypt and, strangely, the flag of Germany, both on tiny plastic sticks jammed in the middle console. Mustafa loved the clinical style with which the Germans played football. "Kampfgeist," he'd said. "The fighting spirit of German national team." There was also his Qur'an, a constant bulge in his shirt pocket behind his cigarettes. Hana's favorite oddity dangled from the rearview mirror. A bright yellow SpongeBob SquarePants, the size of a fist. "My last birthday gift," Mustafa said after he'd caught Hana staring. "My daughter bought me the toy she wanted for herself. I did not give it to her." The doll swung on the mirror every time the taxi flew around a corner. The repetitive motion had the same psychological effect on Hana as a seat belt. If SpongeBob was safe, then she was, too. Hana worried less about Mustafa's lead foot and resigned her fate to the will of the cosmos.

That night the cosmos was in a bad mood. Gridlock on the Qasr al-Nil Bridge meant Mustafa's taxi wasn't going anywhere anytime soon. They were stuck. Possibly forever, judging by the number of cars. The cumulative effect of so many idling engines was a slight vibration in the bridge itself, which caused loose screws or cracked plastic or some other part of the broken door to make a soft rattling sound.

"What's the smoke up ahead?" asked Hana. "Tear gas? Fireworks?"

From a distance, every protest and every celebration in the square looked the same. It was hard, then, for Hana to know whether the revolution was going well or not. She felt bad for not asking more often and worse still for being in a position where she didn't have to know.

"Hm." Mustafa excavated his mobile phone from the middle console. "Let me find out. My friend broke his taxi. He has nowhere to go but the square." Mustafa dialed, chatted, laughed, chatted some more. Several minutes later he hung up. "Not tear gas," he said gladly. "No army today in the square. The protesters are blocking traffic by themselves accidentally. Too many people. Copts, Muslims, atheists, foreigners, even women and children. The smoke is a bus that caught fire from no coolant. My friend says they're dumping water on it."

"Children? In the square? Are they protesting?"

"If the parents are protesting, the children must come."

"The children are safe?"

"The children are bored easily. They don't stay very long. They beg their parents."

"And the women?" Hana had heard about molestation and rape in the square, but felt somehow divorced from the danger. Maybe reading about rape all day at work made the endemic feel as if it belonged in other countries. Or maybe because her entire Egyptian experience had occurred in a building or a taxi. She hadn't even seen the pyramids yet, much less stood in the heart of Tahrir.

"I'm sorry to talk about this, but, yes, sometimes the women are touched. Worse things also happen." Mustafa put his head down as if he found shame in a crime someone else had committed. "I saw once and tried to stop, but the crowd was too thick. The woman was carried away."

Pedestrians on both sides of the bridge streamed freely toward the square. Most faces Hana saw contained some degree of excitement. There were only a few sour faces. Old men, mostly. Maybe shouting protesters kept the old men awake at night. Or the old men were also protesting. Maybe they were kept awake by their own shouting. Hana suddenly loved the old men with sour faces. Not to mention, the way bright scarves floated atop brown shirts, black jackets, and tan pants. There were so many women. Why hadn't she noticed before?

When the bridge finally cleared enough to allow cars through, Mustafa zipped to Hana's building. "Ma salaam. Good night." Mustafa gripped the wheel as if he wanted to peel away. The night's profits were already bound to be low. And lower still if he didn't find more customers before they found other taxis.

"I'll call soon," said Hana, rolling the base fare around her generous tip so that Mustafa wouldn't try to hand back the extra money. It turned out he didn't like accepting more than the journey was worth. "By soon, I mean tomorrow. God willing."

Hana rushed inside as if the repose of home awaited her. That comfort would clear her mind and perhaps even allay her conscience. Wasn't rejecting Dalia's petition the only sensible choice? The elevator door, however, was stuck. "Damn you," Hana said to the door, though her true marks were Charlie, Margret, and the vile creatures Mustafa had seen steal that woman. Hana yanked the handle so hard the door bounced open the other way. How embarrassing to forget to push a door so clearly designed to be pushed. She slipped into the lift to escape the possibility that someone had seen her. The cable whined as floors slid past. When the lift finally came to a stop, it halted in such a way that Hana experienced a fleeting weightlessness. The feeling was hard to enjoy despite her wanting to; she was too focused on whatever feeling would come next. Hana sped down the hall to find out. The polished concrete guided her to a familiar brown door. Though not entirely familiar. The inlaid geometric pattern seemed to get more complicated as time passed. "Here goes nothing," said Hana, fishing in her pocket for her key. Would the repose of home waft out when the door opened? Would every worry fade away as she reclaimed her weightlessness? Alas, no. Her door revealed the same dark apartment poised above the same elusive city. Just like last night. Just like every night. Hana wondered when and if that would change. She dragged herself to the kitchen in the meantime. She wasn't hungry, but nevertheless felt the need to eat. "Food cures loneliness, too," Ishtar had once said, wrist deep in mashed fava beans. "You're with whoever taught you the recipe." Dinner that night was leftovers from the night before: fattoush, chopped garlic from a jar, and falafel smothered in tahini, which was what Ishtar made whenever she didn't feel like spending hours laying pastry or braising meat. Hana had tried to re-create the meal with mixed results. The results were worse after a day in the fridge. She stopped eating to call Ishtar.

"Hello?"

"Mother bear," said Hana. "Update from the front line: still alive, still miss you."

"My bean."

"What bean?"

"My little bean," said Ishtar.

"Not poppy seed? Wasn't that my . . . ?"

"Poppy seed was before you were born. Even when you were smaller than one, I still called you that."

Hana didn't like to think of herself as formerly microscopic, with no ability to bear witness, to bear thoughts, to control anything. She entertained the idea, if only in her head, that she was born at the moment of her first memory. She was three years old. There was cake. She was already in America.

"How did *bean* come about?" asked Hana.

"You were a weirdly shaped newborn. I was just looking at old pictures a minute ago. They reminded me." A single forlorn laugh indicated that Ishtar was still looking at the pictures and secretly wanted Hana to know. "So, what are you doing?"

"Picking ants out of my sugar bowl."

A long pause told her the conversation wasn't going as well as she'd thought. Why not? What happened? Was Hana supposed to ask more about the pictures? Or reminisce about childhood? Or tell Ishtar how much she was missed? Hana had already said that, but maybe Ishtar wanted to hear it again.

"You should call more than once a week." Ishtar's words burst from some confined place. "Really, it's not enough."

"What's your ideal number?"

"Seven?"

They both laughed sadly.

Hana didn't know exactly what she'd called to say, but the vagueness of her want didn't make it less pressing. "Pretend you're still in Baghdad," she said finally, and calmly to make the transition easier. In case it caused Ishtar some grief. "Pretend you need to leave now before something bad happens. Your death, your capture. Or something less dramatic. Theoretically, I mean. Not actually less dramatic. Is a lifetime of forced isolation and poverty really less dramatic than death? This is a formal interview. Your one chance to convince me to help you run. What would you say? What did you say, actually?"

"What a way to change the subject. Wow, really."

"I know, I'm sorry."

"That was thirty years ago. No, more than that. Thirty-one."

"You don't remember what you said?"

"I didn't have to say much. Your sister was in tears. You were a bulge in my stomach."

Hana's sister hadn't been a topic of conversation in some time. It was good to hear her name again. Leilah. Not that Ishtar had actually said her name. All the same, it was good to talk about her. The initial relief gave way to pain and longing. Hana needed to walk. Except the phone had a short black cable. Hana pulled the cable to see if it would stretch. It didn't, but the phone's cradle did fall out of the wall. Meters of telephone cord, formerly spooled in the hollow behind the cradle, unfurled on the floor. Hana was suddenly free to walk wherever she pleased, so long as she didn't mind the sound of the cradle dragging behind her.

"Hello? What happened? Are you still there?"

"I'm here." Hana dragged the cradle toward the balcony.

"What are you doing? What's that sound?"

Before Hana could explain — mounting laughter prevented her from opening her mouth lest a guffaw escape — a new sound filled the air. A buzzing sound, like mosquitoes or bees. Every light in the room brightened. A few bulbs even changed color. Soft yellow became nearly white. "Shit," said Hana. That sound could mean only one thing.

"What?"

"The electricity — " started Hana, but it was too late. The lights went black and the call ended. There wasn't even a dial tone to keep her company. Still Hana couldn't bring herself to hang up the phone. She just held the handset against her ear. It felt comfortable. Then for a reason beyond even her own understanding, Hana continued to talk. "Hello?" she said, testing how weird it would feel to speak with an imagined, silent Ishtar. Weird, but not horribly weird. Not so weird she couldn't do it. "Do you mind if I change the subject again? I know, I'm scattered. You've always said that about me. That I'm scattered." The weirdness plateaued. "I rejected a petition to resettle. A petition? Jesus Christ. Her name is Dalia. I felt terrible. You know, typing the letter. Checking the box on the form. The form lingered in the mail for a few days. Like ten days. Twelve, maybe? Margret says it takes time to disseminate even basic information. Yesterday that information was disseminated. Now I feel much worse. Guilty, even. Why? Because Dalia's from Baghdad? No, that's too simple. And makes no sense. I'm not from Baghdad. Not really. You're from Baghdad, but Dalia's not like you. Not that it would matter even if she were exactly like you. Your history isn't relevant to her case. Or my opinion. Still, it makes me wonder. What if Dalia were from another conflict zone? Sudan, Somalia. I'd have to reject her case all the same, but would I feel the same?" Hana toggled the switchhook in a futile attempt to revive the dial tone. She thought of Rita. Why was that so much easier? "I had good reason, I think, to reject her. Dalia's case wasn't urgent, where *urgent* means . . . oh, I don't even know. How can I know? More importantly, how can I judge? And I got to thinking today in the car. Was your case urgent? Would I think your case was urgent?" Hana toggled the switchhook again, desperately. "Maybe the process was different back then. Another time, another war. I know that. Tell me, what was it like? Were the questions intrusive? Did people look at you skeptically? I wanted to ask before, about a hundred times. Only the story felt like yours and Leilah's. What right did I have to that narrative? I wasn't there, not really. Leilah said my only function at the time was to make you puke. She laughed with a bleak look in her eyes when she said that. You remember the look? It surfaced occasionally. I never figured out what it meant. I think it meant she missed home. You two always had that in common."

Tired of wounding herself, Hana finally hung up the phone. The dark and quiet made a perfect vacuum. To disturb the stillness, Hana searched for the origin of the power outage. She searched as if she might actually find something. As if there were a small chance it wasn't the Supreme Council of the Armed Forces cutting power from afar with a switch. The council loved cutting power to demonstrate its reach. Far and wide, into every person's home. After checking the outlets and the fuse box, which proved inconclusive, Hana finished walking to her balcony. She held the railing with both hands. The chipped paint gave the railing a venerable feel, as if it had witnessed history. The whole neighborhood, as far as she could see, was black except for the white glow of camera phones, which turned every pedestrian into a journalist. The river of light flowed south to Tahrir, where protesters guarded the tent city. Tents provided shade, food, and medical treatment for both protesters and passersby. At night, the same tents became freedom hotels.

Any friend of the cause could sleep for free on the ground. The act of sleeping defended the tent. After all, the army couldn't crush a tent that was full of people. Not without alienating more politically correct allies. Not without risking sanctions. Newspapers celebrated or decried the freedom hotels as per their political slants, but Hana was of the opinion that tents were meant to be slept under. Did that make her a friend of the cause? Would she ever go there to sleep? The idea excited Hana even though the revolution wasn't hers to defend. Then again, whose revolution was it? Having begun in Tunisia. Having spread across northern Africa into the Middle East. Having been broadcast worldwide as a symbol on TV. Tahrir, she knew, living down the street from the square, was a symbol; but it was also a real place with tents that were getting torn down. Not that moment, but some nights when the army rolled in unannounced, armored vehicles kicking up dust that had been lodged in the cracks of the streets for decades. Hana wanted to breathe that dust instead of just watch it plume and eventually settle.

6

"You're the first person to get Alzheimer's in their thirties," said Charlie to himself in the mirror. "Congratulations." The party boat, after all, wasn't the only thing he'd forgotten. He'd forgotten that his brother, who'd ambushed Charlie by surprise and was in Cairo for one day – en route back to Baghdad after his leave of absence – would fly that night on the red-eye back to the war. Even though that war was supposed to be over. *Let's put an end to our feud,* Tim had written via e-mail in advance of his obscene layover. *I'm bored of it. I'll probably never be in Cairo again. Normally I fly through Frankfurt.* He'd offered drinks as penance for a tense childhood and a long, silent estrangement. Not only was Charlie dreading it – his original plan had been to drink a few beers with Tim, then say good-bye in a vaguely hostile way, something like "Good luck in Baghdad" – but now Charlie had more pressing things to do: tell Dalia her case had been rejected without emitting any kind of sorry moan; tell Omran he might never see his wife again without feeling some kind of sick joy that Charlie would still get to see her; finally, locate a straw longer than his whiskey bottle so he could drink the whole thing without moving. Unfortunately for Charlie, the desire to abandon his brother wasn't matched by the capacity. He just couldn't will himself to be that cold. He wanted to, badly.

But couldn't. It was something his mother had told him before she'd died. That deeds follow you. "Shit!" said Charlie to his grimacing face in the mirror. He exited the bathroom, swinging shut the plywood door with more force than necessary but not enough to cause a loud bang. Charlie was disappointed. He'd wanted Aos to hear the door. To look up. To say something.

"Are you ready?" asked Charlie in a deceptively neutral tone. He didn't want to sound indignant. "For tea?"

Every Wednesday after work, Charlie and Aos drank tea on the corniche. They nursed the hot water and watched feluccas — small wooden vessels propelled by giant triangular sails — nearly collide with the bridge. Charlie was anxious to begin the ritual, but Aos didn't indicate his readiness. He just kept translating. His pen seemed to move of its own accord, like a sentient extension of his hand.

"Hello?" Charlie loathed to interrupt such devotion, but needed to get the fuck out of the office. The office contained every ball he'd ever dropped. Not to mention the mirror in which he'd seen his brother. Sad how they shared the same features but not the same principles. Both were handsome, if hairy; left unchecked, their eyebrows would connect and their beards would cover their necks. Charlie suspected he was more Neanderthal than other men. He allayed this fear by keeping a trim image.

"Yes," said Aos. "One second."

Ten minutes later they walked to the corniche, the promenade on the east bank of the Nile. They sat on blue stools and sipped black tea from hot glasses. The glass was so hot that Charlie couldn't hold it for too long. He rested the glass on the red bricks beneath his feet. Aos, who'd developed calluses, laughed at the procedure. He'd been drinking hot tea his whole life from glasses with no handles.

"How do you endure the pain?" asked Charlie.

"What pain?"

Charlie pointed to the steaming glass.

"When I was a boy, my father told me to rub my thumb against my index finger every day for several minutes. He said, 'One day you'll know why.'"

It always made Charlie a little uncomfortable to talk about Aos' dad. He'd been a security guard at the Semiramis Hotel in 1993, the year a disturbed musician played his revolver in the coffee shop. Four people were shot dead. "That's good advice," said Charlie, looking with scorn at his thumb; it was barely callused. He started rubbing his thumb against his index finger. It occurred to him, as the rubbing intensified, that he'd never leave Egypt. There could be no life without hot tea on the corniche. "By the way, I've been meaning to ask. Will you come to El Horreya tonight?"

"I don't think so," said Aos. He'd already reached his weekly quota of nights out: one, maybe two. Not counting protests in Tahrir, which were beyond stricture. "I think I'll just go home."

"Don't tell me you're behind on your reading."

"I am behind."

Aos read the entire Qur'an every month; the routine, on account of being so boring, required a schedule.

"Double tomorrow's pages," pleaded Charlie. "I wouldn't ask if I didn't need you."

"What for?"

"Tim wants to drink warm beer until curfew. I'm worried I'll commit a murder-suicide. Come and stop me?" The joke landed exactly as intended. Aos groaned and looked over his shoulder in the direction of El Horreya. Due east one kilometer. Charlie thought he'd sealed the deal until Aos said, "I'll come if you tell me . . ." But Aos couldn't bring himself to actually make his demand.

"What? Tell you what?"

Aos turned red and took refuge in his tea. "I'm embarrassed to ask. It's about Dalia." The only thing that could embarrass Aos so totally was the topic of sex. He'd always been overmodest.

"Oh, God. You think Dalia and I . . ."

"I'm sorry! It's killing me! I have to know!"

Charlie spit in the river. There was sand in his tea, though it wasn't the tea seller's fault. The tea seller occupied a windy spot by the river. He worked all day for almost no money in horrible conditions without complaint. At least, Charlie had never heard the tea seller complain. Not about the wind. Not even about his fate. Was his fate really that bad? He had a cart, a view of the river, plastic chairs, and at least two regular customers. He didn't look that unhappy. "I can't answer a question you didn't ask," said Charlie. The futile attempt to evade only forced Aos to speak candidly.

"Did you touch her? Did you kiss her? Did you . . . ?"

"No."

Aos relaxed a little. "Then . . ."

"God, Aos. Hurry up. My brother's waiting."

The prodding tightened Aos' orbit around the question he was really trying to ask. "How did this happen?" he said finally. "One day you just woke up in love?" The deceptively shallow inquest contained an army of implications. That Charlie should've known better; that his acumen was compromised; that his work, as a result, would suffer.

It wasn't easy for Charlie to trace the origin of a love he'd spent months trying to put down like a sick dog. The dog in his heart wouldn't die, so he'd muzzled it; the biting pain had subsided, but had been replaced with the constant high-pitched whine of confinement. "I never met a client I didn't like," confessed Charlie. His greatest sin was his bias. "I know I like them because their stories hurt me. With Dalia, the pain became love. I can't explain how or why, exactly. I can only tell you when. The day Dalia called in a terror. 'Come quickly,' she said. 'My bawab is unlocking my door.' The bawab wanted money for an undisclosed building repair. You know the ploy. 'Please pay. Right now. The repair has already been made.' And you pay to get rid of him. Dalia wouldn't pay, so her bawab wouldn't leave. She closed the door in his face. That didn't stop him. He kept a spare key. By the time I arrived, the bawab — a large man made giant by his fury — had burst into Dalia's apartment and pinned her against the wall with his broom. The shaft of the broom was pressed horizontally across her chest. 'Hey!' I cried from a safe, cowardly distance. 'Put down the broom. We can figure this out . . . some other way.' The bawab fixed his hot stare on my shoes. We never made actual eye contact. 'Get out!' he shouted, freeing one hand from the broom to wave me away. 'Unless you came to pay.' I was the invertebrate who produced his wallet. Dalia shouted that no bawab like this should be paid and, enraged a thousand times by the idea of paying him, twisted the broom from his grip. The bawab was stunned and stunned again when Dalia began whipping him. The broom cracked against his back as he ran screaming from the building." Charlie finished his tea with the sand in it; he scraped the sand off his tongue with his teeth, then off his teeth with his finger. "Dalia wasn't even a little calmed by the bawab's absence," rued Charlie. "Like she knew he'd come back, and soon. She began packing her things. 'I need another apartment,' she said. 'I need the only key to my door.' All day I was gone to help her find that kind of place. Being white made it much easier. She was sorry to know that and I was sorry to find out. Somehow we agreed not to mention it."

Charlie was suddenly overwhelmed by the task before him, of explaining himself; he'd failed to describe Dalia the way he saw her. He thought he should've told Aos more about how Dalia gripped the broom without fear and whipped the bawab just enough to send him running, but not enough to injure him. And how she seemed to deeply regret the violence afterward. "I forgot to say . . ." Charlie's train of thought not only derailed, but exploded. He was trying to explain what couldn't be explained. If no poets in history had successfully captured their love, how could Charlie, who was more Neanderthal than most men, possibly shed light on the sick dog in his heart?

El Horreya, known to cure depression, drowsiness, loneliness, and temperance, was hidden on a street leading northeast from Tahrir Square, less than twenty minutes by foot from the corniche. No sign or menu was displayed out front, or other declaration begging patronage. Those who knew about El Horreya either stumbled in accidentally or were told to go. Recently El Horreya had been renovated. The charm of the gritty walls had been lost, but the beer was still cheap and the coffee still cost less than clean water. It was a baladi bar, a watering hole for locals who loved chess and their foreign friends who loved feeling like a part of something. Tables were covered in chessboards, ashtrays, mobile phones, and bottle caps.

Tim was already meandering outside by the time Charlie and Aos arrived. When he saw Charlie, Tim cocked his head like a perturbed animal. "I was beginning to think I was lost. I hate that feeling. The only worse feeling is getting shot in the leg." Then after a pause: "It's good to see you again."

Counting how many years it had been distracted Charlie from the obligation to hug his brother. They walked inside without touching. Charlie led the way to a square table in the back corner, where he sought to let the comfort of his favorite haunt sink in and overwhelm him: the humidity, the smell of lupin beans, the dry beer gluing his elbows to the table. If it hadn't been for Tim's fidgeting, perhaps Charlie would've achieved his tranquil state. As it happened, Tim's body was slightly too big for his chair. Each time he adjusted his position both men grew more ornery.

"I need a drink," said Tim, finally giving up and sitting still. "Is there a menu? A waiter?"

Charlie didn't know how to explain. Not that he wanted to try. He preferred to think the obscure system was beyond account. It was the sort of understanding you had to acquire through experience.

"You have to make eye contact," said Aos.

"With who?" asked Tim. "Also, nice to meet you." His face said it was not nice, that he wanted privacy, that Aos wasn't supposed to be here.

"My pleasure." Aos pointed to the best-dressed gentleman in the room: a man wearing a perfectly ironed button-up, who flew through the seating area with speed and fluidity. The man opened bottles as he set them down, but never actually stopped at a table. Tim tried staring at him, but not for long; the embarrassment was too much. He turned away. "Maintain eye contact!" cried Aos. "You have to earn his attention. It doesn't come easily."

Charlie had, once upon a time, received the same instruction. Hearing it again was almost nauseating. To think, he used to have no idea how to order beer at El Horreya. Thank God that phase of his life in Egypt had ended years ago. Charlie wasn't local by a long shot. He could never be local. But he wasn't a tourist. Not anymore. He knew how to cross the street without getting run over, how to pay utilities without getting ripped off by his bawab, how to use every form of public transport without getting lost. At least, not terribly lost. He even knew how to order groceries by phone and have them delivered by motorcycle.

Tim tried to make eye contact again, but it was no use. "What am I doing wrong?" The question bore an unnamable ache, which proved Tim hadn't changed in the years since Charlie had seen him. He was still a cryptic bastard. The waiter delivered beers only after Tim quit eyeing him. Clearly perplexed, Tim said, "I don't understand. Why, after all this time, did he bring . . . ?" Tim grabbed the bottle nearest to him. "And why did you, after much longer, bring . . . ?" He pointed the bottle at Aos.

"Embrace the mystery," said Charlie. He refused to let Tim's questions get the best of him. If he answered earnestly, the conversation would be free to evolve; as fruit, it would bear other subjects. Brotherhood, for example. Charlie didn't want to talk about brotherhood or anything adjacent to brotherhood. Why unearth what had passed between them? Not just words, but money; not just money, but blood. That tired history began with an accident. Charlie had, after claiming he wasn't drunk, wrecked Tim's car. And Tim's face. Tim was asleep in the passenger's seat. His face beat a hole in the dashboard after the air bag failed to inflate. His personality changed less than his appearance, but nonetheless diminished; he became a darker sort with a shorter temper. To apologize, Charlie spent what had remained of his savings – law school had bled him almost dry – on a used model of the same car. The title changed hands without even a smidge of forgiveness. That destroyed Charlie, who saw no other way to repent. He buried his regret inside his reticence. Soon the brothers stopped talking. Charlie went to Egypt; Tim went to war.

"It's not really a mystery," said Aos, eyes still aimed at the waiter. "If you can figure it out by paying attention, it's more like a puzzle. Puzzles want to be solved. That man wants to sell beer. The trick is convincing him that his best route includes your table."

Tim leaned back in his chair until the wood creaked. "There's no alcohol at Camp Victory. I can't even drink when I'm off duty. There's nothing to distract me from what I really want. My children, my wife. I have to sit there all day thinking I'm going to die before I see them." Just then the button-up guy swung round again, this time delivering lupin beans – large, brown, soaked in brine on a white plate. Tim didn't bother asking who ordered or how the fuck. He just smelled the beans before asking if the button-up guy had peanuts and/or pretzels. "Pretzels," said Tim. "You know pretzels?" He tried to make a pretzel with his fingers. The button-up guy snickered and told Tim in decent English to eat the beans.

The air in the room was humid from the sweat of men playing chess. Charlie, grabbing an unused board from another table – on the fly, gifting cigarettes to the occupants for their generous surrender – said to Tim, "The first time I played Aos, he beat me in less than ten minutes. I'd like to see how long it takes him to beat you." Charlie knew the challenge would appeal to Tim, whose competitive nature had always been disguised as an attention to detail; as a kid he'd been happy to win any game on a technicality buried in the rules somewhere. Tim had called it "planning ahead" or, when he was really proud, "playing with strategy." If Charlie was lucky, the game now would drag on until night fell. Then he'd be able to avoid whatever serious conversation Tim had smuggled into the country. Charlie would look indignantly at his watch and say something damning about Mubarak's curfew: *Why does the army still enforce the tyrant's command? It's unjust! I'm so angry!* They'd have no choice but to call it a night. Then Charlie could go home and stare at the phone until he found the courage to pick it up.

"Uh, sure," said Tim, irked if not yet stymied. Nobody asked Aos if he wanted to play, but Aos didn't seem too bothered. He loved chess enough to play in unsavory conditions. Once he'd played outside in the rain. Tim arranged the chess pieces on the board, turning each piece until they faced the same way. Even the pawns had faces, which were scrunched up. Tim said the pawns were dismayed by their fate. Not as a joke, but as a sad fact: "Their lives don't really figure into most defense strategies." Tim gifted Aos the first move even though Aos was using the black pieces. Thus began a silent slaughter. Aos played slow, decisive chess and never regretted a move. Or else never admitted regretting one. His pawns inched forward the front line while his cavalry hung back with his castles, his bishops, his queen. Even so, Tim's king perished in less than twenty minutes. Fuck, thought Charlie. "Ah!" said Tim, amiable to a fault now that he'd finished his drink; he was downright neighborly. "I see your trick. I know what you're doing." His skin had become a nice pink color. "Rematch? Just one more?" To entice Aos, Tim added, "If you win again, I'll eat all those nasty . . ." He threw a queasy look at the beans.

Maybe chess wasn't such a good idea. It bothered Charlie to see Tim in Cairo having a fine time. Worse still, a fine time at El Horreya. Dirty and crowded insofar as café bars were concerned, but lovely in secret ways. Like how some tables had missing tiles with coins glued in their place. Charlie had laughed, cheered, bemoaned, and even fought at these tables. He'd fought one night when a drunk Egyptian suggested the drunk American was cheating at chess. Charlie had laughed. Not with intent to offend, but still an offense had been rendered. He endured a swift whipping. So swift the man had felt bad and, after apologizing, bought Charlie a beer. Such incidents gave Charlie a rich history in this beloved place. He belonged here more than he belonged anywhere else in the world. Why did Tim have to bring that other world into El Horreya? "I wish you hadn't come," said Charlie suddenly. He gestured to the room, but also beyond it. The walls touched the sidewalk, which touched the street. From there you could reach all of Egypt. "To be honest, I wish you'd laid over in a different city. I have a life here that doesn't involve anything or anyone from Montana." Tim didn't react. As if the cryptic bastard had finally lost his hearing. It was only fair given how many guns he'd shot in his life. How many at people? "I wish you hadn't . . ." Charlie wondered how many times he'd end up saying that.

"I heard you." Tim raised his arm in the air until more beer came. That took several minutes. By then, Tim's arm had drained of blood. He grimaced at the waiter when he came. "There's no condensation on the bottle," said Tim, more or less to himself. "It's not cold." He drank it anyway. Then he stole Charlie's beer and drank that, too. Finally, Tim leaned back in his chair until the wood creaked. When he leaned too far and nearly fell, Aos put his foot on the front leg of the chair, applied pressure, and guided the chair back to the floor. There was a loud bang. Tim didn't flinch — or couldn't flinch. Not after what he'd seen. Not after what he'd done. "I forgot to tell you," said Tim. "Why I really came."

"You told me in that phony e-mail," said Charlie, displeased to discover he remembered it. *In training, my commander asked me what I should carry to war. "My armor," I said. "My map." He laughed the way a hyena laughs before killing something. "Bring the memory of the people you love," he said. "And the fear of losing them. That fear will keep you alive."* Tim had gone on to write about Dad, Karen, the kids. Charlie was listed implicitly. The fear of losing people Tim loved, or had once loved, had thrust him down the rabbit hole. It took several years of war to reach the bottom. The bottom was the same as the top. He was the same man except more confused and depressed. He wanted to go home. He also never wanted to go home again. Finally, he needed to see Charlie. His conviction wasn't paired with any logic; his reason was unclear, except to say that his anger had become his mourning. He was tired of hating his face.

"The truth comes out," said Tim.

"What truth?" asked Charlie.

"You think I'm phony."

"That's not exactly what I said."

Charlie turned to Aos for some kind of support. Maybe a wry smile indicating that such drunken talk couldn't possibly mean anything. But Aos was busy playing chess against himself. He gave both sides the same dedicated attention.

"Karen said I shouldn't come," said Tim. He'd never been one to endure even a short silence. "She said you were a lost cause. That our past was an abyss, not a harbor. Just so you know, she grew up in New England. That's why she uses so many boat metaphors." Tim inspected his mobile phone; his finger pecked the screen as if there were no service. Each time with more force. "I never told her I was shot in the leg. On leave, she felt the scar. We were having sex. She didn't mention it. I saw in her eyes that we wouldn't have that fight until I left the army. But I don't know how to be a civilian anymore. I don't know what to do with my life."

The look on Tim's face — not ugly, just different — affected Charlie more than he cared to admit. He imagined what a good brother would say: *I'm sorry* and *I love you* and *Drink up*. But saying those things earnestly required Charlie to be something he hadn't been in years. Why pretend? How would that help? Instead he turned back to Aos, who was still playing chess against himself. More like speed chess, which was unusual. "Are you ready to go? Curfew in like . . ." Charlie showed his watch, but Aos wouldn't look up from his game. It was neck and neck, a real standoff. Charlie, anxious to escape his own cruelty, tapped Aos on the shoulder. Firmly, but not hard. The prodding thrust Aos so abruptly from his focused state that he accidentally knocked over his beer. He picked the bottle up before any liquid spilled. Foam poured from the top and beer spilled that way and covered the board.

———

Charlie, Tim, and Aos waited on the platform for the train. The Cairene metro was cleaner and usually swifter than the New York or Parisian equivalent. Also more fun because the rules of engagement were off in the Cairo underground. People rushed to board and disembark train cars through the same doors at the same time. This caused free-for-alls at larger stations. Too many people wanted off and too many wanted on. They met between the hydraulic doors of each car and battled. Old women threw elbows. Businessmen used briefcases as shields. Schoolboys hip-checked each other out of the way, while girls in fluorescent head scarves ducked between fat men trying to suck in their stomachs. When the train came and the hydraulic doors slid open, Charlie put his hands on his brother's back and pushed him into the fray.

"I'm bumping into people," said Tim. "Stop pushing me."

"We can't wait," said Charlie. "We'll miss the train. If we miss the train . . ."

"Hurry up," said Aos, who was somehow already inside the carriage.

"There are children here!" said Tim.

"Throw them aside." Charlie considered forcing a laugh, but decided he didn't care if Tim thought he was joking.

Tim made it onto the train just as the doors shut, but Charlie — worried his arms would get stuck in the door and his body would be dragged rag doll through the tunnel, whipping in the wind — stepped back. The train was jam-packed. Both Aos and Tim were pressed up against the interior glass panels. Aos smiled as the train departed and tried to wave, but his arm was stuck by his side. Tim shut his eyes and leaned his head against the glass. Charlie thought he looked exhausted and, if such a thing could be inferred from a man's countenance, afraid to die. The train shot down the black tunnel, and the sound of metal rubbing metal faded away. Then a new crowd lined up for the next train. Their mirth aggravated Charlie's abominable mood. Why weren't they concerned about curfew? Nobody who was concerned about curfew would chat without restraint and carry themselves with such lightness and ease. Everybody in the station, save Charlie, had that kind of levity. Why? He knew curfew wasn't enforced citywide. Not even downtown, really. At least not every night. Tonight? Probably not. The whole city would stay awake and go to restaurants and sit on the corniche or walk along the corniche while smoking cigarettes and holding hands. Taxi drivers wouldn't stop driving and the all-night traffic would stay all night. So what curfew, really, except the one threatened on TV? Nevertheless, Charlie experienced the anguish of wondering if he'd be caught outside after dark.

When the next train arrived a few minutes later, Charlie shoved aboard before the first person stepped off. An old man clicked his tongue angrily. People swarmed and the old man was lost in the crowd somewhere. Charlie felt no shame after he disappeared. The door shut and the train shot down a dark tube. Charlie knew he wasn't just underground, but also underwater. Then appeared the bright lights of the next station, the Opera House. Then another tunnel and another station. El Dokki, his stop. *Dokki* meant "harbor," where houseboats – barely floating boxes covered in gardens and tiny yellow lights – were moored in a line running north along the west bank of the Nile. Charlie lived a few blocks in from the river, but loved walking past the houseboats and breathing the slightly cooler air by the water. He felt less affection for the mosquitoes, but had long ago resigned himself to their companionship.

Charlie stepped out of the train. Aos waited by the stairs, back planted on the wall between two sets of empty benches. "Where's Tim?" asked Charlie as the train behind him departed for the next station.

"What?" said Aos over the sound of metal rubbing metal.

"Tim," said Charlie after the train became a rush of air.

"He walked back to the Sheraton."

"Without saying good-bye?" It was, in a way, a relief. Charlie had avoided what would've surely been a strained farewell: questions about when, even if, they'd finish the fight they'd been having; whether to embrace or shake hands or part the same way they'd met, without touching; and most important, any metaphysical questions about what it all meant in the end. There was no end; therefore, no meaning. In addition to being a relief, it was also more than a little sad. Charlie had been robbed of the opportunity to surprise himself. What if he'd gotten off the train only to discover his heart had transformed in the long black tunnel under the deep, muddy river? What if seeing Tim lean against the wall of the subway station, bummed on the way back to war, had dislodged something? A feeling? A memory? How would've Charlie reacted? What might've he said?

"Tim insisted he knew the way," said Aos. "And that he needed to pack. I thought you'd be mad if I stopped him. Not that I could've stopped him. He had that look in his eyes. Like he'd absolutely made up his mind. He was leaving."

Charlie and Aos climbed the stairs, walked down a hallway, and climbed more stairs into the stink of the city. "Curfew started twenty minutes ago," said Charlie at street level. The more energy he spent worrying about curfew, the less energy he had to think about Tim. And Omran. And Dalia. And the yellow card. And how he couldn't stop failing people. "I'd be lying if I said I didn't want to run home. It's not far. I need the exercise."

Aos made a point of watching people walk by. "I'll see you tomorrow," he said, slipping into the stream of pedestrians. He slipped out a few paces later and turned back. "There's nothing wrong with reunion. You might even get something out of it. A brother, for example. Nephews you can spoil with stories of your adventures. That kind of thing." Aos casually rejoined the stream and was gone before Charlie could oppose the remark.

That night Charlie lay prone on his couch with his head hung over the edge of the cushion so that he could breathe and also see his dog, a short-haired pooch of unknown origin. One day Charlie had left his door open and the pooch had wandered in. He didn't have the heart to send her away, so instead gave her a name. Ruby was curled on the floor in such a way that Charlie couldn't tell which side was the head and which was the butt. He rolled supine to escape the mystery. Then reluctantly took hold of the phone. He called Dalia first. *Get the worst out of the way!* was a philosophy his father had drilled into him at an early age. While Charlie hated his father on principle – the man said he feared God, but rarely abided Him – many of his lessons had stuck. *Get the worst out of the way, quick is painless, less is more.* Not to mention *stop running your mouth.* When Dalia picked up, he minded all these philosophies at once: "Your case has been rejected." The pain of admitting his failure was eclipsed by the pain of not hearing Dalia react. "Hello?" said Charlie after a few seconds. "Are you there?"

"Yes."

Charlie had long imagined another version of this call. In that version he said, "Guess what? Your petition has been approved. It'll be a few more . . . well, months. It's hard to say for sure. Like, before you travel. There's a security-clearance procedure. Not that you should have any trouble. Anybody with eyes will see you're an asset, not a threat." In that version Dalia dropped the phone and cried out and picked up the phone again and finally exhaled her despair. To be rid of it! In that version Charlie said, "This is great" and "I'm really happy." The half-truth would be the only truth he'd ever tell Dalia. He'd keep the nausea and sadness to himself, with the hope that his desire, lacking an object, would die. That his heart would swell from sending his love to be happy, even if that happiness didn't include him. That even if his heart didn't swell, and he sulked in jealous anguish, it wouldn't matter. She would already be gone. Charlie would have no chance to fuck up her life anymore. That version struck Charlie now as far-fetched. He felt stupid and sorry for having imagined it.

"I wish I had better news. Really, I thought – "

"I understand," said Dalia, as if God had trained her to expect bad news; perhaps she'd never imagined another outcome. "I should go. It's late. I'm tired."

Charlie knew then what he'd always suspected. Hearts don't break; they simply continue. His heart beat on like an old industrial engine. For a second, he was even glad Dalia would stay. The gladness burned away like tissue paper when he noticed it, revealing a new and upsetting fear. Charlie didn't trust himself. Not with Dalia stuck in Cairo for the long term. Wasn't it only a matter of time before his longing found a way to escape? "You don't need to be alone," he'd tell Dalia one day when she sounded especially sad or cynical. "Just say the word. I'm here for you." Would she tell Omran? Would Omran come to Egypt and kill Charlie with his bare hands? Such punishment didn't lack appeal; dead Charlie would feel no guilt.

Dalia returned the phone to its cradle so quietly that Charlie didn't realize she'd hung up. The dial tone, like an alarm, accosted him. A better lawyer would've known whether to call back now or wait until tomorrow. Charlie's judgment was clouded by pain, which was clouded by whiskey. The smartest thing he could do was the opposite of what he wanted. He wanted to call now and tell her everything. In that way, it was decided. He'd call tomorrow and tell her only what she needed to know. God willing, Dalia would be ready to talk. Or shout. Or demand answers to formidable questions. What now? Where do I go? How do I live? Charlie wouldn't have any satisfying answers prepared. He couldn't prepare what didn't exist. His gut wrenched just thinking about the several platitudes he'd be forced to offer. We'll figure something out! It will be okay! I promise!

To pass the time until then, Charlie watched Ruby. He still couldn't tell which side was the head and which was the butt. The mystery nearly drove him mad. Charlie grabbed the phone again. Wasn't it his job to spread the bad news like a plague on Omran? He dialed half the number before deciding not to dial the rest. What would he say to him? I'm sorry? I tried? Maybe it was better to call Omran in the morning before he called Dalia. By then, maybe Dalia would've told Omran herself. "My petition has been denied," she'd say. "Stay where you are. Be safe. Earn money." Charlie could hear Dalia saying these things without meaning them; he could hear Omran moaning. "Fuck!" shouted Charlie at the phone. Ruby, a nervous pooch, cowered under the coffee table. Her tail ricocheted between the wooden legs. A rapid tapping. "I'm sorry," said Charlie, petting her. "Good girl." Ruby wasn't the most forgiving dog and slinked away to the bedroom. Springs compressed when she lay on the bed. The sound recalled the screen door, which recalled the office; that recalled every client Charlie had ever failed to help. Their multitude pinned him to the couch. He wouldn't get up for water. He wouldn't get up to piss.

Dark, vindictive hours passed languidly. Charlie thought he was going insane from the solitude and lack of sleep. He went so far as to hold his eyes shut with his fingers. Morning arrived what felt like years later. The sun was still way off, but the call to prayer said the date had changed. Charlie, who was done self-flagellating for the moment, got up to piss his whiskey. Then he reheated yesterday's stale coffee and poured bourbon in the pot to freshen it. He fed, walked, and watered Ruby. He only walked her to the corner store and back because she kept sitting down. Ruby was getting old. Her joints were swollen. "My dear," said Charlie when they reached the stairs leading back inside. The stairs were much harder for her to go up than to go down. He carried her. Once inside, Charlie put Ruby back to bed. Right away she slipped into a dream about yearning. Her paws moved as if she were chasing something. Charlie watched her paws until they stopped. He was glad to see Ruby get what she wanted. Her tongue fell out of her mouth. Charlie's mood continued to improve after that. He paced for a while. He even did a little cleaning. He stacked the books on his coffee table in descending order of size, making a pyramid. A lovely and stable shape. Then, after Charlie couldn't think of more ways to delay, he called Omran. He pressed what felt like a million buttons before the ringing started. Each ring increased his desire to time travel, to go back and redo Dalia's case. Not that he could do much to change the outcome. Charlie had done everything right, to the letter. All his work was to the letter. Maybe that was the problem. Maybe he needed to break more rules. Maybe he needed to break every rule ever written. Nobody would care. Nobody would even notice.

"Hello?" Omran's voice sounded the same as always, if worn a little thin; Dalia, it seemed, had said nothing.

Charlie wanted to throw up knowing it was now his curse to share the bad news. "It's Charlie."

"Salaam, Charlie!" It was kind, the way Omran said the name. He had a way of making Charlie sound more important than he was, more influential. Better at his job. Better at his life. "How is Dalia? When is she coming? I talked to her earlier, but she said there was no news. Tell me she's playing a trick. I can't tell with her. Not always. Not anymore. Sometimes I wonder if she's . . ."

Charlie considered that word for a long time – *trick*, both its definition and etymology. A maneuver intended to deceive or cheat. An optical illusion. From the Old North French and the Vulgar Latin, which Charlie knew from his one-semester stint as a linguist. But no dictionary mentioned the sadness with which Omran used that word.

"There's news," said Charlie. "Just not good news."

"What do you mean, not good?"

"I mean Dalia's not coming. Her petition to resettle has been denied. Really, I tried everything. I'm sorry. I tried."

The silence went on so long it grew teeth. Charlie wondered if he should keep talking. He could apologize again. He could offer condolences. Dalia had, in a way, just died; she was beyond seeing, wasn't she? Unless Omran gave up everything good in his life. His job. His chance at American citizenship. His decent future.

"No," said Omran finally. "I don't accept."

"You don't accept?"

"What you're saying!"

"That's not really how this works, Omran. Look, I'm just the messenger. You know what they say about messengers." Charlie secretly wished that Omran would flay him alive. Somehow it seemed less painful than finishing the conversation.

"Oh, God. My God." Clearly Omran's radar had been too optimistic. He hadn't seen or planned for this. Charlie was glad for the company; he hated being the only one to make such a stupid mistake. "I think . . . ," said Omran as if his thoughts were trying to evade capture. He was panicking. "I have no power. I have no choice." Then, after a pause: "I will come to Egypt! That is the only way I can see to be with her." Something in his voice said he was going to weep, or that he'd been weeping all along and was failing now to hide it. "You tell Dalia that I will be there soon. I will also tell her. Bye, I have to go. I have to pray. Then I have to sleep."

Once again Charlie had forgotten that morning for him was midnight for Omran. He'd made the mistake so many times it had become a habit. "No, you can't. Come, I mean. To Egypt. You can pray whenever you want. Or sleep, for that matter. It's a free country. Your country, I mean. America. Which will be your country if you *stay put*. Egypt's not a free country, by the way. There's no clear route to citizenship. The inflation rate is absurd. The revolution is dying."

"I'm going to very soon."

"You're going to what?"

"Come to Egypt."

"You better not!"

"I'm going to!"

Charlie had a profound respect and liking for Omran, but never wanted to meet the man. Not now. Not here. If Omran came to Egypt, his life would be ruined. He'd arrive, see his wife, and sit on her couch with a great sigh as his body landed. Together they'd find age, poverty, and a future that wasn't one. Stuck in Egypt, not citizens, legally barred from owning property or finding work. They'd discover that love wasn't something they could eat or live inside. They'd work illegally, risking police harassment and fines, even imprisonment. Never earning enough money. Charlie would have to watch them spiral that way into hopelessness. Meanwhile the woman he loved would embrace the man she did, more desperately as time passed.

"How will you find work?" asked Charlie, agitated by Omran's stubbornness. "How will you afford children? How will you make a life you can live and not just sit through? Omran, are you listening? Did you hear what I said? Hello, Omran?"

Omran hung up with less finesse than Dalia, so that Charlie heard the phone whack the cradle. No dial tone had ever made Charlie so sick. He ran to the bathroom. Nothing came out except a hacking sound. That woke Ruby, who peeked in. She was always checking on his welfare. Either by poking him in the crotch with her muzzle or barking loudly in his face. *ARE YOU ALIVE? ARE YOU WELL? DO YOU LOVE ME?*

PART II

THE PLAN

1

Omran's plan was to lie in bed with Dalia no matter what. She'd promised him at least one child. Thinking of her promise made him sweat. He was getting old. Gray hairs grappled for control of his brown beard. Dalia said this made him look reliable. He wanted a child, soon. He wanted his wife. Then the phone rang. Hadn't he just hung up? Ring, ring. Yes, he'd just hung up on Charlie. Ring, ring. His sweaty hand on the phone gave the plastic a sticky feel.

"Hello?"

"Hello," said Charlie in a dour way. "Maybe you forgot we were talking."

What Omran had forgotten was the tea he'd brewed to help him sleep; at least, until the pot's yowl reminded him. A similar cry had burst from Omran's mouth during his torture. And the mouths of other captives held in other rooms. A few men in a dank basement. A woman, too. Or a boy. All begging to die. Omran was still learning to endure kindred sounds, which emanated from teapots, engine brakes, and certain trains. The worst offender was the subway grinding to a stop. He stayed above ground for that reason and avoided areas where the T breached the street.

"What else is there to say?" asked Omran. "Her case is finished."

Suddenly he wondered why Charlie had broken the news in lieu of Dalia. He needed to call her. He needed to know why she'd withheld such vital information and what else she might be withholding. "I'm coming to Egypt to be with the one I have loved my whole life and, I think, even before that."

"You're not listening. You're not even trying to listen!"

Omran's eye socket throbbed on beat with his pulse. The injury had mostly healed, but the area remained sensitive. As if it remembered trauma. Or somehow predicted it. As if his captors' final torture was the clairvoyance of his wound.

"I have to go. I have to call Dalia."

"Wait! I just met with a woman who works at the UNHCR. A friend on the inside. There are other options. Other ways to get what you deserve. A life, Omran. Far away from war. Any war. Look, there's no guarantee. There's never a guarantee. But I'm not giving up. That's what I'm calling about. That's what I would've said before, if you hadn't – "

Omran hung up on Charlie again to call Dalia. Her greeting was plain and languid. "Are you okay?" he asked. Suppressing the urge to yank the truth from Dalia like a rotten tooth was no easy feat. But Omran had practiced the game of waiting. He'd practiced every morning of what felt now like someone else's life. He'd wait for George to come out from under the bed. The cat's nose would appear first, cautiously. Then his eyes. When George saw Omran watching, his head would disappear back under the bed. The process would repeat, each time revealing more of George. His ears, his neck. Omran hadn't understood the ritual, but nevertheless accepted it. George needed to come out in his own way.

Dalia released the truth after a similar coaxing. Omran played his part by pretending he didn't know. He could hear Dalia weeping, though she tried to hide the sound by holding the phone away from her face. Her voice and the crying had a distant quality, as if the sounds were tired from their travels. Omran didn't care so much about the sound he made and cried into the phone with every part of him. He cried until he could think of something to say: "I have always wanted to see the pyramids." The joke's tone betrayed the teller's doubt; it wasn't funny. "I must come. I must see them."

"What?" Dalia's voice exhibited a sudden drop in temperature. "No, don't. You better not. There's nothing here for us."

"Nothing?"

They argued over the meaning of that word.

"No job, no life."

To avoid falling into despair, Omran told himself it didn't really exist. The word should be cut from the dictionary. People at risk of feeling such a thing would have nothing to call it. The feeling would eventually die from lack of attention.

"I'd rather be poor than . . ." Omran's mistake was pausing. He didn't get to finish his thought. That he'd rather be poor than estranged. He was already poor. America was no picnic.

"Don't come." Dalia seized the pause with such force that her interruption seemed irrevocable. "I'm telling you. It's not a joke." The phone line between them was a long wire delaying the transmission of sound by milliseconds, so that in between Dalia's saying something and Omran's responding was a brief, almost imperceptible loneliness. "Don't come," said Dalia for what felt, to Omran, like the millionth time. Her words were all worn-out. It was just as well. His phone card ran out of money.

Omran had been in Boston since September. The flight had frightened him. He'd only been on a plane once before, as a child; he remembered liking it. Since then his opinion had changed. The turbulence caused the plane to move on strange axes. It swiveled from side to side in the air. Omran cinched his belt so tightly that his legs felt cut from his body. For comfort, he thought of Dalia. That only made things worse. He bore one grudge against her for asking him to leave and another against himself for going. It had been a mistake to go alone. Night chased the plane across the ocean. When he finally landed in Boston, there was a frighteningly loud thump. Several people clapped. Omran couldn't tell if they were being sarcastic or if they were having fun. The flight attendant said, "The local time is . . . and the weather is . . ." Out the window, rain fell sideways. "We hope you enjoyed the flight." Omran hadn't enjoyed the flight but still couldn't bring himself to leave his seat; it was a strange feeling. He sat there long after the plane had reached the gate. Even the other disabled passengers had disembarked. "Excuse me, sir," said the flight attendant. "Sir?" Omran felt a poke on his shoulder. Then another poke.

He finally turned. "I left my wife in Baghdad. Please, I left her." He asked what time the plane would go back.

The flight attendant, tired but otherwise cordial, escorted Omran to the jet bridge. "Customs is that way. Just follow the hall."

The hall stretched farther than Omran could see or curved in such a way that it appeared to stretch forever. He forgot what to do next and so fished out the paper that told him. *Pass immigration. Collect luggage. Pass customs. Go to the exit. Find the social worker.*

Jenny had long hair and a smile as wide as her face. She must've been in her early thirties. Omran saw the last hurrah of genuine youth. "As-salamu alaikum," said Jenny. "Welcome to America."

As-salamu alaikum. Peace be upon you. Familiar words that re-minded Omran how far he was from home. "Wa alaikum al-salaam," he said. And unto you peace, for the Qur'an says, *When you are greeted with a greeting, greet in return with what is better than it, or return it equally. Indeed, Allah is ever, over all things, an accountant.*

"This way." Jenny grabbed the larger of Omran's two bags and dragged it to the parking garage. She seemed like the sort of person who would've grabbed the bag even if Omran hadn't a cane or a limp. Her car smelled like coconut. She played Ella Fitzgerald, "Ringo Beat." Omran didn't say he knew the song, but he knew it well. He loved Ella Fitzgerald almost as much as jazz itself, which he loved almost as much as George, whom he loved tremendously. The music gave Omran the feeling that life was good and short. He felt sick and happy. Then just sick because Dalia wasn't in the backseat telling him to adjust the volume. Her ears had always been more sensitive. "I'm going deaf!" she would've whispered, not wanting Jenny to know. "Please, Omran! I'm going deaf!" The love he felt for Dalia was impossible to quantify, except to say it was more than the love he felt for Ella, jazz, George, Baghdad, God, food, water, sex, and freedom combined. He would lose every sense but his sight just to see her.

The long drive into the city and back out the other side doubled as a kind of orientation. Every refugee was afforded the same volume of pity, to be expressed financially. A place to live, a menial job, and counseling if required. The idea being: gone is the trauma, now on with your life. But Omran had spent his whole life taking care of himself. He felt pride for the past and shame now for needing care. Especially care rendered by someone he didn't love. Someone he didn't even know. The pride conjured God's prophet. In a hadith, Muhammad said he who has in his heart the weight of an atom of pride shall not enter paradise. It was hard for Omran not to interpret that literally.

"I think you'll like your job," said Jenny. "We placed you with Faisal, who owns a garage in Medford. Repairs, oil changes, rotating tires. That kind of thing. You won't be building houses or paving streets — your application said you did construction in Baghdad, is that right? — but at least you'll get to use your hands. Most days I just sit in front of a computer doing this . . ." Jenny tapped her fingers on the steering wheel. "It's not satisfying. The best part of my job is when I get to drive to and from the airport. Really, dragging the bags. You know that feeling? Of doing something with your body? Of breaking a sweat?"

Omran's body hadn't felt like his own since before his torture. His dominion had been lost with his eye. "I will be glad to work with Faisal." Omran was gladder still to know the name. It was Arab.

"It's important to have a community. In truth, I don't even like taking vacations. I miss my friends too much. Even my family. Isn't that ridiculous? My father is . . . well, a piece of work."

A red light brought the car to a halt. Out the window was a Walgreens. Jenny deftly changed subjects by explaining what Omran could purchase there. Umbrellas, batteries, milk, cereal, shampoo, over-the-counter drugs, behind-the-counter drugs — Jenny snickered and said pharmaceutical companies were the great American racket — and even cat food.

"I have a cat," said Omran. He imagined George's eyes shining at night by the window. Before the window was the edge of the bed and a bump in the covers. Omran wanted to reach out and touch the bump. He wanted to say, *Dalia*. He wanted to watch the bump roll over, revealing itself as his wife. The shame of leaving her was so great that Omran had to turn away from the Walgreens.

"There are other stores, too," said Jenny. "That you might like."

The red light turned green. The green light lured the car through the intersection. People and trees and road signs and storefronts flew by. The street changed names several times before the car finally turned down an alley. Omran had always lived in and loved alleys, but this one was unlike the others. There was nowhere to congregate. No balconies; no stoops that weren't behind fences. It was as if neighbors in this country had no interest in speaking or seeing each other.

"Welcome to your apartment. It's not much to look at from the outside. To be honest, it's not much to look at from the inside, either. But it's clean and everything works properly. And you can paint the walls if you want. And hang pictures."

After parking the car, Jenny lugged Omran's bags inside. He thanked her excessively. Jenny said she was just doing her job and, besides, was glad to help. Then she gave an exhaustingly thorough tour — not just the location of appliances, which were in plain sight, but their operating instructions, which were self-evident; where to collect his mail; where to leave his trash; where the breaker panel was located. Did Jenny have a meticulous nature or was some training regimen to blame? Omran leaned toward the training regimen. He envisioned a long document outlining how "the social worker" ought to make "the refugee" feel at home. *Plug in the toaster. Turn on the toaster. Wait for the toaster to pop.* Maybe Omran wasn't being fair. Maybe there was some psychological benefit, though he couldn't fathom one. The longer Jenny lingered, the more lonely Omran felt.

The next day, Omran left his front door wide-open. The idea was to let familiar sounds visit from other alleys. Car horns, people chatting, children playing games in the street. If he was lucky, maybe a donkey would bray. Was it beyond reason to think there might be a donkey in Boston? Nobody had told Omran there wasn't. He waited patiently for the hee-haw. A surprise rain came instead and soaked the carpet, which took several days to dry. To escape the damp smell, the quiet, the absence growing on the right side of his bed – there was no worse feeling than waking in the morning and reaching out of habit for his wife – Omran spent his time walking through and even beyond his neighborhood. The hypothetical goal was to find a store that sold hats, but the truth was he needed to stay busy. Or get busy. The job with Faisal wouldn't begin for a week. He walked without any destination in mind, keeping his balance with his cane. The cane, he thought, was a smart invention. The rubber foot especially, which stuck to everything. The wet sidewalk. The wet paint on the crosswalk. Even the wet tiles at the entrance to most stores. Work started eventually, thank God. The cane's handle wasn't nearly so good as its foot; it caused blisters. Omran had to stop walking so far because he couldn't grip the handle without tearing his scabs. He needed another way to fill his time. Inflating tires, changing oil, checking wiper fluid. Even talking to Faisal. Then, especially talking to him. Faisal became Omran's brother. Not overnight, but fast enough that both men were slightly embarrassed. Faisal, a Palestinian, was born in Rafah. His habits were tokens of a life Omran recognized. The food he brought for lunch; the times he prayed; the way he spoke English. After all this time, still mistaking *b* sounds for *p* sounds and mispronouncing vowels so that *biscuit* became *basket* and *protein* became *Britain*. When no customers were around, they talked in Arabic for the immense pleasure of speaking poetry and creating the semblance of home.

They talked a lot about carpets. Once upon a time, as a young man, Faisal had made carpets. They discussed materials, craftsmanship, design. Finally, meaning. A good carpet meant a lot to its owner. When it was prayer time, each man took pride in laying down the one he'd brought to America. Both carpets were symmetrical in design except for the niche at the head end in the shape of a mihrab. Both were pointed due east. In doing so, the garage's cement floor, scuffed smooth, had color. The call to prayer was a cassette tape Faisal said he'd recorded back home when he was still a young man in love with the idea of living in a sovereign Palestine. He'd held a recorder in the air by the mosque, capturing an old man belting out the adhan. The quality of the recording was poor. It had been played too many times and was so old.

Omran spent all night cutting his phone card into tiny pieces. Snip. Ten minutes later, snip. So on until the sun rose. He couldn't understand how it had come to this. His marriage was conducted by copper wire in increments of $10. If the UNHCR had it their way, that marriage would be severed entirely. Omran would assimilate into the local culture as a low-paid nobody with no right to reunion. His wife would be banished as a memory. Wasn't it his fault for trusting the large international apparatus to give a shit? The idea transformed his anger into a bleak feeling, which was decidedly worse. He got dressed slowly and donned both his hat and his coat. It was Omran's day off, but he still went to work. He needed the money. Badly. More than ever. For a plane ticket, for travel documents, for an emergency fund. What if Omran couldn't find a job upon arrival in Cairo? Not having the required work permit would bedevil an already improbable search. What if that period of unemployment dragged on for months? Or even years? What if the Egyptian pound continued to slide on the global market? What if a war started? What if he and Dalia needed to flee again? Land routes were not viable. Libya and Sudan were embroiled in their own conflicts, and Israel's border was impossible to cross without ending up dead in a box. They would have to flee by sea to Italy, Cyprus, or Greece. How much would that cost? How much would that cost a year from now? It was impossible for Omran to know. The only thing he knew was that he needed money. God willing, Faisal wouldn't mind if Omran showed up. He'd never minded before. Why did Omran worry? He knew Faisal's heart contained no register. The long walk to work was nevertheless strewn with guilt. Working extra hours didn't bring in new customers or otherwise increase revenue; it curtailed the bottom line of a modest business, the foundation upon which Faisal had built his life. It was never part of Omran's plan to be such a burden.

By the time Omran arrived at the garage, his cheeks felt as if they were going to fall off from the wind's bitterness. Wasn't it a little late in the season for that kind of thing? Then again, it was Omran's first spring at that latitude. He shoved open the heavy side door. The door was so heavy it swung shut by itself, even with the wind blowing in at what felt like gale force. Sounds of industry filled the garage. The hum of a healthy engine and the sputter of a busted one; a lug nut loosened under pressure of an impact wrench; the radio, almost drowned out. A red light, which flashed repeatedly every time the door opened, flashed now. Faisal, standing over a workbench in the far back, turned. "Salaam, habibi!" Faisal was pushing sixty and his stomach was pushing out. He used the bulge as an armrest. "I had a feeling you'd come. I'm glad I was right. Usually, about these things, I have a sense. I have a sharp mind. My son says I'm not so sharp in old age, but I say that I'm not as old as he thinks. I'm glad you're here. I made tea."

Being so predictable depressed the hell out of Omran; it suggested his life was stuck on some infernal autopilot. He shook Faisal's hand and kissed his cheek, a ritual performed every morning. Though something about the greeting must've struck Faisal as aberrant. He wore a concerned look.

"You seem . . ." Faisal stepped back from Omran to see him better. "Distressed. What happened? Is it Dalia?"

Omran meant to tell Faisal about the case, but thought suddenly that he couldn't tell him. The truth was, mutually exclusive longings battled for control of his want: to stay, to go. To go would be to lose both a reliable income and an even more reliable friend. In Omran's mind, a friend was someone you shared meals with and invited into your home regularly. What could he say to preserve the fondness that had grown from pain, time, music, and money? Come, my friend, to Cairo? Forget the revolution? Forget the cost? Please, visit me? Staying, meanwhile, would forgo his marriage. How could Omran possibly stay? Even if Dalia told him? She had no right to demand such a cruelty. To exile Omran in paradise. Or what she must've thought was paradise. It was Omran's fault. He'd told her Boston was where their life would begin again. They would get by, start a family, be happy. He'd said that being happy started with being safe. One fact they both loved about Boston: it had been more than two centuries since that city had seen war.

"Nothing happened." Omran stepped back and tried to appear steady.

"Ha ha. Tell you what. I'll pretend like I can't read you."

"You see things that aren't – "

"Ha ha," said Faisal sadly.

Omran failed to avoid eye contact. He lost the staring contest handily.

"I don't know what to do," said Omran, giving up. He slung his coat over the back of a chair, then collapsed into it. The chair protested by emitting a pretty serious groan. "Her case has been rejected. What can I do?"

Faisal wiped his hands on his knees, leaving oil marks. He stared at the marks as if someone else had caused them, with an annoyed look. "There's no hope?"

Omran recalled Charlie's inane rambling, his voice both tired and sore. *Wait! I just met with a woman who works at the UNHCR. A friend on the inside.* It wasn't like Charlie to flail blindly for something utterly beyond reach. The UNHCR wasn't on Dalia's side. The UNHCR had never been on her side. "Foolish hope," said Omran.

Faisal said he'd never heard of such a thing. He tried to wipe the oil off his pants with the backs of his hands. Why? He must've known the oil would never come out. He'd been working in the garage business and thus ruining his pants for decades. Maybe it never got any easier. "Are you going home then?" he asked after a long while.

Omran wasn't going home, was he? He wasn't from Egypt and he certainly wasn't going back to Iraq. "My home is blown up or squatted in," he said, slightly miffed by the idea that he could return there without dying. "How can I go back?"

"You forget what home means," said Faisal, perking up slightly. The only thing he loved more than telling stories was giving advice. "Home isn't the place you sleep. You can sleep anywhere. You can sleep in a trash can."

"What! A trash can!"

Faisal pulled Omran out of his chair and led him in the direction of tea. "I hope you haven't forgotten the story about my boy Salman." That boy had grown up, gone to college, and gotten married. Calling him a "boy" was a little misleading.

"There's no trash can in that story."

"Ya Allah! Forget the can. I'm asking if you remember the story."

"Yes, I remember. You've told me before. You tell me every – "

"Let me tell you again." Faisal poured two cups of hot tea and forced one into Omran's hands. "Stories are great weights unless told often."

Now wasn't the time for a tale of woe. Or was it? Maybe disappearing in another man's tragedy would do Omran some good. To know he wasn't alone. That his was a shared suffering. "At least don't punch me in on the clock until the story is – "

Faisal punched him in on the clock. Faisal had said before that a good listener was a precious thing, but this was the first time he'd actually paid Omran to just sit there. It would be wrong to protest such kindness. The only thing Omran could do was turn down the radio. He did just that. Not off, but so low the music was just white noise.

Faisal said his boy was made in Rafah, but not born there. The boy had no ties to his country, his history, or his language. Not even things Faisal thought his son must intrinsically love, such as the sea. Or his mother. Faisal never dared give Salman's mother a name; he feared remembering her death too clearly. "She died of terminal homesickness," Faisal said as if that fact still swallowed him. He said he'd failed to make her happy and was solely to blame for her death. They'd escaped Rafah during the first Intifada by smuggling themselves in wooden crates across the Egyptian border. She'd vomited the whole time and shit on herself, and he'd shit on himself the same way. They'd made it to Cairo by the skin of their teeth. Then to America after several months of paperwork. By then, Faisal's wife was so pregnant she could barely stand up. Though no joy came from their escape. How could Faisal and his wife – with no family, no mosque, no kofta, and no access to the sea – lead any kind of recognizable life? A few months after Salman was born, in the dead of winter – "Colorado was very beautiful, but very cold," said Faisal – his wife wandered into the snow. In the morning, he followed her footprints and found her frozen body wrapped in her frozen robe. The robe, which had been soaked in water, had fused to her skin. Her face was like a death mask covered in silver flakes. Faisal dreamed for years that if he'd only peeled the flakes off, he would've found his wife alive.

Faisal never discussed the police questioning except to say that he was shocked by its nakedness. Did you kill your wife? Come on, did you kill her? Nor did he discuss the funeral except to say that he and baby Salman were the only guests. His story jumped to Boston, where Faisal moved shortly after the police inquiry had determined there was no probable cause. He moved to escape the house, the solitude, the creative neighbors who reported hearing a struggle the night his wife died. "They heard what they wanted to hear," said Faisal. "They never liked us." In Boston, Salman became a city boy. He grew up without prayer or even Arabic. It was Faisal's fault for not teaching him. Hoping his son would assimilate and thus find school to be more pleasant, Faisal had spoken exclusively in English until realizing, too late, his grave error. Salman barely knew the language in which his father thought and dreamed and prayed. By then, Salman was a teenager with gangly arms and terrible acne. Faisal tried enrolling him in language classes, but Salman refused to go. He claimed there was no reason. Plus, the alphabet, besides having too many letters, looked like scribbling. The fight took a turn for the worse when Salman said English was his native language. Hearing that caused Faisal to whack Salman. Not because of what he said, but because of how he said it. With no sense of regret. The boy bled from his lip, but didn't run. He sat on the floor and cried, but didn't run. Faisal turned red not from rage but from embarrassment. He marched around the house looking for Band-Aids. "I can't find the Band-Aids!" he shouted. Faisal loved telling the part of the story where Salman said, "You can't put a Band-Aid in my mouth. It won't stick." Faisal lifted his son off the ground and nearly smothered him in an embrace. "I miss your mother," he said by way of explanation and perhaps apology. "I miss the place you were made."

What did the boy say, so young and apparently beyond his years? He asked, with a lisp induced by the swelling: "What do sad people have in common?"

Suddenly, Faisal knew his son had read the book he'd given him. Faisal was overcome with relief and joy and pride and love for his son. "You read the book! Hafez of Shiraz, the greatest poet ever born! Sure, he's Persian. But I don't hold that against him. It's not his fault." Salman asked again, "What do sad people have in common?" A reference to page 183 in Faisal's shabby edition. The hard cover had become soft from being held so tightly for so long. "It seems they have all built a shrine to the past and often go there and do a strange wail and worship."

Faisal couldn't help but laugh. "Are you trying to teach your father a lesson? I read that poem to your mother on a beach in a war. I know what Hafez of Shiraz said, and, more importantly, what he intended."

Salman scoffed, pulled away from Faisal, and didn't hug him again for a week. When he did finally hug his father — the week had passed in uneasy quietude — he said, "I forgive you, but I don't want to learn Arabic. It's not my language. I've never been to Palestine. It's not even a real country. I'm sorry, but it's not. Maybe one day. Not that it would be my home even if that happened. Home isn't a place. Home is the feeling you get with certain people."

It pained Omran to hear that line again. *Home is the feeling you get . . .* Not one he'd gotten in a long while; he could barely remember it. How terrifying to know his good memories were being gouged out. To make room for what? Nightmares? Omran sprang from his chair to escape the spiral of pondering. He needed to work. He needed to do something with his hands. A ten-point inspection, for example. "I'm sorry," said Omran as he shoved his head under a car hood. "It's just . . ." There was no polite way to say he was done listening.

"Are you . . . checking the oil?"

"I am."

"Don't you think that can wait?"

Omran pulled the dipstick out of the engine and held it up to the light. The oil should've been changed months ago. It was full of particulates. "This oil needs to be changed immediately."

"My friend, come back. It seems you've forgotten how the story ends."

Maybe Omran had forgotten. Not what happened, but how it felt to *hear* what happened. He reluctantly pulled his head out from under the hood of the car, allowing the story to continue without further hindrance. Of course Salman would go on to change his mind about Arabic. He would grow up, go to college, study abroad,

learn a few language skills. Very few, as it happened. He would
return home desperately frustrated. He would move back in with
his father to finally collect what he called "my inheritance." They
would live together for a number of years with one non-negotiable,
stress-inducing rule: only Arabic was allowed in the house. For the
first few months there was a lot of contentious gesturing. A kind of
switch would flip after that. Salman would realize he was too old
to absorb language and would have to work hard to acquire it. The
flash cards, the books, the formidable computer program – these
were just symptoms of a larger change in Salman's nature. In time,
he would learn what Faisal had neglected to teach him when he was
still young and spongelike. A language so packed with idiom it was
like their own lonely code. That code would prove both a pleasure
and a burden to speak. It made strangers nervous. Sometimes hostile.
"We speak English in this country," they'd say as if it were their duty
as patriots. It would take a while for Salman to grow armor, to be
proud. But Faisal had never been so glad as the day he'd heard his
boy, ablaze with pride, speak up to spite them.

Omran shoved his head back under the car hood. There was,
after all that, some relief in hearing Faisal had eventually gotten
what he wanted, but that relief was more or less canceled out by the
distress of hearing how long it had taken and what he'd lost on the
way. Maybe that was Faisal's point. Maybe he just wanted to assure
Omran that it was possible to survive unfathomable tragedy. That
there might be some joy to be had in the end.

Faisal set to work on the car next to Omran. Sounds of industry
precluded the awkward silence that might otherwise have resulted.
"It's your day to choose the music," said Faisal, nodding at the stereo.

"Billie Holiday," said Omran, his voice a little tinny from bouncing
around the guts of a car. He didn't have to think about it for long.
Since coming to America, the Billie Holiday tape had become his
favorite. "If you don't mind . . ."

The relaxed pace at which she sang matched the slow pace at
which Omran worked. His monocular vision affected his depth per-

ception in a way he hadn't quite figured out, which impeded tasks such as plunging the dipstick back into the engine pipe. Though going slow had its advantages. It gave Omran the chance to practice focusing. It also gave him time to think. Returning the dipstick whence it had come was thus almost meditative; he'd made countless discoveries about himself while trying to aim it properly. For example, that he read Rumi to his wife for many (thought not all) of the reasons Salman read Hafez to his father. It wasn't just because the Persians had learned, hundreds of years before the rest of the world, how to cure a dark heart. ("By loving recklessly!" Faisal had said when he gave Omran the book. "This is Rumi, second best to Hafez. I'm sorry. I don't have any Hafez left. Salman took my only copy.") Some other intangible power was at work. Some inkling that told Omran not to read the book by himself.

Omran hoped for more insight as he tried once again to plunge the dipstick into the engine pipe. He missed so many times he thought some insight must come of it. Alas, Omran didn't learn anything he didn't already know. He needed to leave. The only home he'd ever had was waiting for him. But the dipstick didn't entirely fail to be of use. It gave Omran somewhere to hide as he wept, hunched under the hood of an old-fashioned and oft-used Pontiac. The abyss of dirt, soot, and shadow hid all evidence of his unwinding until he regained control and wound himself up again. He had work to do. There were still nine things left to inspect.

2

Charlie had been in love once before. With Karen, weirdly. Before she'd married Tim. Not that it had been much of a competition. Charlie had never told her how he felt. At least, not in plain terms. He'd tried once to convey his love in a gesture. On Karen's twenty-fifth birthday, he shot a pig on her behalf. Regrettably, he struck the gut. He chased the squeal, the smell of the pig's bile, the trail winding in the grass. He had to shoot the pig a second time to end its misery.

Tim, who'd always had ripe timing, who'd heard the shots from afar, found Charlie crying into the pig as he gutted it. "What's the pig for? And why are you . . . ?"

"The party."

"The party tonight? Karen's party?"

"I buried coals. I wanted to cook the pig that way. I wanted it to be special."

"Uh . . . why are you . . . ?"

Charlie wasn't able to explain why the pig's misery affected him. Especially not to Tim, who was the sort of hunter who liked a clean kill but didn't insist. That night Charlie's gift was the most shared, most talked about, most savored. The pig had been cooked to perfection. The coals had imbued the meat with a tenderness its death had lacked. Everyone ate, drank, and danced freely until someone caught Karen kissing Tim. The subsequent and wild cheering surprised Charlie and, soon thereafter, banished him from the party; the only thing worse than seeing Karen bestow her affection on Tim was hearing how happy that made everyone. Charlie ran from what remained of his pig, hid in his brother's car, and drank himself into oblivion. That faint place beyond feeling. Later that night he drove Tim home. Less by choice than by strong suggestion. "Are you drunk?" Tim had asked, giving the keys before receiving an answer. "You don't *look* drunk." The high beams poured through the passing trees like a zoetrope. Charlie imagined ink deer jumping ink brooks. His eyes were so fixed on the trees that, when the road turned, he drove into them.

Lying in bed with Ruby proved Charlie's heart hadn't changed much over the years. How irritating to know he still loved what caused him to suffer. Tonight he suffered a loud and smelly bedfellow. Soon he'd suffer her death. Ruby was old and sick more days than she was well. He promised to put her down when her tail stopped wagging. When her tail stopped, then her heart must; she would be ready to go. "My sweet," he said, petting her. Charlie also suffered Dalia, a bedfellow of a different sort. She made it damn near impossible to sleep. God willing, her death would come as her absence. Charlie would send her away. To be happy, to be safe. To have agency again. To work. To find home. To grow old there, if that's what she wanted; or to go somewhere else, if she disliked Boston. It was boring! It was cold! Dalia would hate it there! The idea of Dalia's hating a place she would be free to leave — well, Charlie had never been so happy and so miserable at the same time. Fortunately, the call to dawn prayer thrust him from that fragile state. "Fuck," said Charlie. He hadn't slept. He hadn't even undressed. That made getting dressed easier. He smelled his shirt to make sure it was fine to wear again. Or wear still. His shirt passed the test, barely. Now Charlie was ready for work. He'd intended to eat toast on the way out, but forgot to toast it; he ate stale bread instead. It tasted like the plastic bag it came in.

It was Friday, April 1. Still early. There was no light in the sky. Nor any cabs in the street. "Funny," said Charlie to God, might there be one cursing him. "You're very funny." He jogged from his door to Sharia Tahrir, the main drag heading east across the river. His rush was spurred by the idea that Omran had started packing. In an ideal world, Omran would calm down. He'd stay in Boston a while longer. Maybe a lot longer. That way Charlie would have time to help Dalia immigrate through legal means. Was a domestic appeal, such as family reunification, a viable option? Could he fast-track Dalia through the visa queue after Omran was granted—well, if he was granted—American citizenship? Or was a green card enough? Could Omran, as a resident alien, sponsor his wife? If so, how long would that take? Maybe a few years. Maybe five years. Worst-case scenario, was five years that bad? Worst-case scenario was more like ten years, or never. The math, stretching toward infinity, convinced Charlie that what remained of the legal route was, at best, impractical and, at worst, a sham. The only real way forward was to finish what he'd started. If Charlie could forge another resettlement petition, an urgent one, before Omran quit his job and got his passport, providing irrefutable evidence that Dalia was coming to America, then catastrophe would be averted. Charlie would be directly responsible for reducing, not increasing, the number of refugees in Egypt. More important, he'd finally atone for the crime of loving Dalia by making it impossible to love her. What yearning not killed by time would be killed by distance. Fifty-four hundred miles of sand and salt water, to be exact.

Charlie jogged all the way to the Dokki metro stop before he saw any cabs. He was yet thwarted. The few cabs speeding by were already occupied; the others, parked by the curb, lacked drivers. "Now you're just being mean," said Charlie, glaring skyward. Next he tried the metro, but found a locked gate at the bottom of the stairs. "Fucking gate." He shook it. "This isn't supposed to be here! Somebody isn't doing their job!" He retreated up the stairs and checked the parked cabs again, just in case. He glared at the sky a final time. "I don't know how people suffer your wickedness." Then Charlie jogged east across the river. The burn in his lungs felt good, but also horrible. He needed to stop drinking. He needed to eat better. He needed a gym membership. The Nile, thought Charlie, was too wide. Jogging across turned his work outfit into a sweat rag. Then, right before Tahrir the street became Tahrir the square, Charlie turned left and descended the stairs to the corniche. He didn't want to disturb the protesters. Or worse, anger them. As if they might intuit his bitterness and, as punishment, beat him to death with their signs. Not that Charlie was against the protesters or their dream of jailing Mubarak and his nefarious sons, who had appropriated public money for private wants. Arresting them was a noble cause, to be sure. Praying they'd die in prison was less noble, but still just. If not just, then justifiable. Still, the whole thing hampered his work. Not only had the revolution scared half his interns out of the country, but it drew Aos from the office nearly every day. Before, after, sometimes even during work. Charlie had long disguised his worry for Aos' safety as disapproval of his desire to protest. When Aos arrived at the office in the mornings straight from the square having not slept and smelling badly of smoke, looking as if he wanted to talk — needed to talk, had witnessed something — Charlie would pretend he wasn't perceptive, hadn't noticed, and couldn't offer to discuss much less relieve any burden. The ignoble behavior was excused, at least in Charlie's heart, by his intentions. A despondent Aos might avoid the square. Thus its danger. Perhaps his death.

The long route to the office — north along the corniche, then east onto Ramses — ended by the Nasser metro stop, named after the pan-Arab and doggedly socialist president who'd survived numerous assassination attempts only to succumb to his bad habits. The heavy smoker had a family history of heart disease and had repeatedly been warned by his brothers' fates. But Nasser's apparent immunity to political rivalry had deafened him to the whine of what must've felt like the lesser threat: his own body. He was only fifty-two when he died. The Lebanese *Le Jour* bewailed that all Arabs were made orphans by his death, not just Egyptians. The headline testified to Egypt's once-great standing as the heart of the Arab world. Politically, but also culturally. The country's greatest exports had been its movies, books, and art.

Crossing the intersection above the metro stop – Ramses going one way, 26th of July Street going the other – was like playing Frogger in real life. The fast-moving traffic refused to stop under any circumstances. But traffic at that hour was light. Charlie dashed across without dying or even thinking he'd nearly died. No chicken heart beat under his cotton shirt. His heart raced for plainer reasons: the long jog, the humid weather, the idea that Dalia could be stuck in Egypt for life. Such pounding didn't mix well with Charlie's unprecedented hangover, which had lasted all of Thursday – he'd taken his first sick leave in four years – and was just now beginning to tail off. He sat on the curb for a few minutes to wait out the queasiness. An errant plane in the sky, revealed in such darkness by the red flashing lights on its wings, reminded Charlie that Tim had flown back to his war. Good riddance, he thought. Also, and reluctantly, good luck.

Charlie carried on to the office after the worst of the nausea had passed. Round the corner, down the block, through the gate. To his dismay, the office door was already unlocked and the lights had already been switched on. Charlie's plan had been to arrive so early there was no chance anyone else would be there. He had things to do that ought not to be witnessed. "Hello?" asked Charlie after the door's spring hinges cried out. First in pain at stretching, then in joy as they compressed again. He felt a twinge of guilt for seeing Aos and still wanting solitude. Couldn't Aos be trusted? Hadn't he already been told? Still, Charlie loved how the office felt in the early morning when the only sounds were his own breathing and the coffee machine failing to work properly. He loved sitting at his desk with an insurmountable task before him, and starting anyway. He loved perching on the edge of a lonely morning only to hear the door open at the right time.

"I couldn't sleep," said Aos. He opened his eyes as wide as possible, then held them open with his fingers. "Like this, all night." The whites were strawberry. "I had work to do, so I came in. A few hours ago, I think. What time is it?"

Charlie's eyes were also strawberry, or at least felt like strawberries. Almost granular. He made a show of parting the blinds and peering out the window. "The sky is barely light at the edges. The traffic is, eh, not the worst I've ever seen. What is that? Five? Six?" He walked to the kitchen and filled the coffeepot with tap water. He'd been told not to drink tap water on account of heavy metals, but, like Nasser, believed greater dangers would get him first. "It's hard to know for sure. I forgot my watch. At home, I think. I hope so." Losing the watch would be an insult to his mother, who'd offered the antique ticker in lieu of a maudlin good-bye. Dying had made her oddly practical and painfully frank. "I know you hate it here," she'd croaked from her bed. It had been late spring at the time. Hail nonetheless pecked the window. "Truth be told, I've always felt the same way."

Aos perched in the doorway between the kitchen and the hall, resting his back against the doorframe as if he was settling in for what looked to be a dismal chat. It was unlike Aos to be so grave. "I almost got run over by a horse on my way here. Can you believe that? There wasn't even a carriage attached. Just a kid on a horse on the sidewalk shouting, '*Whoop, whoop.*' I could feel the animal's hair as it ran past, whipping me."

"Are you sure it wasn't a donkey? And the boy wasn't an old man taking his carrots to the juice shop? And the *whoop* wasn't the driver bidding you to step aside lest he cream you? The old men take their carrots to the juice shops in the morning before the traffic is bad."

"I don't know what I saw." Aos expelled his doubt in a sigh. "There was a lot of wind. If it wasn't a horse, it was a storm."

Charlie hit the power button on the coffeepot, but the water wouldn't drip. He tapped the side of the coffeepot with his finger. When the water finally started dripping, Charlie said, "This machine . . . I'm telling you. What it lacks in reliability, it makes up for in life span." The rhythm of the dripping hypnotized Charlie, who was predisposed to that kind of thing; he'd had more than his fair share of out-of-body experiences. He saw himself in Hana's office failing to change her mind. He saw himself leaving Dalia to perish in the sand. He saw Omran, stricken with grief, wading into the ocean. "I'm just going to say what I've got to say," said Charlie, snapping out of it. "I'm sorry, I should've told you before."

"I didn't know you were withholding." Aos poured his share of the coffee and sipped the hot, black magma without even blowing the steam.

"I'm not going to appeal Dalia's case. . . ."

Aos, in a clear case of jumping the gun, moved to give Charlie a hug. As if he was sorry, but ultimately thought it was the right decision; there was no time to waste on a lost cause, disheartening as that may be.

". . . I'm going to forge a new one from scratch."

"Huh?" Aos froze in an awkward position. His arms had been lifted slightly in preparation for his sorry embrace. "What do you mean, a new case? Dalia's case was rejected. That's it. We move on."

"I went to Hana's office. I had to see her. I told you."

Aos retreated. Then gulped his hot coffee and made a pained face. "I thought you were joking. I mean, having a moment of crisis that would later become a joke. I know how you are. Everybody knows."

"Well, I . . ."

"Oh, God. You really went."

"Look, I — "

"What did you say?"

"Greetings, strange, callused life-form."

Aos tried to smooth his hair. Not that it needed smoothing; the smoothing only made things worse. A lick of hair, broken free from the gel, stuck up. "Please, tell me what you said. Tell me what you wanted."

"A yellow card. It's just a piece of paper. It's not like I . . ."

Aos walked back to his desk, sat down, and resumed translating documents. He gripped his pen with such rancor that Charlie assumed Aos was writing through the paper and on the desk. Soon he'd be writing on the floor. Not even wood could endure such irate scribbling.

"We can't reform the system," said Charlie after a few distressing seconds. "The only thing we can do is subvert it. You said so yourself about Mubarak. 'Subversion is the only way to even the odds when you have no money and no power.' Word for word, I think. We were playing chess at the time. You'd recently taken my rook with your knight."

"I never said that!" shouted Aos. He looked as if he wanted to stand up and march around the room in an angry rectangle. "That's not something I'd say. Without rules, there'd be chaos. I love rules. I follow rules."

"Except the ones declared by your government. Do those rules get their own category? Are they exempt because you chose them?"

"Don't even," said Aos. "I don't want to talk about . . ."

"What? The revolution? That thing lying dead in the street? That thing that has failed and will fail to change anything?"

Aos took a while to breathe again. "I forgive you for saying that."

How could Charlie express regret without apologizing? To apologize at that point in the argument would be to admit defeat. "I shouldn't have gone there. It's not my business."

"Injustice is everybody's business. You of all people . . ."

"Look, my point is – "

Aos slapped his hands together. "You're conflating rules and laws to make a point that's not fair." Aos was calm, but only in comparison to the loud sound he'd just made with his hands. "Really! Rules and laws aren't the same. The former are instituted in good faith, often by committee. The United Nations is a committee, isn't it? They don't wield any real power. Laws are instituted by lawmakers, who are instituted by whoever paid for their campaigns. Who absolutely do wield power! And lack conscience! To say they're the same – God, Charlie. What have you done?"

"Nothing yet. But I have a plan."

"What plan? More importantly, what motive? You're too close. Too biased."

"I am biased. By my conscience. That word you just mentioned. *Conscience.* C-O-N – "

"How can you say that? You can't say that after you tell me you love her. Like you'd do this for everyone else." Then: "You haven't told Dalia, have you? Oh, God. Please tell me you haven't told her."

"What would I say? 'So, we've spent all this time together talking – and entirely by accident, I've fallen . . . and now I'm going to . . .'"

"Oh, no. No, no."

"It's not like I have a choice."

"That argument wasn't valid the first time. Why are you still using it?"

"The heart wants what it – "

"Please, shut up." Aos removed his glasses and rubbed his eyes. "You'll be deported. You'll be hung from the bridge by your neck."

"By who? The government? What government?" Charlie's wild gesture – guns blazing – was meant to indicate that Egypt was like Montana before it became a state; there was no law in those plains. "It's less complicated than you think. There's only one document we can't forge. The yellow card. Only someone inside the UNHCR can issue that. That's why I went to see Hana."

"Don't count me as part of your plan," said Aos. "I don't even know what your plan is."

"I'm trying to tell you."

Aos refilled his coffee, then continued burning his throat. "What did Hana say? She was willing to give you a yellow card, just like that?"

"She'll come around. All we need is leverage."

"What leverage? Wait, don't tell me. I don't want to know. I can't believe I just asked that. I should be ashamed. I *am* ashamed."

By now, Charlie's first cup of coffee was the perfect temperature. He swallowed the contents without enjoying the flavor, then waited impatiently for the effect. Hopefully a clearer mind would make sharper points.

"What do Sabah and Michael have to say about this?" asked Aos. "I can't believe they're on board. Did you brainwash them? Did you promise them paid vacations? You know there's nothing left in the budget for — "

"I'd rather not discuss the budget," bemoaned Charlie. "And, no, I didn't tell them. Nor am I going to. We have other clients and they need lawyers who aren't . . . well, I'll say it plainly. Who aren't involved." Charlie regretted saying *other clients*. He should've said *hundreds of other clients*. He should've said *a legion of suffering*. The legion was growing every day, both in size and sorrow. "Michael and Sabah are liable if they know. Protecting them is the only way to protect our clients."

"What about me? I'm liable, too. Not that I'm going to do this, because I'm not. I could go to jail. Where? Abdeen? Tora Mazraa? Good-bye, hot food or even sufficient cold food. Good-bye, soap and water. Good-bye, personal space. I'd have to use a man's soiled thigh as a neck rest. That's probably not good for my posture and definitely not good for my . . ." Aos had to wash his hands just thinking about it. "Imagine weeks, months, even years of beatings and sleep deprivation. Then at the end of it all you just disappear."

"So, about leverage." Charlie took his turn to lean on the door-frame. The polish on the wood in that spot was long gone from all the leaning. "We write a new case, unrelated to Dalia, and submit it. Mark it urgent. You know, using the medical-necessity angle to our advantage. Really harp on that side of things. Are you listening?" Aos nodded; cold water poured from the sink. "The case is a whole family. There are kids involved. One died already. The older one. Another is sick and declining fast. Probably terminal. Mom's the primary client. Her kid can't be treated in Egypt. Money's not the issue so much as geography. Her kid is twentysomething. I don't know. A little older.

But once a child always a child, right? Parents always love what they make. He's really sick and needs out. Lupus. Cancer. Something. The mother is frantic. We submit the case and it gets stuck, as usual, in the review process. On Hana's desk."

"What's that supposed to accomplish?"

"A week after we first submit the case, we send an amendment. It'll say, 'Please remove X from the file.' X being the name of her son. Hana will know why. There's only one reason that happens. X died because the UNHCR didn't review the case fast enough. The brilliant thing is the case won't have time to be fully processed, so we don't need yellow cards or medical documents. Just a testimony to get us started."

"To what end?"

"To make her feel responsible for the death of a young man. It occurs to me, seeing her in person, watching her hide behind policy, that she may be vulnerable to that kind of . . ."

"Attack?"

"*Approach*, I think, is the better word."

"It won't work," said Aos, clearly relieved by the thought. "It's the same old story. Sometimes people die. It's horrible, but true. We have a lot of clients. They're old. If they're not old, they're sick."

"What if you show up at her door? And act the part of dying son who loves his mother? Things change when you put a face on the ID number. She never sees the people she reads about. Not really. Not in a human way. Interviews don't count. They're rigged. There's no humanity in a room full of resettlement officers prowling for discrepancies in a long, complicated story. We show Hana that this story is in fact someone's life. *Your* life cut short by *your* illness. Whatever that illness may be. A normally treatable condition exacerbated by circumstances in Egypt. Lack of quality medical care being the germane – "

"Oh, no. No, no."

"Hana needs to feel guilty. Guilty people need to forgive themselves. We provide that opportunity. Help us help Dalia! We get a new yellow card. She gets to clear her conscience." Charlie handed Aos a stapled document – a testimony Charlie had spent most of his sick day writing and rewriting – but Aos crumpled the paper and threw the ball into the trash. Charlie, having planned ahead, had e-mailed himself the document. He logged on to the computer and printed a second copy. Then a third copy just to make a point. "I can do this forever," said Charlie. He printed a fourth copy to make his point a second time.

Aos saw the sink was flooding and finally turned off the tap. Then he grabbed the document out of Charlie's hand. He didn't read it right away. He glared at Charlie for a few seconds. Not in a seething way. Just tired and taken aback.

Case Number: 167/2011
Name: Amirah Salih Radi
Mobile: +20 – – – –
E-mail: – – – – @gmail.com
Family: Rami Kamel Salih (husband)
　　　　　 Jalal Radi Salih (son, born 1989)
　　　　　 Sahar Radi Salih (daughter, deceased 2005)

(prepared with the help of the Refugee Relief Project)

Introduction

My name is Amirah Salih Radi and I am an Iraqi refugee living in Egypt with my husband, Ibrahim, and my son, Jalal. We fled Baghdad after the Americans fled the war they started. When they left, the militias took control. Life got worse for everybody, but especially those in mixed marriages. Our family among them. I am Sunni, but my husband is Shia. We had to flee Baghdad because a long time ago we married and since then we loved each other. The militias demanded we divorce or die, so we fled. Egypt was our first stop, but we didn't want to stay long. Of course we thought Europe or America was better — because Sahar, my daughter, was sick. In another world, lupus is not so grim. But with no treatment? First my daughter was tired. Then her skin began to tear itself when she went out in the sun. She lost weight. Her eyes dried, her hair thinned, and her mouth bled when she ate anything too hard. Why was the crust on bread too hard? There was also a rash on her face in the shape of a butterfly. Her knees and elbows, the bones themselves seemed to grow thicker. She never moved because of the pain. She died during a night I slept through in a country that wasn't our home. I dreamed right through the moment she left me.

Now my son exhibits symptoms and my husband refuses to pray. Rami says God gifted us children so He could test us by taking them. I am the foolish one who still hopes. I hope we can leave Egypt. I hope there is a better hospital with better services and access to medication. We are noncitizens with no money. I hope my son will not die from a disease that is treatable, but much later after I have died and he has become an old man. I hope you will understand why we are asking for resettlement. We only have one child left, and I hope to keep him.

Aos folded the document without reading the other four pages — the chronological list of events, including the escape from Iraq and the religious persecution preceding it, and everything detailing Jalal's terminal disease, currently developing. He imprisoned the folded pages in his shirt pocket. Then Aos drew the blinds, causing morning to appear like a fox; it was sudden and sanguine. The hot, red light turned Charlie into a long black shadow.

3

Aos' plan was to forget the lie he'd told. Why say the hair that had brushed against him was horse's hair when the hair belonged to a woman? Last night when Aos had gone to the square, things had escalated unexpectedly. The sound of armored vehicles exceeding the speed limit, then turning sharply toward the crowd — *Leave now or die by our tires!* — had urged the protesters to run. When the protesters didn't run, the armored vehicles stopped to unload their cargo. Each vehicle jettisoned twenty soldiers, who chased protesters from the square and beat the ones who wouldn't leave or couldn't run fast enough. To escape, at the very least, a contusion, Aos had left a woman he didn't know on the sidewalk at the mercy of the soldiers chasing them. His crime was running faster than her. The soldiers, wearing dark green clothes with lots of pockets and carrying thick black sticks, reaching for Aos, had grabbed her arm instead and pulled her to the ground. The black sticks fell, and fell, and fell. He hadn't seen, but heard the falling. Whup, whup. Down the road, when Aos had been a safe distance away, he'd turned back. By then, the woman had been lifted into the rear of a gray van covered in what looked like fencing. Aos didn't know her name, her address, her phone number; he'd met her in the square as water cannons had made sloppy work of the protesters.

After prayer, after shouting slogans, after Aos had lost himself in the volume of his own voice – shouting, desperately, for the Supreme Council to prosecute the field marshal – they'd exchanged happy, hopeless glances.

The plan to forget his lie was really a plan to forget her whupping. Aos would leave the office for noon prayer, then repent in the square by shouting even louder than last night. Arrest the leading members of the old government! Trials for corrupt businessmen! Prosecute the field marshal, leader of the military council, closet Mubarak confidant! Unfortunately, Michael and Sabah cornered Aos as he tried to escape. It was disappointing because he'd taken great pains to skirt past the interns.

"Hey . . . ," said Sabah. "I wanted to ask if . . ."

Aos ducked into the kitchen to avoid Sabah's hot stare. To make it seem as if he weren't running away, but intended to end up there, he started washing his mug.

"Are we bothering you?" asked Sabah. She'd followed Aos into the kitchen; Michael had followed her. The room had never been so small or stagnant.

"Not at all. I'm glad you're here. I enjoy your company." After Aos' mug was cleaner than it had ever been, he began washing other mugs. He just couldn't bring himself to stop washing.

"I sense a tension," said Sabah. "Is something up? Are you and Charlie . . . ?"

"What tension?" said Aos. "I can't speak for Charlie, but I've never been less tense." He shook the soap bottle as if something could be made from nothing if he shook hard enough.

"Don't you sense a tension?" Sabah asked Michael.

"I just wanted tea," said Michael, pointing to the mug in Aos' hand. Though he didn't want tea badly enough to endure any further awkwardness. He tried backing away, but Sabah blocked him.

"Aos and Charlie haven't talked all morning," she said. "When has that ever happened? Normally they're like . . ." Sabah rubbed her hands together. Charlie would've found this to be a curious gesture, but Aos wasn't bothered; he'd grown up in a country where men were free to express tenderness.

"I'll admit," said Michael, "it's very strange."

Sabah finally let him pass. He returned to his desk with a look of mourning. He'd failed to get his tea.

"So what's going on?" asked Sabah.

Telling Sabah the truth required betraying Charlie. How could Aos betray his friend? When he knew, or at least hoped feverishly, that Charlie wouldn't go through with his rash plan? Knowing Charlie, he'd later apologize for being so imprudent and again for being so slow to realize that. Aos chose to forgive Charlie in advance and not betray him. "I nearly got hit in the head with a baton last night. That's all. I didn't sleep." There was nothing wrong with the truth. Aos had nearly been hit in the head with a baton. Was it his fault the woman behind him had been hit instead? Was it his fault for running faster?

"A baton?"

"I escaped. I was very lucky."

Sabah was the only one in the office who could possibly understand. Everybody else — Charlie, Michael, the interns — could flee Egypt at any time. And very well might in the months to come. But Sabah and Aos couldn't flee without scorning God. They were born in Egypt for a reason. To see it become something great. Yet there was and had always been a distance between them. Sabah, so far as Aos knew, never went to the square. She never protested. Aos hadn't asked why, but assumed the worst: that Sabah wanted the revolution to go away. Even if that was true, could he blame her? He knew less about Sabah than he should've, given how long they'd worked together. Maybe the revolution had caused irrevocable harm to her family. Maybe somebody she knew had died or was rotting in prison. Not knowing made Aos a little sick. Why weren't they better friends? Why weren't they lovers?

"If there's ever anything you want to talk about . . . ," said Sabah in Arabic.

Every day Aos nearly forgot what his own language sounded

like. Not because he didn't hear it, but because he didn't listen the right way. He listened only insofar as he needed to translate. It was a pleasure to hear words as they really sounded without feeling the need to change their form and, subtly, their meaning.

"Shukran," said Aos.

Sabah poured hot water for tea into one of the several mugs Aos had washed. "Did you notice Michael didn't get what he came for?" she asked, laughing. "What a coward." That line contained the state of their relationship. Aos knew Sabah and Michael were fucking. He knew they were fighting, too. He'd extrapolated that from what Michael had recently told him about their "situation." Michael had wanted to propose months ago, but lingered in doubt until the revolution started. His problem had since grown several times its original size. Sabah had discovered a notepad on which Michael had rehearsed his proposal. "I didn't want to mince words," he'd said when presented with the evidence. Should he propose now despite her thinking the note was a joke? She'd smirked upon reading it. Should he propose now despite the turmoil in Tahrir? Nobody knew when or even if the revolution would end. Maybe it would end in a war. Should he propose now despite his burning desire to leave Egypt? Aos, blitzed by these questions, said he wasn't the right person to ask. He'd never been in love before. At least, not so much that he'd felt compelled to tell the person. Much less marry them. "I'm sorry," Aos had said. "I want to help, but my advice would be uninformed." Michael, clearly distressed, had quietly left. Soon after things had taken a turn for the worse. The discrepancy between what Michael said and what Michael wanted caused rifts in the pressure seal of his and Sabah's love. Her comment about his cowardice the least among them. Aos figured it would blow up soon enough; then the whole office would know.

In the square, banners read SLOW JUSTICE IS INJUSTICE — a reminder that former president Mubarak, sly devil, had escaped the wrath of the people. He'd been ousted almost two months before and had yet to languish in prison. He wasn't even hiding. He was eating lamb and fish on the coast of the Red Sea in Sharm el-Sheikh with the hills of Tiran — an island with unclear sovereignty — in the distance. Mubarak could kayak there if he needed to escape; should, for example, the attorney general actually charge the tyrant. For the murders, the corruption, the misappropriation of public funds. A fit man could even swim to Tiran in good weather. Aos hoped Mubarak would try to escape by swimming. Even calm and salty water would fail to keep such an old crony afloat. His bloated body, washed ashore, would bring repose to Egypt.

It was Save the Revolution Day and protesters had planned in advance. First, gather. Then, pray. Finally, shame the military council that took power after Mubarak had stepped down. The plan had been the same for weeks now. The council's greatest sins, after all, hadn't changed. Violence, lethargy. The protesters would demand free elections and fair trials for members of the old regime. No exile; no exoneration. The call to Jumu'ah prayer started shortly after noon. Upon Aos' arrival, it seemed. As if God had asked the protesters to wait for him. Slowly at first, the call sounded at a distance and crawled across the city. As more muezzins turned toward Mecca and sang the adhan into microphones, which echoed into the streets through elevated speakers wired to every mosque in Cairo, the hum became a roar. Aos scrambled to wash his arms, his face, his neck, and his feet up to his ankles. He poured water from a one-liter plastic bottle, purchased from a corner store. The water poured clean and freezing. When he prayed, his back curled and straightened. His lips moved and a whisper slipped out. The whole crowd prayed with him. When Aos opened his eyes, he saw what he loved to see: God's choreography. A thousand people bending in unison. More than a thousand. Two thousand, maybe. Or more.

When the speeches began, Aos took pleasure in how little fear he felt. It wasn't always that way. He used to feel vulnerable near Tahrir. If he could hear the speeches, he was too close. He used to sweat even at night in January when the air was so cold. The revolution was still an infant idea back then. Mubarak hadn't stepped down yet. The fervor, and with it the violence, had peaked. Aos had attended the early protests in the safest way possible, by standing back by the bridge. Tahrir Square was just one part of Tahrir Street, which continued west across the river. He'd escaped every time he saw danger or heard that danger would come. Not until after Mubarak had stepped down had Aos dared enter the heart of the square. He'd been drawn by the idea that the revolution had ended. No thanks to him, of course. His fear had turned to guilt. That guilt had lured him into the square, which had gotten him captured. Paid thugs in civilian clothing had come that night to tear down the tents and scare away the protesters. The Supreme Council had declared the occupation of Tahrir not just a violation of law, but also logic. What are you still doing here? Isn't the revolution over? Hasn't Mubarak gone to his palace in Sharm? Go home! Stop blocking traffic! "Mubarak may be exiled, but he's not imprisoned!" Aos had shouted. He'd been one among thousands shouting. "Only the image of the regime has changed, not its practices! Where is the freedom? The dignity? The bread?" Aos had been waiting to say these things for weeks, months, even years; he was born wanting to say them. Grain prices had gone up. Gas prices had gone up. The only thing that hadn't risen was the employment rate. Aos had a job and felt both thankful and like shit. He told nobody. When he and a small group of other protesters — desperate men and women masquerading as brave — refused to leave, they were dragged to the grounds of the Egyptian Museum, a hulking pink building north of the square. The building, formerly noted for its priceless collection, was noted then for its deep basement and fenced yard. The men and the women were separated. The men were stripped naked and their heads were shaved. Live wires were dragged across their wet skin. Wet from bottled water, which had been poured upon them; wet from crying and sweating and spit. Aos took home bruises where he was kicked. Burns, too, where the wires dragged. The burns had since become thin, branching scars. Upon release, the captors bestowed on their captives a gift. "Your lives," they said in all seriousness. "Never return to the square. If you return, we'll find you. We know your faces." Some, including Aos, went anyway. They didn't have any fear left except that the goons would go unpunished.

Aos never learned what came of the women. Were their heads shaved? Were they electrocuted? Or had something worse occurred? How much worse? Aos didn't want to know. He also wanted to know badly. The woman he'd left on the bridge probably suffered their fate. Aos tried not to think about her. What would be accomplished by thinking and regretting? He'd already decided he was sorry for leaving her. Next time he'd sacrifice himself. He'd dive headfirst into the soldiers giving chase. He'd beg for another haircut when the whupping started, just to anger them. Although, would he really? It was easy to believe so; but believing was all he could do besides shouting. Aos shouted until his throat hurt. Arrest the leading members of the old government! Trials for corrupt businessmen! Prosecute the field marshal, leader of the military council, closet Mubarak confidant!

A scuffle erupted somewhere in the crowd of protesters. Nearby, but out of sight. There was a cry of pain. Aos, ears unstuck from the speeches, moved toward the sound. A second cry dispatched his hesitation. He parted the crowd by walking sideways. "Yallah!" he shouted. "Get out of the way!" He found a man bleeding from his nose and a deep gash in his cheek. The eye above the gash was already beginning to swell shut. The man's other eye begged Aos for help. It begged urgency. He was hurt. He needed water. Aos impulsively handed the man his one-liter plastic bottle, which had been drained from all the washing; the man looked confused. The bottle was empty, so he pushed it away. He moaned about a rock or stick hitting him. Maybe both. Or something else. He couldn't say for sure. When he sneezed, blood flew out of his nose. Protesters grabbed the injured man by the arms and a few more grabbed him by the feet. They carried him away to the tents. By the time Aos realized he'd done nothing to help, it was too late. He couldn't even pick up the man's glasses. Someone had stepped on them. Aos was so ashamed of his failure to act that he set off in search of the culprit. Surely a hatchet man hired by the government for the dirtiest work, a member of the baltagiya. These gangs of insolvent men from across the city were paid to scare protesters away from the square. No means were too godless. Aos supposed he could identify the culprit, who would be wearing civilian clothes – the baltagiya only represented the government in an unofficial capacity – by the way he gripped his weapon: so hard his knuckles turned white. White knuckles indicated not readiness to swing, but yearning. Hatchet men were anxious to harm. Protesters, on the other hand, held their sticks, boards, shields, helmets, flags, and signs without squeezing them; their knuckles would be the color of their skin. The relaxed grips declared more legitimate wants. Freedom, jobs, fair elections. Aos sped through the crowd of four or five thousand – the number swelling by the second – eyes moving from hand to hand. He saw no white knuckles. He kept looking, hoping to find a man gripping a board with fear and longing and hate. Aos stopped cold. His own desire frightened him. He needed to get away from the crowd before he started seeing white knuckles where there weren't any. He kept his head parallel to the ground so that he saw only faces, except for the one hand held at head height; when he saw the hand, he directed his attention to the sign it was holding: SORRY FOR THE DISTURBANCE WHILE WE REBUILD EGYPT.

The shade of the Mugamma, the most intimidating government edifice in all of Africa, covered Aos so that he felt cool and dead. The Mugamma, located one block south of Tahrir, was nicknamed the Tall Monster for its colossal block exterior and thin, labyrinthine halls, each like a vein pumping blood through a beast. Normally the blood was men and women in worn-looking office attire who worked on everything from tax-evasion investigations to visa renewals. Now the blood was hot, stagnant air. Today, as on most days since the revolution began, the Mugamma was closed. It relieved Aos to know the building was abandoned, the Supreme Council couldn't govern, the army had no lasting power. Their power would run out with their ammunition, which would run out eventually. Or would it? In a window several stories above the main entrance, Aos saw something move. His heart stopped when he realized it was a man's head.

"I came for the shade," said a voice behind Aos, from the palm garden. "Then I recognized your water bottle. Am I intruding? May I sit?"

Aos turned and saw the man with a swollen eye and a gash coated in what looked like jelly. The shame of seeing him again fit nicely inside the shock of seeing a head in the window, so that he couldn't feel it right away. "Come here!" said Aos, gesturing. "Do you see that?" He pointed to the window.

"What?"

"Is that a head? Not a football? Not a globe?"

"It's hard to say. I don't have my glasses." The man pointed to his bulbous, swollen eye. "The thug was a young boy, I think. Barely as high as my chest. That's why I didn't see him. I'm afraid now for my own sons, who are the same height. Not once have I asked what they believe or what they want from their country. Now I wonder. What if they love Mubarak? What if they want him to come back?"

Aos couldn't think about anything except the head in the window. He wanted to know who it belonged to and what they were doing at their desk. Maybe the Mugamma wasn't really closed. Or only closed to the public for appearances. Maybe the Supreme Council was governing behind closed doors. Not in service to the people, but scheming against them. "I'm sorry," said Aos, standing up. "I'm sorry I had no water and didn't carry you to the medical tent and can't stay here in the shade. Someone is inside the Mugamma." Aos left the man with jelly on his face to recover alone in the palm garden. Then he ran back to the office to tell Charlie what he'd seen. To Aos, a head in the window meant the revolution was in grave danger. Charlie needed to know. The fate of the revolution and the fate of their clients were inextricably linked. Most of their clients would never leave Egypt, so the only way to improve their lives would be to improve the government. The government would never improve if it wasn't overthrown. The government would never be overthrown if the Mugamma wasn't closed due to general civil disobedience. If the Mugamma wasn't closed, the Supreme Council wasn't scared. If the council wasn't scared, they wouldn't hold fair elections. Mubarak would be replaced by a man like him. Only his name would change.

When Aos arrived at the office, news lodged in his throat, Charlie was nowhere to be found. Odd considering how rarely Charlie left the office, even at night. Certainly not during working hours. The weekend counted as working hours; even interns slogged through half days. Aos called Charlie using the office phone since Aos' mobile had been stolen in Tahrir. Not that day, but last week. He'd not gotten round to replacing it. There was no answer. "Where's Charlie?" he asked the office at a slightly heightened pitch. Aos didn't want to react badly in front of the interns, but couldn't help himself. Michael answered with a blank stare while Sabah answered with several questions: "What happened to your shirt?" She gestured to the polka dots. "Is that blood? Are you hurt?" The interns answered with confused looks. Nobody had seen Charlie leave.

Aos' unusual day was only beginning. Later, the office phone rang. He was so sure it was Charlie returning his call that he didn't use his normal greeting. "Salaam, habibi! You won't believe what I saw! A head in the window at the – "

A smoker's cough revealed the caller wasn't Charlie. He wasn't patient, either. "Am I speaking to Aos? If not, I need to speak with him. Tell him it's a matter of life and death. Tell him I'm not joking."

The office phone traded almost exclusively in matters of life and death. Aos had acclimated years ago. "Yes, Aos. That's me." He tried to sound attentive and concerned. "What's your name? Have you or your family been threatened? Injured? Arrested?"

The police were known to arrest refugees caught selling trinkets in the street, which was a common and altogether pitiful source of income for many clients. It was technically illegal. The police would demand to see work permits. When no permits could be produced, they'd demand bribes. The bribes were always in excess of the value of the trinkets. There was no way for the clients to pay.

"No, no. My name is Naguib." The caller said his name as if it meant something. As if they'd been friends once.

Aos cycled all the Naguibs that he knew. His bawab, who collected money for repairs that never materialized. The shrewd businessman from the corner store who sold the best bread in all of Cairo but refused to name its source. Even the boy who came every so often with his cart of nearly spoiled vegetables down Aos' alley. "For soup," he'd say. "Very cheap." Many clients, too, had the same name. Naguib Fakhoury. Naguib Ashhad.

"I'm sorry," said Aos. "I don't – " Aos heard a fist slam a desk.

"Please, remember! The Yemeni Restaurant. On Sharia Iran. We ate there one night in college after class was canceled. I ran away when a machete man outside tried to rob us. I never apologized for leaving you. I should have apologized, but I was so humiliated. How could I come back to class? How could I face you?"

Yes, of course. Naguib. Aos was surprised how vividly he remembered a man he'd not seen or thought of in years. Their friendship had lived a short life. It began at Cairo University outside the locked door of a canceled class. Masters of Egyptian Literature. That week they were studying *The Yacoubian Building*, about the fictional residents of a real edifice by the same name located on Talaat Harb Street, not far from Tahrir. The novel condemned and utterly dismantled a society consumed by a corrupt government, by greed, by lack of principle. The author's reproach, though aimed at the ruling class, had a wide spread; nobody, not even the shirtmaker, escaped blame. Aos read the book but slept through the professor's speculations about which Egyptian politicians and socialites the characters were based upon. The professor's only passion was his theory; he didn't really want to teach.

That night Aos and Naguib had arrived at the locked classroom at the same time. They weren't friends and had barely spoken until that moment. It wasn't either man's fault. The size of the class precluded normal rapport. Naguib awkwardly bent over to investigate the slit at the bottom of the door. "No lights. The class is canceled. Why weren't we notified?" He looked excited and almost afraid, as if he hadn't expected to have spare time and, as a result, would now squander it.

"Are you hungry?" Aos thought spare time was God's blessing. It would be a sin not to use it to eat. It would be a worse sin not to invite Naguib, who looked lonely. "I know this place. It's far, but not very far. It's worth the walk. The bread is . . ." Aos made a large circle with his arms. "Humongous."

They went to a Yemeni restaurant. The restaurant was called the Yemeni Restaurant, located on a street called Iran. Aos went there originally for the strangeness of the name and location, but visited every week after for the hot saltah stew, which he scooped with torn pieces of malooga flat bread. Aos said the bread would, if toasted, make a good shield against an armed enemy. Naguib, in an attempt to make the jest a little smarter, said too seriously, "If Romans ever return to Egypt, I'll lift my bread in defense." He made a strained face when lifting it and, after a few long seconds, let himself laugh. They continued eating and, in between bites, talked about history, art, and, after exhausting their knowledge on the other subjects, literature. Were the characters in Al-Aswany's novel based on real people? Could the professor's theory be believed? Naguib said a professor, out of respect, should be trusted; Aos said a professor, out of duty, should have proof. Not that it mattered much either way. The conversation was an exercise in intellectual heavy petting, and by the end of the meal both Aos and Naguib thought highly of each other and, more important, themselves.

Sharia Iran was a dark and oddly quiet street, but Cairo was a safe city – safe as most cities, at least – and after splitting the bill they walked west toward Al Bohooth, where they would've turned south toward Cairo University. Naguib had another class to attend and Aos had a paper to write in the library. The library was quieter than his apartment. His upstairs neighbors had a habit of watching TV all night. The floors were so thin they may as well not have existed. On the walk, Aos and Naguib passed the Asad Ibn Al-Forat Mosque, the Metro grocery, and the iron gym where men boxed away their bellies with no gloves. The gym's signage displayed one man knocking out another man, who somehow was smiling as he fell to the mat. After the gym was a trash pile that dwarfed the cars parked next to it. Every time Aos walked by that pile – he went to the Yemeni Restaurant at least twice a week – he was reminded of the Zabbaleen, the garbage people of Manshiyat Naser. They traveled door-to-door collecting refuse. They hauled the refuse back to Garbage City, their slum on the edge of the ward, where it was sorted, sold, recycled, reused, or, in the case of organic material, fed to pigs. It was the most effective garbage collection Cairo had ever seen. But those responsible weren't rewarded by the government or respected by the people. Aos tried to start a conversation about the Zabbaleen. Not that he had anything insightful to say about them, other than how he admired their resourcefulness. Maybe it was an overly polite opinion, but nice to say nonetheless. Somehow Naguib found a reason to scoff. "The Zabbaleen? Those weasels? Those rats?" Aos didn't know how to react. Let it go? Or defend the Zabbaleen? He could say weasels were better than racists. Was it even a race issue? Or a class issue? Maybe it was a religious issue. Most of the Zabbaleen, after all, were Copts.

A machete man saved Aos and Naguib from what had become an awkward lull in conversation. He jumped from the shadows into the yellow light cast by the lamp hung overhead on a black wire crossing the street. He demanded two wallets and swung his machete as evidence of his willingness to chop them up to get their money. The swinging was so wild it was almost beyond the machete man's control. His arm looked ready to fly from its socket. Aos, in a bid to keep what belonged to him, said they were students and had no money. Naguib vigorously nodded in agreement. The machete man swung his blade, closer this time, again and again. Naguib turned to run, but slipped into the trash pile. The quick movement of his body falling startled the machete man, who lunged at Naguib with his blade extended. Aos stuck his foot out, tripping the machete man. Aos' foot moved entirely of its own accord. Why would Aos consciously protect Naguib? Whom he didn't know and had discovered he didn't like? Who'd said crude things about the Zabbaleen? The questions disturbed Aos, for they revealed his brain was less moral than his foot.

The machete man landed flat on the pavement in a daze. Aos snatched his blade lest the daze wear off and the machete take to the air again. Then he dragged the machete man to the side of the road in case a vehicle happened past and, mistaking his body for a speed bump, slowed down but nevertheless drove over him. Finally, Aos turned to check on Naguib. Part of him wanted Naguib to be injured from his face-plant into the trash pile. Not so injured that he needed medical attention, but injured enough to regret what he'd said about weasels. If the Zabbaleen hadn't suffered such enmity – the prejudice made it easy for Parliament to imperil their livelihood by culling their pigs – then perhaps the trash pile would've been long gone to Garbage City. To Aos' surprise, Naguib didn't lie sprawled in the refuse. There was only a mark in the pile where he'd landed. Naguib must've stood up and, without concern for the fate of his new "friend," slunk away. "You're the weasel," said Aos to the trail of garbage betraying the direction he'd fled. To prevent that annoyance from becoming anger, Aos shoved Naguib from his mind. He returned to and sat by the machete man. With the adrenaline beginning to wear off, Aos could finally see the man for what he was: thin and tired looking. He gave the man some money. Not a lot, but what he had. The prophet, after all, had commanded it: *If I had a mountain of gold, I would love that, before three days had passed, not a single coin thereof remained with me. . . .* But so, too, did something in Aos' gut compel him to hand over his banknotes and even his coins. The feeling that he'd made an error of judgment. How could he blame the poorest of the poor for being desperate? That was like blaming the fire you'd set for burning you. It was Aos' fault for not giving the money right away. For not giving more often to more people. For not attacking the problem at its source: in government, which fed injustice with nepotism and corruption and greed. For not revolting against tyranny. For not demanding the tyrant step down. The machete man accepted the money, then tried to steal back the blade Aos had tucked under his arm — a lazy and futile attempt to reclaim an identity no man could possibly want.

"I need that," said the machete man.

"I'm sorry." Aos scooted away. He stood up when the machete man scooted after him. "I can't give it back to you." Aos walked east toward the river instead of south toward the school. The machete man didn't give chase, but did yell that he'd been robbed. "Thief!" he shouted from the sitting position. Aos didn't stop until he reached the Nile's bank, a kilometer away. There he let the blade fly like an ibis over the water. A faint splash rid the world of the machete.

That night had been the beginning of Aos' political disposition and the end of his brief friendship with the weasel Naguib. The man, who'd failed to appear again in Masters of Egyptian Literature, had practically fallen out of Aos' memory. He'd barely thought of him again until now.

"You didn't run," said Naguib quietly into the phone.

"I was so afraid I forgot to run." Aos was pleased to discover how easy it was to forgive someone who'd committed a small crime long ago. There was nothing left to discuss. Aos hadn't fostered a grudge. He didn't want an apology. He wanted to get back to work.

"I have a son now," said Naguib.

Aos' job had cursed him with a laconic way of speaking. He'd learned to stay on topic. In doing so, he'd lost the patience required to converse the Arab way—with a strange, rapt interest in knowing everything about everyone. Aos felt sorry that he'd lost the part of himself that had allowed conversations to unspool, to go nowhere, to wind endlessly. "What's his name?" The obligation to ask bothered Aos. The bother informed his regret. He'd changed. He'd lost something.

"Geb."

The name of the Egyptian god who permitted crops to grow, whose laughter caused earthquakes. Aos knew the name from an elective course he'd taken on Egyptology, once upon a time. Geb was, or might've been—at least some archaeologists theorized—related to the divine creator. The divine creator was a bird that laid the world as an egg. The bird was either a goose or an ibis. When the egg hatched, Ra, the sun god, filled the sky. Geb was his cousin or something.

"He's sick," said Naguib.

Ya Allah, thought Aos. Now he couldn't end the conversation in good conscience. He'd have to wait for it to end naturally.

"Sick how?"

"He requires an operation."

"What operation?"

"Maybe I deserve this," said Naguib with a drawl that implied he was drunk or medicated. Why hadn't Aos noticed the drawl before? Perhaps he really had lost the ability to listen. "My life hasn't always been virtuous. I left Egypt for medical school. London, you know. I came back with a nasty habit. Pills, I'm sorry to say. What once cured stress then cured sadness. Years melted away in the sun. Now I work at Hallacare. You know Hallacare? The hospital in Shubra? We tell our patients there is no better care to receive than the terrible care we can offer. My soul is gone from saying that. I wait for God to punish me. But Geb? What could a boy do in four years to deserve this? Geb is four. I don't have the money."

"What money? Why do you—"

"Any doctor in Egypt who would take the surgery would just kill my boy. The system is falling apart. There's no trust. No accountability. Call me a traitor for saying that. I don't care what you say." Then, after calming down a bit: "Two days ago I found a stray goat in the ward with the children. I knew then what I've known for years, but was too ashamed to admit: I should've stayed in London. I should've stayed. But my family said come back. They said come back to Egypt. They said, 'What is our country if all the educated people abandon us?' I had agreed at the time and felt proud. The mistake now ruins my family. Geb, my boy. He's sick." Aos realized too late that he'd also made a mistake. Naguib hadn't called to share his woe. He wanted something. "One hundred thousand Egyptian pounds. I beg you. For the plane ticket and the surgery. Please, I beg you. Geb will die."

Aos felt so uncomfortable that he had to laugh. He felt sick for laughing. "I'm sorry, I—"

"I already called everyone I know," Naguib said plaintively. "I've resorted to calling people I barely knew once, whom I've also offended. I have no excuse. The only thing I have is my son."

"I'm sorry. I don't have the money. I won't ever have it."

Desperation presented itself in the form of stilted breathing over the phone. Aos listened as long as he could bear the noise, but eventually had to hang up. In the dead air grew a strange feeling: this wasn't the last time they'd speak.

4

Hana needed to get out of her apartment. Unfortunately, her plan – go somewhere! – was bedeviled by the day. Friday in Cairo was the same as Saturday in Dearborn. People fortunate enough to have salaries were out spending them. It was the weekend and Hana lacked both the authority and the key required to go to work. Where else could she go? Whom could she bother? If she wanted to ride around the city aimlessly for a few hours paying a man to make small talk, she could call Mustafa. That was pitiful, but was it *too* pitiful? He needed the money and she needed the . . . well, Hana didn't know what to call it. The only thing she knew was that she couldn't spend the whole day alone on her couch. She'd already spent the whole morning and most of the afternoon crying into her wineglass. Did that mean she'd actually drunk her own tears? Maybe so, but Hana had earned such abandon. This day, April Fools', was not a joke. It was the day Leilah was born; also, and irrevocably, the day she was missed. Like their father, Leilah had perished when a bomb shredded her clothes milliseconds before the rest of her body. She'd died the way she came into the world. Naked and blinded by light.

"I'm going outside," Hana said to herself. Saying it aloud made it official. Two shoes sat by the door like dogs desperate to get out. Hana's fingers shook as she laced them. Fear, rage, regret. Why hadn't she begged Leilah the same way Ishtar had begged her? "Don't go back to Baghdad! I don't care if it's for work! Quit if you have to! As your mother, the woman who *made you* and *saved your life*, I'm asking you . . . no, telling you! . . ." Suddenly Hana found herself in the hall punching the call button to the elevator. The apparatus was either broken or taking a break. Hana used the stairs. She flew down two at a time, risking a fall to her death. The wind of her downward movement made her feel like a bird diving into the sea. A brown pelican. An imperial shag. Hana liked the idea of being an imperial anything. By the time she reached the lobby, her mood had improved. Not a lot, but enough to keep her going. The hot stink of the city, pouring through the open door, offered what Hana's air-conditioned apartment had not: the smell of life in its putrid beauty. She followed the smell outside. Then followed the sidewalk until her heart told her where to go. The Khan el-Khalili! The great market! She told herself to get lost in its size. She would sip tea. Or carrot juice, if she encountered a juice seller delicately balancing a tin tray of glasses full to their brims with deep orange liquid and pale orange froth. After the juice she would shop cautiously. She would avoid eye contact. She would scowl at boys who made kissing sounds with their lips or crude gestures with their hands. Kissing sounds, piled upon each other, blown rapidly from groups of boys, who seemed to troll the streets day and night, had done much to keep Hana inside. Not today, she thought. Today she would scowl and, if need be, shout or chase the boys until they fled crying. She laughed at the fear they'd once caused her and looked forward to causing them fear in return.

Hana walked the long way to the Khan, in part because she couldn't remember its exact location. The sun felt good on her face. Talaat Harb Street, starting by the statue of the famous banker; past the underwear shop, the movie theater, the watch sellers; left to Ramses, then right toward the High Court; right again on 26th of July Street to Attaba, a market district, almost a city within itself, akin to the Kahn but less touristy and harder to enjoy on account of feeling like an interloper; then Al-Azhar all the way to the Khan itself. In total, over four kilometers. Though made longer by the heat and the time spent waiting endlessly at intersections. Reaching her destination was most pleasing to her feet. Hana sat on a bench in the packed square by the Mosque of Sayyidna Al-Hussein. Her feet cramped immediately upon relieving them. Flexing her toes only made the cramping worse. "Ouch," said Hana. The stranger sitting next to her proffered a weird look. Hana couldn't tell whether the look conveyed sympathy or surprise. Or something worse, such as scorn. Maybe Hana wasn't dressed properly. It was hard to know for sure. The opinions on dress were so strong and so varied. Hana thought none of them ought to apply to her shirt, but then again she was wearing her shirt in someone else's country. By the time Hana decided how to respond—with a neutral but friendly look, like a Swiss diplomat—the stranger had abandoned the bench. The brusque departure pinched Hana, causing more bother than pain; she spread out so nobody else would sit next to her.

The square was bordered on one side by a series of historic cafés that used to house Egypt's most celebrated authors—among them Naguib Mahfouz, who haunted al-Fishawi for decades carrying his various depressions and an empty notebook to plant them in. He always sat in the interior treasure room beneath a giant Spanish mirror with lotus blossoms carved into the frame. He came for the mirror but stayed for the legendary customer service. Al-Fishawi's claim to fame was that they'd operated twenty-four hours a day for 240 years straight. No customer had ever come seeking tea without receiving it. The doors didn't even have locks. Mahfouz once expressed his gratitude in the guest register. *Loving greetings I present to my beloved home, al-Fishawi. God grant it and its owners long life, fame, and happiness. Your loyal son, Naguib Mahfouz. 1982.* Six years later, Mahfouz won the Nobel Prize for the stories he wrote in their treasure room. Hana loved *The Harafish* more than his other books, even though it was less famous. She carried the first sentence in her chest like a gunshot wound: "In the passionate dark of dawn, on the path between death and life, within view of the watchful stars and within earshot of the beautiful, obscure anthems, a voice told of the trials and joys promised to our alley." From her vantage on the bench, Hana could see into al-Fishawi. Waiters ran down a gauntlet of customers with admirable finesse, carrying glasses of Lipton through two rows of turned backs. The waiters never stopped or spilled tea. Orders were shouted at high volume over impenetrable conversations, arguments, tirades, and the sort of laughter reserved for people who'd just finished working long hours or were, more regrettably, about to start. Hana promised herself that one day she'd not only find an empty chair, but sit down and actually order something. The explicit goal would be to mingle with the ghost of an author. That was somehow less embarrassing than the implicit goal. To finally live in this city. As of yet, Hana had simply witnessed it. From a window. From a taxi. And now, from a bench.

All of a sudden, an ice cream man on the corner rang his bell. That bell was the cold metal cart he whacked with his long metal spoon. Whack, whack. He shouted three flavors, but Hana couldn't hear which three. She was mystified by the movement of the spoon and the taffylike quality of the ice cream swirling on the end. The metal spoon led to an arm, which led to a face; Hana squinted and, swear to God, saw Charlie. Hana figured the illusion was caused by heat bouncing off the sidewalk and her preoccupation with what Charlie had said the other day in her office. Maybe not what he'd said, but what he'd meant. That she lacked compassion. Or even a heart muscle. Hana feared that was true. A few seconds later, she realized what she really saw: Charlie's face on Charlie's body. He was standing behind the man selling ice cream, who'd leaned back to stretch. Hana, agog, marched over. Charlie looked surprised. Then almost frightened. He pretended to play with his phone.

"What are you doing here?" asked Hana. "Are you following me?" It was, in her mind, an absurd question. Of course he was following her. There was no such thing as a Cairo Coincidence. The city was too big. There were too many people.

Either Charlie recognized that or he was too lazy to defend himself. He just wore a sorry look. "You walked past my office. Then walked past again a minute later going the other way. When does fate strike twice? That almost never happens."

Hana tried to remember a moment during her walk when she'd turned around. Had she accidentally gone left on Ramses only to realize she should've gone right? Had she crossed the wrong intersection and had to go back? Her path had been so winding it was only fair to assume Charlie was telling the truth.

"Just, we have important things to discuss," said Charlie. "When I saw you twice through the screen door, I figured only God could make that happen. I don't even believe in God! That compelled me to chase after you and try to catch up. But you were too far up the street and moving too quickly. Part of the reason you're so fast, by the way, is that you cross the street without looking. You almost died about . . . well, more than once. It's a miracle you're still alive."

The ice cream man whacked his cart again. Then told Charlie to choose his flavor or get out of line. There was no line, but that was beside his point. Charlie was blocking view of the cart; therefore, the wild show by a man who'd clearly spent years practicing the art of slinging ice cream on the world's longest spoon. All that hard work was for naught with Charlie standing between him and potential customers. The ice cream man was losing a sale every time a child walked by. No child could see over Charlie's shoulders.

"You could've called," said Hana. "I'll be in the office next week. And the week after. And the week after that."

Charlie started to blather about fate again, but stopped short. "The truth is, there's no time. Dalia is . . . well, heartbroken. But her damn husband has gone insane. Now, I respect the man. But he's gone insane. He wants to trade his life in Boston for a much worse life in Cairo. He's packing as we speak. Actually *packing*. I can't live with that. I just can't."

Charlie's hyperbole had a troubling earnestness. As if he believed his heart would just stop. It caused Hana to feel what she felt some mornings after she couldn't sleep. That her job was pointless and her purpose wasn't to help people cross borders, but to impede the process. Normally she disturbed the feeling during the taxi ride to work by rolling down the window and letting the air slap her face. Now the air was not moving; the feeling would not hide. "I need a drink," said Hana, more or less to herself. It sounded less desperate than she thought it would. "Do you know anywhere nearby that serves –"

The ice cream man whacked his cart again. When that didn't work, he whacked Charlie on the arm. The spoon made a duller sound against flesh than against metal. Charlie startled and finally backed away from the cart with a grimace. "Beer?" he said, side-eyeing the ice cream man's evil spoon. "Please tell me you were going to say beer. Egyptians invented beer, by the way. Did you know that? Now they scorn their own invention. I say at their peril. Scorn beer, scorn God. That's what I think. I think God bestowed beer as an apology for everything else he bestowed. Mortality, in-laws, peanut allergies."

The history of Egypt struck Hana as overwhelming, as if one might ask what the Egyptians didn't invent and actually receive an answer. The cafés nearby had the same kind of illustrious history. Even the sidewalk seemed so old that the British Museum ought to have plundered it. "I was in the British Museum once," said Hana, as if her thoughts had been spoken aloud. "I remember thinking it was an impressive testament to empire. I felt horrible for liking it." Her reward for the peculiar digression was a baffled look on Charlie's face. There was real pleasure in watching the bafflement spread to the rest of his body. He shifted his weight. He inspected his cuticles.

"So, about the beer?"

Hana considered her implied invitation before confirming it. Just in case she'd been impulsive before and had since changed her mind. But she'd not changed her mind. Going anywhere with Charlie still beat going home by herself. She asked if he knew a place.

"Do you know El Horreya?"

"No. Should I? Is it famous? Please tell me it's not famous."

"It's not famous, at all. Or even very clean. It's not far. Not *that* far, anyway. We can – "

Hana's feet protested before Charlie could suggest they walk. "Oh, look," said Hana. "A taxi."

Hana and Charlie sat at a square table covered in bean casings. Several old men in suits and jellabiya played tawla while a few others played chess; entire packs of cigarettes disappeared effortlessly. Hana's beer, which Charlie had summoned by raising his arm, was lukewarm but still satisfying. It satiated a more important want than thirst. "Today my sister was born," said Hana. The idea was to start talking before Charlie had the opportunity to abscond with the conversation. Also to give Charlie a taste of his own medicine. He'd come into her office and implanted his sorrow; now she'd implant hers in return. "Almost forty years ago, today. Thirty-seven, to be exact." Hana knew Leilah wouldn't mind being used in this way. She'd always had a snotty and sarcastic side and, as a child, had loved vengeance.

"Huh? I mean, what I came here to say . . ."

Hana's look told Charlie to shut up. It was her turn. "But the year that really matters, if I had to pick one, was 1980. That year my mother did two things for the first time. She buried my father and immediately fled Iraq, emigrating by plane from Baghdad to Munich to Michigan." Ishtar had called it the "weird year." Egypt established diplomatic relations with Israel. The United States severed relations with Iran. Saddam Hussein even donated hundreds of thousands of dollars to Syriac Catholic churches in Detroit. That was where Ishtar had brought Leilah, who was four feet tall at the time, and Hana, who was still a bulge in Ishtar's midriff – to the Motor City, where Ishtar pushed a pink screaming beast into a blue felt blanket. "The pink beast was me," said Hana proudly. Time passed without declaring itself, so that it came and went. Hana learned to talk; Leilah attended school; Ishtar worked hard on her English. "She called it the No Fun Language to Learn," said Hana, biting deeply into the memory of Ishtar falling asleep on a book. "The studying paid off. She got a job at Wayne State. The library, as it happened. Despite lacking the required degree, my mother advanced quickly to a staff position. She had the gumption to argue she was qualified and proved her point by doing the job better than everyone else." But the intervening years and comparative financial security hadn't made everything well. There was a hierarchy of suffering in the house. Hana, the only one who'd never met her father and had never been to Baghdad, came last on account of being least homesick. How could she miss a place she'd never seen except in photographs? Leilah, who was sad but elastic, came next. Young people just healed faster. Ishtar, however, contender for most damaged person on Earth, was prone to fits. She'd lost almost everything. Her true love, named Somar. Her true home, called Baghdad. Not only where she was born, but where she'd become herself. Baghdad was where she'd learned how to read. Baghdad was where she'd learned how to love. When Hana was very young, the fits consisted of crying on certain occasions. Such as Akitu, the Assyrian New Year, which Hana had never actually celebrated. "Apparently there's poetry and a parade," said Hana. Over time, Ishtar expressed her grief in an increasingly honest manner. On Hana's fifteenth birthday, her mother's gift was a detailed account of how Somar died. Not just the broad strokes—the war, the missile—which Hana had learned at an earlier age, but a visual description of the street, complete with blood and bits of paper flying around in the wind. Somar was decimated alongside a shop selling newspapers and pocket-sized copies of the Qur'an. The only thing Hana unwrapped that year was her mother's bathrobe. "Leilah and I put her into the tub. I sat on the toilet. Leilah sat on the floor. I remember not feeling angry. Just worried that Ishtar would drown in the tub if we didn't sit with her."

Ishtar had told more stories that night. Grander stories, thank God. Mostly about the Mesopotamians. She said Mesopotamians invented not only the wheel, but also the world's first vampire. Take that, Egyptians! Dimme, a female demon who hounded women during childbirth. Dimme couldn't bear offspring of her own, so resorted to stealing and eating children from the human world. In addition to her crimes against newborns, Dimme disturbed sleep, delivered nightmares, carried sickness, ate men, and stomped newly planted crops to deliver the bad news that death was coming to Earth. To defend against such wickedness, Ishtar had carried around an amulet with Pazuzu's image on it. Pazuzu was king of the demons of wind. Storms came every time he exhaled. Droughts coincided with his thirst. While he didn't embody many virtues himself, he was Dimme's rival in Mesopotamian lore. Ishtar thought Dimme wouldn't enter a room Pazuzu already occupied.

"My mother was such a fanatic," said Hana with admiration and sadness and an intense desire to embrace the woman. "The night got better after my mother threw her robe on the floor and sat naked in the tepid water." She envisioned her mother's much-younger skin. "When she got tired, she asked Leilah to say what she remembered about our father. His name, Somar, hung on her lips. Leilah smiled. She said her memories of Father were called little glimpses. Father planting things in pots he kept in the window. Father rubbing his dirty hands on his shirt. Father saying one of his many beloved proverbs. 'One never exits the hammam the same as one entered. I must take a bath!'"

Hana sat now with a past that didn't belong to her. She hated Somar for not surviving the bomb. She hated her sister for missing him so much that she went back to find what remained of his tale. "Leilah left Baghdad with Ishtar in 1980 and returned, alone, in 2008. Not alone, exactly. On assignment. She was a journalist. That was three years ago. Now that I think about it, wow. It feels much longer."

By 2008, Leilah was a woman who'd married, miscarried, divorced, then thrust all her love into her work. She wrote stories other people couldn't write because they lacked either compassion or tenacity. Stories that required long distances and crappy vehicles in which to travel. Once she'd traveled on the back of a donkey, which had made her feel fat when it brayed. In Baghdad, Leilah was embedded with American troops, though not a combat regiment. "She was working on a story about the future," said Hana. "Counting mistakes made, guessing what lessons we learned. Rarely shoot, never panic. These were ideals. Not exactly practical."

January 6, Epiphany Day. The day Jesus was baptized in the Jordan River. More than two thousand years later – 2008, to be exact – the Associated Press bureau in Baghdad called to declare their epiphany, which they were shocked and saddened to report: Leilah had died on assignment. A bomb in a church, they said, though it sounded like a single word said quickly. At least, when spit from Ishtar's mouth in shocked response. Abombinachurch. Ishtar had been the one to answer the phone. She'd pulled out her endless box of cigarettes and shook her head like nuh-uh and not-possible. She'd said, "What do you mean, abombinachurch?" The bureau had almost no information to share. There weren't, at the time, many facts available. No body, either. Hana and Ishtar buried Leilah's record collection instead. It ran the gamut from Nina Simone all the way to *42 Mother Goose Songs* with Alec Templeton. They'd cried over an otherwise empty box while a priest spoke Aramaic, a language he'd seemed to think was encoded into Hana. The longer the robed man spoke, the lower she sank in her seat. She couldn't understand the prayers. She couldn't understand what had happened. She couldn't even understand how she felt.

"Nothing was immediately painful in the nights that followed, but everything was sleepless," said Hana. "I was accustomed to Leilah being gone for long periods of time. Meandering around this country or that one, no phone calls, infrequent e-mails, crumpled postcards with a stamp but no love note scribbled on the back. As if the only thing she wanted to prove was that she was still alive, but not missing us. So her death didn't hurt so much at first. Leilah was always traveling and her passing was just another trip. She didn't seem any farther away. Still impossible to contact."

At the time, Hana still occupied her old bedroom. Not old, because she'd never left home. Ishtar had forbidden it. The bed had grown in width and comfort over the years, and the books on the shelf had changed. But otherwise the old bedroom had remained the same. "We developed a nightly ritual. I escorted Ishtar to the tub and felt no shyness in seeing her disrobe. One night after the bath, when she was completely irrigated with boxed wine, zigzagging as she walked, and smelling like vinegar—by then, I was in bed trying and failing to sleep—she wandered into my room and asked if I was still awake. We had just spent all night talking. Literally just finished. The tub, the stories, her crying, me trying to comfort her. So I rolled over and faced the wall to escape having to open my mouth. Ishtar touched my shoulder and said, 'Are you there?,' like I, too, had left her."

Ishtar poked Hana and asked how she thought Leilah had died. Not where or who killed her, but from the blast itself or the bleeding that followed. How fast did it happen? How much did it hurt? At last, Hana said she didn't know. She didn't want to know! The truth came later when authorities released a formal report. "My father died walking to Our Lady of Peace, Sayidat al-Salaam," Hana said. "A modest stack of stone across the Tigris River from the Green Zone. What we learned was that Leilah had gone to visit the same church in the early morning when the streets were clear. To say good-bye? I don't know. Who was going to stop her? She wasn't famous. Not a guest of the ambassador." The report, quietly released by the embassy, said gunmen stormed Our Lady of Peace during Sunday service when a hundred worshippers begged forgiveness for sins. The attackers shot the lights first. Then the crucifix. Then the people hiding behind the crucifix and in the pews. The executions were followed by a single blast—a suicide vest filled with ball bearings and plastic explosive. The bomb turned the church into a pinball machine. An insurgency group called the Islamic State of Iraq, like they were a country and not men with a violent idea, claimed responsibility. Their statement said, 'All Christian centers, organizations, and institutions, leaders and followers, are legitimate targets for the mujahideen wherever they can reach them.' And: 'Let these idolaters, and at their forefront, the hallucinating tyrant of the Vatican, know that the killing sword will not be lifted from the necks of their followers until they declare their innocence from what the dog of the Egyptian Church is doing.' The Islamic State of Iraq believed, and perhaps it was true, that the Coptic Church in Egypt held parishioners captive if they wanted to convert to Islam.

"How does blowing up a Syriac church in Baghdad punish a Coptic one in Cairo?" asked Hana. "Not that it matters. Fear is more important than justice, anyway. They're not reasonable men. Reasonable men don't wear clothes that explode." Ishtar was so mad at Leilah for visiting the church that she wouldn't say her daughter's name for weeks after her death. "I found it harder to blame Leilah for going," said Hana. "She knew Somar and could miss him. A hole. That's what it must've felt like, the longing to see him again. Or at least to go somewhere he'd been. A hole in the ground where the bomb hit made a hole in her heart so big it made every room feel claustrophobic. How do you live with a chest like that? How do you be happy?"

Hana stacked bean casings until they collapsed, which spilled brine onto the table. The brine cleaned the tiles when she mopped the puddle with her napkin, revealing the burlap color was in fact ivory. For some reason she preferred the burlap and covered the clean spot with her dirty napkin. Then she pretended the only two things in the room were her and her drink. Sadly, her drink didn't last forever. Or even very long. Hana put her arm in the air to summon more beer, but the waiter walked by. He seemed intent on serving the men first. She kept her arm raised until it went numb, then held it steady with her other arm. "Will you also put your arm up?" she asked Charlie. "I want to test something." Charlie raised his arm and the waiter finally came. "What's your problem?" Hana asked the waiter. He didn't hear the question or, more likely, chose not to respond. Hana noticed too late that he *had* silently responded by leaving the cap on her bottle. Now Hana had to pry it off with her keys.

"I didn't know you were Iraqi," said Charlie after a few seconds. He began organizing chess pieces in ascending order of height: pawns, rooks, knights, bishops, queens, and one king. The other king had been lost or wasn't on the table.

"That's your takeaway?" said Hana as if she was disappointed but not really surprised. Of course Charlie was impermeable to all but his own suffering. Of course her story had bounced off his nice shirt. Even so, Hana found pleasure in attempting the vengeance and relief in bringing Leilah back to life. Not even Charlie could take that away from her.

"I just find it . . ."

"What?"

"I don't know. Odd."

"Odd how?"

"I don't know!" said Charlie. "You and Dalia came from the same place. It's just . . ."

"Odd?"

"That's right."

"What are you trying to say? That I owe her something?"

Charlie put his head on the table. Either he'd died or he'd drunk too many beers.

"Are you okay?" asked Hana after a few seconds. Part of her thought Charlie had really died. It would be just like him to do that.

"I'm sorry about your sister," he said finally. "Let's just leave it at that."

Hana had heard people say the same thing for years. They fell into two categories: people who said it because they thought they had to; and those who said it because they, having themselves experienced a loss of some magnitude, assumed correctly that their words would fail to offer lasting comfort, but nevertheless said them with the hope that their tone or posture – or, damn it, an entirely unscientific prickly feeling transmitted through the air itself – would make plain the following: that while the speaker was powerless to intervene, they nonetheless understood what it felt like to suffer. What comfort the words lacked was thus found in the company of the person saying them. Hana was bewildered to know Charlie fell into the latter category. She was sure he would've fallen into the first.

When Charlie finally sat up, he did so with gusto; it was as if a perfectly thrilling idea had shocked him back to life. "I have a friend I want you to meet." He turned eagerly toward the door. The idea had really taken hold of his attention. "I can't believe I didn't think of this before. Are you ready? Will you go?"

This was how Hana had imagined relationships with her co-workers would've begun. A simple invitation. To lunch, to dinner. To a party of some kind. Yet a relationship with those people felt suddenly unattainable. Weeks had passed and she'd made little progress with either Joseph or Yezin, and even less with Noha and Fadwa. The women were practically figments of her imagination. Was that Hana's fault? Or theirs? Maybe Hana was just bad at making friends. The sick rain cloud in her chest poured doubt everywhere. She stood up, revealing the cramp in her ass from the hard chair, and followed Charlie. She didn't care where she went so long as she didn't go back to her apartment. Waiting there would be her sister's ghost and ten missed calls from Ishtar begging Hana to come home.

The dust-brown city turned yellow as the sun died and the street-lights burned to their own deaths, flickering. The taxi stopped in an intersection where the streets met at weird angles. Sharp corners battled wide ones for the title of Most Egregious Urban Planning Mistake. Down one street was a tribe of goats eating garbage. Hana could more or less intuit her location from the length and direction of the drive. North along the corniche to the Imbaba Bridge, then west for ten minutes into the labyrinth. After the taxi dropped them off and became a cloud of exhaust, Charlie said, "This way." He walked toward a set of steps leading to a long yellow hall. There was a man sitting on the steps. He was smoking and drinking a Coke. As Charlie and Hana climbed toward him, he said, "Where from?" To Hana, the question contained an unknowable pain. *Where from?* implied *where going?* The man clearly hadn't gone anywhere in a long time.

"Montana," said Charlie as if that word didn't mean much.

"Michigan," said Hana. The simple answer was unsatisfying. But the real answer was too complicated. "And you?"

"Baghdad." The man's body was a black shadow in the yellow light pouring from the hallway behind him. His Coke smelled like some other drink. "Tomorrow I think I go back." He lay down across his step, covering the entire width of the stairs, and looked up at the sky. Hana looked up at the sky, too, but there were no stars. The light of the city bounced off the pollution so that Cairo looked covered by a shroud.

"This way," said Charlie.

After passing the man — by necessity, stepping over him — and crossing the stone floor, the ascent continued. Five flights of slick, worn stairs. The edges had been rounded by years of bombing by feet. Hana thought the stairs had endured rather proudly. The dark upward climb was intermittently lit by dim bulbs. The higher they climbed, the more Hana struggled to breathe. "The secret," said Charlie, "is exhaling through your nose." Hana told him to stop talking. When they finally reached the fifth floor, the dim yellow bulbs in the landings became white fluorescent tubes in the hall. Hana saw the Arabic number ٥٤ sitting cockeyed on a red door. Charlie knocked. He knocked again and smiled at Hana. She put her hands on her hips, stared at the ceiling, and cursed every cigarette she'd ever smoked, which was not many. One every now and then when she was feeling especially stressed.

"What are we *really* doing here?" It occurred to Hana, later than she might've otherwise liked—the information was no longer useful—that this wasn't the sort of building in which she could imagine Charlie socializing. "And why'd we take the stairs?"

"The elevator was broken. You didn't see the sign?" Charlie continued to knock on the door. When there was no answer, Charlie knocked harder. Then said, "Salaam, Dalia?"

5

Dalia's plan to fall asleep was interrupted by a timid knock on her door. Whoever tapped the wood either regretted the decision or wished to have knocked under improved circumstances. She'd heard a similar knock earlier that day. It had been light at the time; she'd cracked open the door without thinking much of it. A woman named Nura had extended her hand, palm facing God, through the crack. She'd asked for money. As every neighbor, Nura was like the man on the stairs. Seen often but not really known. Was she from Karbala or Basra? Was she married? Did she have children? The grim persistence with which she'd begged suggested she had several. "I know who you are," said Nura. She'd heard, by way of the man on the stairs, or some other man in the hall, or maybe on another floor—she didn't know or wouldn't say exactly who told her—that Dalia's husband had, with God's good fortune, made it to America and, blessed still by God, found work. Nura said she knew there was money, as if Dalia had been withholding that fact. Her timid knock was thus revealed as an imposture. Resentment took hold of her face. "Please. Something small." What Dalia had was already so little. Making it smaller would be the same as making it disappear. She shook her head in lieu of saying no. It felt less cruel that way. "I'm begging you." Nura leaned against the door and started pushing

it. Dalia, seized by the memory of her former bawab, pushed back
with all her might, but Nura, seized by the needs of her children,
was too vehement. The door flew open, thrusting Dalia off-balance.
She fell and Nura fell on her. The air in Dalia's lungs flew away. So,
too, went the urge to inhale. In that instant, totally alone in a still
and dark place in her mind, Dalia finally saw how to leave Egypt.
All she had to do was hold her breath.

Nura rolled off when Dalia gulped air a few seconds later. Though
Nura didn't flee or scrounge for money. She just lay on the floor
next to Dalia while her breathing normalized. The dust of their
scuffle – a specter of ash, powder, and lint – glowed in the light from
the door. A young man walked by, looked in, then kept walking. He
said something like "Dear God" or "What's this?" No such mumbling
could be unraveled. Maybe he said, "My life has been destroyed."
Or, "I have lost everything." Dalia turned to see Nura, who wept
quietly to herself. Then Nura turned to see her. There was no point
in apologizing. The wall between right and wrong had collapsed
long ago. It had been surprisingly fragile. "I don't understand why
you're here," said Nura. "You have a husband in America with a
job. Everyone says you should go." Dalia said it wasn't her choice.
It made no difference whom she loved or where he'd landed. Her
case, besides, had been rejected. "No," said Nura. "Don't say that.
It's not true." One's fate informed the other's fear. That was how
it was and would always be in a building of marooned emigrants.
"My own case is . . ." The way Nura trailed off indicated her case had
been lost in the void. She'd been waiting for months. Probably much
longer. "God willing you have more luck," said Dalia. In the air was
the salt of blood they'd spilled on their journeys. Either that or it
was the sharp smell of wet laundry that had been washed without
soap. In time, both women sat up. Dalia gave Nura twenty pounds,
which Nura was ashamed to accept. Twenty pounds equaled $3,
officially; and only slightly more on the black market. "Shukran,"
said Nura. She left with her head hung so low she couldn't see
and, before Dalia could warn her, smacked her head on the door.

Embarrassment was a waste of energy. She kept walking without saying anything or turning back.

Hours had passed since the first knock had announced Nura. The second knock, alighting only moments ago, sounded just as timid. Had Nura come back for more money? Or did the most recent knock have more insidious origins? Maybe Dalia's former bawab had finally found her. She couldn't imagine her former bawab knocking timidly. Though she could imagine him performing a timid knock. By now, the sun had fallen. Dalia's sole window looked out on a dark alley. The amount of light the window let in was less relevant than the time it indicated. Day just *felt* safer. The timid knock struck again. The height of the knock implied someone taller than Nura. A man, probably. The door's busted eyehole had never been more cruel. Dalia saw an array of colors separated by myriad cracks in the glass. The colors wouldn't coalesce no matter how much she wanted to see what awaited her. "Salaam, Dalia?" said a voice, muffled by the wood it traveled through. "Are you there?" She would've recognized that voice from any distance, through any material, at any volume. "Charlie," she said to herself. She mistook her relief for yearning. In doing so, Dalia cracked open her door. The mistake didn't go unpunished. Her eyes swept past the man she knew to the woman she never wanted to see again. It took all Dalia's willpower to resist slamming the door in her face. What was her name again?

"The rejection notice, I think, was a bit hasty," said Charlie. "Don't you feel that way? Sorry I didn't call first. I know I should have. But this is, as it were, off the cuff. I mean, unofficial. Don't tell anyone we're here. Really, we're not supposed to . . ." He glanced at . . . Hana, wasn't it? "Can we come in? It won't take long, I promise. I wish it could wait. If only Omran weren't so . . . well, you know. I mean, you married him. He's stubborn as a —"

Hana said, "I can't be here," and Dalia said, "I don't think . . . ," at the same time. Why allow them to enter? Why expose her apartment to scorn? The ceiling would sag in the middle. The shower drain, partially but irreversibly clogged, would present the smell of mold like a gift to her visitors. Not the kind who were invited; the other kind, who showed up unannounced without bearing pastries or other sweet treats to abate the badness of their manners. Dalia expected Hana to lack such courtesy, but was surprised by Charlie; he'd always been oddly aware of how she felt and what she wanted.

"Well, we can talk here. That's fine." Charlie looked up and down the hallway as if that wasn't fine. It wasn't fine at all.

A strange and sudden pressure – Dalia's ears popped – sucked open the door when a gust of wind blew past her open window. Charlie and Hana both peered in as if their heads were similarly drawn. Did they see squalor? Or did they see how Dalia had disguised the space? Pictures of her old life owned the walls. The couch defied the stark floor with its plush cushions. Why had the past inhabitants left such a couch behind? Three wooden chairs, each with a piece of bright laundry drying on its back, proved space limitations were no match for a woman who insisted on clean clothing. At least, as clean as possible given the nature of where and how she washed them. (In the sink using tepid water.) A woman on the first floor who had hot water did laundry with soap for "donations" – just a pound or two per piece – but Dalia couldn't justify the extravagance. She'd grown accustomed to telling Omran exactly how she spent his money. Not that he wanted to know. He'd asked her many times not to tell him. The money he sent was *hers*. She deserved it more than him. "Forget the expense," he said. "I'll work harder. I'll work more." In Omran's voice, Dalia heard a man drowning in his want to provide.

"You might as well come in," said Dalia now that her door was open. In a hadith, Muhammad said be generous to guests. There were no listed exceptions. "Please, sit." Dalia gestured to the couch before steeping tea. She used mint to cover the smell of the shower drain. Upon delivering the steaming cups, Dalia imagined spilling them into the laps of her guests. The image of them wriggling in pain was satisfying. Hana should've known better than to come; Charlie should've known better than to bring her.

"How's Omran?" Charlie blew the steam off his cup. He rubbed his thumb against his index finger. Odd, thought Dalia. That rubbing.

Lacking a proper seat of her own, Dalia sat on her laundry. "Determined to 'come back.' He says that like he's been here before. And I must tell you. I don't want him to come. There's nothing here for us. I've told him the same thing many times before. Maybe he has a hearing problem." Dalia turned to the wall of pictures. A four-by-six-inch catalog of everything that had once made her happy. "I knocked the nails in with a book," she said proudly. Omran dancing. Omran holding the cat. Omran washing cabbages in the sink.

"How long since you've seen him?" asked Charlie.

"A long time. I don't count the days."

"You don't miss him?"

Charlie was either stupid or cold. Except Dalia knew he wasn't either of those things. Whenever they met to discuss her case, he gave more than his time. He gave his attention. He remembered everything. He knew what questions to ask and how long to pause before asking them. He knew when to turn off his tape recorder. He knew when to leave the room and for how long. He was, or had been, the rare sort of man who could hear things he hadn't said himself. It had occurred to Dalia many times before that their relationship wasn't entirely professional. Somewhere along the way they'd become friends.

"The opposite reason," said Dalia finally. It took her a few seconds to forgive Charlie for what he'd said. "I thank God every day for the phone."

An eerie thing happened. A phone rang somewhere in the distance. It should've been less eerie. Tens if not hundreds of phones were within earshot. That was life in a dense neighborhood peppered with open windows. Still, Dalia felt the rings were meant for her. Someone far away had something important to say.

"So, about the rejection," said Charlie. Dalia assumed the bad news was about to get worse and stopped listening. "Like I said, a bit hasty. Given that you forgot to answer an important question at your interview." Dalia's small apartment felt much smaller with three people stuffed inside. Three people, she thought, was a fire hazard. "A very important question. All the questions, of course, are important. But this one especially so. I'm troubled you weren't asked before."

"What question?" asked Dalia.

A heretofore petrified Hana leaned in as if she also wanted to know.

Charlie wrung his hands. When Dalia glanced at them, he stopped wringing. "How'd you get Omran back? Tell Hana what you told me. Please, you have to say it out loud. I know it's difficult."

Dalia almost laughed at Charlie's posturing. What did he really know? Nothing. He didn't know what it felt like to tell the world something she couldn't bear to tell her own husband. Why did it matter how she'd secured his release, anyway? The better story was how she'd secured his hand in marriage. Against her father's will! That would go down in history as one of the great rebellions. Maybe not world history, but family history. Dalia looked again at the photo of Omran washing cabbages with more care than they deserved. Practice, he'd said in all seriousness, for parenthood. "I wasn't supposed to marry him," said Dalia. She didn't look at her guests because she wasn't speaking for their benefit. "My father was so angry." The rebellion started with a borrowed car. No, before that. It started when Dalia, at the age of seventeen, fell in love with Omran even though she was betrothed to another man. The betrothal was her father's arrangement, not her desire. She loved Omran. It took them more than a year to kiss for the first time, but by the end of the same week Dalia had removed her shirt and Omran had cowered at the prospect of seeing her in a way he'd thought was holy. Nude as the day she was born. At least, half-nude. More like nude from the waist up, except for the scarf. Sixty percent nude. "I can't," said Omran. He'd always been more devout than Dalia, or at least more afraid of God's judgment. He'd cowered by turning away and saying, "Not yet. Soon, I promise you." Dalia, for her part, hadn't been so shy. She'd turned his head back with her fingers and said, "You're embarrassing me. Look, I'm embarrassed." He'd finally looked; she'd been smiling widely.

Dalia didn't tell Omran she was betrothed to another man until one day, in the last year of secondary school, when she said, "We need to run. I want to marry you. I'm going to borrow the car."

"What car?"

"My father's car. Wait for me in the alley?"

"When?"

"Right now. We have to go. I'm betrothed to another man."

"What other man?" cried Omran.

Dalia knew it wasn't the time to explain, but Omran didn't know that. To spur him along, she kissed him with way more tongue than was normally appropriate given who could've seen. His father. *Her* father. "Wait for me in the alley! Please, will you wait for me? I won't be more than a few minutes. Ten minutes, at most. If I'm not here in ten minutes, then . . ."

"Don't say that."

"I'm kidding. Just wait for me. Will you wait?"

Omran said yes as if the word had to be coaxed from his throat. Then he said the same word several times as his love and fear revealed their magnitude. "Yes!" he shouted. He ran so fast to pack his things that he nearly tripped over his own feet.

"Only bring what you need."

"Pants, shirts, socks, shoes, toothbrush, toothpaste, hair comb . . . ," said Omran, fleeing. His list continued, but trailed off as he turned the corner.

Dalia was suddenly alone in her doorway. She lived by herself in an apartment separate from, but immediately next to, her parents', willed to her by an uncle who'd died in a motorcycle accident. Her uncle had been driving fast on a desert road. What were desert roads for if not driving fast in a straight line into oblivion? He'd lost control and slid a hundred meters across the tar, leaving a trail of clothes and skin. When Dalia had moved next door, her father had been more heartbroken by her departure than his brother's death. The fighting had been loud and remained continuous. He said it made him look weak, that his daughter didn't live in his house. "The buildings share a wall," said Dalia. "But not a roof," said her father. Now she tried to summon the courage required to borrow his car. Lacking courage, Dalia ran next door. She ran the way Omran ran to pack. If she ran fast enough, she would arrive before second-guessing herself. She would have no choice but to say what she wanted. Her father's door was suddenly before her. Would she let herself in? Or would she heed her father's word? He'd said, "If you don't live here, then you must knock." Dalia pounded the door with her fist. The moment before the latch clicked and the door opened extended into painful territory. Dalia spent the time preparing her speech. Father, can I borrow the car? . . . No, I won't bring it back. I suppose that means I'm asking to have it. . . . I know, but please. I'm sorry. I can't tell you where I'm going. Please, Father. In time, I'll buy you another car.

When the door opened, Dalia kissed her father's cheek. He smelled like tobacco and dirt. His cheek felt like paper. He embraced Dalia; she was dismayed. His large, rough hands made her feel so young.

"As-salamu alaikum."

Her father cocked his head at the formal greeting. "Wa alaikum al-salaam. It's good to see you."

"I came to talk."

"Then it's a good day. Your mother misses you."

A code, she knew. Her father never expressed love except indirectly through his wife. He said, "Kiss your mother. Hug your mother. Call your mother." When Dalia did call, her father would commandeer the phone. He'd ramble — on God, school, poetry — until her mother complained in the background about the phone bill. Her complaint was a criticism in disguise. Why wouldn't her husband go next door? Why wouldn't her daughter come home?

"I have a lot to say."

"Not until you kiss your mother."

"Please, it's important."

"Your family is important. She misses you."

"Family is the people you love," said Dalia. "Right?"

"That's right."

"I love Omran."

"Omran?"

"Yes, Omran."

"The boy with no land?"

"Not yet."

"Or even a job?"

"Not yet!"

"Oh my God."

"I'm sorry. I have to go. Can I borrow the car?"

Dalia saw a shadow pacing in the hall. She wanted nothing more than to invite the shadow to become her mother. Her mother would've been a force of reason. She would've taken Dalia's side. In a canny way, to be sure. Father would talk about God to instill obedience; mother would talk reason to fight back. "Don't use the hadiths to effect your ill will upon our daughter!" The fight would change hands and Dalia would be free to abscond with the car keys. Yet something stopped Dalia from calling her mother's name. The feeling that later her mother would be made to pay for responding.

"What do you mean, 'love'?" her father asked.

"I mean I'm going to marry him even though I'm betrothed to another man. I don't care what God thinks. Or what you do. I do care somewhat because I'm telling you. But not so much that I'd abandon my love for your approval!"

Was this really the right way to borrow the car? By telling her father everything? Now instead of later? When time and anger had passed? When Dalia could say with certainty that everything was okay? That she'd made the right choice? That Omran had found a job? That she was back in school? That a small act against God was required in pursuit of happiness?

"You don't care what God thinks?" her father boomed.

"I don't know." Dalia loved God and feared Him for the pain He caused.

"Where did this come from? You're betrothed! You can't borrow the car!"

Dalia grabbed the keys off the dining room table and her father grabbed Dalia by the arm.

"I have to go!" shouted Dalia. "I want Omran so much I would steal your car. Sorry, I'm stealing it!"

"You're going to steal from your own father?"

"I wouldn't have to steal the car if you'd let me borrow it!"

Dalia escaped her father's grip by shaking her arm violently. No grip could've survived her shaking. She was like a hummingbird with Herculean wings.

"Let her borrow the car," said her mother, stepping from the hall into the light. Her presence emboldened Dalia the same way wind emboldens a kite. "She'll bring it back. You will, won't you?"

Dalia locked eyes with her father. "I have to think I'll be forgiven for this. What else can I do? Attend my own wedding as a reluctant bride? Not wanting the man I must have? No, I won't! The Qur'an says that after you've been intimate and made your solemn pledge, you can't take it back. I have made my solemn pledge."

"You've been intimate?" screamed her father.

"I've made my solemn pledge!"

"Oh, no."

Dalia locked eyes with her mother and said everything she needed to with a passing glance: *I love you, but I can't ever come home.* Then she stole the car and drove to Baghdad with Omran sitting wide-eyed in the passenger seat. He shut his eyes when they got sand in them, but left the window open. The wind, he said, gave him courage. Omran couldn't say why, but it didn't matter; Dalia knew what he meant. They married a few months later in a distant village so Omran's par-

ents could attend without being shamed by their neighbors. Other
benefits included a lower cost and a better view than in Baghdad.
Sadly, Dalia's parents didn't make the journey. A note arrived in
their stead. *My star, a gift of admiration. Love and greetings. Your mother.*
Dalia remembered scouring the note for any sign of her father. A
faint smudge mark the size of his thumb. But there was no sign of
him. It was then that Dalia knew she'd been banished.

Charlie — suddenly and loudly — cleared his throat. "Ahem."

It occurred to Dalia that she'd been staring into empty space for
a while now. Her attempt to chase down more pleasant years had
borne sour fruit. It was excruciating to think those years had been
more pleasant.

"Please," said Charlie. "Tell us how you secured Omran's release."

Dalia locked eyes with him the same way she'd once locked eyes
with her parents. How else to tell him what he didn't want to hear?
That it was late. That she was tired. That he needed to leave. Dalia
couldn't just say that. Not after all Charlie had done for her. Had he
really done so much? Not in measurable terms, maybe. In measurable terms, he'd done almost nothing. Though there wasn't much
he could do. Charlie had said so at their first meeting. "I just write
testimonies and submit case files. The rest is up to other people."
Wasn't it Dalia's fault for believing he could do more? He had done
more, she supposed. His optimism had rubbed off. For a few decent
months she'd believed her time in Cairo was temporary. The memory
of those months was precious, for they included conversations with
Omran in which he'd discussed the future by making lists. The lists
had oddly long titles such as:

What We'll Do in Boston Once You Get Here

1. Find a larger apartment
2. Learn to cook the American cuisine
3. Have several children
4. Feed them the American cuisine

And longer still:

How to Have the Children Mentioned in the Previous List

1. Eat a light dinner
2. Put on the romantic music
3. THIS POINT HAS BEEN CENSORED (consult Rumi for clues)
4. Ha! A baby!
5. Repeat as necessary

Dalia had laughed, which had caught Omran a little off guard. The lists weren't intended as jokes. To him, the lists were serious. He'd spent a lot of time considering even his mirthful points. Regarding the American cuisine, he'd said, "I want our children to fit in. I want them to like the food. It's very salty. I had to adjust." Regarding the romantic music, he'd said, "Faisal has shown me many tapes that I've never heard before. Now I have tapes to show you. There are several I think you will like." Dalia had apologized for laughing. She hadn't meant to make fun. It was just that she'd wanted those things so badly she couldn't bear to say aloud that she'd wanted them. The goal now, with all that taken away, was to thank Charlie for making those conversations possible in the first place. Only in such abundance could his optimism actually rub off on Dalia, who prided herself on being realistic. She'd loved the few months when she'd not been exactly herself. The only way Dalia knew how to thank Charlie was to resist the urge to kick him out. If the man had any sense, he'd soon leave of his own accord.

Charlie seemed to deflate when he exhaled and hunched slightly. The hunch grew worse over time. It was as if his body were sinking into and perhaps even through the couch. Dalia couldn't watch him without feeling things that would be rude to say. She watched Hana instead of saying them. Hana looked nervous and ready to bolt. Dalia's steady eye contact made it a thousand times worse for her. Hana sat up straight. She became flustered and distressed. It was sweet, petty, harmless revenge for the way Hana had stared at Dalia during the resettlement interview – as if Hana was, from an official standpoint, curious, but didn't personally give a shit what happened. Dalia planned to stare the same way until Hana fled and Charlie, realizing the party had come to an end, followed her.

Unfortunately, things didn't go exactly as planned. The staring made Hana so uncomfortable that she must've felt the need to speak, as if that would somehow release the pressure that had been mounting since Dalia had opened her door. "Can I have more tea?" asked Hana. The request was inexplicable and infuriating; her cup was still full. What was Dalia supposed to do? Pour more tea into Hana's full cup? Watch the tea spill onto the floor?

"This isn't working," said Dalia. "You both need to leave. Right now. Please go." Standing was made burdensome by the depth she'd sunk into her laundry. She rocked back; she rocked forward. The momentum made it easier. "I'm sorry you've come all this way for no reason." The tea, thought Dalia, would go to waste. A pity. Or the tea would go down the shower drain. God willing, that would help unclog it.

Hana practically jumped to her feet, but Charlie rose more reluctantly. "I want you to know something," he said. Apparently that "something" was more complicated than he'd initially thought. He kept saying *um* and *well*, only to conclude, as each pause hung on for dear life, that he ought not to say that. Charlie finally settled on something vague and therefore more or less appropriate. "I won't give up. Not now, not ever. Emily Dickinson said the heart wants . . . well, something. Mine wants to drive you to the airport."

Dalia found this to be an aggravating sentiment. "It's not up to you. The same way it's not up to me." That left just one person to whom the decision belonged. Dalia couldn't look at her anymore. Not without crying or possibly lashing out. She wouldn't give Hana the satisfaction of knowing the power she bore by beholding the sorrow she'd wrought. That sorrow was Dalia's obscure companion. An eidolon in the shape of Omran hiding in the umbra of her heart.

6

Charlie leaned back against the gray brick wall under a tube of white light outside Dalia's apartment. The rough surface of the brick pressed into his skin. Hard enough to feel, but not hard enough to hurt. He leaned with more pressure. Should he explain to Hana what was supposed to have happened? What Dalia should've said? That she did, per her testimony, get raped? That she saw no other way to free her husband? That her rape meant everything? And meant more now that it was, or should've been, rendered in minute detail? A line in Dalia's letter described the cleric's hands as rocks. That was all she'd written, but Charlie knew there were more horrors to tell. If only she would've told them! Then Hana would know! And knowing would've changed . . . something! Should he remind Hana that the length Dalia went to secure Omran's release was so far beyond kindness and love that no word could describe what she must've felt for him? And how that indescribable feeling was admirable and infectious? And must be preserved at any cost? Should he argue that logic, math, and policy no longer applied? That his heart was beating so fast that, medically speaking, he should die? Or should've died months ago when it started?

Charlie recalled one time that he and Dalia had, entirely by accident, touched. Her hand fell on his arm when, without looking, she'd reached for something. A pen, maybe. Or perhaps Charlie's arm in her peripheral vision had looked the same as Omran's. And Dalia, in want of the man she loved, had reached for him. The damp, incidental, and frightening contact—Dalia's horror-stricken face declared immense embarrassment—had struck Charlie at the time as really sad for them both. Remembering the moment made him similarly wistful. In such a state, Charlie was prone to reimagining the circumstances. He imagined asking to kiss Dalia after every string connecting her to her past life had been severed. By war, by jihadists, by politicians. The politicians were the worst. They started wars in which they didn't fight and for which they weren't punished. The same wars that fueled the anger jihadists used to recruit. The strings connecting Dalia to her past life thus severed by the scourge of the Earth, Charlie imagined asking to kiss her. Or imagined nearly asking. The question, like a timid bird, would never fly from his lips. Instead it would nest there and torment him with its presence. The idea almost made Charlie laugh. It was absurd. He lacked the courage to speak openly even in the imagined world he'd created for himself.

"A few years ago I attended a dinner party that turned out to be a murder mystery," said Hana. Her calmness rattled Charlie the same way deep water rattled him. What lurked was past knowing. "The revelation was obvious, disappointing, almost offensive in its simplicity. Just like tonight. It's uncanny."

"By revelation, you mean . . ."

"Why you brought me here."

Charlie's shirt had tangled in the rough surface of the bricks. Shifting his weight felt like peeling a sticker. "I didn't mean to hide my reason. Dalia still needs a yellow card. It's just a piece of paper. It must cost five cents." He couldn't say what the other reasons were. That he'd just wanted to see Dalia. That she'd had no reason to visit his office since before her interview. That it had been weeks. That he missed her. It would be a breach of duty to say that. Maybe it was a breach of duty just to feel it. Although, did it matter? Given that Charlie had scorned every lawyer's oath he'd ever taken? I will maintain the respect due to courts of justice and judicial officers! I will employ for the purpose of maintaining the causes confided to me such means only as are consistent with truth and honor! I do solemnly swear to abide by and uphold the law! How could he uphold the law when that law upheld injustice?

Hana leaned on the wall next to Charlie. Now she was close enough to strangle him. "You're really going to go through with this?"

"God willing." Charlie's fight-or-flight response sent mixed messages. "Not that I believe in God. I don't know why I keep saying that. Maybe because the phrase is so ubiquitous. God willing, Mubarak goes to jail. God willing, Mubarak dies in jail. God willing, nobody puts up a Mubarak statue. Protesters say these things like God might actually will them."

It occurred to Charlie that Dalia might be watching them through the eyehole. If he were Dalia, he'd be watching. They must've looked stupid through the fisheye lens and sounded even stupider through the wood, like mumbling idiots. He approached the door and peered through the eyehole the wrong way. The only thing he could see was the reflection of his pupil split by cracks in the glass. Or was that Dalia's beautiful brown eye? She had two beautiful brown eyes, but Charlie supposed in that context he would only be seeing one of them. He stepped out of what he assumed was the eyehole's viewable angle, then took a few more steps just to be safe. "Can we talk over here? Or maybe down there would be better." Charlie gestured to the stairs, but meant the landing: the essentially private area between floors where all mention of their small crime, plotted for good reason, would be irretrievably lost in the dimness of a single yellow bulb hung from a tiny metal string. He descended a step hoping that Hana would follow him.

"You haven't told Dalia your plan, have you?" said Hana, who'd not moved so much as an inch. "Is that why you're running away?"

"I'm not running!" hissed Charlie. He lowered his voice slightly. "I'm barely even walking. And, no, I haven't told her. Not yet. Not until it's absolutely necessary. Ignorance is Dalia's only armor. She can't be held liable for something she didn't do or even know about." The sound logic only applied in a just court. But now wasn't the time for Charlie to divulge his opinion on the Egyptian judicial system. It would undermine his argument to say the judicial system was a total joke. That joke was altogether terrifying. That joke let people rot in jail for years without charge or access to counsel. That joke permitted and thus sanctioned "enhanced" interrogation techniques such as choking, beating, sleep deprivation, and induced vomiting by means of oil, salt, washing powder, and just enough water to make the cocktail fit to drink. It was thus of the utmost importance that every aspect of Charlie's plan be executed perfectly.

"You're going to get everyone thrown in jail," said Hana. "You, Dalia, and me just for being here. I haven't even done anything." To Charlie, it sounded less like an outrage than a lament. Her job, like her purpose on Earth, was purely theoretical.

"The police are busy torturing protesters in the basement of the museum. They don't have time to arrest Americans. Nor do they need the public relations nightmare. Don't forget that our taxes pay for their army! Or that the Clintons recently called Mubarak a 'family friend'! Can you believe that? A family friend? Someone you *know*. Someone you *trust*. Someone you trust to do your bidding, maybe." Charlie hated the cynic that lived within him, but didn't know how to exile or execute the dark part of his heart. It caused him to say the wrong things to the wrong people at the wrong volume. "What I mean to say is — "

Suddenly a door creaked opened at the far end of the hall. A man tentatively peered out. He seemed to really *look* at them. It was almost as if he needed glasses. "Ah!" said the man after the longest five seconds in Charlie's life. "Really? Is that you? Charlie?" The man smiled as widely as a man could without looking clownish. When he finally stepped into the hall, Charlie's stomach dropped. Was it Ali? Could it be? The man rushed over and shook hands so vigorously that Charlie thought his arm would fall off. Yes, it was Ali! The man from weeks ago who'd stormed the office with four passports in his back pocket, who'd held a knife against his neck. "Please, I need to leave," he'd said that day. "I have no money. I have no job. My children don't attend school. How can I put them in school? Even if they were allowed, I couldn't buy the uniform. Or pay the school fees. I want to pay the fees! I want to work!" Charlie had failed to convince Ali to put down his knife, to come in, to begin the long application process. Ali had fled in a wretched state after calling the application a sham. Charlie was beyond ecstatic to see him again. To know that Ali had not cut his throat. Charlie didn't realize until now how much not knowing had bothered him. A lot, apparently. Charlie whooped as if he'd won something. And wept from the solace he took in finding Ali alive. Charlie grabbed him by the arms and hugged him. "Thank God, you're alive."

Ali appeared upbeat. He was a new man. "It's true, then? The rumor? The tickets? You're giving them away at the office? That's why you're here? To tell us? I heard from a friend, who said he'd heard the rumor; I told him not to believe what couldn't possibly be true. I said, 'It's not true. You're stupid for believing it.' Thank God I'm wrong! Thank God you're here! You're telling people!" Ali rubbed his hands together as if he were about to eat. His whole family was at the table. He loved them. He loved feeding them. He loved giving them life. "There are two more floors and half a third floor on the west end of the building. Please don't forget the people living at the very top. Tell them, too! About the rumor! Tell them it's not a rumor! It's true!" Charlie, still gripping Ali with all his might, wasn't listening. How beautiful to see him again. How beautiful to find him alive. "I'm going now," said Ali. "I will see you again soon at the office!" He peeled away from Charlie's grip and fled the building. His long legs meant there was no stopping him.

7

Hana watched the color drain from Charlie's face.

"Did he say . . . rumor?" asked Charlie.

"Yes. Apparently you're giving away – "

"Plane tickets?"

"Yes."

Charlie punched the air. "He said that? Tickets? Are you sure?"

By now, Hana wasn't sure of much. Her power to observe without prejudice, fatally wounded by the smell of Dalia's shower drain – not to mention the abominable look on her face after they'd, and with such rudeness, barged in – was in its death throes. But Hana couldn't admit that in present company. If she told Charlie that she was feeling literally *anything*, he would find some way to take advantage. Some way to draw a line between right and wrong such that Hana fell on the bad side, where the devil and Hitler and Ivan the Terrible lived in sorrow and eternal regret. "Yes," said Hana. "Were you not listening? Did that guy not shout in your ear?"

Charlie made the sorriest face she'd ever seen. He ran down the stairs yelling, "Ali! Come back! Don't believe the rumor! It's not true! There are no tickets!"

All of a sudden it was quiet. The solitude Hana had been trying to avoid all day finally caught her. Therein appeared ghosts of the dead. Somar and Leilah — him a numbness, her a yearning — whispered in Hana's ears. *Why'd you ditch your mother?* and *Why'd you let me leave?* Every eyehole drilled through every door bore further judgment. Hana felt as if she were being watched by every person who'd ever died in or run from a conflict zone. Their cumulative weight was almost as staggering as Hana's inability to reincarnate the dead or reunite the separated, despite a yet-more-staggering desire to do both immediately. She ran down the stairs. Not in pursuit of Charlie, albeit technically after him. The curved edges were more precarious on the way down than the way up, though she made it all the way outside before falling. Even then it wasn't the stairs' fault. The man lying across the stairs, who'd once held a Coke bottle but had since finished whatever had been inside — now the bottle contained cigarette butts and spit enough to snuff them — said, "I'm like a river going under a bridge." He spoke right when Hana stepped over him. His voice startled her even though she knew he was there. Or maybe what startled her was the idea that he was a river. That a man who couldn't move had to imagine himself as something that moved no matter what. Even a dammed river evaporated. Hana saw him evaporating into the pollution that hung over the city and falling later wherever he wanted to go. Seeing this, even inside her head, drew her eyes to the sky. She lost her balance. She fell in the sitting position to avoid falling down the steps headlong and more than likely breaking her neck. The man grunted when Hana sat on him. "Oh, God," she said, standing up as quickly as possible. "I'm sorry. Really, I didn't mean . . ." The man was utterly disinterested in Hana's guilt complex, which only made it worse. She couldn't be absolved of an offense that hadn't been rendered. The man just rubbed his stomach and said he wasn't hurt.

"Please, a cab!" shouted Charlie from the sidewalk, gesticulating wildly at the heavens. "God willing! It must be so easy for you! Just snap your fingers! Snap them, damn it!" It was totally delusional behavior. What taxi driver would roam Imbaba at night when he could cruise other neighborhoods for richer fares? Hana, knowing this, or intuiting what locals knew and must've hated about their locality, called Mustafa. As the phone rang, she considered whether to share the ride with Charlie or abandon him. She thought it would feel sugar sweet to leave him behind—revenge for his presumptuous deception, for his guilt trip, for his high horse—but knew she'd regret her decision after making it. Charlie needed to find Ali before Ali spread a rumor that wasn't true. It would be cruel to delay that just cause for petty vengeance. She yelled that Charlie could share the ride if he wanted, but he better not talk now or when the car came or even when they were sitting quietly inside as Mustafa took corners at an unreasonable speed. No more appeals to emotion. No more smart remarks.

Mustafa didn't answer his phone until it went to voice mail. Hana thought she was recording a message when she was actually having a conversation. "What?" Mustafa sounded confused. "What is that you're saying?" Hana repeated herself. She tried not to laugh or cry. Mustafa said yes, he was free, or would be once the disgruntled passenger in his backseat stopped groaning about the price and finally paid him. "Pay what you owe!" he shouted in Arabic. Then in English: "I'm coming in ten minutes, God willing. Remember, don't lean on the door. Please, it's still broken. I don't want you to fall out." Hana wondered if Mustafa would ever fix the door or if it would stay broken so he could collect absurd tips from her indefinitely. Wondering that felt the same as accusing him, which felt lousy. Especially considering how Mustafa only accepted absurd tips when Hana tricked him. Usually he handed them back. "See you soon," said Hana. "All my thanks."

Twenty minutes passed while Charlie and Hana guarded each other against nothing tangible, only the uncanny feeling of being watched on a dark street in a poor quarter. The man on the stairs sat up and started watching them. As a result, the uncanniness increased. When Mustafa finally rolled up, he did so in a style unlike his old self. Normally his humor disguised his lethargy. The look—weary eyes and a wide smile—reminded Hana that he drove all day and not just when she needed him. But that night he looked unhinged, as if something odd and upsetting had happened. Maybe the last fare had run off without paying. "Get in!" said Mustafa. His arm, protruding from the window, beckoned them. "Hurry up! A bored soldier whistled at me on the next street! And waved his radio! I drove away! I saw him running!"

Hana jumped in the front seat while Charlie jumped in the back. She looked past him out the rear window. The bored soldier, flying around the bend at a fevered speed, had become almost rabid. "Go!" cried Hana. "He's right there!" Mustafa floored it, but the soldier refused to give up. He ran like a mad dog after a desert hare. That is, until catching whiff of a better scent. He stopped short in front of Dalia's building and turned to the man on the stairs. Perhaps to collect a bribe; perhaps to commence a whupping. The man on the stairs stood up and grudgingly backed away. The soldier made as if he were going to follow him, but tarried once the man—at last, surrendering his pride—turned to flee. That seemed to thrill the soldier. Hana couldn't see his face from the distance between him and the car, ever increasing, but his strut said he loved scaring people. There was no recourse; no way to complain. He couldn't be touched, beaten, robbed, or held accountable for his behavior. Not while the Supreme Council was in power. He was beyond the law. He was even beyond the dangers of a dark neighborhood aligned against him. He was the real danger. His radio could turn one soldier into a truckload.

The dark maze of Imbaba became the bright lights of Mohandessin, a middle-class neighborhood known more for its shopping than its mosques. The faster route downtown would've been to go east across the Imbaba Bridge, but that would've required circling the block and driving once more past the soldier. "I think it's better if we go . . . ," Mustafa had said, turning south. He promised to make the detour short by driving faster. Streetlamps whipped by at odd angles. Hana had come to trust Mustafa's skill, judgment, and luck, so felt no need to pray for safe passage. Instead she prayed for advice: *What should I do about Charlie? What would Leilah do in my position?* Upon asking the latter question, Hana realized she wasn't praying to God so much as attempting to contact the dead. Admitting that freed her to get on with it. *Leilah! Are you there? Should I help Charlie? He isn't really the point so much as the vector, I guess; through him I can help Dalia. Isn't my job designed to help people like her? Isn't the design flawed on some fundamental level? Might my task on Earth be to change that in some small way?* Hana had been considering her task on Earth ever since Leilah, at the age of eleven, had won a gold medal at a horse camp meant for teenagers. Jealousy had forced Hana, beginning at such a young age, to consider her own future. What was she good at? What could she be? Not an equestrian, since Leilah had already locked that down. A baseball player? A movie star? A famous painter? Ishtar had said, "Why not help people? Even one person. If you can improve one life by the time you die, you've completed God's task." Hana thought she'd be deemed a failure if she died now. Or anytime soon, for that matter. Especially compared to her family, which had nearly been snuffed out by selflessness. Her father had perished on his way to beseech God for a cease-fire. That his country might know peace! Her sister had perished in the very church her father had been trying to visit. To know him better, to fill up on history, to force what she'd learned on the world. That her country was not lost! Hana's mother had perished, at least on the inside, from the frantic need to stay faithful. That she might relentlessly pray for the dead! What sacrifice had Hana ever made to earn her place in such a family? *Leilah! Are you there? Please, I need to talk to you! I need to know what you think!*

Sharia Ahmed Orabi became Sharia Gemeat al Dewal; that became Dokki, which became Tahrir. The Nile, languid and perfectly flat, flowed under the bridge without regard for the troubles of the country it watered. Mustafa hooked left toward Ramses. A few minutes later he made a parking spot where there wasn't one, on a small pile of trash. Several weasels scattered like roaches with tails. Mustafa bid farewell to Charlie, a man he didn't know and hadn't traded words with, in the style of his old self—with well-wishings, with prayers, with his hands in the air, gesturing both goodwill and good luck. Apparently the soldier who had meant so much in Imbaba meant so little downtown; he was long gone on the far side of the river. Then Mustafa turned to Hana and said, "God willing, you call soon." Charlie opened the door, got out, then tried to close the door. The door wouldn't shut. Mustafa told him to kick it. Charlie kicked the door, which mysteriously stuck in the frame. Mustafa pretended to be happy. Hana could see through his bullshit as if it were beach water. The soldier was obviously still on Mustafa's mind. His posturing lasted only until he was paid. Then he sped away looking flabbergasted and bleary-eyed.

Charlie offered to reimburse Hana for the fare, but his mobile rang before he could produce his wallet. "What?" he shouted into his phone. Then Charlie mouthed five words to Hana: *Aos, colleague, translator, trusted friend.* "Yes, I know. The rumor. I heard. From Ali. You know Ali. Or met him once. The man from before. With the knife. . . . Yes, the knife! . . . I know. I'm telling you. I'm outside as we speak. I'll be there in two minutes. . . . Yes, two minutes! I'm right here. I'm with Hana. You know, from. . . . Yes, that's right. The UNHCR. . . . I know! I'm sorry! It couldn't be helped!" The long, somber pause alarmed Hana. She was, and probably had been several times before, the topic of conversation. She couldn't imagine those conversations had been flattering. "I'll explain later! God, Aos! I'm two minutes away!" Charlie consigned his phone to the grave of his pocket. Then he faced Hana, looking ever tired but never dead, and said, "Let's go."

Their feet beat the sidewalk. They turned left at the traffic circle. Then left again at a one-story brick building, which was unassuming in every way. Before them was a courtyard surrounded on all sides by a wall, except for a metal gate that provided a disturbing view. Clients, wearing everything from pajamas to suit jackets, leaned against walls, paced the length of the yard, rapped the screen door, and begged each other for information. Men gripped wives, who gripped suitcases. Their children gripped their younger children, who gripped toys. The younger children wept violently. It was so late. They were so tired. Above it all bobbed Ali's head. He used his hands as a bullhorn. "Who got a ticket already? Who knows where I can get mine? And four more for my family?"

8

Earlier that day, Aos had made a grave error. He'd dialed the wrong number when trying to call Charlie. He'd been forced to dial all twelve digits using the office landline, since his mobile had been stolen in Tahrir. It felt weird and old-fashioned. Had Aos not blundered, he would've reached Charlie and said, "The Mugamma is only closed for appearances! The revolution is in danger! It's always been in danger, but the danger is worse than I thought!" But Charlie couldn't answer a phone that didn't ring. Aos hadn't known that—there'd been no recorded message to reveal his mistake—so pressed redial every thirty minutes on the dot. He'd been blinded by frustration until a moment of panic and despair: when, in late evening, there came a series of impassioned knocks. First on the door, then again on the window. It was entirely unexpected. There were no appointments scheduled. The interns had gone home. Even Michael and Sabah had left. The office, until the knock, had felt more desolate than the Sand Sea beyond Siwa. As a boy, Aos had gone camping there. Not once did he see a fox, a bug, or even a bird. His only company had been his father's voice, the sound of wood burning, and the innumerable stars. His father had said the stars were innumerable because the sky rotated. There were always new stars to count.

Aos answered the door cautiously. What if the knocker was the person he'd seen in the window at the Mugamma? What if the person wore a uniform and absconded with Aos to jail? His crime was seeing what he shouldn't have seen and knowing what he ought not to know. The Mugamma was only closed for appearances. He pulled the door open so slowly the spring hinges didn't whine. Then exhaled in a happy gust. There stood clients he recognized, trusted, and liked. He embraced Ibrahim, who carried two suitcases. Behind him, Nujah held two kids. Nujah was Ibrahim's wife. They'd married at a young age by arrangement, then fell in love at a later date. "She is my al-Kiblah," Ibrahim had said during his intake interview. Al-Kiblah was the old word for Polaris, the North Star. God's compass. "I'm lost without her. Lost like the others. Lost like my son." Their first son had been shot during a botched kidnapping attempt in central Baghdad. A terrible fate, but Ibrahim hadn't had the money to pay the ransom the militia would've demanded. The boy would've died anyway after a long torture. Better his death was swift and, at least by comparison, painless. Ibrahim had cried when he'd said that death was better. The remaining two children, normally little balls of life but asleep now, held tightly in their mother's arms, were named Nada and Ahmed. Behind that family, a few more clients ambled in the yard, a cement rectangle between the office and the street. The yard was surrounded by a high wall cleaved by a green gate. It was bowled in the middle so that when Cairo received rain, a blessed rarity, it filled with standing water. The water smelled bad, but made the yard cooler. Birds visited to bathe and eat bugs. The birds' chirping invariably boosted the mood.

"It's good to see you," said Aos. Though it was less good to see Ibrahim's suitcases. "Please wait." He gestured that Ibrahim should wait outside. Then he shut the door, retrieved his phone, and hit redial several more times until finally seeing his mistake. "Alla," said Aos. "Ya salaam." He dialed the right number, carefully. When Charlie picked up, Aos didn't mince words: "You need to get back here. The Mugamma isn't really closed. I meant to tell you before.

Also, where have you been all day? Ah! The second thing I have to say is much worse than the first. Clients are gathering. They've brought suitcases." Charlie said he already knew. He'd seen Ali, the man with the knife. "Alla," said Aos a second time. "Ya salaam. The man who threatened to cut his own throat? He's still alive?" Aos breathed deeply and held his head in his hands. The first piece of good news he'd gotten in a long time was ruined by the bad news already waiting in the yard to wipe away the sweet feeling.

Clients gathering after hours wasn't unprecedented. The same thing had happened last summer. A misinformed client heard tell that the Refugee Relief Project was handing out plane tickets. First come, first served. The rumor had spread like a virus. A crowd had gathered at the office in the early hours of a cool morning. Their agitation had been obvious. People moved hastily and kept inspecting their phones. Charlie and Aos had been the only two employees on-site at the time. When they'd opened the screen door, confusion had ensued. There'd been some yelling. The Refugee Relief Project had never given and would never give away plane tickets. Why were clients surprised? Where would the money come from? What was a plane ticket even worth without a visa? Charlie had tried to explain this to Aos, who'd tried in vain to translate for the crowd in terms that wouldn't incite a riot. The bleak silence following the translated speech was broken by the sound of glass shattering. Someone had thrown a brick through a window. It had been disturbing at the time and more so after the fact. The brick couldn't have been lying abandoned in the yard. It was a different color from the building in which they worked and the wall surrounding the yard. Whoever threw the brick had brought it with them.

To thwart history from repeating itself with renewed fervor — a fervor borrowed from or feeding off the revolution — Aos boiled water for tea. The idea was to give the clients something. Aos had always believed the act of giving had a hidden significance. What you gave mattered less than the gusto with which you offered it. He practiced saying *tea* as if it meant *ticket*. To England. To Germany. To France.

While the water boiled, he laid paper cups in a grid pattern across the counter. "Where are you, Charlie?" he said to himself. Two minutes had already passed; five minutes were at risk of passing. He needed help filling the cups. He needed even more help passing them out.

The office door flew open so hard the knob lanced a hole in the drywall. "There must be forty people out there," said Charlie as if he'd never seen a bigger number. "They're asking a lot of questions. I said we'd be out soon to answer them." Charlie looked at his watch. He wasn't wearing a watch. The absence clearly disturbed him. "We need a plan. We need something to say." A woman who must've been Hana followed Charlie through the door, backward. It surprised Aos — to be honest, it also relieved him — that she wasn't white. Past experience had taught him the last thing clients needed was another pale face looking sorry for them.

"Forty?" said Aos. "There were only twenty the last time I checked." He looked out the window before nervously arranging the chairs in a grid pattern, akin to the cups.

"What are you doing?" asked Charlie.

"We have to let them in. We have to let them sit down."

Charlie extended his hand and told Aos to slap five. Slapping five was their ritual beginning to seemingly impossible work. Such as when several rejection notices arrived the same day and they were tasked with breaking the news. Such as when the Supreme Council shut off electricity, forcing Charlie and Aos to excavate typewriters from storage. The typewriters were badly in need of repair. Indispensable keys such as the space bar didn't function properly. Aos and Charlie slapped five for several reasons. To make a loud sound. To feel a modicum of pain. To wake up. To mark the start of a race. First to finish the task at hand so another task could be started! Most of all, they slapped five for things they refused to talk about. How glad they were to be friends, to have similar obsessions, to care so much about their clients without ever confessing their emotional attachment to the work. This due to ego and toughness of heart, for both men seemed to believe that muscle functioned best when neglected. The slap cracked so hard it startled Hana, who turned around. She let the screen door swing shut. The door hitting the frame – bang! – startled her a second time.

"There's not enough room," said Charlie, rubbing the sting off his palm. "There aren't even enough chairs."

"I know. You're right." Aos sat down and ran his hands through his hair until it wasn't combed anymore.

"Is there anything I can do?" asked Hana.

Impulse told Aos to eye her skeptically – why was she here and what were her motives? – but he didn't want to be incredulous in case there was a hadith against it. Plus, he needed her hands. "I put tea in paper cups," said Aos. "Will you help me distribute them? Quickly, before the tea is cold." He fetched one tray while Hana fetched the other. Charlie pushed the screen door open using his foot. The sound of the hinges drowned in the sound of feverish mumbling from what must've been sixty clients ambling in the yard. Aos knew immediately there wasn't enough tea to go around. Hopefully the children didn't like tea or were too tired to want it. Clients turned on seeing the glint of the trays. Even the children woke up and turned. "We have tea," said Aos loudly. There were a few seconds of puzzled staring. Then clients began shouting. Are there tickets? Are there *really* tickets? Can I have one? Can I have three? The questions grew increasingly philosophical. Why me? What did I do wrong? Why can't I work? Why can't I leave? Why did I come to this country? Clients started yelling to be heard. As the volume of the crowd increased, so did the unintelligibility. Aos walked down the two stairs leading from the door to the yard. He said *tea* as if it meant *ticket.* "Tea! Please, take a cup! I have tea!" Clients grabbed cups and also his sleeves, to slow him down. What's the status of my case? When can I leave? Where can I go? I need money. I need medicine. I need help. Some of the youngest children cried from tiredness and the fact that their parents were loud, angry, and scared. Children looked at their parents as if they didn't know them anymore. Who is this person holding me? After Aos' tray of tea became just a tray, he tried to silence the crowd by hitting the tray with his hand. It sounded like a gong or a bell. He tried to explain to the whole what he'd already said to the parts. There were no plane tickets. A ticket was no use anyway. Not without a visa or a job set up on the other side. Not without a place to live. These were the responsibility not of the Refugee Relief Project, but of the United Nations High Commissioner for Refugees — Aos thought it would've been dangerous to expose Hana so didn't look at her — and the various nonprofits and service agencies available on arrival in the host country. Should that happen, should your case be approved, should a country take you. Aos affirmed the process was still going. Yes, slowly. Very slowly. He apologized in the loudest voice possible in the simplest Arabic so even the children could understand. Then he repeated himself in English in case the few Sudanese and Eritreans in the crowd, whose first languages were probably tribal and whose second languages were probably Standard Arabic, had trouble understanding the Egyptian. He said the reasonable course now was to go home and wait. "Wait?" a man yelled so loudly the others in the crowd shut up and stared at him. "I've been waiting!" When Aos turned toward the yelling, a suitcase whacked him in the face. The black plastic shell stuffed with old clothes swung heavy. He fell over. The clothes, set free from the suitcase, rained down and covered him. Aos didn't move right away. Not because he couldn't, but because he didn't want to. He was tired. Also his face hurt. So Aos just lay there and listened to Charlie pushing the offender back. "Stay back! Calm down, brother!" Aos could feel the client still whacking him with the broken suitcase through the pile of clothes. The suitcase, relieved of its contents, weighed so little that its impact barely hurt anymore. Aos felt no need to roll away. He just lay there until Charlie, with the help of Hana — "Put the suitcase down!" she shouted — successfully pushed the assailant back into the crowd.

Where Aos lay was quiet and peaceful and dark. He thought he was dead for a second. Then Aos remembered how much he feared death. He feared death because he feared God. That he'd not done well enough by Him. Or that God didn't even exist. That Aos had been wasting his time talking to his hands and to the floor and to his books. He jumped up in fear of where his mind was taking him. "I shouldn't have stood up so quickly," said Aos, squatting until the dots in his vision went away. He stood more slowly the second time. Then he tore away the clothes hanging off him and continued walking on through the crowd, answering questions as best he could with his crushed, bloody nose stuffed in his shirt. He didn't stop until he bumped into a heartsick Ali with a knife on his hip, where his hand also rested. The memory of what had happened last time—Ali running toward what Aos had feared would be a suicide—shoved away his other concerns. Aos touched the man on the arm to convey what there was no material way to say: *You're thought of, worried for, and cared about; I beg you, don't pull your knife or, God forbid, make use of it.* The sorry touch must've conveyed to Ali what the calamity had not. There were no tickets. He wept like the children by him and turned away from the embarrassment of being seen. The back of his head advanced without pause toward the gate. "Wait, Ali!" shouted Aos. "Come back! I beg you, come back!" He tried to give chase, but Charlie, appearing from nowhere, grabbed Aos by the arm and pulled him the other way. "Damn you, Charlie! Let go of my arm! I need to know where Ali's going!" Charlie just pulled harder. He wasn't listening. When Aos turned, he saw why. He saw Dalia. The world's suffering was obscured behind her. Therein lay the cost of Charlie's want. Aos tried not to bump into or bleed on the crowd, hooked as he was like a fish, and more or less flailing like one. "Drop my arm! Do you hear me? I said . . . !" Charlie finally dropped Aos' arm, but by then it was too late. Ali had already reached the gate and had fled into the dark of the city. Aos moaned, but that moan was lost in the loudness of the crowd.

"I heard there were tickets!" shouted Dalia over the ruckus. She wasn't less fucked than Ali, just less evidently fucked. Her pain hid well in her doggedness. "I knew it wasn't true. I don't know why

I came. The cab cost fifty pounds. That's two times the fair price. I know because I asked before I got in. The man said the rate changed after we started. I tried to negotiate." Dalia showed the wet spot where the driver had spit on her. "So I hit him in the face with my money. Next time I must remember to use something else." Her story would've been sadder had she cried or even laughed at the end; as it was, Dalia just asked if there was any tea left. There wasn't. The cups on Aos' tray had all been drunk or spilled. Hana's tray, too, had been emptied. While attempting to tuck the tray under her arm, Hana dropped it. The tray clanged on the ground. They all startled except Dalia. Her blank face troubled Aos more than anything else he'd seen that night. She looked absent of life, hope, love, even fear – like her own recumbent effigy propped curiously in the standing position.

By midnight, the yard had cleared.

"Why do we call it the yard?" asked Aos, sitting on the steps leading from the yard to the hallway behind him. The hall led to the office, which led nowhere apparently. "It's just a cement rectangle."

"One day I'll plant grass," said Charlie as if he knew that wouldn't happen but couldn't stop himself from imagining what it might look like and how it might smell. The futile longing imbued his voice with grief. "And erect benches." He'd taken pains over the years to improve the office and the yard as much as the budget allowed. The screen door had always been Charlie's proudest achievement. It was important to him that clients could see into and out of the office. That they had somewhere to go where they needn't feel trapped.

Hana collected the clothes dropped in the yard by Aos' assailant, which had been scattered by the feet of the crowd. "Why take the suitcase," she asked, "but leave behind everything he cared enough about to pack on short notice?" Clothes weren't the only valuables on display. Amid the scattering was a swimming cap, a harmonica, a black leather belt, a prayer rug, and photos held together by a brown rubber band. Aos dared not look at the photos. They contained the identity of whoever whacked him. He didn't want to know. He already knew it was someone he recognized, trusted, and liked. Knowing who exactly would only complicate his opinion.

"How's your . . . ?" Charlie gestured to Aos' face.

Aos let his finger glide along the bridge of his nose. The bridge felt askew and the slight pressure caused his face to ache and his eyes to water. "Not in need of medical attention," joked Aos. He remembered what he suspected Charlie was also remembering. The night, a few months back, that he'd spent at the Egyptian Museum. "I don't need medical attention," he'd wheezed in the morning upon his return, burned up with a bad haircut. His chest had hurt from being kicked so many times. He'd barely been able to breathe. Charlie finally coerced him into a taxi after shouting for ten minutes that he'd be fired otherwise. Aos had wept on the way to the hospital and punched the back of the seat.

"Look," said Hana. "Tap shoes."

The shoes were rolled in a pair of jeans, but the heal taps poked out. Aos realized then who'd clobbered him. Ghassan, who loved tap; who'd once tapped so hard and so long that he'd split the wood floor he'd been dancing on. The wood floor was just fiberboard pressed in the dirt. That didn't make Ghassan less proud; he was a fast tapper. One of the documents Aos had translated for Ghassan's resettlement petition was an acceptance letter to a dance studio Ghassan had never attended. *We welcome you, Ghassan Sadiq.* Followed by details regarding the date he was meant to begin and the nature of his scholarship. While the document, in context of his resettlement petition, should've indicated loss and proved that Ghassan had drive, passion, and talent — he would've been an asset to any community — in evaluative terms, the document served only to substantiate Ghassan's identity. His drives, passions, and talents mattered so little that, for all intents and purposes, they ceased to exist.

Aos was suddenly ashamed that Hana was the one picking up Ghassan's clothing. He stood up to help her. Charlie, too. The gathering of items was a grim and sodden affair. Ghassan had been in such a rush that some of his garb was still wet from recent washing. "Collect the wet clothes separately," said Aos. Afterward they watched the damp spots on the pavement fade away. With the spots went the last proof of the night's happenings.

"By the way . . . " Hana approached Aos as if she meant to start a conversation, but stood there awhile before saying anything more. It was as if she were condensing a long speech into an essential point, a kind of singularity in which meaning was infinitely dense. "I'm Hana," she said finally. She offered her hand to Aos the same way he'd offered tea to his clients. There was a particular misery in knowing what you had to give would never be enough.

"I know who you are." Her hand wasn't as clammy as Aos had expected. "Though I can't say I'm pleased to meet you. Forgive me for being rude. I'd hoped Charlie was planning something that would never pass." A few meters away, Charlie swept discarded cups into a mound. He told Aos not to talk about him as if he weren't there. "Your presence suggests my hope is in vain. Tell me, please. Are you forging a yellow card?" While technically a question, Aos' voice indicated he was troubled by an answer that he'd absorbed like a sponge from the air. But Charlie, pining for surety, didn't breathe until Hana nodded.

PART III

THE PAYOFF

1

Sunday in Cairo was the same as Monday in Dearborn, except made worse by an awesome and terrifying responsibility. Hana needed to pilfer a yellow card. Summoning the courage to pilfer it took several hours, but the theft itself took only seconds. There was yet no relief to be found. The card was made new and strange by its blankness. No number. No address. No name. What name would Hana choose? "Amira, Sanaa, Fatima," she whispered in search of an alias that fit Dalia's nature as well as or better than the name bestowed upon her at birth. "Habiba, Maryam, Mona." Hana grew less satisfied as the list gained names. "Rabi'a, Sabeen, Uzma." She tried writing the names in both Latin and Arabic scripts on a legal pad. Seeing the black ink tangle on lined paper didn't help. The decision was wrought with too much significance. A name indicated origin, affected the personality, and caused the owner to turn when they heard it. Such a decision would live at least as long as Dalia. Perhaps much longer. If Dalia had children, for example, and didn't impart her real name lest it spill from ear to ear all the way back to Immigration and Customs Enforcement. Then Hana's choice would live forever in the memories of those who loved Dalia but didn't call her that. They'd pass her alias down the line with her story: *Your grandma saved your grandpa's life. She survived the war in Iraq by sheer fortitude. We wouldn't be here without her. Remember her name. It's . . .*

Out of nowhere, a man cleared his throat. "Ahem." Hana froze. Her forgery-in-progress lay bare on her desk. The card was totally blank. Shit, thought Hana. A blank card was a smoking gun. Especially considering its location. The card rested next to a pen with no cap, which rested next to a long list of names. Hana felt stupid for writing them all down. The dots begged connecting and would point like arrows at her guilty-looking face. Why hadn't she closed her door? Oh, right. Closed doors weren't allowed in the office except during resettlement interviews. "Not allowed!" said Margret every time she found a door closed for another reason. Margret said closed doors inhibited synergy, curtailed the natural light, and prevented the air-con from working properly. Hana regretted not testing the rule by closing her door partway. A grubby paw would've had to push the door open before prying eyes fell on her desk. Thus alerting Hana to the meddler's presence half a second before the hacking sound of his phlegm dislodging. She could've used that half second to jumble the evidence presently condemning her. Calm down, thought Hana. Look up! Look up right now! Damn you, Hana! Look up!

Joseph, framed by the doorway, exhibited as two-dimensional: an ominous picture of a man wearing a bloodred bow tie and an appropriately dead-looking stare. Hana was surprised when he blinked and more surprised still when he spoke. "You look tired," said Joseph, becoming himself by stepping into the room. Suddenly Hana's office felt a little crowded. "Not tired in a bad way. Not old or haggard. That's not what I mean."

"What do you mean?" Hana couldn't shake the feeling that Joseph wanted something. Why didn't he say what it was? *Hey, Hana . . . uh, pardon me, but . . . do you have a second? I came to discuss . . .*

"I'm not sure. Maybe I'm the tired one. Do I look tired? Or old? According to my knees, I *am* old. And haggard. It's the weather, I think. My joints tend to swell in the heat. That never used to happen.

What used to happen was I'd wake up feeling fine and I'd feel fine all day and I'd go to bed feeling fine with my life."

"You're not old. You are a bit odd."

And menacing. Hana couldn't pin down exactly why, except to say that she wanted to get the fuck away from him.

"I'm tired and you look stunning. That's what I'm trying to say."

"Thank you."

"Not that my appreciation for you or your work has anything to do with how you look. I barely see you." He said that as if it made him sad. Or perhaps suspicious. What was Hana doing with all her time?

"How do I look?"

"Tired." Joseph sat down in a chair, clearly exhausted in his own right. The weather couldn't have been the only reason. Work must've had some effect. The sheer number of resettlement cases was mind-numbing. Not to mention the revolution. Joseph had made comments before indicating how much it troubled him. He worried that a group of soldiers would take up loitering on his street. Or protesters, mistaking him for some kind of Western diplomat, would throw rocks at his car. "I came to see you for a reason." The longer he paused, the more serious his demeanor became. Eventually his brow furrowed. Oh shit, thought Hana. He sees the yellow card. He's looking at it right now through the side of his eye. "But I can't remember what it was. I think stress has a negative effect on the memory."

"Are you stressed?" asked Hana. Not because she didn't know the answer, but because asking questions – at least, the right questions – would prevent Joseph from remembering the subject he'd come to discuss. Did it involve the yellow card that had mysteriously gone missing? Hana wanted to rest her arm over it, but feared that would only draw Joseph's attention.

"Well, that depends. Is being worried the same as being stressed?"

"Biologically speaking?" It was, Hana thought, the perfect response: answering a question with another question. More still, a question with no satisfying answer. A question like that could murder any conversation. Joseph might even think the abrupt end was his own fault. He ought not to be so candid. It wasn't as if they were close friends who'd gotten drunk at a bar. God willing, the awkwardness would be so bad that even Joseph would notice it. Perhaps then he'd leave.

Joseph thwarted Hana by settling into his chair. "I'm worried I'll never leave Egypt. I'm worried I'll die here of lung cancer at forty. Just living in Cairo — just breathing the *air* — is like smoking twenty cigarettes a day. According to the World Health Organization, that's a fact. I've never smoked and I'm still near dead from smoking. It's not fair. I'm worried my family and friends won't realize I'm dead for months, at which point they'll mourn out of obligation and not actual sadness. Isn't that what happens when you're gone for so long? Don't loved ones find closer people to care about?"

Hana tried not to indulge such a frightening idea. Of course, she couldn't help herself. She imagined Omran trading Dalia for someone closer to him. A neighbor, maybe. Or someone he'd met at the store. The vision, like a Russian nesting doll, contained diminutive versions of itself: Omran had found an American who was liberal enough to accept his affection; Omran had found an American; Omran had fallen in love. The last string connecting Dalia to her past life would thus sever itself. It was only a matter of time. The string, named Omran, would still send money, but only as recompense. The money would subside with his guilt, leaving Dalia in Egypt with no income and no way to escape.

"Do you also have a list?" asked Joseph as if he didn't want to be the only one confessing worries. "It's actually pretty liberating to put it out there."

How quickly the tables had turned. Hana's question without a satisfying answer had been volleyed back as a question with no answer at all. Hana couldn't deny having a list without declaring herself an automaton, with no heart. Nor could she admit having a list without incriminating herself. *Yes, I have one. But my list is always changing. Right now I'm worried that I'll get caught forging Dalia's yellow card. What if you caught me? Would you tell Margret? Whom would she tell? The embassy? My worries only get bigger from there. How would I be punished?*

What country would have jurisdiction? The crime being tangled: committed in Egypt, against the United States, by way of the United Nations. What if I'm not extradited? What if I never go home? No, Hana couldn't answer Joseph's question honestly. Or dishonestly, for that matter. She'd never been a good liar. Nor could Hana explicitly *not* answer it. That would only beg Joseph to wonder why. *She must be hiding something.* Hana took the only course of action left to take. She pretended to consider Joseph's question with the hope that he'd grow so bored of waiting that he'd be utterly compelled to leave. *I'm late for . . . something,* he'd say. But Joseph never grew bored and as such never said that. Instead he grew alert and austere. The startling about-face could mean only one thing: Joseph had seen the yellow card. Oh, God, thought Hana. It's right there. He's looking straight at it.

"The party!" cried Joseph as if those two words caused him indescribable pain. "That's what I came here to tell you about! There's a whole goddamn room of people waiting for us!" He pressed his hand against his forehead as if he'd been shot and his brain were falling out. "Margret sent me to fetch you and I just . . . forgot!" Hana discovered the only thing worse than feeling like a traitor was feeling like a tennis ball. "We need to go! Right away! It's your one-month anniversary! And you're missing it!" Joseph rose from his chair in such a rush that he spilled his coffee. The steaming liquid fell on his pants and also the floor. He winced in pain. He couldn't do anything besides wait for the pain to subside. "Please hurry," said Joseph as soon as the coffee stopped burning him. "We're very late." He rubbed the coffee into the carpet with his shoe as if that would make the dark spot disappear. "Jesus Christ. I've made it worse." The dark spot had spread out without fading. Joseph turned away from the stain he'd created and led the way to the door.

Nobody Hana loved was at her party. The best she could muster was respect. She respected Yezin for being a happy man. Or at least appearing happy. It was quite the trick. She respected Joseph for his bow tie collection. Wearing bow ties required bravery or obliviousness, which had its own kind of value. Hadn't Joseph's obliviousness just saved Hana from getting caught? Most of all she respected Noha and Fadwa. They were intimidating, prickly, unapologetic. Bumping into Noha solicited a *whoops* and not a *sorry*; bumping into Fadwa solicited an actual grimace and sometimes even a clicking sound. Hana craved their friendship so much she couldn't imagine ever having it. She smiled in their direction but otherwise kept her distance. The entire office was in attendance, except for a few local employees who'd left to pick up their children from school. Margret wasn't there yet, but had sent word — via the whiteboard nailed to the wall by her door — that she was coming soon. Her door had been closed when Joseph had dragged Hana past. It was both startling and curious. Why would Margret break her own rule in front of everybody?

"Excuse me," said Joseph, much calmer now that Margret would never know that he'd failed to bring Hana on time. "I need to reheat my coffee. Pardon me. Don't mind me. Coming through." He opened the microwave, inserted his cup, and pressed the power button. His addiction to the bitter nectar presented itself in the rapt way he watched the cup rotate on the tray. Hana fidgeted while Joseph bathed in the toxic yellow light emitted from the window. The uneasy feeling was Ishtar's fault. From an early age, Ishtar had installed in Hana a fear: that microwave radiation could cook a woman's eggs from up to ten feet away. "Those eggs are my grandchildren," Ishtar would say, and not as a joke. She deserved grandchildren. She wanted them badly. Finally the microwave beeped and the yellow light disappeared. "Ah," said Joseph, grabbing his cup. He breathed the steam and seemed to have some kind of religious experience. The desperate look on his face proved to Hana beyond the most exacting doubt that he wasn't dangerous. He'd never been dangerous. Poor Joseph had no chance in hell of connecting any dots whatsoever. He was too bothered generally by the state of his life. So declared the sweat ring on his shirt collar.

Hana felt sick knowing the lies she'd told and must continue to tell by her silence. Taking the yellow card was peanuts in comparison to filling it out, which was peanuts in comparison to attaching the testimony. Her heart punched her from the inside when she imagined who'd read the testimony upon its submission. An elaborate, visceral fiction presented as a tragedy that occurred in the real world. Who would fall victim to that lie? Hopefully not Joseph. His heart was already fragile from years spent neglecting its want. What if Dalia's fake case was the one that pushed him over the edge? Hana saw it happening eventually. One day Joseph would just go home.

The party was brought to an early and rather abrupt end by two strange sounds in sequence: a door being thrown open, then slamming shut again. Nothing had ever troubled Hana more than a room full of people not shoving cake into their cake holes. The social few glanced nervously at each other; the rest glanced nervously at their plates. "I got two calls," said Margret, steamrolling into the kitchen like a coal-powered train. Hana had never seen her look overwhelmed. Apparently nobody else had, either. People ran the gamut from shaken to scared. "One from the Ministry of the Interior and another from the US embassy. Protesters marched on both this morning. Threw rocks, burned flags. Nothing unusual. But plainclothes officers in the crowd reported demonstrators have organized a march on this street later this afternoon. What's on this street besides our building?" Margret let her implication sink in. "We're going to evacuate. Get your work, take it with you."

Hearsay had taught Hana that plainclothes officers were the worst of the worst of the worst. They infiltrated Tahrir by shedding their uniforms. They spied and attacked when commanded and swarmed by surprise, arresting the most vulnerable: women, whom they'd strip down to their underwear to embarrass; old men; injured men. Anyone who tripped while fleeing. They'd drag their prisoners away for interrogation. They'd ask women if they were virgins and men if they were terrorists. Then force confessions by threat of torture in the form of rape and further beating. Confessions came in high pitch or low moan, depending on the prisoners' degree of resistance and therefore the degree of force used against them. We're not virgins! We are terrorists! Followed by imprisonment for crimes committed against God and government. They said God was government. In addition to being famous for disguising their cowardice as rage, these impostors were also known as propaganda police – men who would dress down and say anything.

"Did anybody hear what I said?" asked Margret. "We're evacuating."

Nobody moved.

"Go! Right now!"

Nobody even breathed.

Margret's pink face alerted the room to the weather. A storm was coming. "Don't make me . . ."

Someone threw his cake in the sink and said, "Shit."

Someone else said, "Are we really evacuating?"

Margret asked if anyone had ever – really, ever – heard her tell a joke. Then Margret engaged the staff in a staring contest and slayed the room. Whoever threw his cake in the sink said, "Shit," again, but at a lower volume with the digraph drawn out – *"Shhhhit"* – so that he sounded utterly defeated and depressed. Hana knew without looking that it was Joseph. He hated working from home. He hated his neighbors. More accurately, he hated his neighbor's children. The children didn't attend school or seem to have friends or even relatives to visit. "They're always home," Joseph had bemoaned on more than one occasion. "Fighting, wrestling, laughing, and hitting the wall with their fists." By way of contrast, he remarked once how his own child had been "quiet." Hana discovered later that "quiet" meant "stillborn." Yezin whispered that the unbearable strain of the death had killed Joseph's marriage, and that Hana should never mention it. Joseph's sorrow wasn't buried very deep.

The staff oozed like syrup from the kitchen to an open area full of filing cabinets and copy machines. Normally people went here to get slightly high on the smell of toner. Now they continued past,

down the hall, out the exit. Hana dodged the exodus by hiding in
the supply closet. Hiding was the only way to finish her forgery
without witnesses. No more witnesses, anyway. The idea relaxed
her, despite the fear of protesters swarming the office, breaking
the windows, burning it down. Would protesters really march all
the way from downtown? An hour's drive, normally? And a day's
walk? Even if they did come, Hana would be gone by the time they
arrived. How long would it take to forge a yellow card, then write
and file the documents required to show it was real? A few hours, at
most. Nobody could do a day's walk in a few hours. Especially not a
group of people marching in the heat and traffic and smog. A day's
walk would take several days in those conditions.

The closet door swung open just as Hana was beginning to trust
her solitude. Fucking Joseph again! "Great minds do think alike," he
said, pushing in. "I can't work from home. It would drive me insane.
The noise is like . . ." He imitated kids chattering. The sound was so
precise that Joseph seemed to get on his own nerves. Yezin appeared,
too, seconds later. He pushed in the same way. "Ya ilahi," he said,
shutting the door behind him softly but decisively. Then he flicked
on the light. "I can't believe there's enough room in here for all of
us." He smiled even though what he said was barely true. The plastic
smell of new pens and rolled tape, and the indescribable smell of a
room that had never been occupied for more than a few seconds – as
if the carpet were still new after ten years – gave way to the smell of
stale cake on hot breath. Hana wished both Joseph and Yezin would
leave. Not that she believed wishing so would make it happen. There
just wasn't anything else she could do. She couldn't push them out.
The door was shut. Even if the door were open, pushing them would
just start a fight. An argument, at least. It depended on how hard she
pushed and whether they fell over. Either way, not a good way to stay
hidden. Margret would hear Joseph's cry of surprise. She would stomp
down the hall, shouting wildly, *What are you doing? Why are you here?*

"Put your hand on the knob," whispered Hana.

"What?" whispered Joseph.

"In case Margret tries to open the door. Put your hand on the knob. That way she'll think the door is locked."

"This door doesn't have a lock," whispered Joseph.

"Just do it! Or let me do it!"

Joseph gripped the knob so tightly his face turned red. He didn't move or change back to his normal color for almost twenty minutes. It was both impressive and a little sad to see a man dedicated to such distressing work.

At last, Yezin said, "I have a feeling we're safe." They were all bone-weary from breathing one another's hot breath. Joseph was even worse off with one noodle arm from holding the door. When he opened it, room temperature felt like air-conditioning. They all took deep breaths. Then Yezin leaned out of the closet and cautiously looked both ways down the hall. He gave the all clear – 3ala mahlak, meaning "in haste there is regret, so go slowly." Yezin went and Joseph followed him. "Protesters can't march this far," said Joseph, as if there were no chance in hell the protesters would take buses. As if that convenient thought would keep him safe. Hana, the sloth of the group, hung back. Her idea was to be alone for a second to remember what she was doing and why she was doing it. The solitude didn't turn out to be constructive. It made her think, which made her doubt. That made her terribly afraid again. Hana fled the closet in a rush.

The slick metal slide of cabinets opening as two men perused documents was an assault on the sanctity of what had become a quiet place. Hana proceeded with her plan despite them. Two potential witnesses minding their own business was a lot better than an office full of prying eyes. Nevertheless, Hana discovered choosing a name was just as hard as it had been. Harder, in fact. With an elevated heart rate and sticky fingers from cake and, strangely, the same nervous feeling of standing close to the microwave. It was as if the whole office had somehow become irradiated. Hana consulted with Charlie to mitigate the responsibility of finally making a choice. She called him on her mobile from the women's bathroom. With only two men left in the building, the women's bathroom was the safest place.

"I need a name," whispered Hana into her phone. The phone was so cheaply manufactured that Hana expected, any day now, that it would fall apart from the pressure of being held. "The same one you're going to put on the testimony."

"Who's this?"

"Who do you think?"

"Hana?"

"Oh my God. Yes. Hana."

"Why are you whispering?"

"I'm forging a yellow card!" she said at a slightly higher volume. Her guilt rose from the dead. Hana almost wished she'd be caught, fired, shamed, and sent home. She missed Ishtar.

"Hm. How about Salih? For her surname."

"And a given one?"

Charlie paused as if he'd been waiting his whole life to say her name, but it pained him now to say it. "Farah," he said finally. "It's Arabic for 'joy.' That's the goal, isn't it? To give her some?"

The logic wasn't exactly sound, but it was comforting. It also covered Hana's guilt with something more palatable. Pride, maybe. She'd accomplished more in one minute using a toilet as a desk than she had in more than a month using an actual table. Now Dalia, who deserved to leave, would get to. "Farah Salih," said Hana with leery satisfaction. How long would the good feeling last? "The card will be ready tonight." She hung up, exited the bathroom, and found Dalia's old files. She shredded everything except the two-by-two photo of a woman not smiling. For the first time, Hana really looked at the picture. Just stared at it and tried to imagine what Dalia thought when the flash had blinded her. Sadness? Anger? Hope? Hana wrote the name Farah Salih on the blank yellow card and affixed the old photo with two staples. To the UNHCR, the woman known as Dalia officially ceased to exist.

2

um was the word on Friday's near riot in the yard. There was no way to control the story if word got out. Interns asking questions like "What exactly happened?" would lead to Sabah and Michael asking questions like "Why didn't you call us?" There was no telling where that would lead. Mum was also the word on whether Aos was on board with Charlie's plan now that Hana had agreed to forge the yellow card. Aos had tried all morning to deflect Charlie's entreaties, which were conveyed primarily through eye contact – *Please, help* and *I need you* – but eventually capitulated. More to protect himself than to serve his friend. Aos' myriad opinions on the Egyptian judicial system, the police, and the prison complex had been distilled into a single decree: avoid them at all costs. If that meant seeing Charlie through the mess he'd created, then so be it. The consequences of Charlie's capture were too great to ignore. Police would cast a wide net in search of coconspirators. Dalia for being the object of the plot; Hana for being the vehicle; Aos for not reporting it. Sabah and Michael, too. They weren't aware of the scheme, much less involved; but if the police could be trusted to do anything, it was to cook up false charges. Perhaps even the interns would be interrogated.

The question became how to tell Charlie that he'd capitulated without arousing suspicion in the office that something was up. A rumor mill was the last thing Aos needed. The interns were scurrying about, which precluded any kind of privacy. Sabah was also causing problems. She'd been staring at Aos' broken nose and black eyes all morning, even after he'd excused them as blows from the protests. She kept checking in and saying things like "Do you . . . want anything? Water? Tylenol? Just to talk?" To escape, Aos finally came up with the idea of inviting Charlie to lunch. He scorned the interns by saying it was a lunch meeting. The information to be discussed was beyond their pay grade. The unpaid interns seemed not to understand the joke, but nevertheless accepted its premise. Aos scorned Sabah and Michael by asking them to come discuss the budget. Sabah and Michael hated the budget with vitriol. Michael had once called it a cruel bitch. "Fine," said Aos. "Don't come." He was pleased that he'd tricked everybody. When he realized how much he'd enjoyed tricking them, he felt awful. More awful knowing his trick was meant to stave off danger they didn't even know they were in.

Aos and Charlie ate at Taboula, a Lebanese restaurant located in Garden City just past the Canadian embassy. The embassy was demarcated not by a sign but a red maple leaf emblazoned into a gray wall. They sat at a round table in the back of the restaurant, where nonsmokers were relegated, and discussed the menu before venturing on to a tougher subject. Charlie insisted on splitting dishes: "That way no one will feel food envy or regret for ordering the wrong dish." Aos didn't feel much like sharing, but felt even less keen on saying that. Knowing Charlie, he would've taken some imagined offense. When the appetizers came — a salad and a plate of labneh — Charlie said, "Please, eat." Then rotated the tabletop, which was somehow disconnected from the supporting pedestal. Aos stabbed the salad with his fork and cut a small piece of labneh before rotating the table back to Charlie, who attacked the salad and cheese without restraint.

Mum was *still* the word on the topic Aos had come to discuss, even though the menus had been taken away. Aos found it surprisingly difficult to say, *I've capitulated. I'm willing to help.* Maybe because Charlie wasn't astute enough to infer why. Aos would have to tell him: *If your ship sinks, I sink with it! Not because I want to! Because you tied me to the side of your boat!* Deep water appeared in Aos' mind. At the bottom, in the silt, lay a police van. *If you're caught—and let's be honest, you're useless without me; utterly sloppy and impatient—we're both going to jail. Not that we'll suffer the same! You, the American, will get a beating; but I'll disappear after a long, inhuman imprisonment.* What Egyptian didn't know the stories? Thirty inmates crammed into a five-by-five-meter cell. A single en suite toilet that wasn't private and rarely worked, so that inmates came to accept their foul as an immutable companion. Daily beatings with electrical wires. Daily mocking, which must've been even worse. It was said that inmates were hung naked from their shoulders in a room. Guards came to laugh, point, jostle. More evil was the Manwar, a place in the infamous Tora prison where inmates were stripped and sexually assaulted with pipes and hoses. Broken bones and anal fissures killed some men and injured the rest in ways that could never heal. The crimes had been recorded in letters; the letters had been smuggled out of Tora and prisons like it for years.

It was much easier to get mad at Charlie than stay mad long enough to administer a tongue-lashing. It was in Aos' nature to excuse the errant behavior of his friends. The more he cared, the harder he tried to excuse them. Didn't Charlie want to save the woman he loved? Not to see that love returned, but to send his love away? That she might be happy? Aos' desire to forgive wasn't exactly altruistic; he just found it easier than holding a grudge. To brood on others' faults, to hope for and perhaps even expect others to change—not only was it exhausting, but it generated bitterness. Wasn't it better to let things go? The strategy wasn't foolproof. Certain people were beyond forgiving: Mubarak and his cronies, for the despair they'd wrought in Egypt and in the lives of Egyptians abroad who'd left and hoped one day to come back; and the disturbed musician who'd shot his father. Aos knew he'd bear those grudges for life.

Just as Aos was about to say he'd capitulated, loud arguing erupted on the other side of the restaurant. A headwaiter quarreled with a smoking patron who wanted more coals glowing hot red for his shisha. It was an absurd request. The hot coals were already piled high. Any more coals would've rolled off, fallen on the carpet, and started a fire.

"What are they arguing about?" asked Charlie, enthralled by the fracas.

"Never mind." Aos hated translating nonessential conversations. If Charlie wanted to know so badly, he should've spent more time learning Arabic and less time complaining about the emphatic consonants. "It's not important. What is important, and I pray you hear what I'm saying, now that I've decided to say it, is this: I know someone who can make Dalia sick on paper using whatever name you provide. The doctor isn't an insidious connection. He's an acquaintance—just barely an acquaintance—who reached out a few days ago for help I couldn't offer. He begged a hundred thousand Egyptian pounds. Not a fortune to those who have one, but a fortune to those who don't. You, better than anyone, know my salary. I will give you his name and the name of the hospital where he works under two conditions. First, you pay what he asks. He has a good reason for the whole sum. Second, never again do you put your friends, your employees, the office, and *our* work in such jeopardy. This is a onetime offer. Next time I call the police." Aos knew he'd never call the police, but Charlie didn't necessarily know that. God willing, the threat would never be tested.

"Fine," said Charlie as if he would've accepted any terms Aos had proffered. Charlie bowed his head slightly. He didn't look ashamed; more grief stricken. It made sense. Dalia had never been so close to leaving Egypt.

The rest of their food arrived by hand of a young waiter. Perhaps the headwaiter's son. Some kofta on a stick and lamb cubed in yogurt. The young waiter brought water with no ice. He brought juice with a layer of foam bubbling and pulp bobbing on top. The juice was warm because it had just been squeezed from oranges that had, until then, been resting on the counter. Aos had seen the young waiter pluck the oranges from the bowl as if they'd grown there. The young waiter was quiet and distracted after placing the food and the drinks. He didn't leave the vicinity of their table; indeed, he leaned against one of the empty chairs. The young waiter watched the headwaiter carry hot coals toward the smoking patron. The young waiter's shoulders slumped. Had the headwaiter really acquiesced? Aos' heart sank to witness reason's failing: the headwaiter stacking hot coals on top of hot coals. Only his delicate and ingenious positioning saved the tower from collapse.

After agreeing to Aos' terms, Charlie received in return Naguib's name and place of employment. Hallacare, in Shubra. A neighborhood still east of the Nile but north of downtown and therefore beyond walking. The next day Aos and Charlie "went to lunch" again. "The budget is smaller than we thought," Aos said to Michael and Sabah. "We have a lot more to discuss. Come if you want to help stretch the money." Michael and Sabah impolitely declined. They said they were lawyers, not accountants. Aos felt guilty for tricking them again. It was too easy. "Okay," said Aos. "There's tea on the stove for the clients. Just turn on the burner when you need it. It's already prepared. The tea helps the clients relax, which helps the interns conduct their interviews. Please don't forget how much the tea means. Also, Sabah! Don't forget to sit in on the interviews. The interns are crap at Arabic. I mean, they try hard. But you know. They're crap." Then Aos and Charlie taxied to Shubra. A short call the night before to Naguib's office had set the time. God willing, noon. Or thereabouts. Not because Naguib was willy-nilly about when to meet. It was hard to say on account of the deluge of patients always descending upon him. When Aos and Charlie arrived at Hallacare, Aos led the march toward the door. He was drawn by his own anxiousness. He could see his anxious face in the glass. The nearer he got, the more anxious he appeared. Aos tried to relax by not looking at his warped reflection. The glass on the door wasn't perfectly flat. He looked unlike himself in such a way that he couldn't identify the difference except to say there was one. What a relief to finally reach the door and open it. In the waiting room patients coughed, sneezed, and slept while sitting up. A girl played a game by herself on the floor with a plastic ball. The game was to drop the ball and see if she could catch it before it hit the floor. Every time the ball fell, it made a rapping sound. Rap, rap.

"Does your friend know we're here?" asked Charlie. "Should we ask for him? Or should we sit down and just hope he notices?"

Aos thought *friend* was the wrong word. *Acquaintance* was also the wrong word, though he'd used it the day before at lunch. Even *stranger* didn't seem right. What to call a man he barely knew, didn't trust, and yet pitied? "That's him." Aos gestured with his head to a man in a lab coat by the reception desk. Either time had been cruel to Naguib or he'd mistreated his body. His gut, his hairline, his very alertness — the compulsive way he chewed his lip while scrutinizing the waiting room — indicated a man who'd die young. Stress, depression, heart disease. He acknowledged Aos without waving or even making eye contact. There was just some sense that they'd seen each other. When Naguib called the name of his patient, an older woman stood up. He motioned for her to follow him through the swinging doors. Time passed slowly because Aos and Charlie had to stand. There were no empty chairs, except the one vacated by the older woman. Aos didn't want to sit there in case she came back. Meanwhile, the girl on the floor failed to catch her ball about a thousand times. Rap, rap. Rap, rap.

"So, about Naguib," said Charlie after what couldn't have been more than two minutes.

"What about him?"

"Is he amenable? Like, a good guy? A reasonable person?"

"I don't know how to answer that."

"Does he . . . negotiate?"

The word *negotiate* licked Aos like a whip. Had Charlie agreed to terms he could not or would choose not to meet? "You said you'd pay the whole sum! You said – "

"I said what you made me say!" whispered Charlie, though he tried to yell at the same time – a sort of hissing sound. "Really, it amazes me that you think my salary is bigger than yours." Charlie looked at his watch; he'd finally found it. It was old, but nice. Possibly valuable. A gift, Aos remembered, from his mother. "I can come up with *something*. I just can't come up with *that*."

It had never occurred to Aos that Charlie would spend the budget in such a way, without giving preference to himself. Charlie worked harder and longer than anyone else and bore the weight of being the lawyer clients knew and thus contacted in the middle of the night begging for things beyond reach. A passport. A stamp. A plane ticket. A place to live. Even money to pay for medicine, food, and fines from the police. Had those burdens really gone uncompensated for so many years?

"Oh, God," said Aos. The budget must've been even smaller than he'd imagined. He'd imagined the budget as the hole a pin leaves in the cloth it pierces. "I don't know whether he'll negotiate. Like I said. He's not my friend."

Charlie started chewing his nails. He chewed his nails until the old woman who'd gone through the swinging doors came out again. She looked even sicker than before. Sick of not knowing her fate. Sick of waiting. She pushed open the doors with all her grief. The doors swung open, shut, and open the other way. Each oscillation brought a waning view down the hall behind the doors. Aos saw Naguib seeing him. Their faces contained opposite apologies. One for what had passed between them; the other for what was about to pass.

"Let's go," said Aos. He reached the doors even before they finished oscillating. Walking through delayed their rest. How to greet Naguib now that he was standing before him? Fondly? How fondly? Aos considered a handshake. He considered a plain verbal greeting, with and without a smile. He considered a kiss on the cheek. Though a kiss implied a certain level of friendliness they decidedly lacked. Aos settled on the plain verbal greeting. Not with a smile, but neither without one. The greeting was said and returned equally. As-salamu alaikum; wa alaikum al-salaam. A few awkward seconds floundered by. Aos glanced at the floor tiles. The tiles appeared dirty but Aos could tell they weren't. The rubber soles of his shoes stuck nicely to what remained of the wax.

"Please, my office." Naguib pointed to the end of the hall. He rubbed his neck as if money were lost in the knots.

Naguib's office used to be something else. Some kind of storage room, probably. There were no windows. He took a chair and lit a cigarette before offering Charlie and Aos the same raw comfort. "Shukran," said Aos. The conversation, conducted in Arabic, was stiff and obligatory. Family, worries, work. Even politics. Naguib asked Aos if he'd heard about the police station. Yes, he'd heard. The station burned yesterday. What about the boy who died under the water truck? No, Aos hadn't heard. Naguib was sorry to tell him. Soon after the burning, the army ran over a boy standing near the edge of the crowd. Not the whole army, but a uniformed man in a water truck. The boy spread across the sidewalk like warm butter. Was it an accident? Was it a message? *Your children are not safe!* Naguib said there would be a march tomorrow to honor the boy. He wanted to attend, but wasn't able to. He would be stuck at work trying to climb an imaginary ladder leading to an imaginary place where he earned more money.

"Medical documents," said Charlie out of the blue. He was clearly annoyed by his exclusion from what had become a long conversation. That conversation swerved faster than the army's water truck. "That's why I'm here. I don't want to talk. I don't even want to smoke." He threw the cigarette Naguib had given him, which had never been lit, into the trash. Charlie had never been much of a smoker. He'd always called it a suicidal tendency and didn't think of himself as quite that depressed.

Naguib snuffed his cigarette so completely that the butt flattened in the ashtray. He looked absolutely ready to discuss. "You know how much I need?" asked Naguib in English. "Aos told you?"

Charlie declared his salary a crime against – well, something. Apparently he couldn't find the right word. The point was that Charlie had worked many years for next to nothing. Not even his own benefit. "I'm not a rich man. I work for no pay. I guess some pay, but so little it's invisible to the naked eye. You need a microscope to see my paycheck."

"A poor lawyer sitting in the office of a poor doctor," said Naguib. "In a different life, I might find that funny." Naguib tilted his computer monitor to better see the screen. The monitor was a hulking, microwave-size box that appeared to have time-traveled from the last century. Every time he tilted it one way, it fell back. Aos couldn't watch the futile adjustments for fear of seeing the screen. What if Naguib was running Windows 98? What if Aos laughed? The way he'd laughed that day on the phone? The day Naguib had unexpectedly called and asked for one hundred thousand Egyptian pounds. It wasn't funny so much as uncomfortably ludicrous.

"Is that Geb?" Aos pointed to a frame on the desk. It contained the picture of a healthy boy that had, like the computer, time-traveled. Not sick yet. Waving at the camera. Making a face. Aos imagined a second picture hidden behind the first. That picture was Geb on a gray table with his body cut open under a white light.

Naguib turned the frame away from his visitors. He asked for a hundred thousand Egyptian pounds. He said he wasn't a selfish man. He needed the money.

"I can't afford that." Charlie started chewing his nails again. "That's what I'm trying to tell you. Please, be reasonable. Do I look rich? Am I dressed well?"

Naguib glanced at Charlie's watch, which put an indignant look on both their faces. Aos feared they were nearing an impasse. Pride would get in the way. If not pride, then Charlie's tunnel vision. He saw only Dalia. What if Naguib were infected by the same narrowness and saw only Geb? Each man's plight would be subordinated to the other's. At that point there could be no terms both men would accept.

"Give a number," said Aos. "Someone give a number."

Charlie and Naguib engaged in a staring contest. Who could appear more in control of his fate? While they were doing that, Aos finally stole a look at the computer monitor. He couldn't resist the draw of knowing the truth. His worry was confirmed by the teal desktop and gray taskbar – Windows 98, still in use after all these years. The truth brought the awful feeling that nothing was destined to change.

"A number!" shouted Aos. His shouting was implied by his tone, not declared by his volume. Anyone could be listening. Aos was ever conscious of that.

Charlie scoffed at the prodding, but eventually bit his lip. A good sign. Aos knew Charlie only bit his lip when he was doing math. How much he had minus how much he needed to survive, arriving at what he could spare. The math was made easier for a man who needed little and wanted nothing except Dalia. He would never satiate that want, so would excise it from his life. Right now. This was it. "Fifty thousand." Charlie repeated the modest sum as if it contained his life's work and he was surprised, in a bad way, by its smallness. The words just leaked out of his mouth.

Naguib sat up in his chair, excited if not exactly impressed. "Aos told me you have a client that needs to appear sick beyond treatment in Egypt. Tell me exactly what you need. Hurry up. Please, I have patients waiting. If they wait for too long, my boss will ask why."

Aos exhaled his relief only to discover in its wake a pressing question. Why was Naguib so pleased by the modest sum? The number itself indicated less than the currency in which it was paid. Less still than the conversion rate into whatever currency Naguib needed. Dollars? Euros? Pounds sterling? Fifty thousands was not a lot, all things considered. The answer to Aos' question presented itself in the way Naguib wrung his hands and gripped the picture of his son.

It wasn't really money that he wanted. Just hope enough to believe, despite the evidence, that Geb could live.

"I need to prove this woman is terminal." Charlie slid a Post-it with Dalia's fake name and associated information across the desk. "I need lab tests, X-rays, and an examination report. I need certified copies with your signature on the bottom. If the UNHCR calls to verify the authenticity of the documents, I need you to verify. It's easy work. So easy it should cost — well, much less."

"I see." Naguib lit another cigarette and inhaled wildly. "Aplastic anemia," he said to himself. Then to Charlie: "It's a blood disorder. The symptoms aren't visible to the untrained eye, except in later stages. Then only if you're paying attention. The patient gets very pale. They develop arrhythmia. The gums bleed. We had a fatal case last year. I can switch the names and dates and reprint everything but the death record." Naguib paused to look at the name on the Post-it.

"Aplastic anemia," said Charlie. The words seemed to please him. It was as if they'd changed meaning inside his head. They didn't connote disease, death, or mourning; they declared that Dalia would leave Egypt. God willing, before Omran showed up and ruined everything. "How long will this take? Not long, I hope. I'm a little tight on — "

"I have your number." Naguib stood as if now was a good time for Charlie and Aos to get out, and they did so with the promise that the good doctor would call soon.

3

"Hello?" said Omran.

The buzz of the line gave way to a voice. The background noise — typical garage sounds such as the radio, the hydraulic car lifts, and the invariably disgruntled customer arguing that something was wrong with his bill — faded away. Some function had developed in Omran's brain that parsed sounds. He heard only what he needed to hear. Right now he needed to hear Dalia.

"Call me back," she said.

Why was the call to Egypt cheaper than the call from there? They both hung up. Then Omran dialed a toll-free number followed by the PIN on the back of his phone card followed by the country code followed by Dalia's mobile number. His fingers had memorized everything except the PIN, which changed constantly. Every time he bought a new card. He'd tried buying cards of higher value to avoid the abundance of change, but quickly learned to hate spending $50 on a single piece of flimsy plastic. It was somehow easier to spend $10 bills on five separate cards. Hence his trouble remembering the PIN. Finally, the buzz of the line gave way to a voice.

"Hello? Omran?"

"Yes, I'm here. Can you hear me?"

Omran said, "Hello?" and Dalia said, "Hello?" at the same time. They laughed at the delay in order to not let it break them.

"Any news on the revolution?" he asked. "Were you safe today?"

Omran let Dalia report her version of occurrences without contradicting her, despite what he'd seen or read in the news. Her lies flowed over him like calm water: "The same old fight."

"No protests?"

"On my side of the Nile? In Imbaba? Where there are no government buildings? No, I think the protesters will, God willing, stay on the other side of the river."

"God willing." Omran fiddled with the TV remote. First, power. Then, mute.

"Today was a strange day."

"For me, too." Omran couldn't turn away from the TV. He waited impatiently for Egypt to appear. Heads were currently jabbering about the stock market. Down forty points! No, forty-two points! No, forty-four! Omran had come to accept that catastrophe was always imminent in America.

"You go first."

"Nice try."

Missing her felt like pinpricks. Not the good kind resulting from a lover's touch; the uncomfortable kind resulting from paresthesia, the feeling one gets when awkward positioning inhibits blood from reaching the nerve fibers. It felt as if Omran's entire body had fallen asleep.

"I needed vegetables, so I walked to the corner store," said Dalia. "On the sidewalk I found picture frames. The perfect size and very nice wood. The glass panels were gone, but who needs glass panels? They were lighter and easier to carry without them. I replaced the old frames, which were scratched up. Then I stepped back and looked at the wall. I felt like I was in a museum. Our old life was long gone, a historical artifact. You know that feeling? In a museum? When you can't touch anything?"

"Yes," said Omran. "I know."

"You felt even farther away in the nicer frames. I had to put the scratched frames back up."

The background noise reappeared when Dalia stopped talking. Faisal was still smooth-talking the customer out of his irate state. There was no saying why the customer was so upset. His car ran flawlessly. There wasn't, as it turned out, anything wrong with the bill. Maybe Faisal had forgotten to hang an air freshener from the mirror or hadn't put the driver's seat in its original position after sliding it all the way back. Faisal had freakishly long legs. His nickname in Rafah had been Spider.

"Today my papers came," said Omran. "I paid for rushed service. Not a frivolous expense, if you ask me. You'll like the passport photo. I look like a movie star." Bewildered. Depressed. As if the flash had accessed the dark pit where Omran stored his fears. Most of those fears were questions he couldn't ask Dalia about what their life might look like or how their love might feel. He called these questions his "wonderings" and sought to banish them lest they reach his mouth. They revealed a man's split heart. Two roads, as it were, in a wood. Omran despised the part of himself that wanted to stay in Boston. The part that wanted to send money until such time as Dalia could come to America through other means. The part that would wait five years or ten years for a chance in hell that they would be reunited in the United States. That part, like cancer, had grown; the longer Omran stayed in America, the easier it became. "I need to see you," he said. "The sooner, the better. No more than a few days. I just have to buy my ticket." The truth was, with Faisal's help, he'd already purchased it. God said all Muslims were brothers; the money wasn't a loan, but a gift.

"I told you before! Don't come. It's not safe. There's nothing here for us."

The old fight sped like a drunk driver toward Omran. He saw it coming and craved the sound it would make. He craved the fight the same way he craved Dalia. He would see her again, no matter what. Even without her approval. Even if she never forgave him.

Even if she never spoke to him again. He would speak to her. He would speak to her until she told him to shut up. Her silence would be broken that way.

"I will come," said Omran. "There's no choice." His words assumed other meanings. That he wouldn't leave his wife to suffer alone. Not anymore. He was ashamed of leaving her. He was ashamed of waiting so long to come back. Any additional shame would instantly crush Omran to death. How useful was a flat, dead husband five thousand miles away?

Dalia seemed to decode at least some of that. "None of this is your fault. If anything, I'm the one who's to blame. I said we shouldn't leave Baghdad until I finished school. Then after I finished school, I still didn't want to leave. Remember? The years just sort of passed. And the war started." Omran tried to interrupt, but Dalia talked over him. "Nevertheless! You seem not to understand what I'm saying. I love you, but don't come."

"I must," whispered Omran.

Dalia heard the whisper and, as a result, made several threats. She threatened to leave Omran at the airport until he returned to Boston; if he refused, and somehow made it of his own accord to her apartment, then she'd just bolt her door.

Omran said he'd kick the door open, if necessary. "Do you have hinges for the repair?" he asked. "Or shall I bring hinges?" Another man saying that could only be telling a joke. Not Omran the builder, the digger, the paver, the oil-changer, the all-stuff-can-be-repaired man who tinkered with old things until they were new again.

Closing time wasn't marked by a bell or even a clock, but by the moment the last customer's oddly pungent body odor had dissipated. Omran's last day of work was officially in the books. His last pay, too, was in his pocket. It felt like the wrong pocket. The only remedy was a quick trip to the Western Union. "I'm going to the store," he told

Faisal, donning both his coat and his hat. "I'll come back to collect my things and . . . to say good-bye."

Faisal was set to leave in the morning on a weeklong vacation with Salman and his family; Omran was set to fly in a tin can over the cold ocean before the week's end. They'd not discussed what that meant. It was easier to just let it happen.

"God willing," said Faisal. "Hurry back. I'll make tea and warm milk on the . . ." He pointed to a portable stove, a relic purchased at a garage sale for, he claimed, $1. He said he'd sooner risk blowing up the garage than heat milk in the microwave.

Omran pushed open the door. Then he followed wet black trees and wet gray pavement for more than a mile only to discover the Western Union he patronized every week—reluctantly, for the clerk always had a crude remark prepared—had closed. Why had it closed so early? The Western Union was just a window embedded in the back wall of a corner store. Omran put his hands through the metal bars and tried to slide open the locked window. "What the . . . ?" he asked the glass, the bars. He shook the bars with all his strength. The employee tending the register on the other side of the store asked him to stop shaking. Not that it was her business. The Western Union was technically an independent establishment.

"You're making me nervous," said the employee, slouching in a tall chair behind the register. Scrambled hair sat in complete disarray on her head. "Don't even think about it!" she said when Omran reached for the bars again. "Shit's closed. I told you."

"I have money to send. Right now, I have money. My wife—" Sending money was his only respite from the shame of leaving her. That brief moment when he got to write Dalia's name on the form and slide the paper through the depression in the counter, under the window, into the hands of the clerk. Who cared what the clerk said about where the money was going or what the money was for?

"Do I have to call the police?" asked the employee of the corner store. "I have no problem calling them. You'd be surprised how many times I've called them before."

Omran wanted to tell the employee to go ahead. Call the police. Report the true crime, that Dalia was trapped in Cairo. Ask the police to do their job. Ask them to prevent the tragedy.

"If you're not going to leave, then I'm going to have to . . ." The employee put her hand on the phone.

Omran's gesture — arms out, palms up — asked why. "Please, let me wait here until the clerk comes back. The clerk has to come back. It's still early. The sign says the Western Union is open for another . . ." He turned to read the sign, but didn't have time; a faint but frightening dial tone indicated the employee had picked up the phone.

"I'm calling the police in ten seconds if you're still here."

Perhaps Omran had been rash to imagine a life where armed men didn't appear randomly. He hurried out before the employee could threaten to call them a third and probably final time. The bell on the door planted a seed of heartache in his chest. Ring, ring. The only thing to stop that seed from growing wildly was the cold slap of the night's air. The outdoors, if not the great outdoors — absent was the solitude, the smell of pine — still reminded Omran of the American poets he'd been reading to acquaint himself with the spirit of their country. When he closed his eyes, he saw Robert Frost. The specter said, "The woods are lovely, dark and deep, / But I have promises to keep, / And miles to go before I sleep." Frost was decidedly less ecstatic than Rumi or Hafez, but considerably more determined. Omran feared he lacked that quality and thus had to borrow it from the poem. He recited the lines again in his head. Then Omran set off in search of another Western Union. He couldn't walk fast enough. Nor could he run. Not with his leg in such sorry condition. His eye socket was even sorrier; it still ached in the bone and felt odd in the shower, as if hot water seeped into his head. Omran tried not to blame his body for failing to become whole again. Now wasn't really the time. Not with cash stuffed in his pocket that he needed to send. The money was life, safety, and rest; in a way, it was even an advance on his apology. I'm sorry for leaving you. I'm sorry for taking so long to come back.

Omran had dreamed of his reunion with Dalia so many times it felt destined to pass as he'd imagined it. Dalia would shout or look at him in a painful way when he finally arrived in Cairo. It would be hard to maintain eye contact. The urge to hide the breadth of his scar by turning his head slightly would be almost overpowering. Omran would try to resist. He'd say home wasn't Baghdad. Not Boston, either. Not even the city in which they now found themselves. "Home isn't a place," he'd say like no truth had ever been so evident. "Home is the feeling you get with certain people." God willing, Dalia would accept Omran's hand when he offered it. Then a long, silent car ride – hands still grasped, palms still sweating – would take them deep into the maze of the city. West on the raised road; west across the Imbaba Bridge; west still on Al Matar Street until they turned north toward the alleys. Walking into the building and up the stairs would be just as quiet. Upon reaching the apartment, Omran would collapse on the couch. Dalia, with no crippled leg to burden her, would sit more naturally on the cushion next to him. For a few seconds they wouldn't touch. Then some combination of want and need would compel them to begin undressing. Slowly, cautiously. Like time had changed more than they thought. Their bodies; their opinions of each other. The fear would make it hard to strip beyond their socks. Dalia would hold her zipper; Omran would hold his belt. The infinite moment would feel absent of matter, of light. And very cold. But Dalia, who'd always been the braver one, wouldn't let the moment persist. She'd close her eyes and finally pull her zipper. Soon their modesties would be reduced to piles of clothes on the floor. Two hearts would beat so hard you could dance to their sound. Omran and Dalia would dance, in their own way, with their hands and later their lips.

The wet black trees lining the street weren't like the trees Frost must've looked upon in the forest. They weren't so old or nearly so many. Still, a tree was a tree; joy was to be had in its presence. The April snow was supposed to be an anomaly, but somehow it felt right; Omran knocked the powder off branches that were low enough to whack with his hat. There, finally! A Western Union. The yellow letters appeared above a lit window. "Thank God," said Omran. "May your kindness last a while longer." He blew hot breath on his hands and rubbed them together vigorously. Then God's kindness did last. For the time being, at least. The clerk inside didn't snicker when Omran gave him the money. He didn't even snicker when Omran read the line on the form indicating the money's destination: Cairo, Egypt. Totally unlike the clerk in the other window, whose remarks had grown sharper over time. Are you funding terrorists? Are you buying a bride? Omran's whole body felt lightened now that he'd sent the money, and without a remark to ruin his mood. "Thank you," he said to the clerk. He put his hand on the glass since it was impossible to shake the clerk's hand through the depression in the counter, which wasn't deep enough. Barely a finger would fit. "No problem," said the clerk, oblivious of the gift he'd bestowed. Even Omran's feet were affected. His stride was longer than normal as he walked back to the garage. He sped down the sidewalk at an unprecedented speed. Good fortune apparently killed pain. The unintended side effect of such hustle was that Omran arrived too soon. He wasn't ready to say good-bye to Faisal. He waited outside while his heart settled. Snow fell on his coat and his hat. The flakes reminded him of a day in January 2008: the first time in living memory that snow fell on Baghdad. Two opposite air flows had kissed in the skies above Iraq. Though snow had barely accumulated, children had played wildly in the streets. He remembered one girl, a child, who made her sled out of cardboard. She'd cried when the sled didn't fly down the flat sidewalk. It was somehow lonely to remember such a happy day. Knowing that it would never come again. To remember Dalia's warm hand on his neck before she ran out to comfort the girl. Omran had opened the window to hear what Dalia would say to her. "God willing, my sweet. Let me pull you." The girl was reluctant at first, but finally allowed it; she held on for dear life as she sailed down the block.

———————

The garage was Faisal's only solace besides Salman. It contained both his purpose on Earth and the record of his life so far. That record was mounted above the workbench and ran the width of the garage: antique license plates, old photographs, and bobbleheads collected on a road trip he'd taken with Salman to see each of the world's largest roadside attractions on the Eastern Seaboard. Their first stop had been the world's largest clam box in Ipswich, Massachusetts. There were postcards from other places Faisal had been, with and without his son; he'd posted these cards to himself. More postcards were from places Salman had traveled by himself or, more recently, with his wife. These cards were a record in and of themselves: the story of his son growing up.

When Omran pushed open the side door, Faisal poured two cups of hot tea. "Finally. You're back. An old man was growing impatient." He put the two cups on the break table. "Come sit. Please, hurry. Before the milk is cold and the tea is lukewarm. Who wants to drink warm tea?"

Omran shook free the snow lodged in the brim of his hat. He watched the snow finish its descent to the ground, where it melted.

"Stop! Come, sit."

"Stop what?" asked Omran.

"That. What you're doing. Come, sit."

"What am I doing? I'm shaking snow off my hat."

"You're bowing down to the grief. I know you are. I'm old. I can see everything."

"I thought you said you were very young." Every conversation they'd had on the nature of time passing unspooled in Omran's memory. Faisal arguing that people were the age of their behavior. Faisal arguing that people were the age of their heart. Faisal arguing that he was, according to those rules, between nineteen and twenty.

"Of mind, yes; of body, no. Just look at me." Faisal slapped his gut like a bongo. "If I died now, my son would say I lived a good life. His mourning would be short. The way it should be, I think. Remember what my mother used to say: 'Never miss the dead. You will see them again soon enough.' She invented the saying after her sister, a mourning widow whose husband had just died, drowned by chance in the sea. I can see how my mother would've been awash with grief forever if not for the lesson she'd learned from the sequence of tragedies."

Omran stuffed his hat in his pocket and took his sweet time removing his coat. He knew leaving Faisal would be like excising part of his own body. That part would be lopped off when he sat down to drink tea and, after a long goading, said good-bye.

"Will you sit already? I'm going to fall asleep if you make me wait any longer."

That wouldn't be so bad, thought Omran. There were many things he wanted to say without the embarrassment of saying them. How do you tell a grown man that his friendship meant everything?

"Please," said Faisal stiffly. "Sit."

Omran finally sat and drank tea. Though he didn't drink much. He mostly just breathed the steam swirling above the mug. There was something newly discomforting about swallowing the same black tea he'd been swallowing his whole life. It implied a stability his life had lacked. Who was to blame? The Americans, who cared not for the people displaced by their wars? The Iraqi security forces, who couldn't protect their own country? The militias, under the guise of God, who committed wickedness beyond understanding? No, Omran couldn't blame the wretched powers; the powers had always been and would always be wretched. He could only blame himself for not begging Dalia to run away with him to another country when they still had the chance. He'd asked, but he'd not begged. He'd not beseeched God for help in convincing her.

"Tonight let's listen to . . ." Faisal's stiffness evaporated as he gazed at his tapes.

"Billie Holiday," said Omran. "If you don't mind."

"You love that tape."

"I've always loved it. I think even before I was born."

The tapes had been alphabetized, but sloppily; Omran had learned months ago to put Billie Holiday in a specific spot. He fetched the tape and shoved it into the stereo, thumb falling hard on the play button. Right away a woman sang about moving mountains. Her mountains, which ran with history past suffering of all kinds, made other mountains look flat. Omran heard pain in her voice when she sang about moving them.

Was this how they planned to say good-bye? Without talking? Without even looking at each other? Omran hoped so. It would be easier, if less satisfying. He would let the tape speak on his behalf. The lines he wanted Faisal to hear were jammed between lines about a woman loving a man, or losing a man, or leaving a man and thus being rid of him. And lines such as "I get no kick from champagne." It was an impossible exercise in selective listening and interpretation, but Omran thought Faisal was up to the task. By the time the tape ended, Faisal would know he was loved and would travel with Omran to Egypt as a memory. Faisal would know that memory would be kept safe by being told often as a story. Omran would tell Dalia about the garage, the bobbleheads, the tape collection, even the snobbish customers. He'd tell her about Salman and the wife Faisal had never been able to name. "I think he loves her now even more than before," Omran would say. "I can't imagine how much that must hurt. Wishing his love had gone with her body, so that it would stop tormenting him." Omran would tell Dalia every detail he'd not told her over the phone. The long calls would've cost too much. He'd tell her in bed at night when they were kept awake by their worries. Faisal's modest but nevertheless mirthful ending would present a life they could look forward to.

Things didn't go according to that admittedly far-fetched plan. By the end of the tape, Faisal had fallen asleep. Thus he couldn't have an epiphany about what the tape had meant. He looked dead with his mouth open. "You are an old man, after all," said Omran. "I knew you were." Omran had been taught to let his elders sleep, and so grabbed a pen and paper with the idea that he'd write a short note conveying what his mouth would've blundered. The note spiraled in length over several pages. When the note was finished more than an hour later, Omran rubbed his palms dry on his pants. "I didn't want to wake you," he said to the unconscious flop in the chair. Omran rolled closer and placed his folded note in Faisal's shirt pocket, with the corner sticking out so Faisal would notice it. Then Omran sat there for a few agonizing minutes trying to muster the courage to leave.

4

Why had Charlie agreed to pay Naguib a sum he couldn't afford? The question, to Charlie, was rhetorical; he knew damn well that Naguib wouldn't have accepted less. Charlie was lucky to get the number down as far as he did. Still, he didn't have fifty thousand Egyptian pounds the same way he didn't have a hundred thousand. Even after consolidating his bank accounts – he'd left some money in America, but not much; plus two accounts he'd opened in Egypt, one ostensibly for retirement – he'd come up with a little more than twenty thousand. Would Naguib snub the number and, to seek vengeance, destroy the documents? The image of him shredding paper appeared in Charlie's nightmares three nights in a row. He told himself these were just stress dreams and not bad omens. His plan, he thought, would work: at the time and place of exchange, Charlie would offer his pittance along with a regrettable but logically sound argument. Wasn't it better to have some money than none? It wasn't an ideal way to conduct business, but it wasn't as if Charlie had much of a choice. He didn't have the money and couldn't get the money without stealing it from the Refugee Relief Project. In a drunken fit one night he told himself that wasn't such a bad idea. *Steal the money from the budget. Pay it back later. Or don't pay it back. It doesn't matter. The money is wasted. The endeavor is vain. The* appeal of such wickedness lasted only as long as Charlie's bender. He woke up with a different opinion. The endeavor was still vain, but the budget was not wasted. It kept the office open and that kept his clients alive. How could they live without hope?

The pain of waiting for Naguib to call was compounded by the frustration of being unable to reach Omran. Charlie had tried phoning him about a thousand times from the relative privacy of the office kitchen. He left furtive messages such as "When we last talked, you said you were coming and I said you ought not to, as there were a few plans in the works; those plans are coming to fruition and, well . . . call me back, please. As soon as you get this. It's urgent. You know my number. Just in case, it's . . ." Followed by twelve digits. "That's . . ." Followed by the same twelve digits. As of yet, Charlie hadn't heard back.

To make the intolerable situation even worse, Michael and Sabah and the interns had been throwing Charlie side-eye, or what he perceived as side-eye, for days. To avoid engaging them in anything more than a short conversation, Charlie kept his head down and his hands busy. He scribbled pointlessly on a legal pad for hours on end. He also went to "lunch" every day with Aos to "discuss the budget." The constancy of that illusive conversation made Sabah and Michael think they were getting fired. By midweek, Sabah was certain enough to ask Charlie if there was a severance package. Her voice said she didn't want to ask, but needed to. The embarrassment was symptomatic of her salary, which was symptomatic of what Charlie called "the inherent financial constraints." Or, when no interns were in earshot, "the fucking budget." The budget was symptomatic of an irrevocable backwardness in the world. Money funneled where it was needed least. No way was there a severance; no way would there ever be one. Tragedy was avoided only because Charlie wasn't firing Sabah or anyone else. "I'm not firing you," said Charlie. "Not now, not ever. I need you, Michael, and the . . ." He gestured to the younger and, in his imagination, shorter people in the room. The display only made Sabah more paranoid. What kind of boss promised never to fire you?

Hana, too, was testing Charlie's patience now that forging the yellow card had unleashed her craven side. She was worried, nigh obsessed, with the particulars of the card's delivery: exactly how to get it into Charlie's hands. "We don't know who's watching," said Hana. "The army. The embassy. The police." Charlie felt this was overly cautious, but couldn't expect Hana to feel the same way. People disappeared in Egypt all the time. Rarely foreigners, but still; he saw how that might unnerve a person. Charlie's goal was to assuage Hana's fear and thus bring a swift end to their impasse. This by suggesting inconspicuous places to meet. Places where such a handoff would be the last thing anybody cared about. "We could go back to El Horreya," said Charlie. "People there are blind drunk and generally carefree. You've been there. Nobody heard a damn thing we said. Or, if you prefer, we could meet on the corniche. People walk this way, that way, chat, shout, drink tea, catch fish. Not even sore thumbs stick out on the corniche." Charlie enjoyed having what he thought were two good ideas in a row, so was less than pleased to discover Hana was of a different mind: "You want to meet in public?" She made no effort to hide her contempt for his suggestions. "During the day?" Charlie was so vexed by her seriousness that he couldn't think up more places to meet. Much less quiet, empty places. Was there even such a thing in Cairo, a city that wouldn't be itself without its crowds? Charlie sensed that continuing their conversation as such would only test their newfangled and unproven relationship. He said he'd call back later with new ideas. Hana told him not to call back unless the new ideas were also much better. The pressure was like a vise on Charlie's head. By day's end, he was ready to put his head through the drywall. An idea only occurred to him when Aos inadvertently brought it up.

"It's getting late," said Aos. He began packing his things. Everyone else in the office had left more than an hour before. "I'm going home unless you need me. I'm hungry, exhausted, and, to be honest, a little depressed." The revolution, he said, hadn't been going well. Then again, had it ever?

What felt like an epiphany drastically improved Charlie's mood.

"That's it. Home. My home. Well, my apartment. It's quiet. More importantly, it's desolate. Almost no life means almost no witnesses. The only witness will be the blob on my couch known as Ruby." Charlie hadn't felt this good in some time. He called Hana straightaway, but kept talking to Aos while the phone rang. "My apartment really is the perfect place. I never have guests and barely have neighbors. They're recluses, I think. Hoarders, maybe. I can hear them through the walls stacking boxes of – "

The call finally connected. As Hana recited her scripted greeting, Charlie experienced a short-lived pang of guilt. Why had he interrupted his conversation with Aos? It had been so long since they'd just chatted. "Hello? Hana? Is that you?"

She answered in the irked affirmative. Hadn't she just said her name?

"I have good news," said Charlie. "I know a place we can meet. My apartment." It had sounded less debauched in his head. "Before you say no, let me explain. The apartment is impervious to the goings-on. It's a few stories above street level and on the back side of the building. The view goes absolutely nowhere."

Hana was surprisingly amenable to the idea. Still, she said she'd only agree on condition that Aos would also be there. She wanted to meet him. Charlie reminded Hana that she'd already met Aos the night of the near riot in the yard. Hana said that wasn't her point. She wanted to know him better. Was he reliable? Could he be trusted? Charlie tried vouching for Aos, but Hana told him not to bother. She preferred to make up her own mind.

"Fine." Charlie put his hand over the receiver and told Aos he couldn't leave. Not yet. Please, he was needed. Aos' face tensed slightly. Charlie grimaced at him. "Aos will be happy to come," said Charlie into the phone. He scheduled the "party" for that night at ten o'clock. "The sooner, the better," he said. "With this over, we can all get back to work." Nothing had ever made Charlie so happy as the idea that he'd be swamped again without any respite in sight.

Somehow the "party" turned into an actual party. How did the duty-free whiskey Charlie had been saving get off his bookshelf and on the table? It was too late now to correct the error. He poured three drinks: one for Hana, one for Aos, and one slightly shorter pour for himself. This was a tried-and-failed method of controlling his immoderate thirst. Shorter pours just became more glasses. "A word of warning," said Charlie. "If you drink this, you'll never want to drink anything else. Not even cold water." Aos and Hana drank freely while Charlie mourned the death of a friend: his whiskey. Eventually Hana set the yellow card on the table. She placed the card with a certain hesitation, as if it signified her final and irrevocable commitment to a plan that frightened her. Charlie stared at the card for a few seconds before touching it. A strange feeling. Not joy. Not even relief. The feeling that this should've happened much sooner. What a tragedy that it took so long and the means were so devious. Charlie thought he should give some kind of speech.

"I'm not delusional," he said. "I don't think we're changing the world. We're not even changing the system. We are doing something, though. That's important. Doing something. Not talking about doing something. Not giving money to someone else who promises to do something on our behalf. Doing something with our own hands. We used our hands, didn't we? When we get the medical documents, we'll use our hands to mail them to your office." Charlie gestured to Hana. "And, Hana, you'll use your hands to . . ." He mimed the reception of documents and also their filing. "The result is that Dalia will go to Boston and Omran will get to weep openly at the airport. Wouldn't that be funny to watch? *Funny* is probably the wrong word, but I think I would just have to laugh. To release the pressure of the moment. If I were there, I mean, to witness it." Charlie frowned, but not intentionally; his face just got tired. "I won't be there, obviously. I'll be here. Working on another case. There's always another case. I can't imagine a time when there won't be one." Charlie's life stretched before him. One day leaked into the next until he saw himself as an old man with a picture of a dead dog.

It was unclear what was supposed to happen now that the yellow card had been placed on the table and Charlie had given his speech. Would Hana remember that she'd wanted to interrogate Aos? *List three times you were especially trustworthy. . . .* Would Aos somehow fail the test in question? If that happened, would Hana take back the yellow card? Charlie slid the card nearer to him and finished his drink. Then poured a second glass, which freed Hana and Aos to do the same. In short order they were drunk enough to relax, if not to enjoy themselves. Charlie tried to savor the equanimity by making it last. He tried to make it last by not talking. He knew, though was pained to admit, how prone he was to ruining the mood. Nobody liked being bad tempered, contrary, unpleasant, and not fun. Charlie wasn't born that way, he didn't think. He'd acquired his nature from reading the news. People the world over were suffering. And the few that weren't suffering didn't give a shit.

The phone interrupted and thus stalled a party that was just becoming itself. The phone? At this hour? After the city had fallen asleep? Charlie thought at first it was Naguib and tensed up. Oh, God, he thought. I don't have your money. I don't even have *half* your money. The phone kept ringing. Hana and Aos stared each other. "Are you going to answer that?" said Aos. Charlie told himself it couldn't be Naguib. Not at this hour. It was Omran, obviously. That made more sense given the time change. Also given that Charlie had left about a thousand messages. He was propelled to his feet by the comfort of his assumption and walked at an angle to the phone. He imagined the pleasure of explaining in veiled terms that the winds of Omran's fortune had changed. He would see Dalia again soon enough. Stay put, stop packing. "Hello?" Charlie pressed the handset against his head so hard that the cartilage in his ear more or less flattened against his skull. He fell into his armchair. Years of sitting in the same spot had scuffed smooth the upholstery. Ruby, who had until that moment been a dark blob on the couch, woke up, climbed down, walked over, and sat on Charlie's feet. He loved her so much and regretted how he treated her. Not badly, of course. He remembered to feed Ruby on a mechanical level, as part of his morning routine, and pick up her shit – most in the alley, but some in hall when she was too tired to go all the way out – but the duty to keep her alive resided in his subconscious. There wasn't enough time in the day to give her the attention or tenderness she deserved. He apologized to Ruby in his head for the unfairness of it all. There was nothing whole or round about their relationship. "Hello?" said Charlie again into the phone. The tone of his voice, high at the end of his question, excited Ruby, who beat the floor with her tail. Whack, whack. Charlie told Ruby to stop. Her tail was distracting him.

"Stop what?" said the voice on the phone.

For a second Charlie thought Ruby, grouchy all of a sudden, was talking back. He was mystified and a little afraid. Would she disavow his cruelty, come in the form of neglect? Would she ask Charlie why he failed to tend to her the way an old pooch ought to be tended?

"Hello?" The voice on the phone was fevered now. "Are you there? Is this Charlie? Stop what? I haven't done anything! I only called. You told me to call when the papers were ready. They're ready. You must take them. Right now. We have to meet. Charlie? Hello, Charlie? Are you there?"

Charlie's heart beat his chest the way a hummingbird beats the air with its wings. He whispered, "Yes," with the faint hope that Naguib wouldn't hear and would, out of frustration, hang up. Then call back tomorrow. Though Charlie needed the papers, he couldn't use them that night and didn't want them right now. His mind-set was wrong. He was a little drunk. He still needed to prepare his logical argument about how two-fifths of fifty thousand was admittedly less than the agreed-upon five-fifths, but was still much more than zero fifths – the zilch Naguib would receive if the deal fell through.

"Zamalek, on the north side of the island by the water," said Naguib in a gust of wind. "No army will be there, I don't think. No protesters. The rich people send them away. There's a one-way street along the bank with cars parked on both sides. I will be there in one hour. Bring the money in a brown sealed envelope. Fifty thousand Egyptian pounds."

Charlie didn't have any envelopes in his apartment. Much less brown envelopes. Much less brown envelopes that sealed automatically. Like, without licking them? More than half the money intended to go inside the imaginary envelope was also missing. "Why don't I have any money?" Charlie screamed at himself in his head. Again, the question was rhetorical. He'd spent his money on clients who called or showed up at the office with simple pleas. Rent, food, medicine. Were the pleas not just? Were the pleas not worth everything? Charlie skimmed what he could from the budget, then skimmed more from his pay. His pay had become a fragile thing. It covered expenses only. His expenses included the whiskey he got at the airport when he faked flying in overnight on the red-eye. He'd bribed and had become acquainted with the janitor who mopped the floor by the duty-free. So was born their relationship. He paid good money for the whiskey every few weeks, after a long taxi ride in which he sometimes got dropped off in the wrong place. The taxi driver would demand more money to go to the right terminal. Of course, Charlie would pay. The money he didn't use for the ride or food or rent or whiskey or the electricity required to freeze the cubes he dropped in his glass, which he barely washed on account of thinking the glass saved the flavor, was spent on people who would always and forever need it more than him. His clients. Charlie didn't have fifty thousand Egyptian pounds the same way he didn't have all the money in the world.

"I'll be there in one hour," said Charlie. He hung the phone up as if he wanted to hammer a nail in with the handset. Then he made coffee to sober up. The sink poured water. The stove poured flames. Soon the kettle made the sound birds make as the sun rises. At last, Charlie said, "Naguib has the documents. He wants to meet. I don't have the money."

In Mustafa's taxi—Hana had insisted on using a driver she knew personally—Charlie struggled to explain to Aos why he kept making promises he couldn't keep. Lying to Naguib was, in a way, lying to Aos, who'd vouched for him. It was an egregious crime. Aos was, or had been, Charlie's true brother; the only man on the planet Charlie felt comfortable touching despite his unreasonable fear of male-on-male contact. The fear was a souvenir from his boyhood in Montana, where Charlie's gender and sexual orientation had been assailed without pause for more than a decade. Not because he was small for his age, gentle, or feminine. He'd just been an affectionate boy. He remembered holding his mother's hand. He remembered making friends in the first grade and trying to hold their hands for the same reason. He trusted them. Charlie became known as "the girl" for a few years and "the fag" after that, once puberty had increased the boys' viciousness. Whereas Egyptian men held hands, leaned against each other, and walked arm in arm chatting happily. All the while maintaining their vehement homophobia. It was confusing. It was freeing, too. Charlie and Aos didn't hold hands, but they hugged when something good happened and leaned against each other on packed trains shooting unseen beneath the city. "You know I'm not rich," said Charlie. "My salary is almost as small as yours. In a way, it's your fault for thinking I had fifty thousand." Pride surfaced as a detached look, as if he didn't care whom he hurt so long as he got what he wanted. That wasn't really what Charlie believed. It was just the message he delivered to protect himself. Had Charlie really not changed since grade school? "I'll pay what I have," he said, trying to change now for the better. He'd always wanted to be a decent man. "And the rest when I have it until the whole sum is paid. That's what I'm trying to say."

Aos said it didn't matter. "By then, Geb will be . . ."

Charlie's only solace was knowing that Naguib hadn't named what ailed his boy. Aos couldn't say how, when, or even if the boy would perish. For all Aos knew, Naguib was playing them.

"Who's Geb?" asked Hana from the front seat. The radio was too loud and the windows were rolled open. Most of what Charlie and Aos said had been sucked out of the car.

"What?" said Charlie. Not because he didn't hear, but because he wouldn't say. Why burden Hana by telling her?

"Geb!"

Charlie mumbled something under his breath.

"What?" Hana said.

"A boy!" shouted Charlie.

Hana didn't press for more information. She must've intuited the fruitlessness of her endeavor and decided to quit. Charlie admired the ease with which she let go. Letting go required forward thinking, something Charlie had always lacked; he couldn't see even ten seconds into the future. Or maybe he was just too afraid to look. That cowardice warped time and resulted in Charlie's blind spot for consequences. Whereas Hana obviously saw consequences from far away. If she learned who Geb was, she'd feel responsible for what happened. It was better not to know.

Mustafa drove to the eastern shore of Zamalek, the river island that split the Nile and marked the center of the city's richness. What little richness remained congregated in those tree-lined streets north of the Gezira Club. The rest of Egypt's money had left the country or at least the capital, choosing instead the gated communities on the outskirts of Cairo, where the urban rabble could be kept at bay and where the revolution ceased to be more than an impolite conversation. Trees blurred together as Mustafa annihilated the gas pedal. City lights glared as they flew by and looked like stars shooting through the car window. Those counterfeit stars bounced off the river and were yellow, green, and red. They bounced home to the night sky, which blushed with their color.

5

Aos avoided Zamalek for economic reasons. The restaurants inflated prices for poor views of the river. Still, he knew every street on the island by heart. His youth had been spent wandering there and other neighborhoods within walking distance of Dokki. With no brothers or sisters to distract him, the city had been his best friend and only companion after his father died. He spent many afternoons in Zamalek trying to sneak into the Gezira Club to feed the horses. Approaching the club from every angle had taught Aos the name of every street. Mustafa stopped on the narrow Kamal Al Taweel, named after the famed composer and member of Parliament. Aos thought using fame to win office was better than nepotism; at least fame came from the people. Directly to the south, the Hungarian embassy sat fat on a corner. Directly to the north, the overpriced Sequoia. A strange name for a Mediterranean restaurant. The tablecloths were stiff and bleached so white they blinded patrons. An appetizer cost ten times a plate of koshari from a food cart. Aos had gone once to scorn the food only to discover it was pretty good. It had been a troubling experience.

"Here we are," said Mustafa, bringing the car to a halt. Hana asked him to wait. She promised it wouldn't take long. Somewhere between two and twenty minutes. "Very good," said Mustafa. "Call or walk up the street when you're done." He said he'd be listening to a song or sleeping with his seat reclined. "Do not worry if the car looks empty. It is not empty. I have not gone. I will only be hidden like this." He used his hand to show that he'd be horizontal and thus obscured from view. If he wasn't sleeping, he'd be talking on the phone with his wife. More likely, his daughter. His daughter, who had the bad habit of staying up too late, had been teaching him English vocabulary she'd been learning in school. Lots of words and phrases starting with *b*, as they'd just embarked on the long journey through the alphabet. *Beguile, behemoth, beholden. Betwixt* and *between. Beehive. Bouncy balls.* "She's so smart I can't understand where she came from," said Mustafa proudly. "Another man? Another planet?" He peered out the window at the smog. The smog imprisoned every celestial light. "Hm," said Mustafa when he was finished gawking. He gestured up the street with his head. "I will park over there for your privacy. Shout if you want, I still won't hear you." He released Hana, Charlie, and Aos onto the sidewalk by smiling in the mirror at each of them. "See you soon." When they were safely on the sidewalk, Mustafa pulverized the gas pedal. The air smelled like rotten eggs and burning plastic. The stink revealed Mustafa's speed. He was gone before his passengers could thank him.

The streets of Zamalek were darker than downtown. People who could afford to live there needed their sleep. Aos had goose bumps, like one gets from a stiff wind in cold weather. There was no wind except the heavy breathing of people who demonstrated the physical symptoms of fear: hearts in a horse race against each other, beating faster the longer it took for Naguib to show himself. Fear of failure. Fear the documents wouldn't materialize. Fear the names wouldn't match, the copies would look tampered with, or Naguib, realizing there was no money, or not the sum he was promised, would release the documents into the river like fish.

"Salaam," said Naguib from the shadows. He called their attention by rapping his leather folio against the bench on which he sat. His presence might've startled them had the folio not been so slim and his voice so languid; as it was, Naguib was more strange than scary—an abstruse man who'd arrived early to sit by himself in the dark. He rose with some trouble and tottered when he finally stood up. He leaned against a parked car to steady himself. Either Naguib didn't know or didn't care how that made him look. Weak, tired. Possibly drunk. He tucked the folio under his arm as if that were his only concern. Protecting it was protecting Geb. The good doctor approached with foreboding: gazing down the road, up at the windows, out at the river. He eyed Hana for a time, but didn't impugn her presence. He wasn't in a position to remonstrate. Naguib stopped a little more than arm's length away. He said fifty thousand Egyptian pounds was God's apology for His error in judgment; Geb ought not to be sick. "The brown envelope goes here," said Naguib, extending his hand.

Aos found it odd that Naguib wanted the money presented so specifically. Odder still that Naguib couldn't see the regret displayed plainly on Charlie's face. Anybody with eyes could see there wasn't money.

"There's no money," said Charlie. "I mean, less than you're expecting. Two-fifths, to be exact. Twenty thousand." He showed the notes, which weren't stuffed in a brown envelope; the best he could do was a bag. Not just any bag, though. A brown paper bag. Hopefully that would suffice. "So you know, I intend to pay. The rest, I mean. When I have it. Please, I'm not a rich man. I will pay more when I can. Soon, I promise you."

Naguib's face evolved before them. Confusion. Anger. Finally, he wore the look of a cornered animal. "Soon Geb will be dead." He tightened his grip on the folio. Aos couldn't help but think back to their meeting at the hospital: Naguib clutching the picture frame with the same yearning to keep hold.

A penitent Charlie stared at his shoes while a distraught Naguib stared ambiguously into the air, giving him a glazed look. "Ahem," said Hana after the autonomous staring contests had gone on for too long. Their eyes, called her way, fell harshly; apparently Charlie and Naguib loathed to be interrupted even when they weren't doing anything. "About those papers," said Hana, gesturing to the folio. "Is twenty enough or isn't it?"

Naguib scowled. "Are you sure you don't have fifty thousand?"

Aos had observed this phenomenon before. People asking questions to which they already had answers, often more than once. Clients were especially prone to such behavior. My case has been rejected? Are you sure? Are you *certain*? The coping mechanism had practical implications. It increased by a few seconds the time a person had to absorb the pain of the truth. More time would spread the pain a little thinner.

"I don't have fifty thousand!" said Charlie for the last time; his tone said he was finished apologizing. "But I will pay. Didn't I say that? That I would pay?"

"And I said Geb would be dead! Do you not understand what *dead* means? You can't pay the dead to come back!" Naguib turned around and walked away, though would never escape at his pace; it was as if snails carried him.

"Come back," said Hana. She followed Naguib, who plodded off with his folio.

Not knowing what Hana wanted distressed the hell out of Aos. He knew what everyone else wanted. Naguib wanted money. Aos wanted his boring life back. Charlie wanted his love to go away. What did Hana want? To know what it felt like to steal something?

Before Aos could express his concern, Charlie set off to help Hana procure the folio. Naguib's errant despair made it easier. It was a bad time to be so moved that he couldn't walk normally. Hana sped ahead, blocking Naguib's path; then Charlie approached Naguib from the side. "Please," said Charlie, taking hold of the folio. Two fingers resting lightly on the nearest edge. "Be reasonable. Take the money. Twenty thousand is still a lot. More than these papers are worth, considering they're just photocopies." A tug-of-war erupted when Charlie's two fingers became his whole hand. "No!" said Naguib, who jerked the folio the way a dog jerks a rope. "Geb," he said, tugging.

Charlie so clearly controlled the situation that intervening on his behalf would've been a shameful use of force. Aos didn't want to feel more guilty than he felt watching the folio slip from Naguib's hands into Charlie's. One final tug was all it took. Naguib fell or maybe sat down. Was he giving up? Was he letting Geb die? He lay down on the road. A day's worth of sun leaked from the hot tar. "My son is sick. Please, the money. Fifty thousand. You said you'd pay." Naguib put his hand up for the whole payment. Charlie gave him the portion he'd brought and tried to explain that two-fifths of the promised sum was much better than the zero fifths he'd otherwise be getting. Plus, the papers were of no value to Naguib. He couldn't sell them to anyone else. Why keep the papers? That wouldn't help Geb. That wouldn't help anybody.

Naguib held the money in the air above his face. He counted the notes. He counted them again, to be sure. "No." He threw the notes in the air. They descended erratically. One note even ascended to head height before descending again. Naguib moaned when it returned to him, alighting like a bird on his chest. He crumpled the note and threw the ball down the riverbank. "You have no idea!" said Naguib. He made no further attempt to mask his state. He was inebriated. When he sat up, he fell back again. He didn't slur exactly, but some of his words grew tails. "What if my boss asks about my quota on the copy machine? I've run through my week's quota in one day. To make the perfect copy! Like an original print! Have you ever made an original print with a copy machine that doesn't work properly? What original print is this badly crinkled?" Naguib waved his hand in the air to illustrate crinkling. "And my boss, he sees me with papers in my hand. What am I supposed to do? I can't throw them away. What if he looks in the bin? The questions he'll ask! The accusations he'll make with his eyes! He already accuses me of something every day. What is the thing that I've done? In his mind, I've done something. I've done something grave. I don't know what it is. Even on the best days when all my work is finished and the patients are out of the waiting room and I am stuck organizing files. Stuck from my wife and my son. He says I'm lazy. He says that late at night when I'm still working. Is he still working? Or just watching me fail to meet some imagined standard? So he can threaten me? And accuse me of a crime? What crime, I don't know!" The terrified look on Naguib's face proved he was a good father. He'd risked everything to help Geb. "People now everywhere in Cairo—you must understand, it's not just me—in all parts of the city, are suspected of grave crimes against the government. So what if the government is gone? Not really gone, for the Supreme Council is comprised of the same men! Please, the money! The money you said you would pay!"

Aos wanted to scream now that Geb would die. Geb would've died anyway, but now Aos bore part of the blame. And Naguib would suffer more for having come close, in his mind, to saving him. What if Aos screamed? What if one of the dark windows above, in the array of dark windows that filled the buildings that lined the street, brightened? And a head appeared? The head would call the police, who would call the army; the army would come in trucks and take them for "questioning." God's just punishment would be turning a blind eye to whatever came next.

"Are my pills in the folio?" asked Naguib. Though he looked to know the answer. "Can I have them, please?"

"What pills?" asked Charlie.

"Please, the pills." Naguib climbed to his knees. He eyed, then leaped for the folio. The movement was sudden and stupid. He lay prone after that with his face on the tar. He wept and said the name of his son over and over. "Please. I will die if Geb dies. Please, I will die."

Aos wiped his sweaty hands on his pants and said prayers as reparations for his crimes and other crimes committed by other people. He prayed for Naguib to stand up, for Geb to get better, for Hana to go back to America. He prayed Charlie would come to his senses. What would Charlie do with normal senses? Would he repent for his lie? Would he call his brother to borrow money? God willing. Then Geb would live, Dalia would leave, and Aos would have what he wanted. His dull life appeared in his mind like the ghost of a dead love. He almost reached for her.

All of a sudden, a piercing whistle sounded from up the street. It was the noise a parent makes when calling to and also scolding a child for disappearing in a public space. Fingers jammed deep in the mouth, air blown steadily. When Aos turned, he saw a uniformed man walking toward them. "Oh, no," said Aos. "No, no." The figure smoked a cigarette and carried a club. A rifle was strung over his back. Aos couldn't see the gun, but could see the strapping. In truth, the club made him more nervous. A long black stick. "As-salamu alaikum," said the soldier when he was close enough to talk without shouting. He wore the smile of a man who'd stumbled upon a profitable opportunity: foreigners out after curfew. "Don't move. If you move, I'll have to . . ." The soldier gestured to his radio, which connected him to an army of like-minded men. Aos, Hana, and Charlie were thus outnumbered by a factor of at least a thousand. Naguib, given his state, didn't count in their favor. He looked as if he'd fallen asleep. "You know," said the soldier, moving closer, "there is curfew. You know curfew?"

The word meant different things to different people. To mothers of young children, whose offspring lacked agency, curfew had a more literal meaning. It meant don't go out after dark. It was disruptive, but not debilitating. It forced loud children to play inside. To mothers of older children, who were almost certainly protesters — young men and women who'd moved out or didn't abide strict rules — it meant no sleep and sore eyes from nights spent staring at mobile phones, ever waiting to learn their children were safe. Fathers obeyed or disobeyed curfew according to politics they'd developed or, more likely, inherited from their parents. If they disobeyed curfew, it was usually to smoke shisha on the corner with their friends. To protesters, curfew was a crime against the cause of freedom and justice and was to be disobeyed at all costs. To Charlie, curfew was little more than an intangible thing he could fear. He'd once defined the word with a dictionary in a failed attempt to dissuade Aos from protesting. *A regulation requiring people to remain indoors between specified hours, typically at night.* The definition had offended Aos at the time, but seemed fitting at this juncture; indoors would've been a fine place to hide from the soldier. Aos hated being the kind of person who wanted to hide. Choosing not to was a constant battle. Why couldn't he be brave by nature? Nature never failed. Nature never changed its mind.

"We were just leaving," said Charlie. "It was nice meeting you."

Right away the soldier began jabbing people. He jabbed Naguib in the ribs with his foot, presumably to check if he was still alive. The groaning sound was, according to the soldier, "good news for you." Then he jabbed Charlie in the shoulder with his club. Charlie stepped back to soften the blow, which seemed to please the soldier. Who didn't like being all-powerful? Aos received the next jab, though his was much harder on account of being "from here." The soldier said Aos ought to know better. Aos absorbed the impact without moving, which caused the soldier to jab with increasing vitriol until Aos finally stepped back. The soldier celebrated his victory with another jab. "I think I have seen you before. You're like every boy in the square. You're a tough guy. You have an attitude. I correct that with my . . ." He waved his club in Aos' face. Hana's face, too. The soldier's threat wasn't prejudiced. "Whoop," he whispered. Hana, who looked surprised that curfew applied to her, pushed away the soldier's club. "What's this?" asked the soldier, laughing. A woman who resisted was a joke. "And what is *that*?" He reached for the folio, which Charlie had given her. Hana was meant to determine if the papers looked right. Her position at the UNHCR made her uniquely qualified to judge their authenticity.

"Used tampons," said Hana, dodging the soldier's hand. "Dead rats."

The soldier's face turned red when he reached for the folio a second time.

"Don't touch me," said Hana, dodging his hand again.

"Give him the folio!" pleaded Aos. He knew what Hana didn't

want to know. Her liberties hadn't traveled with her from America. The soldier would touch or take what pleased him. Withholding the folio would only make it worse.

Charlie tried to intervene, but the soldier clubbed him on the arm where there was no muscle or fat as padding: the side of his elbow joint, where bone lay naked under thin layers of skin. It sounded like a rock falling on a softer rock. The impact turned Charlie into another man. He was still. He was quiet.

The soldier laughed and reached for the folio a third time, lazily. Hana slapped his hand instead of just dodging it. The slap made sense using pure, unadulterated logic. The old method wasn't working; only a fool would continue trying it. Aos' logic had, however, been contaminated by certain realities. One such reality was the soldier before them. The soldier was serving in an army that had become a government. His actions, no matter how rash, were beyond law. It was no surprise, then, when he grabbed Hana by the hair. Or when he pulled her away from her companions. Or when he wrapped his arm around her like a snake and began squeezing the air from her lungs. Aos and Charlie lurched forward, but the soldier commanded them to stay back. He threatened injury, imprisonment, even death. His threat was nonverbal. The soldier just touched his radio with the butt of his club.

Hana tried to free herself by stomping on the soldier's foot. His boots were stiff leather with steel toes, but that didn't discourage her. Hana tried to bend the metal and perhaps even lop off a few toes by stomping repeatedly with all her strength. But the metal toe was designed to endure far worse than Hana's futile effort. The soldier must've known that and let Hana wear herself out. "Let go," said Hana after she couldn't stomp anymore or hardly even breathe. "Not yet," said the soldier. His nonchalance threw gas on a dying fire. Hana used the last of her strength to throw her head back like a battering ram. The soldier's height protected fragile targets such as his larynx or his nose. Her head landed square on his chest, causing no damage except perhaps to his ego. The soldier had been hit again by a woman. "Garbuuʒa," he said. Hopping desert rodent. You fucking bitch.

What created such a man? Not God, thought Aos. Though something nearly as omnipotent. The Egyptian Armed Forces, in which all men had to serve. Aos had only been exempt because he lacked male siblings. The Ministry of Defense wouldn't deprive families of their first and only sons lest they be called a plague to Egypt. As a result, Aos had never learned ruthlessness. Instead he'd watched his friends disappear into an architecture of ideas – about honor, about duty – only to appear later as changed men. Nervous, depressed, lonely. Not wanting to kill, but able to. Estranged by way of their sadness. They wouldn't talk to Aos because he'd not served. He'd become no more than a woman to them.

Aos, perched on the balls of his feet, stared at the soldier's radio. His impertinent gaze broadcast a question. How do you plan on using that device without freeing your hand? Short of growing a third hand, the soldier had two choices: drop his club or release his prisoner. A soldier's quandary. No soldier would drop his club or free his prisoner. No Egyptian soldier, at least. Egypt started history and survived the wrath of time by the strength and will of its military. That military fought valiantly to the last man. Thus even their losses were honored. Such history must've informed the soldier's decision to tighten his grip. Fuck the radio. He didn't need it. The soldier's arm was a vise powered by what must've been thousands of push-ups doled out as punishment for not making his bed correctly. *Stop*, mouthed Hana, but no sound escaped from her throat. Her body lacked the air that would've otherwise given it voice. Life, too. Her eyes dilated. The soldier loosened his grip at the last second and laughed when Hana breathed the most desperate breath. The fear of death had made her docile.

"Money," said the soldier through Hana's hair. "This much." He gestured with two of five fingers holding his club that the stack should be thick enough to interest him. Or disinterest him from foreigners in Zamalek at night, the man they'd left in the road, and the woman they'd stupidly enmeshed in their business. Not to mention the beautiful leather folio. "Money now or you go to the museum." To prove he was serious, the soldier walloped Hana on the bridge of her nose. He used the same club he'd used to tap his radio, though with more force. A spring opened somewhere inside Hana's head, allowing the soldier to choke her without squeezing. All he had to do was prevent the blood from draining by holding back her head. Hana gasped, spit, and swallowed her blood to get rid of it. To Aos, the sound of Hana's choking was even worse than the sound of black sticks falling on the woman he'd left on the bridge. Whup, whup. He ran maniacally at the tangled strangers, legs powered less by anger at this soldier than shame left by many like him. Aos collided with Hana and the soldier at full speed. Their bodies flew away from each other like birds frightened by a gunshot. Each body landed with an appropriately dull thud in the road. There was yet no rest for the weary. A scramble erupted. The scramble grew in intensity the way a spark grows in dry grass. The spark grows wildly. Hana scrambled for air. The soldier scrambled for his gun, his club, his footing. Not to mention, his radio. The radio bounced around on a coiled wire. Aos scrambled faster and found the club first. He gripped the club so hard his knuckles turned white. The soldier barely had enough time to raise his arms in defense before the club fell upon him. Whup, whup.

6

The whupping lasted so long the sound changed. Aos pounded the soldier's head into something a little softer. Bone mush. Bone soup. Hana stood over the pacified body. Her face was bloody and she held the folio against her chest like a child. She jabbed the soldier in the ribs with her foot the same way he'd once jabbed Naguib. What comes around goes around. Hana cried when that phrase appeared in her head like a road sign she was driving past on the expressway to feeling vindicated. How sick to be in such a rush. "I'm sorry," whispered Hana to the body. The ducts connecting her nose to her throat had already swollen shut. It sounded as if food were in her mouth. "I'm so sorry." Hana tucked the folio into her pants and rolled the soldier toward the riverbank. His body had become, pained as she was to admit, evidence. That evidence needed to disappear. Its discovery would drop an early curtain on her life. Not to mention the lives of Mustafa, Charlie, Aos, and the indubitably unconscious Naguib. Their imprisonment or deportation would beget a more pervasive suffering. Naguib's and Mustafa's families would join the tangle along with Charlie's office and Aos' work. That work — thousands of translated documents — was not without consequence. Tragedies clients told needed to become English tragedies before they could become case files.

An obscene number of lives, mostly innocent, would thus unravel if the soldier's body was found. Knowing that didn't make it easier to roll him. "I'm sorry," said Hana again. She repeated her apology every time the soldier's hands struck the pavement. "I'm sorry. I'm sorry. I'm sorry." Clop. Clop. Clop. From the riverbank, one final push was all it took. The angle of incline conspired with gravity to roll the soldier on Hana's behalf. His hands clopped a few more times before a modest splash sent ripples into the blackest water she'd ever seen. Once settled, the soldier's body was close to neutral buoyancy. His face and toes barely sailed above the surface. The weapons that had once given him power now weighed him down. His gun, his club, his radio. The Nile bore that cargo without complaint. A relentless haul befitting the stubborn river, which had survived desert, dam, and drought. Nothing short of God's will could stop the Nile, or the rubbish contained therein, from reaching the Mediterranean. People had a way of disappearing in the vastness of that sea. Migrants, for the most part. Drowned by the hundreds on ill-fated journeys of hope.

Charlie sat on the curb with his head down and gripped the spot where the soldier had slapped him. The bone on the side of his arm. The soldier had used his club but hadn't wound up or followed through on his swing. *Slap* was the more appropriate word; he'd not really *hit* Charlie. In retrospect, it was a shocking use of restraint. Why forgo the standard pummeling? Wasn't pain the seed of fear? Wasn't fear the seed of obedience? The grim error had cost the soldier his life. His blood, pooled on the black tar, was less pronounced than it would've been on another surface. It was just a shimmering, like oil in a puddle when it rains. Aos, clearly tormented by the sight, spread the blood so it would dry faster. He used his hands, not his shoes. Hana was aghast only until she realized that hands could be washed in the river without falling in. Not shoes. Not dress shoes with no grip. Not dress shoes with blood on the rubber and the man wearing them perched gravely above the water on a rock. The intimate nature of the spreading appeared to cause Aos no small pain. He sobbed and mumbled in Arabic while coating the road. The vocabulary was too advanced for Hana. Something about God. Something about mercy.

"We need to leave," said Hana after Aos climbed to and from the water. His arms had disappeared at the elbows and were a different color when they reappeared. "Before . . ." Well, there was no saying. Before the police arrived. Before the army arrived. Before a stranger happened past and called whomever. The sooner they left, the better for everybody. Except leaving speedily required a car, which required Mustafa. Calling him felt worse than rolling the soldier. Wasn't he a man with a family? Didn't calling him put them at risk? Yes, thought Hana as she dialed. She stopped dialing before reaching the last digit. Mustafa was a man with a family. Then Hana finished dialing for exactly that reason. She decided, without considering Mustafa's nature, to warn him away. Leave now! Go quickly! Hana breathed each time the phone rang. Knowing when to breathe made it hurt less. The soldier's arm had left a tenderness running diagonally across her chest, beginning at her clavicle. The discomfort predicted a long bruise, like a sash worn in mourning.

When Mustafa finally picked up, he said, "So sorry. My daughter was telling me how to spell *barnacle*. B-A-R-N . . ."

"You need to leave without us," whispered Hana. Her urgent plea was beyond polite timing. "I'll explain later. Please go."

Mustafa scoffed as if she'd blasphemed the holy code of taxi driving. How could he abandon his fare? "God only knows what you mean. I will be there soon. Five minutes."

He hung up before Hana could beg no and didn't answer when she called back. "Fuck!" whispered Hana at her phone. There was nothing else to do now but wait. Five minutes was a long time to drive some hundred meters. Except the street was one-way, so Mustafa had to go around. Most streets in Zamalek were one-way. Taxi drivers joked that the only way to go back somewhere you'd been was to start over. That required leaving the island. Mustafa wasn't that sort of comedian, who told jokes to swindle passengers. But he wasn't a desperado, either. Mustafa, law-abiding as one could be, wouldn't drive the wrong way. He'd go around.

Meanwhile Aos unbuttoned his shirt, which was strewn with blood. The unbuttoning was slow and morbid; his hands were rendered almost obsolete by an inescapable shake. When Aos finally got the shirt off, he turned it inside out. Then he tried to put the shirt back on. Aos swore at the bunched sleeves while forcing his arms through. The effort was all for naught. Most of the blood had soaked through the fabric. As a result, the myriad spots had only slightly reduced diameters. There was no hiding them. Aos moaned, yanked the shirt off his back, and crammed it down a storm drain. His arm followed the shirt to ensure it plunged beyond light's purview. That purview was arm's length. Yonder that lay a twisting sewer in varying states of decrepitude. What human would ever go down there?

Two headlights appeared suddenly at the south end of the street. Mustafa's hand waved out the window as if to say, *I'm over here.* He parked in the only free spot available, loath, as he was, to idle in the middle of the street. No more than thirty meters away. The lights, the waving, the idea of escape – all that must've cured Charlie of the soldier's slap. He shucked off the impotence imbued by the strike. Free of that, he stood up and ran toward the car. "No!" whispered Hana to Charlie's back. "No!" she said a little louder when he didn't stop. He still didn't stop! Hana ran after Charlie to prevent him from destroying Mustafa's life. The future prosecutor's case against Mustafa would hinge on whether he was a willing participant. Didn't sitting in his car make it so? Mustafa would be charged with aiding and abetting criminals. Conspiracy. Fraud. Accessory to murder. Or murder outright. Or treason, for killing a soldier. If only Charlie's legs weren't so long. If only he didn't run so fast toward more suffering.

It was too late by the time Hana arrived. Charlie had already enlisted Mustafa as their wheelman. Mustafa looked happy enough to be of service, and Charlie looked damn pleased to have secured a ride. He nearly ripped off the broken back door when he opened it. Then he leaped into the car the way a fish leaps to freedom after escaping a fisherman's grip. Yet arriving in the backseat didn't seem to comfort Charlie. Maybe because the car wasn't moving yet. "What are you doing, Hana?" Charlie glared at her. "Get in!"

Hana wanted to say no, but Charlie's desperation assaulted her cogent heart. That heart was wildly powerful. It convinced Hana of things that weren't true. Or weren't necessarily true. That more soldiers were on their way. That Mustafa would be caught at the scene of a crime. That the future prosecutor's case wouldn't need evidence beyond that. Mustafa would be imprisoned in one of the Great Egyptian Atrocities. It didn't matter which prison. They were all the same. Wasn't leaving with Mustafa the only way to keep him safe? The presumed answer to that question forced Hana into the car.

"Where's Aos?" asked Charlie as if he were the sole missing passenger.

Hana leaned out the window to get a better view of the goings-on. Charlie did the same, but on the other side. Mustafa, too, in the front. An unbelievable sight lay before them. Aos was dragging Naguib down the street. He looked like an ox driving a plow meant for two oxen. Fits and starts. One foot at a time.

"Oh, God!" said Charlie. "Hurry up!"

Aos was long gone in his pulling. He didn't seem to hear or even feel anything. Not exhaustion. Not anxiety. Not fear. He'd been drained of all that. The only thing he seemed to have left was a tight grip on Naguib's arms. There was no leaving him.

Mustafa, having recently acquired a sense of urgency, put the car in gear and drove so close to Aos that he nearly ran over him. Of course that didn't happen. Maybe it wasn't even possible. Mustafa was too precise in all his movements. He parked where he'd previously not wanted to park: in the middle of the damn road. "God forgive me for breaking the law," said Mustafa. He got out to help lift Naguib into the backseat. Hana got out to hold open the door. Charlie also got out, but there wasn't anything for him to do. He paced impatiently. "Oh, God," he said. "Please hurry."

Together Aos (by the wrists) and Mustafa (by the ankles) lifted Naguib in the air. He drooped like a puppet lacking his master. Though he was breathing normally. A good sign, thought Hana. Maybe Naguib hadn't overdosed. Maybe he would be fine in the end. If Aos and Mustafa could just get his tattered ass in the car! The maneuvering was surprisingly complicated. Aos backed into the car through the broken door that Hana held open, then slid so far across the seat that Charlie, who'd rushed to get back inside before the rest of them, was squished against the far door. He emitted a disapproving groan. Then Aos pulled Naguib by the shoulders and Mustafa pushed Naguib by the feet. His tattered ass slipped across Aos' lap and part of the way onto Charlie's, whose groan deepened. Hana sealed the mess by slamming the broken door. To ensure it had properly latched, she gave the door a swift kick.

"Yallah!" said Mustafa. He jumped into the driver's seat while Hana ran around the car and jumped into the passenger's. She still wasn't used to sitting up front. It was strange viewing Mustafa from the side and agonizing to see him look so frightened. One minute he was talking to his daughter, the next he was stuffing an unconscious man into his car. He slammed the gas and the car flew up the street toward Sequoia, the nice restaurant on the north end of the island. After just a few seconds Hana could see a few well-dressed pedestrians ambling in a warm yellow light. They smoked so many cigarettes that they looked to be standing in fog.

"Turn here!" said Charlie. "Left! Left!"

"I know where to turn," said Mustafa. "If I didn't know where to turn, I wouldn't be a . . ."

Charlie's head bashed the window during the turn. The loud whack left a grim silence. Mustafa, who by nature was diametrically opposed to quietness – hadn't he spent every ride yakking with Hana about life and love and war? – turned on the radio and, as if that weren't yet enough, flattened the gas pedal. The engine roared and shook the car. SpongeBob SquarePants, dangling from the mirror by a string, swung like a pendulum toward the back of the car. The doll hung at its apex for a time, made weightless by the acceleration, before returning to equilibrium. The car had finally reached its top speed; it wasn't possible to escape any faster.

Weeks after choosing to care less about things she couldn't control, such as whether Mustafa's taxi would careen into a building, Hana discovered the front seat had what the backseat lacked: a seat belt. An ironic laugh died just before leaving her mouth. Her chest hurt. She still couldn't breathe easily. She could smell blood. She could taste blood. She could feel mostly dried blood in her hair. It was still a little sticky. Hana wrapped the seat belt around her body. Crumbs, which had once clung to the strap, clung now to her fingers. She didn't care. Or cared less than she would normally. Normally Hana would've felt an immediate and intense desire to wash her hands with antibacterial soap. That wasn't possible right now. For all Hana knew, it would never be possible again. Did they have running water in Tora prison? She rolled down the window and brushed the crumbs into the wind. The folio, exhumed from her pants and held now in the crook of her arm, whipped violently and made a slapping sound. The same sound her hand had made when she'd hit the soldier. Regret blossomed and filled her entire body. How would the night have ended if she hadn't slapped his hand?

Mustafa rolled up Hana's window as soon as her arms were back inside. He said he couldn't hear the radio. He pointed to the radio as if it were the only thing that had ever made any sense. The change in air pressure caused Hana's ears to pop. That cleared way for the soap opera full of exaggerated laughing sounds. A mother found her child in the kitchen eating — well, something. Hana didn't know the word but apparently it was funny. Nobody in the car joined in the laughter except Mustafa, who sounded more nervous than amused. As if he had no idea what he'd just done, except to say that it wasn't good. Not something he should brag about. Not something he should tell to his wife. Streetlights were spotlights looking in, incriminating them. There you are, we know you did it.

Then, out of the blue, Naguib stirred to life. The sharp turns must've got his blood pumping and jostled his brain. "The brown . . . sealed . . . envelope," said Naguib, pulling himself off Charlie and out of Aos' lap. He leaned the other way, against the broken door. Before Hana could warn him about the precariousness of that spot, he said, "Please, the money. The money you promised to pay." Hana didn't think it was possible for the mood to get any worse, but it did. The mention of money drained all hope from Mustafa's face. Money implied business, which implied all kinds of things.

The one-way street became a two-way bridge to Dokki. Past the traffic circle and the metro stop, and down an alley — irrevocably away from people — Mustafa parked his car. "Hena quayes?" he asked, which meant "Is here good?" but sounded more like "You need to leave" mixed with "Don't ever call me again." His voice wasn't angry so much as totally unnerved. "Hena quayes?" he asked again. Aos, Charlie, and Hana unloaded onto the sidewalk. Naguib, however, didn't exit so gracefully. He fell out of the car after leaning against the broken door with too much pressure. The door swung open and Naguib fell out with a surprised cry. He lay in repose in the street. Though he only lay that way for a few seconds. When Naguib sat up, he made the strangest face. The look an animal has immediately before attacking or running away: tense, but ultimately devoid of emotion; instinct had kicked in. Aos hurried over to hold him still. Though Aos was sort of sneaky about it. He made it look as if he were just helping Naguib to his feet. But Hana could see that Aos was gripping him.

"Why is your friend not wearing a shirt?" asked Mustafa. He'd rolled down the window to be heard. Though he didn't look at his passengers. He looked straight ahead at the road. "And who is the other man? The . . . ?" Mustafa made some loopy gesture indicating drunkenness.

Hana sensed that Mustafa was speaking only to her. Were they not friends? Could she not bring his old soul some rest by saying Naguib was her cousin? Or her lover? Or something? That he was drunk? That he'd gotten sick on Aos' shirt, which had been thrown in the river to avoid getting any mess in the car? That the money Naguib mentioned was borrowed or lost in a bet? That no business had been conducted? And that despite the blood and the swelling evident on Hana's face – at least, it *felt* evident – nobody had been hurt?

"Well?" said Mustafa.

Hana yearned to say everything would be fine in the end, but couldn't bring herself to tell such a palpable lie. "It's really important that I pay for your door. Tonight. Right now." Hana knew she could never see Mustafa again. It would be an inordinate and entirely unnecessary risk to continue their relationship. Hana tried not to think about it lest she change her mind. She just dug in her pocket for the cash she'd picked off the street. The same cash Charlie had offered Naguib. The same cash Naguib had thrown in the air. Or the portion she'd been able to collect while Aos had been washing his arms in the river. The money was evidence, too, like the blood. She couldn't just leave it there. Hana guessed a few thousand pounds were in a little grubby clump. It was both a pittance and a bonanza: much less than Geb needed, but more than enough for the door.

Mustafa wouldn't look at Hana or touch the money. "Please," he said, more serious than he'd ever been in her presence. "Step away. I don't want to run over your feet."

Hana abided, but not easily; no step had ever caused her more pain. Then Mustafa drove away in a hurry. Hana tried to throw money in the window, but missed. Banknotes flew everywhere. A few notes, caught in the invisible pull of the car, followed Mustafa for a short time before finally resting.

7

That night Charlie couldn't sleep. Visions plagued him. He saw a sodden man in the water. He saw money amiss in the street. He saw himself bending over a thousand times to pick up every note, even though Hana was the one who had picked them. He saw those notes tendered as a diminutive, blood-covered payment to Geb. Didn't he owe a boy, not a father? Plus, Charlie's bed was too small for both him and Ruby. The dog had spread herself diagonally across the mattress. There was nowhere for Charlie to extend himself. He got up slowly so as not to wake the old pooch. He needed to borrow money. He should've borrowed money before, but lacked what every fool needed: a time machine. The only thing he could do was borrow money a little late. God willing, not too late. Geb, he thought, could live.

It wasn't that Charlie hadn't thought to borrow money last week; he just hadn't known whom to borrow from. No rich people were in Charlie's life; not even any financially stable people. Aos, Sabah, and Michael would've been destitute without their jobs. Even with their jobs they were nearly broke almost all the time. There was nobody back home, either. Not that Charlie still knew. Much less still knew their phone numbers. And Tim had never crossed Charlie's mind. Some combination of grief and ego must've blocked him out. The only thing that had changed was seeing in hindsight what his ego had done. Charlie imagined excising that ego and cutting it into little bits. He walked to the phone while that figment still meant something. To reach Tim, Charlie had to call Karen. Her number had arrived in a letter some years back. *Love from your family back home. Your brother misses you. He'll never tell you that. Write him, please. Will you? Please, for me. I'm asking. Call and I'll give you the address.* The phone rang the way tides oscillate. At a slow, reliable interval.

"Hello?" Karen sounded confused and possibly upset. As if she knew it was Charlie even before he'd said anything.

"Yeah, hi." It unsettled Charlie to think she was prescient. Did she know he wanted money? Would she say how disgusting it was that he'd called after all this time for nothing more than a handout? "This is . . ."

". . . Charlie?"

Maybe Karen just had caller ID. The sheer number of digits, beginning with +20, would've indicated the call was crossing a border. Probably even the ocean. How many people did Karen know that lived across the ocean besides her husband? Tim's number, while similar in length, would've begun with +964. Karen would've known that. She would've seen his number hundreds of times over the course of his deployments. There was only one person +20 could be.

"Yes, Charlie. I'm hoping you can connect me with Tim."

Despite everything, he tried to sound chipper. Charlie didn't want the conversation to devolve into some kind of vaguely hostile catching up. Did you receive the letter I sent? Why didn't you call? Why didn't you write to your brother? Why did you treat him so badly at El Horreya after he'd traveled so far to see you? Yes, he told me! We're married! We talk!

"You want to talk with *Tim*?" said Karen, as if under no circumstances was that possible.

"I owe him an apology. Look, it's better late than never. Do you have a way of reaching him or not? It occurs to me that I don't actually know how that works. The whole 'keeping in touch' thing. With a soldier. I guess it's complicated."

Karen made an awful, protracted moaning sound. Charlie couldn't help but think of the pig he'd once shot in the gut. It sickened him to remember the screaming and the terrified look in its eyes. When enough blood had seeped from the wound, the screaming stopped and the moaning started. Charlie remembered thinking at the time that it was almost human sounding. The evidence presented now was inescapable. It was human sounding. The pig had been afraid to die. Just as Karen was afraid of . . . what, exactly? She managed to comfort herself before Charlie could think of something to say. Karen did so by holding her breath. Some kind of breathing exercise, presumably. He imagined her counting to a predetermined number. Five, maybe. Or six. And while in that place — wherever she went while counting — telling herself that everything would be okay in the end. Whatever had gone wrong would go right again. Whatever had gone wrong would go right.

"Tim was injured in an explosion," said Karen. She made the moaning sound again, though it was less pronounced the second time. Charlie still didn't know what to say. He didn't know what to feel, either. He wanted to feel something. Anything. A strong emotion of any kind. Something that proved he was still human and not just humanoid. Karen breathed as if there weren't enough air in the room. Then three letters leaked out of her mouth: "IED." A buzzer went off in Charlie's brain. He saw an armored vehicle rolling by a lump in the dirt. He saw a bright white light engulfed not in fire but in dust. Finally, he saw a dour soldier playing a bugle in the rain. Taps, of course. At dusk. In a cemetery.

"Is he . . . ?" Charlie couldn't bring himself to say *dead* or *dying* or even *possibly dying*. He'd read somewhere that saying things, believing things, even just imagining them for long enough, could actually change the chemistry of the universe and alter the course of events. Charlie had tried not to take the article seriously, but for some reason it had stuck with him.

"The doctors are optimistic."

The way Karen said that word—as if *optimism* were listed in the *Diagnostic and Statistical Manual of Mental Disorders*—made Charlie sick. He retched, but nothing substantial came up. Just some bile and the smell of whiskey he'd drunk earlier that night at the party in his kitchen. The party had been just a few hours before, though it seemed much longer. Ages. His entire life. All of time.

"Are you okay?" asked Karen.

"Yes. Are you?"

Karen laughed a little. Then cried so hard she had to hang up. "I'm sorry. I have to go. I have to pick up the boys from day care. The boys are . . . well, they're fine. I haven't told them yet. I don't know what to say."

How could Charlie ask Karen to wait? How could he beg money from a woman who might need it soon? "Tell Tim I said . . . well, if he ever . . ." But Karen had already hung up. The dial tone foretold at least one more death. If not Tim's, then Geb's. Charlie had nobody else to call and thus no money to borrow. He mourned by waking Ruby. The old pooch, reluctant to sit up, made a whining sound.

Charlie went to work at the first hint of a new day: when the call to prayer disturbed the chickens in the alley, which disturbed the cats. The office provided respite from the memory of that truly awful sound. The hallway inside was musty and cool and dark. Charlie hit the light switch several times before conceding the damn thing didn't work. He looked out the window and saw the streetlights were off, too. They must've turned off just a few seconds before. The Supreme Council was having a fine time fucking with people. Charlie felt his way into the kitchen, where a street-facing window stole light from passing cars. He saw shapes when those cars sped by with their headlights shining. A long box was the counter. A tall box was the fridge. Charlie approached what looked like a snake bowing over an abyss. He scrubbed the sticky feeling off his face. Tears, sweat, Ruby's drool. Then he blindly drank the tepid coffee someone had left in the pot. Just to exile the last of the whiskey still floating around in his blood. He needed a clear mind. He needed to wake up. "Wake up!" shouted Charlie. He rubbed more water on his face. Then he found his desk, burned a candle, and began writing the fake testimony he would present later that morning to Hana and Aos. He'd demanded – voice shaking even more than his hands – that they come at sunup. Hana and Aos had shared bewildered looks before finally nodding.

Since there was no electricity, Charlie wrote the testimony on a legal pad. The oblong yellow paper turned orange in the candle's light. Crushed orange balls of the same paper were the only proof that time was passing. Each failed iteration of the testimony tore up Charlie's heart. That it had come to this. Tears slipped off his chin until morning crept through the window. At last, he'd achieved a draft. It was a wretched, beautiful thing. A kind of love letter to a woman who would never know. Charlie stared at it while waiting impatiently for the screen door to swing open. His heart raced when, after what felt like ten years, the hinges finally whined. Why was he afraid when he knew it was either Hana or Aos? He told himself to stop being so afraid all the time. It wasn't becoming. "Stop it," whispered Charlie so quietly he couldn't even hear himself; the words were just vibrations in his throat. The police hadn't come to arrest him; the army hadn't come to execute him quietly. Nobody would miss the soldier who'd disappeared. Not in a revolution full of injury, havoc, betrayal, and abduction. Wouldn't the army presume that some among them would die? Wasn't that the inherent price of their crimes against the people of Egypt? And the refugees stuck in their midst? Charlie had paid a price, too, in fighting back. The price was his conscience. What did his conscience matter in the scheme of things? In a world full of people who'd done much worse for lesser reasons?

Thank God it was just Aos. He appeared and stood at an angle in the doorway. Like the legal pad, he looked orange in the light from the candle. Charlie saw that he'd showered, changed his clothes, and combed his hair. Though Aos still managed to look disheveled. It was more his demeanor than his dress: a bowed head, a slack body. Neither man was able or willing to speak. It was as if each feared what the other might say. They were only spared a painful moment by the lights, which flicked on suddenly. The refrigerator made a humming sound. The ceiling fan started to click. And hot, blank paper inexplicably spewed from the printer. For some reason that always happened after the power went and came back. Nobody understood why and thus couldn't stop it from happening.

"A gift from the overlords," said Charlie, nodding to the lights. He was glad to have something boring to talk about. The Supreme Council was only boring because it was so predictably unjust. He grabbed the blank paper the printer had spewed out. "In ten minutes this will be a testimony." Charlie shoved the pages back in the tray, turned on his computer, then set about typing what he'd scribbled on the legal pad. He pounded the keys the same way Bach once beat his piano. As if it wasn't his choice, but his calling. Or his compulsion. Or his curse.

"I couldn't stop hitting him." Aos took a chair from the desk next to Charlie's. "Even when I saw his eyes had rolled back in his head. The whites were a pink color."

Charlie didn't stop typing or turn to look at his friend. He dreaded where the conversation would take them. Just thinking about it made him type faster. It was impractical at that point to consult the legal pad. Charlie wrote by memory, accursed by rage. He pressed the keys so hard sometimes the letters appeared twice. "Damn it!" he shouted at the delete key. Soon the printer spewed hot paper covered in black ink. Charlie thrust the pages into Aos' hands. The pages were still hot. They were so hot they were still a bit sticky. "I want you to be the first to read this. I want you to know what we've done." Hadn't they done their jobs? Hadn't they done them well?

Aos held but didn't read the pages. "I should've stopped hitting him. I could've stopped if I'd really wanted to. He was knocked out. He might've already been dead. But I kept hitting him. I remember thinking he wasn't dead enough."

What if Aos had stopped? What if he'd stopped and the soldier wasn't dead? Just injured and pissed? And got hold of his rifle? And gunned them down? And used his radio to call more soldiers to keep gunning them until their bodies were spread down the block?

"If a man deserves a dent in his head, I say give him one." Charlie tried to believe what he'd said so that Aos might also believe it. This required rejiggering Charlie's principles. To that end, he reimagined the day he'd shot the pig. He saw the pig as a wild boar. He saw the boar had long tusks. He saw the long tusks coming straight at him. In this reimagining, Charlie was forced to shoot without restraint until the boar was gone. Bang! Bang! Bang! Not out of vengeance, but out of fear. To protect himself. It was a relief to know he felt nothing when the boar fell.

"I gave him twenty!" cried Aos. "Or was it more? Oh my God, was it more?"

No anguish was worse than watching Aos try to count how many times he'd whacked the soldier. Charlie reached out to touch Aos' arm. Charlie wanted to tell Aos how he viewed him. As his true brother. Didn't that mean Aos' crime was committed in defense of his family? Hadn't God addressed such crimes in the Qur'an? Hadn't Muhammad addressed them in the hadiths? "Aos, you're my true – "

"I could've stopped."

"He deserved it!" said Charlie, exasperated. "That almost never happens. People deserving their fate."

Aos leaned forward and rested his head on the desk. Each second of silence begged the next, endlessly. Charlie watched the flies by the window. They bounced off the glass again and again, kiss-kiss-kiss, as if the best solution to the problem in front of them was to smash against it.

8

On the ride to the Refugee Relief Project, Hana's taxi driver – a nice man, but not Mustafa – told her Zamalek, of the Egyptian Premier League, would be playing Haras El Hodood in football later that day. And to please pray for Zamalek to win. Hana must've seemed rude for not responding and ruder still for not making eye contact at the end of the journey when she reached forward to pay. The exchange was merely transactional. Not because she disliked the driver, but because he wasn't the one that she missed. Hana took her time walking from the curb, through the gate, across the yard, into the office. She wasn't sure if she was going to throw up or not. By the time she made it inside, Charlie had fallen asleep and Aos was in a kind of trance by the wall. He stood by the world map, staring at a tiny speck in the South Atlantic Ocean. "Where could I go and be happy?" said Aos. Either he was talking to himself or he'd heard the whine of the hinges. Hana thought someone should oil them. They were horrendously loud. "Should I need to flee?"

Hana had also thought about fleeing. In the dark of her apartment, she'd stripped naked and stepped into the shower while it was still cold. She'd scrubbed the red pigment from her skin. Her blood and the soldier's blood had inextricably mixed in the shower drain. Hana still hadn't felt clean. Not after the water had become transparent again. Not even after the brand-new bar of soap had become half its original thickness. (So long and harsh was the scrubbing.) It was as if Hana couldn't get the soldier off her body. He was stuck under her nails, in her hair, deep inside her sinus cavities. The swelling had trapped both the smell of his unwashed uniform and the much worse smell of his breath. Hana had tried closing her eyes to forget him. She'd told herself to think about something else. Such as the water coursing down her back. She'd told herself to come up with five words to describe the feeling. But Hana hadn't been able to think of even one word. Instead she'd thought of the soldier's hands clopping the pavement as he rolled by himself toward the river. (He was smiling. He was laughing at her. He kept saying, "You'll remember this for the rest of your life.") Hana had cried and hit the wall with the showerhead until the apparatus had fallen apart in her hands. That had brought an abrupt end to her cleansing. She'd gotten out and tried not to look in the mirror, which had made it even harder not to look. She'd stolen a quick glance, then run from what had become of her face. To her bedroom, where she'd thrown on her clothes. To her office, where she'd grabbed her passport. To her living room, where she'd called her mother. Hana had asked Ishtar if she could come home. The question had been "hypothetical" so as not to frighten her. Ishtar had been so excited that she'd not inquired after the cause of such a "blessed change of heart." (Her words, not Hana's.) Ishtar had said only that Hana would be welcome and her room would be ready. It had taken all of Hana's will *not* to go directly to the airport. Wasn't there a Delta flight from Cairo to New York? Didn't it leave daily at like . . . 1:30 a.m.? Might there still be a seat available? Hana had gotten so far as to start packing before she'd talked herself down from that ledge. The ledge was just a guilty feeling, which lessened of its own accord as the Tylenol began to wear off. Hana was left with nothing but the pain in her face. For some reason it settled her to feel what the soldier had done. What else might've he done had Aos not clobbered him?

"There's nowhere to go!" shouted Aos at the map. "That's what I've learned. That's what the map has taught me."

"How long have you been standing there?" asked Hana.

Aos pulled the map off the wall and crumpled it into a giant ball.

"A while then," she said.

Behind the map was a clean spot on the wall. Aos seemed drawn to the color. He put his hand against the paint. "The whole office used to look like this. Not even that long ago. I don't understand how it went to shit so quickly."

Hana couldn't watch Aos anymore without shaking him. She turned her attention to Charlie instead. "Is he . . . ?" She gestured to what looked like a wax statue awkwardly flopped on the desk.

"Asleep?" said Aos, finally turning away from the wall. "Yes. I think so. I don't understand how it's . . ."

"Possible?"

"Yes."

Together they approached Charlie's desk. There was a faint breathing sound. Hana thought Charlie's brain had probably just shut off to avoid processing whatever resided inside. He was like one of those myotonic goats that fainted every time they were scared. Charlie had fainted on what looked like a testimony. In the header, Hana saw the name she'd spent hours trying and failing to think up. Farah, meaning "joy." The name Charlie had produced so effortlessly, as if he'd been waiting his whole life to say that one word.

"Is that the testimony?" Hana couldn't stop herself from touching it.

"I have to warn you. It reads . . ."

Hana shoved Charlie's floppy arm aside to extract the papers. Then she read the testimony the way the desert drinks water when it rains:

Case Number: 243/2011
Name: Farah Salih
Mobile: +20 – – – –

E-mail: – – – – @hotmail.com
Family: Dead and/or missing

(*prepared with the help of the Refugee Relief Project*)

Introduction

My name is Farah Salih. I am from Baghdad, Iraq. (See Attachment 2, UNHCR Yellow Card.) Though I fled Baghdad to escape danger and can never return for the same reason. Where would I return to? My home is knocked down or occupied by militants! I live in Egypt now. It is better, but not much better. I am not a citizen. I can't work or own property. There are other reasons, too, that are more difficult to list. I mean history, which is really a story, which is really the path I took to get here. Importantly, not the path I chose. Much less the path I wanted. It all began with a death. My daughter, who was born in . . .

Hana folded what remained of the testimony into a neat, impossible-to-read rectangle. Every word was trapped inside the fold. "What's this?" she asked, jabbing Charlie in the back. Hana's finger plunged repeatedly until she hit a nerve. Charlie sat up with gusto. His hair went everywhere. He looked as if he'd walked through a wind tunnel. "Ouch," he said, trying to rub the spot. It was a few inches beyond his reach. Charlie turned, probably to glare at Hana for jabbing him. But his eyes never got that far. They stopped at the bare spot on the wall. It took him a while to remember what used to be there. "What happened to the map?"

A forlorn Aos presented the map as a huge paper ball. He tried to explain what the map had taught him and how frustrating the lesson had been. The world was small; the borders were impervious.

The story annoyed Charlie more than anything else. He said he knew Aos would never leave and therefore didn't need somewhere to go. And the map! The map, said Charlie, was expensive. It was printed on cotton and linen fiber. Like some money. More important, the map had symbolic value. It allowed clients to touch places they'd only dreamed about. That was why America, Canada, Australia, and most of Europe lacked the bright colors exhibited by other countries. Thousands of fingers had rubbed away the ink.

"Stop talking about the damn map!" Hana flung the testimony. The folded papers landed squarely in Charlie's lap. "Whoever reads that will ask questions. 'What lawyer wrote this crap?' It is crap, by the way! The tone is way off! It's barely a legal document! 'What UNHCR employee conducted the interview?' A fake interview, by the way! 'Where did the medical documents come from?' Forged documents, by the way!" Suddenly Hana felt like one of those myotonic goats. She needed to sit down before she fell over. There was nowhere to sit except the floor, unless she wanted to grab a chair from the adjoining room. Hana thought she'd pass out before she got there. As a last resort, she sat right where she'd been standing. "What if the UNHCR calls Naguib? What if he says the documents aren't real? What if he says they were stolen?" For the first time, it occurred to Hana that Naguib might have been conscious enough to observe the murder. Maybe he was at the police station right now reporting it. Aos had, after all, insisted on escorting Naguib back to his home. "He needs to sleep!" Aos had shouted. At the time it had seemed like a perplexing but nevertheless tender gesture. Now it seemed like a terrible mistake. Wasn't the bed a good place to sober up and start recalling things?

Aos flattened the crumpled map with his hands, as if, given enough time and pressure, the fibers would relinquish their wrinkles. But the map refused to flatten. Aos tried using thumbtacks to pin down the rogue corners, but that didn't pan out. He just stabbed himself in the hand several times. Aos was so incensed by the map's unwillingness to return to its former state that he crumpled it again and threw the giant ball across the room. The surface-area-to-weight ratio must've been pretty high; the ball hung ever so slightly at the peak of its arc.

"Naguib won't talk," said Charlie, sounding sure and somehow heartbroken at the same time. "He can't report our crime without also confessing his own. Is he not complicit in the forgery? Will he not rot in jail with the rest of us?" The supposition, like a gift from on high, seemed to rejuvenate Charlie. He asked if anyone had seen the folio. He searched for it by flinging papers everywhere. He finally found the folio on his chair. He'd been sitting on it. "Please," said Charlie, expelling his duress in a sigh. "We have what we need. The rest is just paperwork. I'll rewrite the testimony. I'll fill it with meaningless legalese. It will be formal and boring. I swear to you. This is just a draft. I was just . . . after what happened . . . I just . . ."

9

The hinges whined before Aos could watch Hana punch Charlie in the face. Aos sensed that she wanted to. It would've achieved some kind of equilibrium had it gone off that way. Charlie was, after all, the last person in the room without black eyes and a nasally timbre to his voice. Punching him in the nose would've fixed that. But the hinges caused Charlie to freeze and Hana to uncurl her fists. Looking utterly horrified, they turned toward the source of the sound: the hall, which behaved like an amplifier such that the hinges' cry was made both plaintive and soul crushing. Who the fuck opened the door? Like his colleagues, Aos wanted to know. Badly. He just wasn't as afraid as them. He almost craved punishment. That the footsteps belonged to a soldier. That the soldier, being magically informed of the night's happenings, would storm in and beat Aos to death with his club. Aos shut his eyes to await his comeuppance. He saw God. He saw his father waiting for him.

"Hello?" said a voice that sounded like Michael's, but only if Michael were gasping for breath and in desperate need of some water. Aos held out hope that it was yet a soldier. Perhaps an English-born Egyptian from a military family who came home to serve in the army. Not because he was proud, but because he was shamed by his parents. "Is anyone here? Hello?" The panic evident in the voice gave way to the rushing sound of feet beating the floor. Nobody reacted when the footsteps came to a halt. Aos opened his eyes only because he was still alive to open them. He was disappointed to see Michael. It was a weird feeling. The man's normally red face was much redder from sprinting some unknown distance. He looked back down the hall as if he was waiting for someone. Sabah, also red in the face, appeared moments later. She rested her head on Michael's shoulder. They both looked utterly asthmatic. "They're planting grass in the dust bowl," said Michael, keeling over to catch his breath. Sabah keeled with him, though not quite so far. It appeared she was in slightly better shape. Perhaps because she took a walk every afternoon while Michael just brooded at his desk. "I mean it. Actual grass. They're planting it." The dust bowl was what Michael called Tahrir. He called it that because the traffic circle was made of nothing but dirt. The dirt was kicked up by protesters, passing vehicles, donkeys, whirlwinds, occasional car accidents, and stray dogs that were either fighting or fucking. It was hard to tell the difference, so wild was their yapping either way.

"What do you mean *grass*?" said Aos as if his only sanctuary was under threat: Tahrir, the place he went to escape uncertainty. His life could be torn asunder at any time. If Charlie ever grew tired and left Egypt, for example. If funding cuts precluded keeping a full-time translator on staff. If the new "government" clamped down on nonprofits and shut down the Refugee Relief Project. Where would Aos live? How would he make money? In Tahrir, these questions actually had answers. You live here. And fuck money.

"Grass!" said Michael. Clearly he hadn't slept the night before. Or even closed his eyes. His hair, like Charlie's, stood at weird angles. "The green stuff. Grass. You know grass?" Then, a few seconds later: "I don't understand why you don't understand what I'm saying! I'm speaking English! Isn't it your job to know that language? Isn't that why Charlie hired you?" Weirdly, Michael's tone wasn't condescending; it was as if Aos' question had actually boggled him.

"You idiot!" shouted Aos. Not because Michael was actually an idiot, but because Aos — miffed that Michael knew something about Tahrir that he didn't — just felt like calling him one. What was Michael doing in the square? Why had Sabah taken him? When she could've taken him to the movies? Or out to dinner? Or back to her apartment? "I'm not asking *what* grass is. I'm asking *how* they're planting it. Are they throwing seeds on the ground or are they laying sod?" It seemed to Aos that the army's method declared their intent: whether they were trying to improve the city over time or, more likely, hoping to end the revolution overnight by some nefarious means involving sod. He didn't understand exactly what those means were, except to say they were nefarious. The quickness of it bothered him. As if it was some kind of trick. Some sleight of hand. "Seeds or sod? Tell me! I need to know!"

Hana's sneeze was all it took to divert Michael's attention from Aos' shouting. Michael's eyes widened as he watched Hana wipe a small drop of blood from her nose. It was as if he'd not realized she was there until that moment and was startled to find a stranger in their midst. New faces weren't so odd during working hours, but considering the office was closed and would be closed until at least 10:00 a.m. and, also, the severity of Hana's facial bruising — well, Aos understood why Michael was so nonplussed. What Aos couldn't understand was why it had taken Michael so long to register her presence. Maybe his one-track mind genuinely had only one track. "Who's she?" Michael asked both Charlie and Aos, though he didn't actually make any noise; he mouthed the question while furtively nodding in Hana's direction. It was unsubtle. He might as well have made a cardboard sign and waved it around in the air: WHO IS THAT WOMAN? WHY IS SHE HERE? WHAT IS WRONG WITH HER FACE?

For the first time that morning, Aos assessed the damage. Hana's bruised eyes were connected by a bruised nose. She looked like a raccoon. Brave, possibly rabid. The bruising had gotten much worse since she'd rolled the soldier. In his head, Aos thanked Hana for rolling him. He knew he couldn't have done it himself. He'd been too busy painting the road with the blood. It was all Aos had been able to think about at the time. Getting rid of the shimmer. In a way, he owed Hana his life. She'd protected him at the expense of her own innocence. That meant something to Aos, even if he couldn't tell her right now that it did; he tried telling her anyway by thinking it hard enough and praying Hana would know.

"Fuck the grass!" shouted Charlie at the two who'd come to report it. His tone said far more than his words. *You're interrupting what doesn't concern you!* and *Why are you here, anyway?* and *Go home, damn it!* At best, it came off as dismissive. At worst it was actively hostile.

Michael, as was his nature, retreated from what was or could've easily become an argument. Sabah looked disgusted that she loved such a meek thing. Nevertheless, she loved him. That much was made clear by the way Sabah squeezed Michael's shoulder before shoving him aside. "You have no idea how much the grass matters!" said Sabah with barefaced contempt. It pleased and also surprised Aos. He'd never thought of Sabah as especially opinionated. His misguided and swollen-headed prejudice heaped regret on top of his guilt. Why were they not friends? Why hadn't they been friends for years? Why didn't they go to the square together and shout loudly for the dissolution of the impending autocracy? Wasn't that the real goal of the military council? Not to maintain government until such time that it could be passed back to a civilian authority, but to rig the system such that the military would stay in power indefinitely? Aos had been dreaming for weeks that Egypt's constitution had been classified. Every night he woke up in the same cold sweat.

"You think I have no idea?" asked Charlie as if he was aghast that such a thing could be said about him. Wasn't he informed about everything that mattered? Or else, everything that mattered to him? His love. His plot. "You have no idea! All you see is Tahrir! Tahrir, Tahrir, Tahrir! It's just a traffic circle!"

Aos couldn't bring himself to watch this other place he loved – the office where his uncertain life could be put to some use – devolve into nothingness. Instead he watched the ceiling fan fail to cool the room.

The blades moved so slowly that they didn't appear to blend together. It was as if the electricity had somehow been turned on only partway. Where was the missing energy, the life of Egypt itself, the power that began, in a way, with the sun? The sun had made the Earth, which had made the Nile. The dam in Aswan converted that stubborn river's persistence into a reliable source of electricity. At least, it used to be reliable. Not anymore. Not since the Supreme Council took power.

"It's sabotage!" said Sabah. "Why else lay sod? So tomorrow the army can erect signs that say, 'Don't step on the grass.' On symbolic land! Our one place to gather! No walking, no sitting, no tents! What do you think is going to happen?" Sabah looked at Charlie as if he ought to answer; Charlie looked out the window. "I'll tell you what's going to happen. *Don't walk on the grass* means 'Don't congregate.' Get it? The grass is a barrier between the people and their ambition to live in a free Egypt. Their right to gather and shout loudly about the changes they wish to see in their lifetimes. How clever of the Supreme Council! And I thought they were only good at shooting rubber bullets into people's eyes. Watch. Just watch. I'm telling you. Tomorrow the soldiers, wearing their stupid red berets, will walk along the brick wall marking the perimeter of the circle and they'll shoo away people who get too close. This time the people will abide. The grass is new. The grass is beautiful. The army, they'll say – grudgingly, but still they'll say it! – is improving the city. 'Maybe we should give them a chance.' The apathetic and tired protesters will go home first and fail to congregate. After that it will be ten times harder to mobilize. What then? A million protesters in Tahrir are replaced by one gardener working part-time without benefits. The revolution dies in a flowerbed and the people coo at the beauty of it."

Sabah turned around and ran back outside as if she'd only come for reinforcements. Michael ran after her shouting, "No, Sabah! Don't!" Aos ran after Michael. Hana ran after him. By the sound of it, Charlie was also running and shouting. To come back, to sit down, to start working. "Please, don't go to the square!"

10

To make way for the water trucks, a battery of soldiers shouted for pedestrians and protesters alike to get out of the road. They shoved people who didn't move fast enough. Charlie, Michael, and Hana were separated from Sabah and Aos in a skirmish that spawned from the undue physicality. One brazen protester had the gumption to return from where he'd been pushed. It was impossible to see what became of him. First there was a rush of soldiers. Then a rush of protesters to defend the one among them that had been singled out. The hissing sound of a gas canister acted as an accelerant to the chaos. People shouting the fiery and ever-urgent word – Yallah! Yallah! Yallah! – damn near caused a stampede. The die-hard protesters ran away from the gas, but not to safety. They ran the rest of the way to Tahrir, which was no more than a block away. Why would they run there? Tahrir, being a traffic circle, was wide-open and prone to being surrounded. To Charlie's surprise and dismay, the diehards included both Sabah and Aos. They'd gone like bees in a line to await the arrival of the water trucks. Presumably to stop the freshly planted lawn from being watered. The sod would fail to take root and die later from thirst.

The more cautious protesters and pedestrians inadvertently caught in the fray, who wanted to be safe but didn't necessarily want to leave the vicinity, filtered into several colonial buildings surrounding the square. Charlie, Hana, and Michael were swept into one such building, up the old colonial stairs, and finally, near the top, into an old colonial apartment with high colonial ceilings. Once upon a time, some rich British diplomat must've held fancy soirees in those rooms. The rooms held just enough of their former beauty to let one imagine how good the soirees must've looked and how provincial they must've tasted. With champagne and shisha and jokes at the expense of the rabble. Charlie preferred the current shabbiness over the grandeur he saw in his mind. The people living there now weren't nearly so wealthy as those who'd lived there in the past. That was an improvement, wasn't it? The residents of the apartment were three men who looked to be in their early twenties. "Welcome," said the one who'd originally opened the door. "Please, yallah. Hurry. Please. Come in. Everybody." According to the many textbooks on the table and the many tinfoil containers of mostly eaten koshari, he and the other two residents were students. They were preparing for some kind of exam. They must've been preparing for days. Such was their desire to achieve a high score, a good job, a way out. Soon the apartment was filled to capacity with people who'd run from the gas. The students, after greeting everybody, immediately turned back to their work. Charlie admired their ability to stay focused. To keep going no matter what.

It was well known that people living in the buildings surrounding the square had a kind of open-door policy at dire times. Protesters and pedestrians alike, fleeing goons in all the garb they came – police garb, riot-police garb, army garb, dressed-down pedestrian garb – had, in the early days of the revolution, just ducked into the entryways of the buildings surrounding the square. This to escape being captured or to avoid breathing gas. The residents were glad to invite them inside. If not glad, then at least willing. As if it was their duty as residents living so close to the square to shelter people from danger. That was why so many of the famous photographs of the giant crowds covering every inch of Tahrir and spilling beyond its boundaries—at its peak, Tahrir was buried under the feet of more than a million people—were taken from the vantage of such apartments. Not because so many photographers had conveniently been living there, but because so many had been invited inside. Photographers were especially welcome to hide because they were so tyrannized. Goons just loved whacking the press. Especially free-lancers. The young men and women with cameras but no credentials, who were hoping to begin their careers.

Charlie, Hana, and Michael crowded around a window facing the square. It was a tight squeeze, but they were rewarded with a fine view: Tahrir, the streets going into and out of Tahrir, the Mugamma, the protesters, the water trucks, the traffic created by their obtrusive parking, the smog, and, between the Arab League and the InterContinental Hotel, a glimpse of the river. They were four or five or maybe six stories up. The protesters in the square were small, but not tiny. Charlie could see, if he squinted, some of the facial expressions: stoic, scared, impatient, angry, confused, lost, tired, and one young man looking enamored of another young man he was holding. Not in an especially romantic way. Just by the crook of his arm. The romance was contained in his face. One man pressed against the other before moving away again. Nobody cared. Or, more likely, nobody noticed. It was sad and beautiful and hard to watch. It was also hard not to watch it.

The water trucks prepared to spray the protesters by spraying the road. Presumably to test the strength of their cannons. Even though the pressure wasn't turned all the way up, the water made a slapping sound when it struck the pavement. It pained Charlie to imagine the sound it would make striking flesh. He scanned the crowd for the two people he loved desperately. "Where the fuck is Aos? Or Sabah? Where the fuck is Sabah? Do you see either of them? Will you point them out?"

The crowd wasn't huge, but the protesters were huddling in groups and turning to face the different water trucks positioned at various points around the square. What protester wanted to get hit in the back by the water cannons? They just kept turning because there was always a truck aiming at them from behind. Such was the fate of protesters who'd been surrounded.

"There's Aos!" said Hana.

"There's Sabah!" said Michael.

"Show me!" said Charlie, still not seeing them.

Hana and Michael pointed to the same place: a man and woman standing shoulder to shoulder and, unlike their compatriots, not moving. It made them harder to see. Aos and Sabah must've accepted the water cannons would be aimed at their backs no matter what direction they faced and so had just chosen one. East, thankfully. Toward the colonial building in which Charlie, Hana, and Michael had perched.

Charlie tried waving to them. When that didn't work, he cupped his hands and shouted into the makeshift loudspeaker. "Go back to the office! Or home if you must! Please don't stay in the square!" Neither Aos nor Sabah looked up. They didn't even look around. Charlie tried to shout louder and cup his hands at a more perfect angle. "I swear to God I'll fire you if you don't leave!" But his voice just wouldn't travel that far.

The trucks began "watering the grass." One at first, then the others, until all the trucks were spraying water. The pressure, which had been turned way up, accomplished the opposite of the presumed goal. Instead of softening the dirt beneath the sod, it just tore the sod away. The protesters, too, were torn. They were torn off their feet. Some were even torn out of their clothes. A scarf went flying. Shoes went flying. As more water sprayed at higher velocity, more of the sod was torn up. Eventually one of the trucks turned left to spray a different part of the square. A few protesters in that section were still dry. The spray became a kind of mist as the truck turned into the wind. Every second the light got more ironic. Soon a tiny rainbow was in the cannon's mist.

"Would you look at that," said Hana.

"I can't watch anymore," said Michael, but he kept watching.

"It's horrible," said Charlie, the most mesmerized of them all. "It's sick." It was impossible not to look at the catastrophe unfolding in muddy slow motion. The stream of water making the rainbow, once aimed properly, hit a protester in the chest. He fell back, stood up, fell back again. He rolled a meter or so before coming to a stop. He stopped in the sitting position. The spray of water followed his trail in the mud. The protester didn't bother moving. He must've known there was no escape. He covered his face with his hands as mud covered his body. When the spray moved on to another protester, the mud-covered man looked as if he'd met eyes with Medusa: he'd become a dripping statue of his former self.

"I asked Sabah if we could leave this place," said Michael, as if he were recounting an argument that had started months ago and had continued ever since. He wasn't even mad anymore. Just beat up. "She said she'll never leave home in this condition. But if home were in better condition, there'd be no reason to leave. Get it? She tricked me." Michael turned to leave, then turned to stay, then turned to leave again. "I don't know what to do." He faced away from the square. "I don't know what to say to her."

Charlie, hypnotized by the violence before him, couldn't turn away from the sight of Aos and Sabah shaking their fists at the water trucks. Mud covered them when torrents converged near their feet. Inexplicably, they ran toward the water. It punched them to the ground. They stood up and ran again. The water punched them in the face this time. The way their heads flew back convinced Charlie that they'd been internally decapitated. While their heads were still technically on their bodies, in Charlie's mind no neck bone or spinal cord could've survived such a blow. Thankfully Aos and Sabah rose from the dead before Charlie could panic or faint. It looked as if they had bloody noses. Or mud had gone up their noses and was coming back out a more vibrant color. They shouted—obscenities, probably—at the water trucks. And ran toward them again. A new and profound fear accosted Charlie. What if Sabah and Aos actually reached the water trucks? What would the soldiers do? Pull out their rifles? Shoot without warning them first? The fear abated when the water punched them to the ground again. Aos and Sabah slid back to their starting positions. The cycle repeated itself until exhaustion overwhelmed their rage. They sat down in despair. Mud covered them again when torrents converged near their feet. Aos kept shouting, though he'd switched from obscenities to what must've been prayers. His head bowed just slightly. God let the army stand down! God let the army stand down! When those prayers went unanswered, Aos stood and ran again toward the water trucks. He broke away from the group he was with, including Sabah. He was alone now. The water, having nowhere else to go, blasted him squarely in the chest. Aos fell hard and slid back in a weird position. He was lying facedown in the mud. "Stand up!" shouted Charlie. "Don't lie that way!" But his voice drowned in other voices shouting other things. "Stand up! Aos! Please!" Charlie leaned so far through the window that he seriously risked falling out. He could feel either Hana or Michael holding him. "Stand up, damn it! Aos! Stand up!" Protesters in the square shouted and waved at the soldiers to divert their spray from Aos' body. But the soldiers weren't heeding the call for mercy. The water just kept pounding him. Charlie finally pulled his head from the window. He couldn't watch anymore. This wasn't happening. "God would never kill such a good man," Charlie said to himself. He just kept saying that.

11

The second-to-last thing Omran did before catching a bus from South Station to New York, where he'd catch the EgyptAir flight to Cairo, was read the newspaper. An odd report appeared before his eyes. The army had planted grass in Tahrir. Twice, actually. The grass had been torn up the first time. The reporter suggested the grass was a gesture of goodwill that protesters had misinterpreted. A promise by the army not just to beautify, but to maintain Egypt until a good replacement for the despot could be found. Grass in Egypt required constant attention; the army would become an army of gardeners. It was a nice idea. Omran didn't trust it at all. The last thing he did, after returning the newspaper to its rack — fittingly positioned by the tabloids — was call Dalia for a final argument over the phone. From then on, they'd fight in person. As God intended, Omran thought. He called from a pay phone using a handful of quarters. The conversation was thus limited to a few choice words.

"Will you be there when I arrive?" asked Omran. "EgyptAir. Two thirty a.m."

A man at the next pay phone turned to look at Omran with an uncomfortable amount of concern; apparently something was odd and perhaps even dangerous about an Arab man using a phone in a bus station that was also a train station that was also across the street from the Federal Reserve. Was that really a coincidence?

"No," said Dalia. "I won't. I told you."

The sound of her crying freed Omran to do the same.

The man at the next pay phone made wide eyes; now that the Arab had said good-bye to his family, he was ready to blow himself up.

"I have to go now," said Omran. "My bus leaves in – "

His quarters ran out before he could say *Good-bye* or *See you tomorrow*. Omran directed his frustration at the man who was staring at him. "Stop watching me! I'm not a TV!" The man didn't bother finishing his call or even hanging up. He dropped the phone and speed-walked to the other side of the terminal. He glanced back about halfway to make his disgusted face. It looked like something he'd practiced.

Omran hardly breathed until his bus was on the interstate. He almost whooped with joy when the driver pressed the gas pedal and the engine shook the bus. The joy was in fact a different feeling he couldn't name without admitting it existed. Boston eventually became New York; the bus became the subway, which became the plane. "Welcome aboard," said the flight attendant. Just before takeoff the pilot said bad weather would jostle the plane. "Please," he said, "buckle up for the entire flight." Night fell and passed brutally. An infant with an earache in the seat in front of Omran wailed into its mother's chest. The mother sang to her little siren quietly. Omran listened to the song. Not the words, just the rhythm of it. Her song also calmed him. Few people were on the plane, and the empty seats made the turbulence worse. Omran's entire row was empty except for him. He prayed for God to fill at least one seat. That Omran might have someone to look at, talk to, and, in the event of an emergency, pray with: an all-purpose companion with whom to fly.

"Hello, brother," said a man's voice behind Omran. Was this really the prayer God had chosen to answer? Of all the prayers Omran had sent? He turned and peered down the aisle. A head poked out a few rows back. A young man with a full beard. The hair was healthy and black.

"Hello," said Omran. "Feel free to move up, if you want. The whole row is . . ."

The man was glad to move. He smelled strongly of apple tobacco and aniseed. How funny, thought Omran. The man's last joy in America had been a uniquely Arab delight. Shisha, the water pipe. He must've been glad to leave. That made Omran glad, too. He was going somewhere people wanted to be. Cairo, Egypt. Where history and science and poetry and math and language and perhaps even life itself had started. It was beautiful, wasn't it? And sacred? And blessed?

"I'm going home for the first time in ten years," the man said proudly. He wore a tie for the occasion. When he straightened it, Omran saw his hands shaking. "I left Cairo on scholarship. My parents made me promise that I wouldn't stay in America forever. That I would come home, even if the money was worse and the position was less prestigious. I thought now was the time. I've been away much longer than I had planned at the outset. Isn't it sad how fast years pass? At some point my parents got old." The man pulled out a picture of his mother and father from his wallet and said their names. Yosra Rateb and Anwar Olwi Rateb. He held the picture against his heart.

Ten hours later, Omran landed nineteen minutes late at Cairo International Airport. It was almost 3:00 a.m. The plane touched down, taxied, and parked at what Omran thought was the gate. The noise of the hatch opening cued the passengers to shuffle forward and out of the plane. The shuffling progressed to the back. Omran was glad to finally stand up and move his feet, but was surprised to discover, on reaching the hatch, that no jet bridge stretched from the plane to the terminal. Instead, stairs led to the tarmac; that led straight to a bus. His journey wasn't over quite yet, it seemed. The bus was so air-conditioned that Omran felt cold standing in line to board. He found room in the back by the window. Then looked out the glass pane at the yellow city in the distance.

The line through immigration wasn't a line so much as a mob

of people desperate to be reunited with whoever awaited them. It took a long time to get to the front. Omran didn't know how long. He couldn't bear to look at his watch. When he finally got there, the immigration officer asked him the usual questions. What are you doing in Egypt? How long will you stay? Do you have any monetary instruments in excess of a thousand Egyptian pounds? Followed by more pressing questions, but asked so lazily Omran wasn't sure the officer really wanted the truth. Do you have a camera? Are you a reporter? Are you a spy? Do you plan on protesting? Omran said he was just a tourist on the wrong end of a nonrefundable vacation package. He'd booked the trip months ago before the revolution started. "Bein fakkeiyy il-kammaaša," said Omran, meaning "between the pliers' jaws." Like a rock and a hard place. "I have always wanted to see the pyramids. Now there are no crowds. I suppose God blesses me that way." The immigration officer stamped Omran's papers and said, "Mawwart Masr," then motioned him to move along. He was blocking what remained of the mob. Omran stared at his ninety-day tourist visa and wondered what happened when those ninety days were up. "Yallah," said the immigration officer. "Get out of the way."

Immigration spit Omran into baggage claim, where bags slithered under black flaps. Behind the flaps, Omran could see flashes of men working. Harder, perhaps, than he would've liked. His blue suitcase arrived before he was ready to pull it off the carousel. Omran let it do another lap. The bag contained his whole life: four collared shirts from before the war, washed and ironed; four pleated pants, with stains on the knees and the ass from working the ditches; miscellaneous socks, undergarments, and toiletries, including an ointment designed to give his scars a more natural pigment; a prayer rug worn in five spots—where his knees, hands, and head had rested; and a card from Faisal to Dalia saying, *Thanks for letting me borrow your husband* and *You can have him back now*, but in the Arab way. Poetry and proverbs. Ending, of course, in a question. Who can subsist without love? It was Faisal's attempt to help Dalia understand why Omran had to come back.

The blue suitcase came round again. Every other passenger was less reluctant to collect his or her things. The mother with the formerly crying babe, sleeping now, and the man who'd wept into his tie after showing Omran the picture of his parents. The man's hands were still shaking, but his smile was bright. A slew of other strangers, all with a story about why they were returning to Egypt today. Today, like yesterday and also tomorrow – stretching indefinitely into the future – was the middle of a revolution. Why didn't anybody around the carousel look afraid? Or even annoyed? They were pleased to see their bags, to grab them, to go. Omran thought he should also be pleased. Wasn't Dalia there? Wasn't she waiting for him?

Customs officers waved passengers through as if they didn't care what came into their country. Drugs? Guns? Bombs? No bomb could do any real damage in comparison to the waste laid by the revolutionaries. The officers, thought Omran, were not revolutionaries. They were part of the old regime. They had government jobs. Now that the government had abandoned post, wouldn't those jobs become vacancies filled by other men with better connections to the military? Omran heard families and friends reuniting for the first time in months or even years, and taxi drivers shouting loudly about low fares and fast drives into the city. Omran heard laughter leaking through the frosted-glass wall between him and the rest of the world.

Finally, the blue suitcase came round a third time. Before Omran could decide whether he wanted it, a security officer pulled the suitcase off the carousel. He glared at Omran, who couldn't meet his eyes. Omran's conviction and bravery were gone like hand luggage he'd left on the plane. Except not on the plane. He'd left every virtue he'd ever had in Baghdad, where he'd also left his wife. How could he face her? Having no way to excuse what he'd done?

The security officer set the blue suitcase next to Omran, who was the only passenger left by the carousel. The officer, a young man with a stern face, said, "Yallah." Not just a command, but a threat. Go, now! Or else! Omran grabbed the suitcase and hurried toward customs. The official sitting there at the desk waved him through like a cow toward a slaughterhouse. Omran paused before the frosted-glass door. Though he only paused for a moment; the door, detecting his presence, opened automatically. He wasn't near ready, but had no choice but to go. The officers were watching him. The crowd on the other side of the frosted-glass door was smaller than he'd imagined it. Families were still laughing after having met; taxi drivers were still shouting about fares and arguing with each other about whose car was in better condition. Then Omran saw Dalia standing at the back. Behind the families; behind the drivers. His heart beat like boots on a wood floor. Could everyone in the hall hear the sound? He walked toward her more slowly than he thought he ought to. On the plane, he'd imagined running and grinning widely. Omran stopped a few feet from the woman he loved. Something told him not to touch her. When and if to embrace must be her choice. He'd already done his fair share of the choosing.

"I told you not to come."

"I know. I'm sorry."

Dalia wrapped him up as if she were trying to keep him warm. They remained that way — entwined — until the security officer, the same one as before, approached and commanded, "Yallah." This time the security officer said the word not with anger so much as sadness. Maybe the officer missed his own wife and wished desperately to go home and kiss her. Omran wanted to kiss Dalia right there, but couldn't do it; not in front of the officer. Instead he and Dalia heeded the command by leaving the terminal. The hot night air hit their faces when the glass doors slid open. The taxi ride was no less hot, even with the windows rolled down and the air whipping them. Omran and Dalia held hands as the car sped on the raised highway. Their fingers stuck together with sweat. The whole ride, other than the noise of the wind and the driver hitting the car horn, was silent. When they finally arrived in Imbaba, the taxi driver sped off without so much as ensuring his passengers had fully exited the vehicle. The driver left behind an alley that seemed to stretch endlessly toward other alleys, with only a few yellow streetlamps dotting the darkness. Dalia and Omran stood alone on the curb.

"Today from Baghdad?" asked the voice of a man on the stairs. Omran turned and squinted at him. He saw a man holding a cigarette in one hand and what looked like a warm Coke in the other. The man threw his cigarette on the ground. The orange sparks went dancing.

"Boston," said Omran. "Before that, Baghdad."

"A long journey," said the man.

It occurred to Omran that his journey shouldn't be measured in distance but in time. And that he should apologize to Dalia for taking so long. For failing to get her to America. For having no virtues left. He even felt like apologizing for having one eye. The scar would never go away. Every day she'd have to look at it.

The stairs became a stone floor leading to more stairs leading to a red door five stories up. The door led to an apartment Omran had envisioned many times, but had never seen. He stood in the center of the room and looked at pictures of himself on the wall. He wanted to say something. Needed to say something. He needed a bright new way to tell Dalia the same old truth. That he loved her. That he had to come back.

Dalia didn't linger in the silence for long. She stood between Omran and a lamp, which she flicked on. Dalia became a black shadow with yellow edges. Her head scarf was a feather floating to the floor, but her dress dropped like a rock. The last thing she removed were her socks. She threw each at Omran, who collapsed onto the couch under the weight of her gaze. Dalia jumped on him. It took her a few seconds to remove his belt because her hands were shaking. Omran's hands also shook. He didn't know where to put them. He put them in his pockets, on her thighs, in her hair. They didn't talk because their mouths were busy kissing. What was there to talk about, anyway? The future? Instead they let their bodies move the way celestial bodies do, toward and around each other with desperate inevitability.

PART IV

MOTHER OF THE EARTH

This midnight who has come like moonshine? It is the messenger of love, coming from the mihrab.

— Rumi

D alia and Omran, standing ankle deep in the sand, watched a stiff wind rough up the bay. Six months had passed but only some two hundred kilometers. Alexandria stretched behind them into the green fields of the Nile Delta. They'd come this far on a train and would continue their journey by boat. To Italy, God willing. Should the fisherman show up as promised. Should his vessel be seaworthy. Should the weather not take a turn for the worse.

Dalia fiddled with the letter in her pocket to avoid obsessing over what she couldn't control. She felt the torn edge where she'd ripped off the postscript warning against exactly this form of transport. *Don't trust the smugglers*, the postscript had read. *Please don't trust them. Whatever you do.* It had been a sorry end to what was otherwise a beautiful letter. Dalia had found it one morning shoved under her door. It was from Hana, which had shocked Dalia so badly that she hadn't been able to open it right away. In fact, she'd almost thrown it in the trash. Dalia was glad now that she hadn't done that. The letter, endeavoring to make amends for what had passed between them, spiraled through time and across continents. It told Hana's own tale of woe. Her deceased father and sister figured prominently. There was a bomb and another bomb. There was a bathtub and a bathrobe in a pile on the floor.

At first, it had seemed odd and perhaps invasive to read such an intimate portrait of Hana's family. As if the letter weren't meant for Dalia even though it was addressed to her. As if she were stealing something. Only after reading the letter all the way through, then keeping the letter hidden for a few days before reading it again, did Dalia realize Hana's intent. Hana was giving her story in return for the one she'd tried to steal that day in the conference room. "Was the threat of rape just a threat, or . . . ? Please, I need to know. Ahem. Dalia. I need to know if you were ever . . ." The story of the cleric, of course. Who'd done what he'd done and came back later to do it again. The story Hana had tried to rip from Dalia to lay it bare on the table for that other woman to see. What was her name? Margot? Margery? Hana wasn't proffering an apology so much as squaring a debt.

The letter went on to say that Hana was going home. Though not exactly by choice. *My mother is sick,* she'd written. The prognosis, which was notably absent from the letter, made itself known surreptitiously. The ink had run in the spots where Hana had wept. Dalia remembered the time she'd wept on her own letter in Charlie's office. She found solace in knowing Hana's grief had been recorded in the same insane way. The feeling allowed Dalia to put Hana somewhere else in her mind. In the way back, where she needn't be thought of so frequently and not always in a bad way. Hana was another Iraqi, wasn't she? Whose life had been torn up by war? That meant something. That bound them in some powerful way. It would've been a shame and an injustice to wish anything upon her but luck.

The letter ended with the dreaded postscript, which was Hana's failed attempt to be of some practical use after rambling for so many pages. *P.S. It occurred to me that someday you might try to find your own way to leave Egypt. Not legally, I mean. I felt compelled to tell you. Don't trust the smugglers. Please don't trust them. Whatever you do.* The postscript was longer than any postscript Dalia had ever read before. The smugglers, it said, were cash-strapped and known for overloading their boats. That inadvertently lifted the centers of gravity. It was dangerous to do that. The boats rolled more easily in rough seas.

Coast guards around the Mediterranean (and the UNHCR, being informed through official channels) were well acquainted with the results: bodies floating lifelessly in the sea. The postscript didn't befit the rest of the letter. Plus, Hana wasn't telling Dalia anything she didn't already know. Thankfully the writing appeared on only one side of the page, so Dalia was able to remove the postscript without tearing a hole somewhere else in the letter. She kept the remaining pages and read them from time to time. Dalia liked to think that somehow Hana would know.

The fisherman arrived more than an hour late, looking skittish. He kept peering back at the road. "*Um al-Dunya* leaves tonight," he said in a hushed tone. The fisherman gestured ambiguously to the landing spot. The implied vessel was of unknown size and seaworthiness. "Nine or ten, depending. No refund if you don't show. Bring food unless you're not hungry for three days. Four days, maybe. The weather is . . ." Out of respect or possibly fear, the fisherman bowed to the sea. His baggy pants fit poorly and weren't suitable for a man of his trade. Then again, he'd not been a fisherman since he'd become a smuggler.

Omran handed over the last of their cash. The agonizing exchange belittled the Herculean task of earning money. After all, hawking trinkets in the alleys of the Khan el-Khalili was dangerous work with paltry margins. When Omran and Dalia hadn't been on edge—lacking, as they did, the required work permit—they'd been actively fleeing the police. Normally Omran and Dalia saw the police ahead of time and ducked behind other touts or into shops, where they escaped by pretending to be customers. They'd been caught by surprise only once, but with dire consequence. Dalia and Omran had been rearranging trinkets at the time. This after a distracted passerby had tripped over them. The trinkets had scattered like birds after a gunshot. "God gave you two eyes so you could open at least one of them!" Omran had shouted at the passerby. A policeman had approached in the time it took them to clean up. He'd asked for a permit, a license, a national ID card, a bribe, and, albeit implicitly, the utmost respect. "Huh?" asked Omran. "What did you say? A permit? What permit?" The policeman had rolled his shoulders until muscles had bulged from his neck. The sight had caused both Omran and Dalia to panic; the panic had caused them to run. Thank God the policeman hadn't been so fit as his neck had suggested. He'd sped after them through the winding alleys, but wore out after just a few turns.

Omran and Dalia nevertheless paid a steep price for the crime of trying to work: their hats, their bottles of water, their trinkets, and the rug on which the trinkets had sat. Everything had been stolen by a competitor or confiscated by the police. The rug, designed to seduce even the most incredulous passerby – the beautiful red symmetry had drawn eyes and thus wallets – was the hardest of the losses to take. The rug had been their only business plan. Their way of distinguishing themselves from other sellers hawking the same crap. But the rug, a hefty investment, hadn't yet paid for itself. How then could it be replaced? "Our business is doomed," bemoaned Omran. He might've been right had it not been for Dalia's resource-fulness. Her idea wasn't elegant, but it was effective. She walked the Khan until men whistled, hissed, or made crude remarks. "Do you fuck?" "Are you married?" These men were easy to find and could be trusted to follow her. "Where are you going?" "Can I come?" "Can I come on you?" She'd led them to Omran's spot on the side-walk, where a wry look would shame them into buying something. If the wry look didn't work, Omran would say, "I see you've met my wife." His vaguely homicidal tone would scare vulgar men into becoming reluctant customers. They'd buy small trinkets, bundles of tissues, or individual cigarettes sold at a negligible markup from one-twentieth of the pack price. Omran was pained by the scheme and feared it would wreck Dalia, but she told him to stop worrying; she liked earning money, was enlivened by it. The truth was a little

more complicated. Dalia needed to collect on these men's vileness.
A similar vileness had twice cost her a great deal.

The fisherman stared blankly at the money in Omran's hand.
Dalia suddenly and vehemently hated the fisherman. He must've
felt undervalued by the operation to which he'd pledged his vessel.
Hadn't he quit fishing to get rich? How would he get rich at this
rate? His grubby paw finally grabbed the money.

The long and wending path to the beach started in the most un-
likely place: the Refugee Relief Project one week after Omran had
arrived in Cairo. "What are you doing here?" Charlie had said when
he'd finally, and after such a long wait, embraced a man he'd only
known as a voice. The meeting should've been an evolution in their
friendship, but turned out to be the opposite. Charlie seemed agitated, distracted, in some kind of pain after touching Omran. "You
shouldn't have come! I told you not to!" The bad reaction had grown
more severe by the second. Charlie had laughed in complete disbelief. He'd shaken his head. He'd even reached out to touch Omran
a second time. As if he wanted to be sure he wasn't hallucinating.
"My dear Omran," said Charlie, apparently so heavyhearted that he
had to sit. "What have you done?"

Thereafter Omran hadn't been able to visit the office without
enduring some bitterness. Dalia had tried to visit on his behalf to see
if Charlie might help Omran apply for asylum. This to prevent the
otherwise necessary crime of overstaying his tourist visa. But Charlie
had lost some part of himself. The drive to go beyond where other
lawyers would go. He'd said Omran had come to Egypt of his own
accord. "Not under duress. The official definition of that word is, I'll
admit, a little flawed. Damn it, very flawed. *Duress* should mean all
kinds of things it doesn't mean to policymakers. But I can't change
that. I can't make them understand. I can't even ask that they try
to understand. The people who make decisions are insulated by

people who don't. Any criticism launched at such machinery just disappears in the void." Charlie spoke as if he was reporting the news and not decrying injustice. His heart, it seemed, had changed. Had grown armor. Had shrunk to fit normally inside his chest cavity. He'd become a more practical man. Also strangely bereaved by that metamorphosis. It was as if Charlie missed his old self.

Dalia was glad not to be alone with that longing. She missed his inhuman persistence. The fire, she called it. The shedding of sparks as he worked like hot metal struck with a hammer. She even missed the curious personal concern that used to embarrass her. The absence of those familiarities stole the last of her hope the way black holes steal light from the cosmos. It was a quiet, invisible obliteration. Even Dalia didn't notice it. Not until the screen door opened and slammed closed again. The sound reminded Dalia what was waiting outside: the same unknowable fate that had always been waiting there. Somehow it was nearer than it had been. Would she ever leave Egypt? Would Egypt ever change? For the better? These questions rose anew from the pit in her stomach where she'd buried them.

Dalia couldn't bring herself to leave the office even though its usefulness had run its course. She needed a few minutes to absorb that she and Omran were on their own. The idea gave her a kind of vertigo, the feeling she was slipping ever deeper into a life that was beyond control. She leaned against the translator's desk to steady herself. The smooth, clean surface called attention to the desk's emptiness. Why hadn't she noticed before? The work normally conducted there was vital and the man who normally conducted it was cherished. Dalia didn't feel comfortable asking Charlie outright what happened. Instead she asked why he'd not filled the vacancy.

Watching Charlie bow his head scared the shit out of Dalia. Suddenly she didn't want to know; suddenly she was ready to leave. That readiness grew into something more desperate. She needed to leave before Charlie answered her question. There was no polite exit on that timeline, but Dalia tried nonetheless. She said she'd forgotten something. It was urgent. Salaam. Bye now. I'm going. Then Dalia ran down

the hall, down the stairs to the yard, down the street, down the stairs
to the subway, and finally down the platform to the women's carriage.
She rode the train impatiently under the river. A few women gave her
nasty looks for tapping her nails on the pole. The looks couldn't stop
her; Dalia tapped away until the train came to a stop at the nearest
station to her apartment. It wasn't close at all. She hailed a cab from
there. It was a ludicrous expense but she couldn't bear any further
delay. "Charlie's hands are tied," said Dalia when she finally arrived
at her apartment. Her desire to slam the door was precluded by the
more prescient desire to stay calm in front of Omran. "He can't help.
Something about machinery." She tried to sound optimistic and not
scared when she said they needed to find work. Any way they could.
Hawking trinkets in the Khan, if it came to that. They would save
money and, God willing, flee to Italy. She'd heard talk of these boats.
"Europe," she said as if that one word might yet save them.

Um al-Dunya was a strange name for a vessel in a shadowy fleet of
vessels known for sending their passengers to heaven. *Dunya* meant
"world" and "Earth." Everything a living person could touch. The
terrestrial. The mundane. It was a strange name, too, for the place
Dalia and Omran were trying to flee. Cairo. Masr. Um al-Dunya.
The mother of the world. That title hadn't been appropriate in
several thousand years. Since then, mother had grown old. Since
then, mother had died. Now despots followed each other into
oblivion. The army generals had followed Mubarak. Who would
follow them? Dalia was relieved to know she needn't worry. If the
boat sank, she'd die. If the boat didn't sink, she'd be long gone
in another way. She and Omran, having made it to Italy—either
stopping there or continuing by land farther north—would start
another life. A lonely life, to be sure. Far away from the call to
prayer, which kept company as much as it kept time. A kind of
companionship. Omran said children were the obvious cure to that

quiet problem. Dalia supposed he was right. And that she might want children. Having Omran in bed again had reminded her.

Dalia shifted her weight in the sand. Standing on such an uneven and ever-shifting surface for so long had revealed all kinds of new muscles. Eight had become nine, which had become ten. They hadn't left the beach out of fear the boat would've come and gone in their absence. Moonlight turned seawater into what looked like coal tar. "I can't remember the last time I was this cold," said Dalia. A sudden gust of wind felt like God's way of telling her to go back. She refused. She refused to even turn around. There was nothing behind her except a conflict bordered on three sides by worse conflicts. Israel, Sudan, Libya. The sea may not have offered safe passage, but it did offer a way out. So long as the weather cooperated and the captain did his job properly.

"Did you know I can't swim?" asked Omran, as if they were young again and smitten and playing some kind of guessing game to learn each other's embarrassing secrets. "I can't think of a reason I would've told you before now."

Dalia thought of a reason, but didn't mention it: the vacation they'd nearly taken (years ago) to the gulf. The American war had put a hopeless kink in their plan. They'd arranged to drive south to the water. They were going to stay in a hotel. Dalia, remembering their conversation, found it almost funny. She remembered Omran saying he couldn't wait to "dip" his feet in the water. It was easy to see now that he was confessing something. "I can't swim, either," said Dalia in a hasty attempt to comfort him. She regretted the lie even before she'd finished telling it. Omran knew the story about how she'd learned to swim. Her father, in a blessed and rare mood, had woken Dalia one morning before dawn. She was young. No more than ten years old. "Let's go swimming," he'd said. "The Great Zab River awaits." It had been one of the few times he'd permitted Dalia to behave outside the bounds of his crushing morals. She hadn't been allowed to play football, wear makeup, or read books in which people married. The man who'd imposed these rules and others like them had also taught Dalia to swim. The delicious mystery had gone unexplained for years. Then Dalia had realized the truth. Her father's morals had crushed him the same way they crushed everybody. A man such as that must've had days when he loathed his zealotry, seeking to escape God by regarding something besides Him. His wife, his daughter. It was deplorable. It was pure cowardice.

Omran turned away from the lie, out to sea. "What if the boat doesn't come?" His tone said he hoped it wouldn't. They could go back to Cairo and make some kind of life. Couldn't they? Wasn't it possible? "What if the fisherman just . . . well, you know. Took our money."

Dalia found it hard to be leery and desperate at the same time. She'd chosen, early on in the process, to ignore all feelings of doubt. Even after the man on the stairs said he'd attempted the same journey and had lost everything. Even after he'd written the smuggler's number – "To be rid of it," he'd said as if scribbling the digits would cleanse them from his memory – on the back of a leaflet that must've been distributed by protesters. A foreboding message had been on the front side: *The martyr*, followed by an illegible name, *is dead!* After calling the number a dozen times and receiving no answer, she'd tried again the next day with more luck, which convinced Dalia that her original strategy – to ignore the sinking feeling – was actually the right choice.

"What do you want?" the trafficker had said. Dalia had only gotten partway through her request before the smuggler, disinterested in her personal circumstances, said the cost of the journey was $2,000 per head. As if she and Omran were just cattle. The cost, he'd said, was non-negotiable. The cost wouldn't be refunded under any circumstance. The smuggler had been clear on that point. He wouldn't be held responsible for the weather, the coast guard, or even the condition of the boat. He'd said he was just a man. The operation was another entity. If these provisions weren't acceptable, then passage wasn't for sale. "You can try to swim if you want. Or walk, but it's longer. Go to Israel. Then Lebanon, if you make it that far. Keep going around the sea until you get where you're trying to go." It was a shrewd way to conduct business. Dalia had practically begged him to take her money.

"The boat will come," said Dalia. "I know it will."

Omran looked inland but Dalia, a stalwart, faced the water. The clouds in the distance illuminated. Dark gray turned bright white. A flash of lightning? Or a figment of her imagination?

"Maybe we should – " started Omran.

Dalia lifted her finger to her lips. Hearing a clap of thunder from so far away required total silence. That silence yet eluded her. She heard Omran breathing unsteadily. She heard her own pulse. It was strangely languid. *Lub-dub, lub-dub.* Finally she heard an engine sputtering – and there in the dark was a boat.

ACKNOWLEDGMENTS

This novel was supported by a Fulbright Program grant sponsored by the Bureau of Educational and Cultural Affairs of the United States Department of State and administered by the Institute of International Education. A debt of gratitude is also owed to the Binational Fulbright Commission in Egypt.

Many thanks to Emily Forland, Daniel Loedel, Rosie Mahorter, and Dan Cuddy. Thanks also to the friends and advisers who read early drafts. To Michael Byers, Kirsten Valdez Quade, Renée Zuckerbrot, Kate Osterloh, and the many fiction writers I came to know and trust during my time at the Helen Zell Writers' Program.

Additional debts are owed to the abundant works of both Jalal al-Din Rumi and Hafez of Shiraz; to Naguib Mahfouz's *The Harafish*; and to Alaa Al-Aswany's *The Yacoubian Building*. Also to their generous and masterful translators.

Finally, and most importantly, thanks are due to Erica and Ruby. Love to you both.

LIVE FROM CAIRO

IAN BASSINGTHWAIGHTE

TOPICS AND QUESTIONS FOR DISCUSSION

1. One of the first things we learn about Hana is that her father died in a 1980 bombing in Iraq, forcing her pregnant mother to flee to America. Why do you think readers are given this information so early on? How important is Hana's family history? How would the story be different without Hana's past?

2. During her interview at the United Nations High Commissioner for Refugees, Hana responds to Dalia's initial statement by saying "That's what happened to your country. I'm asking what happened to you" (page 20). In what way are characters defined by their countries? How is identity embedded in location and nationality?

3. What was your reaction to Dalia's testimony (pages 59–67)? How did you feel when Charlie responded by saying "Please tell me there's more?"

4. What role does shame play in the novel? How are the characters differently influenced by shame? What about guilt?

5. How does Mustafa, Hana's cab driver, enrich your understanding of life in Cairo? What do we learn from him that we don't from other characters?

6. During a phone call with her mother, Hana asks if "a lifetime of forced isolation and poverty" is "really less dramatic than death" (page 78). How would you respond? Hana also wonders whether she has a right to her mother's narrative. What does she mean?

7. After receiving the rejection notice for Dalia's petition, Charlie tells her husband, Omran, not to come back to Egypt. He is worried that Omran and Dalia would "discover that love wasn't something they could eat or live inside" (page 101). Where, then, do you think love should rank on a list of priorities?

8. Faisal and his son spoke only Arabic to each other, and it made strangers so nervous they would often say, "We speak English in this country" (page 119). How did these statements impact Faisal and his son? Discuss the power of this sentiment and its presence in the United States.

9. On page 128, Charlie says "Subversion is the only way to even the odds when you have no money and no power." Do you agree? Why or why not?

10. Is it ethical for Charlie to make Hana feel responsible for the death of a young man in order to convince her to provide an illegal yellow card? To what lengths would you go to protect the people you love?

11. How does this book portray insiders versus outsiders?

12. On pages 155–56, Hana reflects on a sentence by her favorite Egyptian writer: "In the passionate dark of dawn, on the path between death and life, within view of the watchful stars and within earshot of the beautiful, obscure anthems, a voice told of the trials and joys promised to our alley." Why do you think this passage resonates with her so much?

13. Discuss what you would have done in Charlie's, Dalia's, Omran's, and Hana's positions. What would you have done differently? How difficult would your decisions be?

ENHANCE YOUR BOOK CLUB

1. As mentioned in the novel, Naguib Mahfouz is a renowned Egyptian writer. Expand your knowledge of Egyptian literature by reading some of his work.

2. *Live from Cairo* is set in Cairo during the turbulent aftermath of the January 25 Revolution. Research the recent events in Egypt and the ousting of President Mubarak. How does the political landscape as described in news compare to that of the novel?

3. Research traditional Egyptian recipes and have members of your book club bring different dishes for everyone to try.